Harper
Monogram

Seasons of Love

ELAINE BARBIERI
LORI COPELAND
KAREN LOCKWOOD
EVELYN ROGERS

HarperPaperbacks
A Division of HarperCollins*Publishers*
A Sutton Press Book

This is a work of fiction. The characters, incidents, and dialogues are products of the author's imagination and are not to be construed as real. Any resemblance to actual events or persons, living or dead, is entirely coincidental.

HarperPaperbacks *A Division of* HarperCollins*Publishers*
10 East 53rd Street, New York, N.Y. 10022

Winter Moon © 1995 by Sutton Press, Inc., and Elaine Barbieri. *Gentle Rain* © 1995 by Sutton Press, Inc., and Evelyn Rogers. *Summer Storm* © 1995 by Sutton Press, Inc., and Karen Finnigan. *Golden Harvest* © 1995 by Sutton Press, Inc.; special thanks and acknowledgment to Lori Copeland for her contribution to the anthology. Published by arrangement with Sutton Press, Inc.
Cover illustrations by Jeff Barson

First printing: August 1995

Printed in the United States of America

HarperPaperbacks, HarperMonogram, and colophon are trademarks of HarperCollins*Publishers*

❖ 10 9 8 7 6 5 4 3 2 1

*Sutton Press, Inc., dedicates this book to
Lydia and Maxine*

CONTENTS

CONTENTS

I

WINTER MOON

Elaine Barbieri

1

Winter, 1892
Benton Falls, Vermont

    Holly adjusted her small, wire-rimmed spectacles with the tip of her finger as she looked out the window of her cabin.

The downy drifts, glittering in the morning sun, extended beyond the clearing in front of her door to tall evergreens and sugar maples, heavily laden with snow. Anxious chickadees and a brilliant red cardinal fluttered among the branches, blurred spots of color against a glorious azure sky. The pristinely beautiful scene was marred only by the footprints she had made during the past week. So tranquil was the view of her little forest domain that she might have been miles from town, instead of a convenient distance from the road on the outskirts of a bustling rural Vermont community.

Holly tucked a stray wisp of hair into the severe bun at her nape and drew herself to her full height, her back rigid. She turned to survey the room.

Granted, it wasn't much in the way of elegance. A smoke-stained fieldstone fireplace dominated one wall, before which sat a worn couch, an end table, and an overstuffed chair. At the opposite end of the room, a much-abused table and chairs stood on an oval hooked rug. Nearby, under a window, was a sink that afforded her the convenience of pumping water straight from her own well. And a few feet away was a large black cooking stove, a gem that had produced minor culinary miracles during Holly's short month of residence.

She glanced at the bedroom doorway and nodded. The two rooms adequately met her needs, especially since the good-sized bedroom had a potbelly stove that was quite effective against the winter cold, and a great brass bed that was more comfortable than any she had ever known.

Best of all, the cabin was hers.

Her throat suddenly tight, she inhaled deeply. There was nothing quite like the fragrance of freshly cut pine wreaths, which she had hung on the walls; nothing more cheerful than holly boughs, with which she had decorated the mantle and doorways. As always, the scent and the colors brought back cherished memories of her mother, whose features had grown dim over the years, but whose words never would, words as clear as if the dear woman had just spoken them.

Pine wreaths and holly, aren't they lovely! They warm the heart and fill the senses when the winter cold sets in. You'll be lovely someday, too, Holly. You'll fill a man's heart with beauty and he'll fill yours, just like the holly boughs.

As a child she had believed those words. But as a woman she had set her sights on more practical and realistic goals.

She glanced sharply at her nemesis, hanging on a hook on the wall, and her stomach tightened. A pair of ice skates. She shuddered. Then, suddenly ashamed of her cowardice, she raised her chin with renewed determination.

She had gone through so much in the past two years. Her maiden Aunt Ellen, who had raised her after her parents died in a fire, had become ill and gradually worsened. When she had become too sick to care for herself, Holly had been forced to resign from her teaching position at a small private girls' school. Then Aunt Ellen had died, and because their savings were depleted, Holly had had to sell their possessions to cover their debts and the funeral expenses. She had then moved from Boston with her few remaining personal belongings to take up a teaching post in this small Vermont community. The school board had provided her with this simple log cabin for the duration of her employment.

She had accomplished so much. Surely this unexpected hurdle, just when she had begun believing she was winning the town's acceptance, would not be her undoing. Her eyes narrowing, she gritted her teeth. No, she would not allow it to be.

She pulled on her coat, drew on her boots, pulled an old wool hat down low over her ears, and wrapped her muffler high around her neck, leaving little more than her wire-rimmed spectacles and her nose exposed. Then she tugged on her gloves, snatched the ice skates from their hook, and strode toward the door.

A wintry gust raised a fine spray of icy snow to flay Judd's face, tightening his frown and eliciting a soft curse as his horse continued its plodding pace along the frozen forest trail. The morning that had begun at the break of dawn was stretching into eternity, and Judd was damned tired. He was also hungry, not having taken the time to eat anything more than a few strips of dried venison for breakfast. He had been too intent on fixing the damaged wagon wheel, just one of many problems that had slowed his progress on this trip.

He glanced back at the otter, beaver, and raccoon skins carefully baled in the wagon bed. The deer carcasses beside them would provide for him and his neighbors, the Sloans, and bring additional money from the town's tavern. But the injury to his horse and the damage to his wagon, sustained in an encounter with a bear, would eat heavily into his profits.

The worst result of the mishaps was the delay. He was more than a week late in returning home. He had been away for more than a month, and he knew that as happy as his nephew Daniel would be to see him, the boy would not quickly shed the anxiety of wondering if Judd would, indeed, return.

Agitation numbing him to the frigid bite in the air, Judd lifted his cap and ran his hand through his hair. His brows met in a frown as he replaced his cap, then rubbed his hand against his bearded chin. He hadn't taken the time to shave or bathe in more than two weeks. He knew he looked as unkempt and disreputable as he felt, and that he didn't smell much better. His frown deepened. He didn't like returning to town like this.

Daniel had been only four when his father, Judd's older brother Todd, died two years ago. Remembering little of his dead mother other than a flash of pale hair and eyes, Daniel had grown close to his father. Daniel had been left with a neighbor when Todd went on the hunting trip from which he never returned. A search party found him and his horse at the bottom of a ravine, victims of a rockslide.

It took Judd nearly two weeks to reach the outpost where Daniel awaited him. Judd had arrived looking as he did now. Daniel had not recognized him and had become almost hysterical when Judd first tried to take the boy with him. Judd believed that Daniel relived that day's fear whenever Judd returned bearded from his hunting trips, so Judd usually came back clean-shaven. But Judd sensed that as he and Daniel had grown closer over the past two years, Daniel's fear increased that one day Judd, like Todd, would not return at all.

A great sadness swelled in Judd. At six, Daniel was already tormented by painful memories. Judd knew how deeply those memories scarred. There was a time when he had thought he would not survive his. But Daniel had changed all that. Now Judd knew that although he could not forget, he could go on.

Because Daniel needed him.

That thought renewing his agitation, Judd slapped the reins against the weary Yankee's back, urging the animal to a faster pace.

Straighten up, Holly! Walk tall! You are young, intelligent, and your own master. You are capable of achieving any goal you set for yourself if you attack it with determination and vigor. Determination, vigor, and independence. Remember, no man controls your destiny, and if you're smart, you'll see to it that no man ever will!

The echo of Aunt Ellen's words rang in Holly's ears as she trudged along the narrow path through the snow, her ice skates dangling uncomfortably from her gloved hand. It amazed her even now that Aunt Ellen and her mother had been sisters, so different had they been in personality. Whereas her mother had been gentle and almost subservient, Aunt Ellen had been strong-willed and proud. She had scoffed at those who pitied her for never having known the bliss of married life, insisting that such bliss was too often another word for misery and subjugation. She had decried some women's use of artifice to enhance their God-given features to catch a man, and had laughed at those who called her plain, replying that being plain had emancipated her. She had lamented that Holly was "pleasing to the eye like her mother," saying that beauty, far from being an asset, was a liability that often trapped a woman. Aunt Ellen had also debunked the belief that a woman needed a man to take care of her, when all too often in a marriage the woman ended up taking care of the man, without receiving any benefit from, or credit for, her efforts.

Holly's shoulders stiffened as a cold gust briefly rocked her. She had loved Aunt Ellen, and she had admired the small, spirited woman who had retained the courage of her convictions right to the end. Her tribute to Ellen's efforts on Holly's behalf since Holly's early childhood had been to conduct her own life with the courage and vigor her aunt had advocated.

With some discomfort, Holly acknowledged that Ellen's teachings had left her deficient in some areas. Her unusual concept of a woman's place in life had strained her personal relations with men, and she truly resented the male condescension with which her valid opinions were often received. She was aware that some men saw her as an ice maiden, but she had not wasted much thought on that. She was, after all, her own master and a woman who excelled in other areas.

For example, she was a good teacher. She was truly fond of children and had come to realize that without sacrificing control in the schoolroom, she could relate to the students individually in a positive way. She also derived genuine excitement from opening young minds to learning, and held the conviction that all children could learn. And while the learning capacity varied from child to child, satisfaction did not, for either the teacher or the student, when the child achieved his or her full potential.

A brief smile flickered across Holly's face. Her desperate financial situation had forced her into accepting her present, uncertain teaching position when she had been unable to find work in Boston. She had, however, found a challenge she had not expected in the one-room schoolhouse attended by children of various ages. She knew she was doing well even though some of the school board members would have preferred an older, more experienced teacher. She was intensely aware that any weaknesses in her performance would be seized upon by those few to be used against her when her probation period ended and the time to offer a firm contract arrived.

Any weaknesses in her performance.

The ice skates dangling from Holly's hand seemed to burn through her rough woolen gloves. How could she possibly have anticipated that an annual preholiday skating party was a traditional event in this community? And how could she possibly have foreseen that as schoolmistress, she was expected not only to help plan the party, but also to participate in it?

Planning?

That was no problem.

Skating?

Holly shuddered as a subtle throbbing began in her ankle, reminding her of the skating accident that had caused the nasty break in it when she was twelve.

She remembered vividly the bloody sight of splintered bone protruding through the flesh and the endless months of pain before she had been able to walk again. An occasional limp was the only physical reminder of that traumatic day, but emotionally . . .

Coward! an inner voice railed.

Remember, you are capable of achieving any goal you set yourself if you attack it with determination and vigor!

Determination and vigor.

She swallowed and squared her shoulders as the pond came into view. She had three weeks to conquer the fear that set her heart pounding, at this convenient spot a moderate distance through the woods from her cabin door. Most people in town preferred the community pond where the annual party was held, but she could fight her demons in private here. She could overcome them.

She *would* overcome them.

Swallowing again against the ever-burgeoning lump in her throat, she walked to the pond's edge and sat on a snow-covered log. She pulled off her boots, refusing to look at the ice reflecting the gold morning sun as she slipped her feet into her newly purchased skates and began lacing them. Somewhere in the back of her mind a warning bell sounded, but she forced herself to remain deaf to its knell as she stood abruptly.

Tottering uncertainly, she inched her way toward the ice. She stepped out onto the slick surface, her heart racing.

Oh, dear.

The wagon rattled on as Judd's stomach clenched tighter with every laborious mile that passed. After a brief acceleration earlier, Yankee had settled back into his former weary pace, and Judd had not dared press him. The horse's foreleg had been badly injured, and Judd had wondered if the old fellow would be able to haul the wagon back at all. But the willing bay was managing admirably, if slowly. So very slowly.

Judd glanced up toward the morning sun reflecting in an almost blinding glare off the ice-encrusted snowscape. He remembered that Betty had been fascinated by the primitive beauty of winter, that she had never seemed to tire of it, no matter how prolonged the season. The nights they had spent in their cabin isolated by winter storms during the four short years of their marriage were among his most cherished memories.

Betty, his chum in childhood, his friend in adolescence, his lover, his wife. His life.

The pain of the moment when Betty's eyes closed for the last time returned in an overwhelming swell. He had promised her then that no one would ever take her place in his life or in his heart. In all intimate encounters with other women in the years since her death, he had had no difficulty in keeping that promise. He knew he never would, for nothing would ever match the joy of seeing the flash of Betty's red hair and the spontaneous grin with which she had always welcomed him home. It had made him feel good all over. He remembered the warmth of her lips, the matchless joy of her arms closing around his neck as he drew her close. And when she had lain in his arms.

He halted his thoughts, forcing Betty's image and the familiar anguish it stirred from his mind. Daniel's small, serious face and forlorn blue eyes appeared automatically instead. Judd had not thought he would survive Betty's death. The realization that others had suffered similar losses during the outbreak of influenza that had swept the area three years ago had been little consolation, but Daniel's need had somehow over-whelmed his own. It seemed a bitter irony that in losing his brother, he had found a reason for living.

His eye catching a familiar landmark, Judd felt his anticipation surge. Barring any additional unforeseen incidents, he would be at the Sloan cabin within the hour. He'd pick up Daniel and take him along when he dropped off his furs for sale. Daniel would like that.

From somewhere in the woods came a sound. Drawing himself suddenly erect, Judd listened intently. There it was again! Pulling back on the reins, he halted the wagon, straining to identify the faint echo. It was a voice, a female voice calling for help!

His heart beating erratically, he jumped down from the wagon, hesitating briefly to confirm the direc-tion of the sound. Suddenly certain, he snatched his gun and a coiled rope from the wagon bed and started through the knee-deep snow at a run.

Frozen more from fear than from the numbing cold of the ice, Holly shuddered uncontrollably. Her throat was raw from her frantic, unanswered calls for help, and she rested her chin briefly against the ice, swallow-ing painfully. Had she not been so terrified, she might have been tempted to laugh at the utter absurdity of her position as she lay on her stomach on the ice, her arms and legs spread-eagled, her hands clinging to the frozen surface like the claws of a panicked cat.

But she had no inclination to laugh, nor did she dare move. The cracks in the ice beneath her worsened with even the slightest movement, and the water rising through them had already soaked the front of her coat.

How had this happened? The ice had seemed
solidly frozen. How could it not have been? The temperature had not risen above freezing for more days
than she could remember. The pond in town was far
larger than this and had supported countless skaters
for the past two weeks. She had not noticed any
thawed spots when she had stepped out onto the pond
more than an hour ago.

Her precise academic mind corrected that last
thought. In truth, her concentration had been directed
solely on remaining upright on her legs, which had
quaked furiously from the first moment she slipped her
feet into her skates.

She briefly closed her eyes. It was a nightmare!
She had no more than touched her skates to the ice
when she had fallen on her backside with a resounding
thump. Numerous attempts to get up had resulted in
such varied humiliating positions that she could not
recall them all, except for the countless painful areas
on her body that were gradually growing numb.

Nor was she certain when she had heard the first
cracking of the ice. It made little difference now. Her
last few determined but unsteady strokes across the ice
had deposited her flat on her stomach, and now great,
seeping cracks stretched out from her inert form like
rays of the sun.

Another sharp pop. Another crackle.

Water surged against her chin. Panicked, Holly lifted
her head as frantic thoughts exploded in her mind. The
ice was going to give way! She was going to drown in
this frozen pond! She would never see the seasons
change in this beautiful place that she had believed
would become her home! She would never accomplish
any of her goals! She would never carve a noble niche
in the world with hard work and dedication. She

would never see her students grow to successful maturity as the result of her guidance. She would never age a day past her twenty-two years and look back and see that she had truly made a difference.

She would not live to grow old!

That last thought petrified her, and her eyes widened. "Hellllp!"

A flicker of movement at the pond's edge sent hope surging through Holly. A tall figure stepped into view, his broad outline in dark relief against the glare of the late-morning sun behind him.

But the man didn't move. Instead, he stood staring in her direction for endless, silent moments.

Her relief turned rapidly to concern. Why was he waiting? Didn't he realize that her situation was critical? Didn't he know that although she was nearly frozen, the ice beneath her was not?

"I need help!" she called out again through chattering teeth.

The silhouette's deep, resounding reply was unexpectedly harsh. "Be quiet, will you!"

"Be quiet?" Her response was a frozen growl. "Be quiet?"

Not deigning to reply, the shadowed male form slipped abruptly from sight. An embarrassingly pitiful rasp escaped from Holly a moment before the silhouette reappeared, swinging a rope over his head. Within moments the looped end was within inches of her reach.

"Take hold of the rope!"

"I can't reach it!"

"Try harder, damn it!"

Damn it? How dare that coarse individual use profanity when addressing her?

She stretched toward the tantalizing loop. "I can't reach it!"

A deep, muttered curse preceded the withdrawal of the rope and another toss that landed it closer. Holly reached toward it and her frozen fingers closed around the rough coil.

"I've got it!"

"Hold tight. I'm going to pull you in."

The rope tugged. Holly's body moved. The ice cracked loudly.

The rope slipped from her grasp and recoiled with a sharp, snapping sound, followed by the man's pained grunt.

"You'll have to think of something else," Holly shouted in a trembling voice. "The ice cracks when I move!"

The rope slapped back against the ice. "Take hold of that rope and *hold onto it*," the voice instructed with obvious irritation, "or I'll leave you here!"

He wouldn't!

She swallowed.

He would.

She grasped the rope and closed her eyes. The loud popping and snapping of the ice that punctuated her progress as she was dragged with painstaking slowness toward shore struck terror in her heart. She was still lying on the ice when she heard the sound of a step near her. Her eyes flew open. She was a distance from shore and her rescuer stood beside her. She gasped aloud.

"Stand up, damn it!" Strong hands drew her roughly to her feet. "The ice is safe here."

She looked up into an angry bearded face and black, snapping eyes as her rescuer held her and all but dragged her toward shore.

"What were you doing skating out here all alone, anyway? And how could you be so stupid as to skate

so close to the underground spring? Everybody knows
the pond doesn't freeze solid enough in that spot to
support skaters!"

A hot anger began invading her numbness. "M-
maybe everybody knew it," she protested, her teeth
chattering, "but I didn't!"

"You should've checked!"

Firm ground under her feet at last, she shook off
the ruffian's grip, her anger overwhelming her. She
would not be treated like a village idiot simply
because . . . Because she had shown the judgment of
one?

She stiffened. "I d-don't need your help any
longer. I can get b-back home by myself."

The dark eyes narrowed. The bearded cheek
twitched. Holly knew she was tall for a woman, but
this man dwarfed her in height and in breadth as he
glowered down at her. "No, you can't. Your coat is
soaked and you're too stiff to walk back to town. Sit
down and wait. I can be back with my wagon in a few
minutes. I'll drive you."

She did not bother to correct his assumption that
she lived in town. "I s-said, I don't need your help
anym-more. Thank you. You may leave."

The bearded jaw locked. "I said, sit there and
wait!" In the next instant her obnoxious rescuer disappeared as quickly as he had appeared.

Fuming despite her shivering, Holly waited only
until the stranger had disappeared through the trees
before pulling off her skates with her fumbling fingers
and putting on her boots. Standing stiffly, she
snatched up the skates and walked back up the path
toward the road as fast as her unsteady legs could
carry her. She was perversely pleased that the tracks
she left in the snow would be lost when she reached

the well-traveled road, and she took great pains not to leave a fresh trail as she headed home.

Entering her cabin a short time later, she slammed the door and slipped the latch. Shivering, she threw the skates across the room and stripped off her stiff coat with an unladylike epithet.

Whoever her savior had been, he was not a gentleman! She had done her duty and thanked him for rescuing her, but he was still a boor!

As far as she was concerned, she hoped she never set eyes on him again!

Where was she, damn it! He was wasting valuable time, and Daniel was waiting.

Standing at the pond's edge, Judd scanned the area briefly before following the unknown woman's tracks back toward the road, his irritation soaring. He realized he hadn't bothered to ask her name. The truth was that he had been furious when he arrived breathless at the pond's edge to see a grown woman who had irresponsibly endangered her own life. He would not have expected such stupidity from a child! Even worse, she had had the gall to tell *him* how to rescue her when she hadn't been able to do more than lie on the ice like a frozen fish!

He cursed again when he reached the road and the woman's tracks disappeared in the rutted mass. He paused, fuming.

Well, if that was the way she wanted it, that was the way she would get it! She had stolen enough of his precious time!

He climbed into the wagon and slapped the reins sharply. Growling under his breath, he decided that if he met the woman on the way back to town, he'd pick her up and take her home. If he didn't see her, he'd just leave her to find her own way home, as she obviously preferred.

It occurred to Judd that the woman was probably the cousin the Trumbulls had been expecting to visit them from the city. Anyone else would have had better sense. He realized he probably wouldn't even recognize her if he met her again. He hadn't been able to see much more of her face than those god-awful glasses and a small, red nose.

He sniffed. Well, he had done his duty and rescued the woman, even if he hadn't quite met her standards of conduct in doing so.

She had barely had the courtesy to thank him, the ungrateful twit.

As far as he was concerned, he hoped he never set eyes on her again.

Teacher's pet. Holly winced as the phrase came to mind. She surveyed her silent schoolroom. She had distributed assignments to the various age groups, ranging from six to sixteen, and all the children were working diligently to complete them. They really were dear boys and girls, the desire to learn as strong in the oldest child as in the youngest. She supposed that was true partly because they had been deprived of school for almost two months, when their former teacher, Mrs. Ballough, had been summoned to the bedside of her critically ill sister shortly after the beginning of the fall term. Mrs. Ballough had been unable to return, providing the opening Holly had filled. After a month, she had formed a true attachment to all twenty-three of her students.

But she had been shocked to realize that she did, indeed, have a pet.

Her eyes momentarily filled. She had been immediately drawn to the fair-haired boy in the front seat whose great blue eyes were trained on the alphabet he was struggling to write. She was uncertain if it was his soberness, which hinted of sadness, that had touched her. Perhaps it was the way he seemed to study her when she talked. She had learned from Mrs. Sloan, who was caring for the child in his uncle's absence, that although he couldn't remember his mother's face very well, he was certain his mother had been as pretty as the new teacher.

Holly was amused to realize that she had enjoyed a compliment about appearance for the first time in many years. She found it somehow gratifying that her attractiveness had given the quiet six-year-old a measure of comfort. She recalled with stinging clarity her own insecurity and fear at being orphaned and sent to live with a relative she hardly knew. She remembered her severe sense of displacement that had lingered despite Aunt Ellen's efforts to provide a warm home. Holly had been fortunate that her aunt had been so understanding.

Holly frowned. Unfortunately, fate had not been as generous to Daniel.

The little boy glanced up and smiled shyly. Holly smiled in return, but her smile faded when his attention returned to his work. Inquiries had revealed that his uncle, the boy's only remaining relative, left him with the Sloans on a regular basis for extended periods of time. Although most people spoke highly of the man, citing his congenial personality and his affection for his nephew, Holly had her doubts. Clearly Daniel's uncle did not see that the little boy needed more security than the man was providing. She had already written to him, requesting a meeting when he returned home. His response would reveal all she needed to know about him.

Forcing these concerns from her mind, Holly looked up at the wall clock. School had come to an end for another day. She glanced out the window. The afternoon had remained clear and cold. Daylight would last for several more hours, and it would not take her long to get home.

Holly drew herself slowly to her feet, stifling a groan. Her unpleasant experience on the pond two days ago had left her bruised and stiff. Embarrassed, she had told no one about it, not even Emily Danton, with whom she had struck up a friendship since arriving in town.

She had slept poorly after her encounter with her boorish rescuer on Saturday, with images of cracking ice and dark, angry eyes flitting in and out of her dreams. She had been so stiff on Sunday morning that she had hardly been able to get out of bed to attend church. She had been ready to put the episode behind her, however, when the new school week had begun this morning. Unfortunately, her aching muscles and bruised posterior were not as ready.

Making a valiant effort to ignore her discomfort, Holly squared her aching shoulders under the plain, high-necked black dress that had become her unofficial teaching uniform. She raised a hand to her bound hair to check for errant wisps that might mar her orderly appearance, and adjusted the annoying spectacles that had slipped down her nose. She then spoke clearly and distinctly in the teacher's voice she had carefully cultivated.

"You may put your books away, students. School is dismissed."

"Miss Collins," twelve-year-old Harry Blight called anxiously from the back of the room. "I haven't finished my assignment yet."

"Anyone who hasn't completed his assignment may take his book home with him and finish it there," Holly replied, addressing the entire class.

A chorus of farewells came from the students filing out the door, but Holly responded absentmindedly to them as she noticed Daniel lingering. He waited until the others were gone, then approached her desk tentatively. Her heart melting, she sat down again and leaned toward him, resisting the urge to slip her arm around his erect little shoulders.

"Is there something you wanted, Daniel?"

He was no longer smiling. "I gave my uncle your letter when he came home."

"Oh?"

"He asked me if I did something wrong." He paused. "Did I, Miss Collins?"

"No, of course, you didn't!" She was unable to resist placing a comforting hand on his shoulder as she fought her annoyance at his uncle's insensitivity. "I just thought it would be nice to meet your uncle, since I've met most of the other parents." She paused, proceeding carefully. "What was his response?"

"He's coming. He says he wants to meet you, too."

Judd approached the schoolhouse, stopping short as the door opened and the children poured out. He drew back to give them a wide berth, returning the greetings of the Simpson girls and the three Sloan youngsters, and nodding to several other children whom he could not identify with as much certainty.

As the children scattered in all directions, he remembered that Mrs. Ballough had always seen to it that her students filed out in an orderly manner. But then, Mrs. Ballough had been a teacher for twenty years, had been married for even longer before her husband died, and had two adult children. From what he had learned since his return, Miss H. Collins, who had stated in her presumptuous letter that she felt he was unaware of his nephew's "state of mind," was inexperienced as a teacher and a frustrated spinster in the bargain!

The path to the schoolhouse cleared, and Judd resumed his approach.

Unaware of his nephew's state of mind.

The words grated. He hadn't liked the tone of the letter, and he had better things to do than to waste time conversing with a dried-up old maid about something that was none of her business. Nor did he like the uncertainty he had seen in Daniel's eyes when Judd had read the letter. Well, he would set her straight.

He ran his hand absently against his clean-shaven cheek. Bathed, his hair cut, and wearing freshly laundered clothes, he was a new man and ready for anything.

Finding the door slightly ajar, he pushed it open. A woman sat at the desk at the front of the room. Daniel stood beside her.

He paused. "Miss Collins? I'm Judd McBain, Daniel's uncle. You wanted to talk to me?"

The woman's head snapped up and she stood abruptly, staring awkwardly at him through small, wire-rimmed glasses.

Through *familiar* small, wire-rimmed glasses.

He blinked.

It couldn't be.

The meeting was not going well.

Judd's eyes narrowed as Daniel's teacher continued speaking. Daniel had been sent out to play, and she had started the conversation without the courtesy of a smile, choosing to treat their previous encounter on the pond as if it had never happened. Satisfied to do the same, Judd had decided to listen and wait. In that time, his greatest fears had been confirmed.

Miss H. Collins. He could only guess what the *H* stood for. Probably Miss Heavy-handed Collins, or Miss Haughty Collins. Either would be an apt description of the woman's personality. He would not have believed a second encounter with her could possibly irritate him more than the first.

Did Miss H. Collins actually think he didn't realize that Daniel was troubled and insecure? Did she really believe he didn't know that his extended absences were aggravating the situation? Did she truthfully think he didn't care?

She did, and Judd's irritation surged.

Holly stood her ground, hoping she didn't appear as shaken as she felt.

This *boor* was Daniel's uncle? The poor child.

"So you're telling me that my neglect of Daniel has contributed to his insecurity."

She swallowed. Something about Judd McBain set her on edge to the point that she had difficulty concentrating. She was not accustomed to such a debilitating reaction to a man.

"Miss Collins."

"I think you're restating my words a bit strongly. I simply said—"

"I know what you said. You said Daniel is too quiet and sober for a boy of six. You said he's insecure. You said 'my attitude' toward him contributes to his insecurity." He paused, anger slowly coloring his face.

"What makes you think you know anything at all about 'my attitude' toward Daniel?"

Her jaw locked. Why did he unnerve her so? Why she was reacting emotionally instead of in the cool, professional manner she commonly used in dealing with her students' parents? "I said there was a definite *possibility* that your attitude toward Daniel was contributing to his insecurity."

"Miss Collins."

"Yes?"

"You're dead wrong."

Her temper flared. "So you choose to deny any responsibility without even discussing the matter!"

"I don't have to deny anything to you!"

"You would if you cared!"

He took a few steps closer and was now within inches of Holly's stiff frame. She didn't need that. She was already reacting confusingly to the heat emanating from his dark eyes, to the play of emotions across his strong, even features, to the fascinating way his lips pulled back against his startlingly white teeth as he sneered. Somewhere in the back of her mind, she noted that he smelled as fresh and clean as a pine forest in the sun.

A pine forest in the sun?

She inwardly groaned.

"Miss Collins," he said quietly, "let me set something straight before I go. No one cares more about Daniel than I do. And no one is going to tell me how to take care of him! Is that understood?"

Her lips twitched. The man was despicable despite his white teeth.

"Is that understood, Miss Collins?"

Her posture grew rigid. "I was merely worried about Daniel."

"You can stop worrying."

"He's a very needy child."

"His 'needs' are my concern."

"All right!"

Intensely aware of the warmth of his sweet breath against her lips, Holly took a firm grip on her emotions. "It appears we have nothing more to discuss."

His mesmerizing eyes bore into hers. "It looks like we've finally found something we can agree upon, Miss Collins."

She grimaced in an attempt at a smile. "Good-bye, Mr. McBain."

"Good-bye, Miss Collins."

In the next moment he was striding back across the classroom. Holly was somehow unable to tear her eyes from his broad back as he pulled open the door and slammed it closed behind him.

Slammed the door! When she was only trying to help!

The man really was a boor!

She hoped she never had to see his face again!

Judd strode down the walk, struggling to control his anger. He had never met such an aggravating woman, or such an opinionated one! In fact, he had never met a woman who was such a total disaster in every way!

Except for her looks. She was a damned handsome woman, despite those ugly glasses.

He sneered at his inner voice. He didn't give a damn about her looks!

He turned as Daniel approached. The boy's expression was hesitant.

"Is everything all right, Uncle Judd?"

Judd forced a smile. "Everything's fine. Your teacher and I had a good talk."

Daniel nodded, then slipped his small hand into Judd's. They walked a little and then Daniel looked up again, his eyes sober.

"Miss Collins is nice, isn't she, Uncle Judd?"

Judd choked, then made a quick decision. "Yes."

And he hoped he never had to see her face again.

A few more feet and she'd be there.

Holly took a deep breath and continued steadfastly along the frozen path. She wasn't going to let her heated encounter with Mr. Judd McBain a short time ago upset her plans.

The pond came into view and a shiver ran down Holly's spine. She had visited briefly with Emily after leaving school and had then gone directly home, pausing only to change her clothes and pick up her skates. She would not make the same mistakes again. She had learned from Emily that the pond was safe for skating if one avoided the area where it was fed from an underground spring, where the ice never froze solidly.

Holly gave a nervous laugh. A bit of knowledge she almost had received too late.

Halting at the edge of the pond, she sat on the log and removed her boots. She pulled on her skates and began lacing them, repeating a familiar litany in her mind.

She would learn to skate.

She would learn to skate well.

She would prove she could do it.

She would show that Judd McBain.

Daniel was none of her business? Mr. McBain obviously wished that were true, but she was Daniel's teacher and she had become his friend as well. No matter how dark the threat in Judd McBain's eyes, she would not abandon that boy.

In the meantime, she would come here every day until she was as at ease on the ice as she was in the classroom.

She would do it if it killed her!

Gritting her teeth, momentarily regretting her poor choice of words, she stepped out onto the ice.

3

The light snow that had begun to fall an hour ago had already covered the ground, but Judd paid it little mind. He did not expect it to last long.

He lifted his ax again and drove it down into the log, splitting it into two uniform pieces of firewood. He had spent the afternoon chopping wood, one of many chores that had gone undone during his month-long absence.

He turned at a sound behind him. Daniel had returned from school, quickly stored his books in the cabin, and come back outside to help. Daniel's "help" with stacking the wood would end up costing Judd time, but he knew how much it meant to the boy to be able to work beside Judd. It strengthened the bond between them, and Judd enjoyed the time they spent together just as much as Daniel did. His eagerness and youthful, well-intentioned fumbling never failed to warm Judd's heart.

Signaling Daniel toward the freshly split firewood, Judd frowned, awaiting the inevitable. It was not long in coming as the boy scrambled to the task of retrieving the wood while resuming the conversation he had begun earlier, in his characteristically sober tone.

"Miss Collins says I write my letters very well, and that I'm one of the best students in the class."

Grateful that Daniel had already started back toward the woodpile and was unable to see his expression, Judd grimaced. Torture, that's what it was! Since his visit to the schoolhouse a week ago, the boy had taken every possible opportunity to introduce the aggravating Miss Collins into the conversation.

Miss Collins told us a story.
Miss Collins taught me to draw a robin.
Miss Collins is teaching me to read.
Miss Collins says . . .
Miss Collins did . . .

Miss Collins, Miss Collins, Miss Collins.

Miss Collins, who had the distinction of making him angrier than any woman he had ever known! As if he could forget her!

Standing another log on its end, his jaw tight, he raised the ax and brought it down with a crashing blow.

"Miss Collins is pretty, isn't she, Uncle Judd?"

Not again.

"Uncle Judd?"

"I didn't really notice, Daniel."

Liar.

He had noticed, all right. He supposed he had noticed because his dear Betty and the irksome Miss Collins were such startling contrasts in appearance and temperament that they somehow demanded comparison.

Betty had been small and petite, hardly reaching

his shoulder when he held her in his arms. Miss Collins was tall and full-figured. Oh, not that she was overweight! She was slim, in most places. The drab witch's garb she wore in the classroom had not concealed her generous bosom and her surprisingly narrow waist.

Betty's red hair had been a fiery burst of color that she had often worn unrestrained because he had liked it that way. Miss Collins's tightly bound hair was a silvery blonde. Betty's eyes had been a lively amber that had danced when she talked. Miss Collins's eyes were as gray and cold as the ice on which he had first found her.

Betty's cheeks had been well-rounded, often flushed with color, and dotted with a fine spray of freckles that never completely vanished during the cold months. Miss Collins's face was finely sculptured, with unmarked, creamy skin.

Betty had lit up a room with the warmth of her personality. Miss Collins was so cold that she left the sting of frostbite in her wake.

"Miss Collins said the skating party is going to be bigger and better than ever this year."

Judd closed his eyes.

"She said she's going to plan games for the children, and there're going to be prizes."

Judd looked at his nephew, amazed. Daniel didn't look frostbitten. Could the boy and he possibly be discussing two different people?

"I don't understand how you didn't notice that she's pretty, Uncle Judd."

Judd glared, then set up another log and carefully raised his ax. Seeing clear, cold gray eyes instead of the target awaiting his blade, he brought the ax down with a powerful crack.

The log split in two.

So much for the bothersome Miss Collins.

"She has nice hair, doesn't she, Uncle Judd?"

Judd groaned.

The light snowfall that had begun earlier in the afternoon continued. The pale curtain of white swirled in a sharp gust of wind as Holly prepared to step out onto the pond's frozen surface, but the lingering snowfall was the least of her problems.

Her stomach knotted. Her heart pounded. She hesitated.

It wasn't working. A full week of perseverance, of coming directly home from school, changing clothes, and going immediately to the pond where she remained until dark, had little effect on her aptitude as a skater. She still spent more time sitting on her derriere than she did standing, and what little forward motion she managed was spastic and jerky. When all was said and done, she had yet to accomplish the simple feat of skating across the pond without falling. The only difficulty she had conquered was clearly marking the dangerous area of the ice in her mind, and managing to avoid it.

The rest of her life was going relatively well. She was extremely comfortable in her cabin and took the greatest pleasure in the small decorative touches she had managed on her limited income. She was satisfied that her cabin was now a home that reflected a part of her personality that she carefully concealed from most people.

Her students continued to respond to her efforts, especially Daniel, who appeared to have grown increasingly comfortable with her during the past week. He had made it a point to approach her desk after school every day for a brief, shy conversation. The effort had touched her heart. Of course, he used the words "Uncle Judd" frequently. The boy obviously adored his uncle. Did Daniel see something in the man that she had missed, aside from the dark-eyed intensity that had so shaken her, and the indefinable quality that had imprinted his image so clearly on her mind that she could not seem to elude it?

Choosing to avoid that question, Holly reviewed her plans for the skating party. All was progressing smoothly with Emily's willing help. She was wonderful, one of the few women she had met who had a truly generous spirit. Aunt Ellen would have liked her, even if Emily did have an eye for the opposite sex. Emily was perfectly respectable, of course, but definitely in the marriage market, and aghast that Holly was not.

Aside from that, Emily had given her the benefit of her experience in helping Mrs. Ballough plan the skating party the previous year. All that was left was to confirm a few more arrangements, to make certain that the innovations Holly had added were carefully noted, and to write up her report to the school board for the necessary funds.

The report would go to Mr. Cartwright, head of the school board, who favored an older teacher. Holly's apprehension heightened. She had become more convinced than ever that for her, much more hinged on the outcome of the skating party than a few hours of winter fun.

Fun. Was that what skating was supposed to be?

She shook her head despairingly, then adjusted her glasses, pulled down her wool hat, and determinedly straightened her scarf. She would skate across the pond, and do it today, if it was the last thing she ever did!

She stepped out onto the ice, furious as her knees immediately began knocking. She had to do this! Everyone was depending on her, especially her students. Their excitement was contagious, and even Daniel had begun looking forward to the event with enthusiasm.

Holly stroked cautiously across the ice. Daniel had begun interacting with the other children more comfortably since his uncle had returned. It was obvious that Daniel needed the man. She only wondered if Judd McBain knew how much.

She sniffed, annoyed as his persistent image again returned to mind. As for herself, she knew she would not know a moment's regret if the man disappeared forever from the face of the earth.

She sniffed again. The man was a boor.

He was a conscienceless oaf.

He was a—

Her feet flew out from under her and her posterior hit the ice with a hard smack. She sat on the ice, momentarily stunned and hurting. Tears filled her eyes and she brushed them away. She rose to her knees, then drew herself to her feet and stood.

Glancing upward as the snow thickened around her, she felt her frustration soar. If the snow continued, she would be forced to leave the ice. Only a little more than two weeks remained until the party, a frighteningly short time when she considered her lack of natural ability for the skill she was attempting to master.

Her jaw locked with resolution as she scrutinized the far edge of the pond. Progress sometimes came an inch at a time. Wasn't that what Aunt Ellen had always said? The trouble was, she was tired of inches. She would make it across the pond without falling, and she would do it today, whatever the cost!

Her gaze fixed on the far shore, she set out boldly. The fine layer of snow on the ice did not impede her as the rhythm of her strokes grew smoother. The particles of falling snow abraded her face and clouded her glasses as a slow confidence built within her. She was doing well, better than she had ever done before! She was moving over the ice with less trepidation. She was almost enjoying herself! She was—

Her blade caught on a rut and she lurched awkwardly forward. The world spun crazily around her as she fell, striking her head against the ice with a resounding crack.

A few moments passed before she realized that she was lying on her stomach, that the snow was still falling, and that the darkness rapidly closing around her meant that this time, she would not get up.

Whirlwinds of falling snow stung Judd's face as he walked along the familiar road, but his seething exasperation left him immune to its chilling abuse. This afternoon had been the final straw. The usually quiet Daniel had never stopped repeating Miss H. Collins's name, and Judd would not have been surprised if Miss High-handed Collins had had a hand in it. He would not put it past her to use Daniel to get back at him for his outspokenness a week ago. Well, whatever she was doing to mesmerize the boy, he would put an end to it, before another hour passed!

He inhaled angrily. Mary Sloan had not questioned him when he dropped Daniel off at her cabin. He supposed he had owed her an explanation, but he had had no intention of giving her one. This interview with Daniel's teacher was strictly between her and him. He'd straighten her out before he returned home that afternoon, or he'd know the reason why!

His eyes narrowing as the old Thomas cabin came into view, Judd slowed his step. He hadn't been in that cabin since the old man died two years ago. As much as he disliked Miss Hard-headed Collins, he had to admit it was a dirty trick on the part of the school board to give a lone woman that dreary shack, even though she probably deserved it!

Judd's step slowed as he approached the door. His brow furrowed. Small boot tracks led to the doorway and then away again. Judging from the amount of snow in the tracks, the imprints leading away from the cabin were the most recent, indicating that Miss H. Collins was not at home.

That was strange. Judd again scrutinized the tracks. If Daniel's teacher had headed toward town, she hadn't left too long ago, and he would have met her along the way.

He stepped up to the cabin door and knocked, then knocked again. He peered in the window. It was dim inside, but he could see she was not at home. He turned away from the cabin.

Trepidation knotting in his chest, he started back down the path, following the small footprints. He trudged on, losing the tracks on the road and walking without hesitation toward the trail to the pond, where the tracks resumed.

A strong sense of foreboding suddenly forcing him into a run, he covered the ground in long, reckless strides. Catching his foot on a rock, he took time only to regain his balance before continuing at a rapid pace.

The snowfall had thickened when he arrived at the edge of the pond. A pair of woman's boots rested beside a log. His stomach twisting, he strained to see through the swirling flakes, his gaze sweeping the surface of the pond.

On the ice halfway across the pond lay a still, snow-covered form.

Unconscious of all but a burgeoning fear, Judd was on the ice within seconds and kneeling beside the inert figure.

"Miss Collins?"

Cursing that he did not know her given name, he carefully turned her over. Her woolen hat was pulled low over her forehead, and her muffler was high around her face, so he could see no more than he had first seen of Miss H. Collins: a peek of eyes, which were now closed, and a small red nose. The only addition was the purple lump on her forehead that was too close to the temple for safety. But she was breathing.

"Miss Collins, can you hear me?" Panic began to invade his mind. "Miss Collins?"

Surprisingly long dark lashes fluttered, and Judd's heart leaped. He was momentarily unable to speak as he looked into large, disoriented gray eyes. They were the most beautiful eyes he had ever seen. They closed as she groaned and mumbled.

When she opened them again, her words were clear and unmistakable. "You must think me a complete fool."

Miss Heavy-handed Collins embarrassed?

"I'm all right." She tried to sit up but couldn't. She frowned. "I *think* I'm all right."

He helped her sit up, supporting her with his arm when she swayed unsteadily.

"You're groggy. If you saw the size of the lump on your forehead, you'd know why."

"I hit a rut in the ice and fell."

"I'd say you did."

"I'll be all right in a minute. You really needn't stay. I can make it home by myself."

He was getting annoyed again. "You can't even sit up by yourself."

Her gray eyes searched his uncertainly. He felt the tug of an emotion he chose to ignore.

"You have good reason to be annoyed at having to rescue me again," she said. "But the truth is I'm not up to an argument right now, so if you don't mind, just go away."

He almost laughed. This woman was sitting on a frozen pond in an isolated area during a blinding snowstorm, unable to stand up by herself, much less walk, and she was telling him to leave!

"What kind of a man do you think I am?"

Her eyes fluttered. "I don't really know, except that you're angry, and I'm not up to it."

"I'm not angry." He frowned. "I suppose I am angry." And he didn't know exactly why. He scrutinized the small visible patch of Miss Collins's face, realizing her color was poor. "Look, this isn't the time to go into any of this. You're hurt. Let me help you. Do you think you can stand?"

"Yes."

"Let's try."

He slipped his arm around her waist and gently helped her to her feet.

Steadying herself as he held her, she looked up at him frankly through a veil of falling snowflakes. "You see, I told you I'm all right. You may leave."

Choosing not to respond, Judd dropped his arm from her waist. She swayed and grabbed for him.

"Satisfied?" he asked.

"Mr. McBain, I suppose I am in need of your help.

May I impose upon you to accompany me home?" Her tone was formal, but he could feel her trembling.

He felt a swell of reluctant admiration. "Certainly, Miss Collins."

They had taken an unsteady step forward when she abruptly stiffened.

His heart jumped. "What's the matter?"

"My spectacles. I need them. I can't see any farther than a foot in front of me without them."

It occurred to Judd that a foot was far enough to see in certain situations.

He was vexed with himself for entertaining that thought even briefly. "Can you stand alone for a few minutes?"

"I think so."

Searching the surrounding ice, he found her glasses and handed them to her. His arm circled her waist as she wiped the snow from the glasses and slipped them on.

"Come on," he said. "Let's get off this ice. My feet are getting cold."

The heavy snowfall continued as Holly's pounding head kept time with her steps along the frozen trail home. She leaned heavily against Judd's side. Her legs felt rubbery, and she was short of breath.

Judd pushed open the cabin door and ushered her inside. He lit the lamp and turned to help her remove her frozen outer garments.

"I was a fool to think I could have made it here alone," she said.

His eyes met hers briefly before he stripped off the coat she had been unable to remove with her stiff fingers, and helped her toward the chair beside the fireplace. In a moment, the fire was blazing. He shed his coat and hat, then crouched beside her.

"How do you feel?"

He was so close. His presence was comforting and she felt so . . .

"Terrible."

He smiled. It was a beautiful smile.

She sighed. "I suppose I can't blame you for smiling at my sad condition. I have the feeling I jumped to unfair conclusions about you and acted badly."

His smile faded. "I have the feeling that might go both ways."

"Oh." The pounding in Holly's head increased, disturbing her train of thought. "I think I'd like to lie down."

"I don't think that's a good idea."

"Really—"

"Miss Collins—"

"My name is Holly."

His lips twitched.

"That seems to amuse you."

"No, it's just that I wasn't expecting the *H* to stand for Holly. It doesn't suit you."

Somehow that statement hurt, and she thought he realized that and regretted it.

"My name's Judd." His smile flashed. "Now don't tell me you don't think my name suits me either."

"Oh, I knew your given name. Daniel speaks of you often."

"No more often than he speaks of you, I'm sure."

"Daniel speaks of me?" If she weren't feeling so poorly, she was certain she would have been elated. She raised a hand to her throbbing forehead, felt a great protrusion and gasped. She saw concern return to his gaze at her obvious pain.

"I'll take care of that." He disappeared momentarily through the front doorway and returned a moment later with icicles he had snatched from the roof. "Do you have a clean cloth?"

"There's one beside the sink."

Back beside her in a moment, he pressed a makeshift ice pack gently to her forehead. "Hold it there while I make us some tea." He paused, meeting her gaze. "You do have tea, don't you?"

"Mr. McBain—"

"Judd."

"Judd. Of course I have tea."

"Good. Just hold the ice on your forehead and I'll do the rest. And don't fall asleep."

"Why?"

"Because it's impolite to fall asleep when you have company."

She *had* misjudged him. She managed a smile, realizing she did not resent his gruff commands as he stood and turned toward the stove.

Judd crouched beside the shivering Holly and tucked the blanket he had taken from her bed more securely around her. She trembled as she sipped her tea, though the fire was blazing and the room was adequately warm. He supposed the perilousness of her situation had begun to set in. The bump on her head had stopped swelling after the application of the ice pack, but she was obviously still suffering the effects of her fall. He had checked her eyes for an indication of a more severe problem than was immediately obvious, but the only problem had been his own when those great gray eyes had risen to meet his and his throat had gone suddenly dry.

"Are you sure you don't want me to get Doc Peel?" he asked again.

"No, please!"

"All right, don't get upset. I won't." He paused. Miss H. Collins was a puzzling woman. If he needed proof that he had misjudged her, believing she was a cold witch, he had only to look around the old Thomas cabin.

He hardly recognized the place. He supposed it wasn't the furniture that made the difference, since there wasn't a piece that didn't show signs of extended abuse, and there certainly had been no major renovations on the cabin's basic structure. Rather, there were subtle differences, some almost intangible.

Most obvious was the fact that the cabin was meticulously clean and orderly, but he wouldn't have expected less. What he had not expected were the simple white curtains trimmed with crocheted lace adorning windows that had always been bare. A matching tablecloth covered the table a few feet away, in the middle of which were a bowl of nuts and a nutcracker with hand-painted wooden handles. He was fairly certain the crystal hurricane lamp on the table nearby, and the matching lamp he had seen on the bedroom nightstand when he had fetched the blanket, had not come with the cabin. Nor, he believed, had the delicate dishes placed with artful effect on the dish rail, or the two small framed watercolors of pastoral scenes hanging nearby.

The feeling of warmth those subtle changes conveyed was as unexpected as the hidden side he was still uncovering of the woman sitting only inches away. But nothing conveyed the cabin's homey feeling more than the pine wreaths she had hung at the windows, and the holly boughs with which she had changed an old, smoke-stained fireplace into an inviting, fragrant asset to the room.

It was the kind of thing Betty would have done.

A brief wave of familiar pain accosted him, but he forced himself to consider Miss Holly Collins once more. Her light-eyed gaze that was no longer frigid flicked away when it met his. A spot of warmth expanded inside him as he realized with considerable surprise that the discomfort he had seen in that gaze had more to do with shyness than with dislike. He had to learn more about this contradictory woman.

"Why won't you let me get Doc Peel?" he asked softly. "He's a nice old coot, even if he's a little past his prime."

"Oh, it's not that." Holly shook her head, the movement obviously causing her pain.

Judd reached spontaneously toward her with concern. He stroked back a silvery wisp of hair from her cheek, noting the silky feel of the strand.

"It's just . . . " She hesitated, searching his face. "I feel like such a fool."

A strong protective instinct rose in Judd. "You're being too hard on yourself. Accidents happen."

"It's not that. I—I don't want anyone to know what I was doing on that pond."

He was momentarily confused. "I thought you were skating."

"I wish that were true." She shuddered. "I was *trying* to skate."

He was still confused. "Why wouldn't you want anyone to know that?"

"It's embarrassing. I'm uncoordinated. I'm ungainly on skates. Anyone who saw me would laugh." She took a deep breath. "No, that's not even the whole truth. I didn't want anyone to know that the real reason I can't skate is because I'm afraid."

"Afraid?"

She averted her gaze. She was proud. It had obviously been difficult for her to admit her fear, especially to him.

"Does it really make that much difference whether you can skate or not?"

Her eyes snapped back to his. The torment he saw there affected him strangely, touching a spot deep inside him that had previously been numb and cold.

"Yes, it does," she said. "The skating party is only two weeks away. Historically, the schoolteacher is in charge of the entire event, and you must know that it's one of the highlights of the season. Everything I do will be scrutinized. I'll be evaluated on how well the party turns out. My future here is almost directly dependent on how I present myself that night."

"You were hired to teach the three R's, not ice skating."

"I'm a good teacher, I know I am." She paused, clearly distressed. "But I don't relate well to some people. Some members of the school board want an older teacher with more experience. Others don't feel I . . . fit in."

"What would make them think that?"

Judd was momentarily aghast. Had he really said those words?

Holly shuddered, her discomfort growing more obvious. "Some men don't like me. They think I'm difficult."

He frowned.

"I don't mean to be, but I feel that a woman has a right to say what she thinks. I won't compromise that principle, but I also know that adhering to it leaves me vulnerable in many respects. This skating party will display my weaknesses instead of my strengths. I'll be the subject of silent ridicule, and when it's time for the school board to offer me a contract at the beginning of the year, those who resent my 'progressive' attitude will have the opportunity to demand that the school board find another teacher."

She halted abruptly. She shook her head, obviously regretting it a moment later as she raised her hand to her forehead, then shuddered again. "It's such a mess."

Her shuddering increased, and Judd's frown deepened. "Are you feeling worse?"

"I'm all right. I just can't seem to get warm. My feet are still numb."

Judd lifted the blanket he had tucked so firmly around Holly only minutes ago and uncovered her feet. They were bare. She had apparently removed her stockings when he had gone to retrieve the blanket. Her feet were also a bluish color and cold to the touch when he took one into his hand. He heard her gasp as he began massaging the warmth back into it, but she did not protest. Somehow, he had known she would not. Minutes later he looked up to see her that eyes were drifting closed. Satisfied that the color of her foot was almost restored, Judd tucked it back under the blanket and began the same procedure with her other foot. This time, however, his attention remained fixed on her face as her eyes closed completely, allowing him to study her more closely.

She was younger than he had thought and lovelier upon closer inspection, despite the ugly swelling on her forehead. With her cold facade stripped away, she was appealingly honest and unexpectedly vulnerable. He also realized as he massaged her that she had incredibly dainty feet for a woman of her height, and that he enjoyed touching her more than was totally safe.

She sighed, and Judd's throat grew thick. Yes, he enjoyed it far more.

*　　*　　*

Holly breathed deeply. Her head was pounding and her thoughts were jumbled, but somehow it seemed perfectly natural for Judd McBain to be massaging her foot with his strong hands while she all but purred.

Her thoughts wandered. Had she really revealed herself so completely to this man, the same man who had stirred such animosity only a few hours ago?

This Judd McBain, however, did not seem to be the same man. She recalled opening her eyes after her fall to see his concerned gaze searching her face. She had been humiliated, but he had dismissed her humiliation. She had been frightened, but he had dismissed her fear. Instead of the ridicule she might have expected from him a few days ago, he had given her comfort.

She opened her eyes to find him studying her intently. She attempted a smile that emerged as a weak grimace.

"Does your head feel worse?"

"No."

His eyes darkened to a deep velvet. "Tell me the truth."

"It's not worse. But it's not better."

He tucked her foot back under the blanket and rose abruptly. "I'm going to get Doc Peel."

"No!"

"Holly." He stood towering over her for long moments before he sat beside her. She was strangely aware of the pressure of his thigh against hers as he leaned close, his voice a husky whisper. A chill raced down her spine as he touched her cheek with his callused fingertips. "You may have injured yourself more than you realize. You may not be reasoning well, and it's up to me to see that you're taken care of."

Nobody had taken care of her in so long.

"No."

"It isn't up to you to make the decision."

"No."

"I've never met a more stubborn woman!"

"It's one of my failings."

"Or a woman more capable of confusing me."

"Perhaps that's because I'm confused, too."

His gaze intensified. "What are you confused about?"

The throbbing in Holly's head forced her eyes closed. "I'm too confused to know."

"Holly."

She opened her eyes again and saw Judd's acute concern. "Wait just a little while longer. Please." Then she realized that she was imposing on his time. "I'm sorry, I wasn't thinking. Daniel—"

"Daniel's fine."

"He might be—"

"He's well taken care of. I'll wait a little longer, and if you aren't feeling better, I'm going to get the doctor."

She closed her eyes. She didn't have the strength to argue. Her feet were warm now and she was tired. She lay her head back against the pillow Judd had placed behind her. "May I sleep now?"

"If you want to be impolite."

"You'll forgive me, won't you?"

He mumbled something she couldn't quite make out as she began drifting off. She wasn't sure, but it sounded like, "Right now I could forgive you anything."

Darkness had fallen. The cabin was filled with the aroma of toasted bread and of the smoked ham Judd had discovered in a cold box outside the door. He turned at the sound of movement behind him, his gaze narrowing assessingly as Holly stirred.

Sitting beside her moments later, he waited as she opened her eyes. He had sat in that spot without moving for a long while after she had fallen asleep. He had told himself that he had to remain there so he could be sure she was breathing normally. He had continued to watch for a rise in her temperature, even though he eventually realized that when he touched her incredibly smooth cheek, he was thinking very little about the heat there.

Holly's eyes opened. They were an extraordinary shade of gray, more like velvet than ice. She managed a weak smile that left him oddly shaken.

"How is your head?"

She touched the lump on her forehead and winced. "Better, I think."

"Do you think you can get up?"

She glanced at the window and was obviously taken aback to see that it was no longer light. She looked back at him. "What time is it? Yes, of course I can get up. It was thoughtless of me to sleep so long."

He helped her to her feet, drawing her close to his side for support as she wavered. Her head reached him mid-cheek as she turned toward him. Her breath was sweet against his lips as she glanced up briefly, and her hair smelled like flowers.

"I'm sorry I took so much of your time. Daniel must be waiting for you. He'll be worried. Please don't feel you should stay any longer."

"Daniel's fine. You aren't." She fit comfortably into the curve of his arm as he urged her across the room and stopped beside the table set for two. "Do you think you could eat something?"

Her stomach growled and Judd laughed, noting that he was reluctant to relinquish her as he drew out a chair. "Sit down. I hope you don't mind my inviting myself to dinner, but I'm hungry."

"Of course I don't mind."

He waited until she was comfortably seated before he turned to the stove. Minutes later, Holly met his gaze soberly as he sat down across from her.

"Thank you. For everything."

"It's my pleasure."

Strangely, Judd realized it was.

She was feeling much better. Her head was no longer pounding and she was steadier. But she knew that her inner warmth had little to do with the lessening of her physical discomfort, as Judd donned his coat and hat and turned back toward her, his hand on the door latch.

They had eaten and talked, or rather, she had talked. She had begun slowly, and then the words had rolled off her tongue, telling him about Aunt Ellen and her life before she came to Vermont, and her thoughts about teaching and all it meant to her.

She didn't truly understand why she had gone on so. It could have been that the fall had knocked her off balance in a way she had not expected. Or the way Judd had looked at her, as if he were unwilling to miss a word she said.

Her throat tightened. "Judd." She paused, suddenly at a loss for words. "I have more to thank you for than I can possibly express."

Standing tall, incredibly broad, and darkly serious, he studied her face with a gaze as palpable as a caress. She felt it touch her forehead, her cheek. She swallowed as it swept her suddenly trembling lips, then returned to meet her eyes.

"You're certain you're all right now?"

"Yes."

He touched her forehead assessingly, and a thrill shot down her spine. "No fever there," he muttered thoughtfully. "Other than a lingering headache and an ugly bruise, I don't think there'll be any problem. If you're not in school on time tomorrow morning, I'll come and check on you."

"I'll be fine."

He opened the door and her heart sank. She realized to her surprise that she did not want him to leave.

Suddenly he turned back to her, as if a thought had occurred to him. "I'll teach you to skate."

She was too startled to speak.

"Good night."

He had closed the door behind him before she could respond; and then she realized that, indeed, had she tried to respond, she would have been unable.

4

"Uncle Judd?"

Judd turned toward Daniel where he sat at the table, his notebook in front of him. Daylight was fading fast as Judd cooked their evening meal and Daniel did his homework. The ritual of spending time in companionable silence had been established shortly after he had first brought Daniel home.

It was obvious, however, by the seriousness in Daniel's eyes that homework was not on his mind. "It's almost time for the skating party, you know."

Judd winced. How well he knew. He had been secretly meeting Holly for lessons that entire week. She was not doing well.

"Yes, I know."

"Are you coming to the party?" Daniel's gaze did not budge from Judd's face.

Judd shrugged. "I usually go, don't I?"

"You didn't last year. I went with Mrs. Sloan."

"Oh, that's right."

How could he have forgotten? Betty's cousin, Jean, had been visiting last year at the time of the skating party.

Jean, who so closely resembled Betty with all that red hair and freckles that his heart had almost stopped at the first sight of her.

Jean, whose voice was so reminiscent of Betty's in tone that it had set him to quaking.

Jean, who had brought such vivid memories of Betty to mind that he had been unable to make love to her.

Jean, so much like Betty without really being like her at all, who had made him realize more clearly than ever before that no one could ever take Betty's place in his life or in his heart.

A familiar pain stirred. He had made that promise to Betty as her eyes had closed for the last time, and he had been faithful to that promise.

"Uncle Judd?"

Judd snapped back to the present.

"I'd rather go to the skating party with you, Uncle Judd."

Judd chastised himself for his selfishness. Daniel had suffered as great a loss as he.

Judd nodded. "I'm going this year."

"You're sure?"

"I'm sure."

Instead of the smile Judd expected, Daniel returned to his homework as sober and thoughtful as before.

Holly looked up from her desk after dismissing her class for the day, focusing her gaze on a small patch of sky through the schoolroom window. It was a bright blue and the sun was still shining, despite the dark clouds rapidly approaching in the distance. She had to get home quickly if she were to have any time at all on the pond.

Her face flushed as Judd's dark-haired image flashed before her mind. She refused to admit that her eagerness for the hours she spent on the pond had more to do with the man she would be spending them with than with her determination to master skating. Judd had been truly wonderful, endlessly patient with her awkwardness and uncertainty. She knew it was difficult for him to understand why she could not conquer her fears. He had natural balance and was completely at ease on the ice, while she had yet to relax enough to attain a smooth stride.

In truth, the sensation of Judd's strong arm around her waist as he guided her on the ice, the intensity that flashed in his gaze when he looked down at her, and the deep, rolling timbre of his voice as he spoke soft encouragements did little to still the anxious fluttering of her heart. His occasional smile made her heart pound, leaving her either breathless or chattering like a fool. But, somehow, there was little that she felt she could not say to Judd.

Though she was at a loss to explain her feelings, Holly knew that they were not based solely on Judd's appearance, even if the sight of him had begun to stir a longing within her that she could not quite comprehend. Aside from that, it did seem that Judd grew more handsome each time she saw him. She was not certain when she had first noticed that the lashes rimming his dark eyes were incredibly long, or that his eyes were so deep and black as to appear bottomless when he drew her into the curve of his arm to skate. She knew only that while sheltered there, while supported against his side and leaning against him for balance, she never felt more secure or more—

More what?

Unsure, she could not describe her feelings except that when she was close to Judd and he smiled down at her, she was . . . happy.

She considered that thought. She was *almost* happy. Draining heavily on the joy of the moments she spent with Judd was the realization that although she spoke freely about herself, Judd seemed reluctant to do the same. She knew only what was general knowledge, that his wife had died a few years ago. He had reportedly been devastated by her death. Emily had told her that Judd's friends had worried for a time that he would not survive.

Holly's brow tightened. Emily had also supplied the unsolicited information that although he was friendly with the unmarried women in the area, Judd had shown no special interest in any of them. Emily had sniffed with disapproval when she repeated the rumor that Judd took care of his intimate needs while away on trapping trips, and that he was often delayed in coming home because he had a woman somewhere.

Holly's lips twitched. That was Judd's business, of course, but she didn't believe it. Judd had been on his way home from a trapping trip the first day she had met him. He had been irritable, bearded and unkempt, totally unlike the Judd she had come to know, and definitely not in a condition that would indicate he had been spending time with a woman.

Since she had come to know him better, she realized that he had doubtlessly been agitated because he had been late in returning to Daniel. It pained her to realize how deeply she had misjudged his sense of responsibility to the boy.

Yes, Judd was nice. He was more than nice. He had been gentle and caring when she was injured, and he had been true to his word in trying to teach her to skate.

Which brought to mind the second and even more wearying drain on the moments she and Judd spent together. Her skating had not improved despite her best efforts. At first Judd had seemed amused by her awkwardness, but she knew that his amusement was fast fading. She feared he would soon grow as impatient with her as she was with herself, and for some reason she could not bear that thought. She had never wanted a man to like her the way she wanted Judd to like her. She had never wanted a man to respect her abilities the way she wanted Judd to respect them. She had never enjoyed a man's company the way she enjoyed his. She had never entertained thoughts of a man the way she entertained thoughts of him, and she had never felt so deep a desperation as she did at the thought that he might not feel the same.

In a way that was somehow inexplicable, Holly had the feeling that time was growing short in many aspects of her life, that she had to do something quickly or she would lose far more than she had ever dreamed when she first came to Benton Falls.

"Miss Collins?"

Snapping from her reverie, Holly turned toward the familiar voice. Her heart warmed as she met Daniel's gaze. The special spot of tenderness she reserved for Daniel alone expanded. He was such a sweet boy.

"Is there something you needed, Daniel?" she responded softly, forcing herself to maintain a professional distance.

"No. I just wanted to tell you something."

Her throat filled with emotion. The once silent,

uncommunicative Daniel was neither silent nor uncommunicative with her any longer.

"What did you want to tell me?"

His slow smile melted her heart. "I won't be going to the skating party with Mrs. Sloan this year."

"You won't?"

"No. My Uncle Judd is taking me."

"Oh. Didn't he take you last year?"

"No. He was sad last year, sad like I was when my father went to heaven."

She was momentarily silent. "Did someone in your family pass away?"

"My Aunt Betty." He paused. "She went to heaven a long time ago, but my Uncle Judd is still sad sometimes, just like me."

"Oh."

"My Uncle Judd is a good skater. He won a race once."

"He did?"

He inched closer. His eyes grew solemn. "My Uncle Judd is nice. He thinks you're nice, too."

She remained silent, letting Daniel continue.

"I know he does because he doesn't get mad anymore when I talk about you."

She was at a loss for a reply.

"When I tell him you're pretty now, he doesn't say he didn't notice anymore, either."

She flushed.

"Do you think my Uncle Judd is handsome?"

"You'll be late getting home if you don't leave soon, Daniel."

"That's all right. Mrs. Sloan's been taking care of me in the afternoon because Uncle Judd's been helping a friend with a couple of sick horses all week."

Sick horses.

"Mrs. Sloan will be worried if you're late."

"No, she knows I sometimes dawdle. Miss Collins?" He paused. "Do you think my Uncle Judd is nice?"

"Daniel—"

"He is, isn't he?"

"I think you should go home now, Daniel."

His blue eyes did not relent.

"I'll see you tomorrow morning. And don't forget to do your homework."

The little boy smiled. He had a beautiful smile. It reminded her of his Uncle Judd's.

Her heart gave a little leap. Daniel's *nice, handsome* Uncle Judd.

The wind had grown colder. Judd looked up and saw that the sun had disappeared in a sky that had grown gray and grim. No one had to tell him what that meant. Within the hour the frozen pond would be covered with a fresh layer of snow, and Holly's skating lesson would be over for the day.

Watching as Holly's heavily bundled figure moved cautiously across the ice a distance away, Judd caught his breath. She was going to fall again! He started toward her, then stopped abruptly as she regained her balance. How she had managed to stay on her feet was a mystery, and a minor miracle.

Judd shook his head. Holly had not exaggerated. She was ungainly and uncoordinated. Anyone who saw her efforts on the ice *would* probably laugh.

He had laughed at first, but not now.

Skating toward her with strong, swift strokes, he caught up to her and slid his arm around her. Her waist was narrow even through the heavy coat she wore. He drew her closer as she looked up at him uncertainly, steadying her in the curve of his arm. He was momentarily stunned at the pleasure it gave him to hold her.

But then, the time they had spent together skating during the past week had brought him more pleasure than he had either expected or desired. He supposed that was true because each day had revealed another intriguing facet of Holly's personality.

Somehow, he had not expected that the stiff, cold, and arrogant Miss H. Collins he had met on this same pond would have a sense of humor, or the ability to laugh at both her anxiety and her awkwardness on the ice. That had been fortunate, because her wild, frantic arm movements as she struggled to maintain her balance, her short, chopping strokes before she fell, and her panicked yipping as she started going down had been truly comical at first.

But he realized that beneath Holly's humor lay a grim determination.

He could not count the times she had been headed for another fall, only to smile or laugh aloud as he caught her. He wondered if Holly knew that the smile that lit her face also lit his heart. He wondered if she suspected that thoughts of her had begun invading his mind throughout the day, and that last night he had also entertained her in his dreams.

He drew her closer and she looked up again. She wasn't smiling anymore, and he felt himself tense. The day had gone badly from the first moment she had stepped onto the ice. He had been successful in saving her from four falls, and unsuccessful in saving her from another three. It was obvious that she was unaccustomed to failure, and that she was becoming more frustrated and angry with herself with every passing moment.

He realized suddenly that she was waiting for him to speak.

"You're trying too hard. You're too tense. Relax and everything will come naturally."

"I'm perfectly willing to relax if you'll tell me how." She shrugged, then glanced away, obviously upset. "I don't know what's the matter with me. I'm starting to think I'll never master these skates in time for the party."

"That's strange talk from the woman Daniel quoted only this morning as saying, 'You can do anything you want to do if you set your mind to it.'"

She glanced back up at him, unexpected torment visible in her clear eyes. "What's wrong with me, Judd?" she asked softly. "There isn't a child in my class who can't skate better than I can."

"I don't know if that's true."

"I do. And even if it weren't, I think I'm safe in saying there isn't a child in my class who looks as foolish as I do on the ice."

"You're too impatient with yourself."

"Impatient?" Her eyes widened. "How can you say that? It's been days, and I'm still tottering and chopping around instead of skating!"

He frowned. "Maybe you can think of a way to avoid putting on skates at the party."

"So you do think I'm hopeless!"

He knew he shouldn't have said that.

"I suppose if I were a more generous person, I'd free you from your promise to teach me to skate."

"Holly—"

"It must be terrible for you to come here every day and watch me clomp around on the ice."

"Holly—"

"You must be wishing at this very moment that I'd give the whole thing up and—"

"Holly."

She clamped her mouth tightly shut and turned

away. Cupping her cheeks with his hands, he turned her back to face him again. Her warmth surged through him although her skin was chilled. He knew instinctively that although her lips were also cold, they would warm easily under his. And they would taste sweet. He suddenly longed to taste that sweetness.

"Holly, I—"

"Are you disgusted with me, Judd? Because the truth is that I'm disgusted with myself."

Disgusted with her? No.

He searched her eyes. How could he tell her that far from being disgusted with her, he had suffered with her every frustration and setback that day; that each time she had fallen, he had been barely able to restrain himself from soothing her in his arms.

Filled with emotion, he halted his thoughts abruptly. "I said I'd teach you to skate," he whispered, "and I will. Do you believe me?"

He watched uncertainty flicker across her wind-reddened face. It was a beautiful face, despite those ugly glasses and the bright red nose.

"Yes, I believe you."

He dropped his arms back to his sides. Solemnly, determinedly, he took Holly's hand.

The silence between them stretched long and taut as Holly trudged back from the pond at Judd's side. She had tried so hard. She hadn't wanted to disappoint him. He had been so certain he could work the magic that would turn an awkward duckling into a graceful swan on the ice. She had been almost grateful when the snow had begun falling so heavily that they had been forced to stop for the day.

She looked up. The wind had stopped, allowing

the glittering flakes to fall straight down in a thick curtain that blocked out the sky. The unrelenting veil of white enclosing her and Judd grew more beautiful by the moment. She had never noticed the true magnificence of winter before she had come to this backwoods community where each snowfall transformed the surrounding forest into a land of enchantment.

But there was no magic or enchantment in her situation. She was still the ugly duckling, and the possibility of ever emerging as a graceful swan grew dimmer every day.

Raising her head as she neared the door to her cabin, she faced Judd squarely for the first time since she had picked herself up off the ice for the last time and headed toward the pond's edge.

"I'm sorry," she said, hating the tears that choked her throat.

"Sorry for what?" he snapped with unexpected anger.

"For being such a dunce."

"Stop that, Holly."

"I'm so disgusted with—"

"I said stop that!"

Incredulous at his tone, she felt a slow anger alter her maudlin state. "I won't have you raising your voice to me, Judd."

"I'll raise my voice if that's what it takes to make you realize you're acting like a damned fool!"

"I won't have you cursing at me, or treating me like a child, either."

"Even if you're acting like one?"

"Acting like a child?"

"Only a child gives up when she's frustrated."

"I haven't said I've given up!"

"What would you call it, then?"

She was silent for a moment. "Why are you so angry?"

"That's a stupid question."

"Is it?" She swallowed against the lump in her throat. She had never seen this part of Judd. His attack was unexpected, and undeserved. She had tried to follow his instructions, but somehow gliding as easily as he did on the ice was beyond her.

"Skating doesn't come as naturally to me as it does to you."

"That's an excuse."

"I don't have to make excuses to you, Judd."

"Then why are you making them?"

She paused. That was a valid question. Why *was* she making them?

"I suppose because I felt I owed you an explanation for—"

"You don't owe me anything."

No, she didn't owe him anything. Her jaw locked. Unspoken was the other truth Judd's statement had implied. He didn't owe *her* anything, either.

She realized that Judd could not possibly have made himself any clearer without saying the words. He had tried his best to help her, but his efforts had been to no avail. He was tired of it all. He wanted a way out and knew no other way but to use his anger to put an end to the lessons.

Pride surged to Holly's rescue. "I think we've gone as far as we can go with these lessons, Judd. I appreciate your help, but I'm freeing you from your promise."

"I thought you said you hadn't given up."

"I haven't. I've just faced the fact that certain accomplishments are beyond me. That's my choice to make, I believe."

"Now you *are* acting like a dunce!"

She stiffened, amazed at the anger she saw in his eyes, at the tight lines that destroyed the tenderness she had seen in his face only a short time ago. How dare he? What gave him the right to criticize her?

"Good-bye, Judd."

"What?"

She drew herself erect. It took all her strength to raise her chin and remain cool. "Good-bye. I appreciate your effort, but I think you'll agree that we've both gone as far as we can with this."

"Have we?"

"Yes."

His expression turning as hard as stone, he stiffened. His broad shoulders had never seemed so massive, his features so hard, the tightly suppressed anger so menacing.

"Yes, I suppose we have," he said. "Good-bye."

He turned abruptly and within moments had disappeared into the falling snow.

Feeling suddenly empty, Holly entered her cabin. The fire was still burning and the room was comfortably warm. But she took none of her usual pleasure in returning home as she removed her outer garments, smoothed her dress, and hung the damp clothes beside the fireplace.

Suddenly realizing that several heavy strands of her hair had worked loose from the bun at her nape, she pulled out the pins, allowing the pale mass to fall freely over her shoulders. She was uncertain of the moment when she realized that her tears were falling freely as well.

Sobs suddenly wracking her, she covered her face with her hands. Judd was gone and he wasn't coming back. She had told him to go. Damned fool that she was.

*   *   *

Damn her!

Judd strode angrily along the familiar road. It was over and done. Miss H. Collins had dismissed him with the same ease with which she dismissed her class for the day. It made little difference to her how he felt about it, or that she had torn his insides apart, wounding him with each word she had uttered against herself!

What *was* wrong with her? Didn't she realize she was worth ten of those fools whose scrutiny she feared? Didn't she know she was far above those backward few who searched for a flaw in her performance as a teacher? Didn't she recognize she was to be admired for the principles she had devoted herself to pursuing, instead of being scorned?

And didn't she know that with each fall she had taken that afternoon, that with each time she had dragged herself to her feet and tried again, he had wanted her more?

Yes, wanted her more, damn her!

She said he had treated her like a child.

He stopped, truly considering her accusation for the first time. Perhaps he had.

His expression tight, he turned back in the direction from which he had come.

The tears had started and they wouldn't stop.

Holly sank to the edge of the sofa, too weak to stand. Somehow it had all gone wrong. She had wanted to make Judd proud of her, not angry. She had wanted to prove to him that she was strong and worthy.

Worthy? Of what? Of whom?

Her throat choked painfully. Worthy of *him*, of course.

Daniel's softly voiced questions returned unexpectedly.

Do you think my Uncle Judd is handsome?

Oh, yes, she did. She was only now brave enough to concede that he was the image of the man she had never admitted to entertaining in the back of her mind, the man who would enter her life one day and become to her all the things her father had been to her mother.

Do you think my Uncle Judd is nice?

Yes, she had thought he was nice. She had thought he was more than nice. She had thought he was strong and sincere, gentle and considerate. She had felt he cared, and she had cared in return.

But she had been mistaken. He had been angry with her when she had not met his expectations. He had become sharp and critical, and in doing so, he had broken her heart.

But why did she feel *she* was to blame? Why did it hurt so much to realize that Judd would never come back to knock at her door, to talk to her, to take—

The door of the cabin burst open, and Judd stood silhouetted against the falling snow.

She gasped, somehow unable to move as he entered, shook off his coat and hat, and closed the door behind him.

"What are you doing?" she asked, her voice hardly recognizable to her own ears.

Judd's gaze was hotly intense as it met hers. A slow shuddering began inside Holly as he walked toward her, halting so close beside her that she could feel his warm breath against her. He looked solemnly down at her.

"I came back to tell you that you were right."

Her heart pounded in her ears. "I was right?" she said softly.

He moved closer. "I *was* treating you like a child."

He raised his hand to her cheek. His hand was cold as it stroked back a strand of her hair that had adhered to the trail of tears there. As he brushed away the dampness with his palm, Holly felt only the heat of his touch.

"If I hadn't been treating you like a child, I would have told you how I feel. I would have told you that I was angry because I couldn't stand to hear you denigrate yourself. I would have told you that every word you spoke against yourself caused me pain. I would've said that I didn't want you to feel alone, because you aren't alone. I would've said that I want you to lean on me."

"To lean on you?"

Holly realized with sudden clarity that those words spoken by any other man would have incited her to instant fury. But they hadn't been spoken by any other man. They had been spoken by Judd. The same Judd who was stroking her cheek with a trembling hand. The same Judd who was drawing her close. The same Judd who was looking down at her with a gaze so earnest and loving that it seared her heart.

"I don't want you to torment yourself anymore, Holly," he said in a ragged whisper. "Let me hold you in my arms for a little while so you can forget everyone and everything but the two of us." His voice was hoarse with emotion. "Let me do that for you, Holly."

Then his mouth was on hers and his arms were crushing her close. His strength, his warmth, filled Holly with joy. Unaware of the moment when her arms slid around Judd's neck, when she urged him closer, she felt an aching need unlike any she had ever known.

This was what she had wanted! This was what she had felt was meant to be from the first moment Judd's eyes had met hers! Fool that she had been, she had been unwilling to admit to herself that Judd was the realization of the hope she had secretly cherished within her heart, and that once she had met him, her only true fear had been admitting all that she could never be without him.

His kiss deepened and she responded with every ounce of love she possessed. She had never dreamed she could feel this way. His lips awakened her. His touch incited her. She was alive in his arms.

Uncertain of the moment when Judd stripped away his coat, Holly knew only the thrill of his heaving chest against her breasts and the mutual pounding of their hearts. She felt his hands in her hair. She heard his passionate rasps. She felt his touch.

Returning touch for touch, caress for caress, she was swept up into a raging maelstrom of emotion that blinded her to all but the wonder of Judd's arms as he carried her to her bedroom.

His strong body shuddering, he halted abruptly, then set her on her feet.

"Holly, are you sure?" he asked, uncertainty in his voice.

"Am I sure?" Her throat was tight as she sought to reply from a font of love deep within that was marked with Judd's name alone. "Yes, I'm sure."

His mouth met hers passionately. His hoarse whispers touched her inner core as he brushed her forehead with kisses, as his lips lingered against her brows and fluttering eyelids, trailed to her cheek, then to her mouth with a ferocity that made her quake.

Beyond thinking as Judd stripped away the impediment of clothing between them, Holly felt the softness of the bed beneath her. A sense of joyous predestination swept over her as his naked flesh met hers at last.

There was no greater glory than the sweet beauty of the moment as Judd worshipped her with his lips. There was no greater splendor as he explored the hidden contours of her body with his kisses. There was no greater bliss than the loving ardor that rose in great, overwhelming swells, silently declaring all that had gone unsaid between them.

Her wonder soared. She had not known love could be so strong, that it could bring about a metamorphosis so absolute that she now realized it was this moment for which she had been born.

Judd moved atop her and she caught her breath. His hard male flesh tight against her moist softness, myriad emotions flashing across his impassioned face, he hesitated briefly before plunging deep and full inside her.

Tears unrelated to the brief, stinging pain flooded Holly's eyes as the rhythm of loving began. Raising herself to Judd's thrusts, she joined him in the ageless cadence of love, breathtaking emotions assaulting her in wave after wave. Hunger. Rapture. Ecstasy.

The moment abruptly upon her, Judd's harsh gasp echoing in her ears as he clutched her close, Holly met his passion full measure.

The heat of passion spent, his powerful body still and replete, she felt Judd stir. Raising himself slowly, he searched her face with eyes of fathomless, liquid onyx. Too filled with love to speak, Holly saw an unidentifiable emotion flash briefly the moment before he lowered his mouth again to hers.

Judd's kiss caressed her lips. A whisper. A sigh.

And the loving, the sweet, sweet loving, began anew.

*   *   *

Silence within. A snowy twilight without. A heady, womanly scent in his nostrils and the warmth of soft, feminine flesh pressed against his.

Judd awakened from a light sleep to the semidarkness of a small room. Holly's long, silvery hair lay stretched across the pillow beside his as she lay tucked against his side. He felt the press of her breasts against his chest and the light fanning of her breath against his neck as he turned to look down at her. She was sleeping. Her expression was serene, content. Lush dark lashes lying against flawless cheeks, delicate lips slightly parted, a clear, high brow and small, perfect features. She was beautiful.

Judd shuddered. Oh, God, what had he done?

Anguished, he closed his eyes. A red-haired, laughing-eyed image flashed before his eyes and his pain increased. He had been with other women since Betty's death, but they had meant nothing. The exchanges had been brief, a matter of physical satiation that had not impinged upon his love for Betty and the promise he had made her.

Betty's image flashed once more, this time pale and still as she had been when her eyes had closed for the last time.

Betty, his love, his life.

Betty, so young to have had her life stolen from her.

Betty, whom he could not allow to slip into obscurity, to fade from his memory as she had from the face of the earth, as if she had never lived at all.

No one will ever take your place in my life and in my heart. I promise you that, Betty, my darling. I promise you.

He opened his eyes and torment stirred anew as he looked down at Holly's sleeping face. She was not like the other women. She was not to be taken casually. Her warmth, her depth, were not to be wasted on a man haunted by a lost love, a man who could never love her as fully as she should be loved and whose heart was not truly his to give again.

But Holly felt so right in his arms.

No.

He wanted, he needed—

No.

Holly deserved more than he could ultimately give her.

She was not for him.

Reality returned abruptly as Holly opened her eyes to her partially lit bedroom. She was naked under the coverlet, and she was alone.

A sudden panic assailing her, she searched the shadows. Relief surged when she saw Judd dressing silently in the far corner, his trousers and boots already donned, his muscular back turned to her. He reached for his shirt, turning so that his profile was etched against the silver light streaming through the window, and Holly's throat squeezed tight with an emotion so intense that she was almost undone. She had not believed herself capable of loving a man, but she had been wrong. Judd had not said the words—she was uncertain whether she had, either—but they had rung over and again in her heart. She heard their echo still.

Silently throwing back the coverlet, Holly reached for the wrapper nearby and slipped it on. Her feet bare, she moved across the room, reaching Judd's side before he heard her approach. She slid into his arms, a silent sigh sounding within her as his strong arms closed around her.

"It's late," he said, his voice hoarse as he whispered against her hair. "I have to go."

A sudden chill of premonition crawled up Holly's spine, and she drew back. "You have to go?"

"Daniel's expecting me." The shadowed room did not allow her a clear view of his expression as he raised a hand to stroke her cheek. "I'll see you tomorrow."

"Tomorrow."

She swallowed as he stared down at her for long moments before lowering his mouth to hers. His kiss was filled with hunger. It lingered, growing more passionate as he crushed her closer still, as his hands roamed her back, tangling in her hair, as he separated her lips under his, groaning.

He drew back abruptly, leaving her unsteady and breathless. "Good-bye, Holly," he whispered.

She stayed him with a light touch on his arm as he turned toward the door. "Tomorrow," she said.

She was still standing where he had left her as the harsh sound of the door latch reverberated in the silence.

Ironically, her skating had improved.

Standing on the frozen pond, Holly stared across the ice to the far shore where she had stepped out an hour ago. Despite the cold, the day was bright and clear.

It had not snowed for three days, since the afternoon Judd and she had made love. Since then, the wind had blown the snow from the trees, and the woods had lost their enchantment. As had her life.

Taking a deep breath, she started back toward the two figures standing on the opposite shore. She had skated back and forth across the pond five times without mishap, her strides growing increasingly smooth and strong. She was almost at the point where she would be comfortable enough on the ice to face the skating party. Under other circumstances, she would have been ecstatic at her accomplishment.

She watched Judd's expression as she neared him and Daniel. It was sober, assessing, and impersonal.

"You're doing fine, Holly."

"You're doing fine, Miss Collins."

Daniel's childish echo of his uncle's words brought a flicker of a smile to her lips. He was such a darling boy. Were the situation different, she would have been delighted to have him there.

All traces of a smile faded from her face.

Tomorrow. The word had rung with promise when Judd had spoken it three days ago, the beauty of the intimacy they had shared still fresh between them. But she had only been fooling herself. Tomorrow had come and he had appeared at her door as promised, Daniel at his side, a small, smiling, deliberate buffer between them. The two days since had been the same.

She had been at a loss to explain it at first. She had wanted to say so many things to Judd that could not be said with Daniel there. She had told herself that Judd would find a moment for a tender word or touch that would convey the same wealth of emotion she felt, or that he would return to the cabin at a later hour so they might talk. But he had not.

She had made excuses for him, telling herself that he was merely being discreet. But the excuses had paled, and reality had loomed painfully clear.

She skated to a halt beside Judd and looked up at him. He appeared the same. His hair was still thick and black, his eyes still dark and intent, his features still stirringly handsome. He still stood tall and broad of shoulder, self-possessed power innate in his carriage.

Yes, he appeared the same, but he was not.

She lifted her chin, ignoring the sudden, blustery gust that raised a spray of glistening snow around them. "I think I've had enough for the day."

He did not respond.

"It's not late, Miss Collins," Daniel piped up, his voice cheerful despite his disappointed expression. "It's fun out here, isn't it? You're skating much better. Uncle Judd said so."

She managed a smile. "Yes, I think I've done well, too, but I'm tired and I have some papers to mark at home. You wouldn't want me to disappoint the children who are expecting to learn the results of their tests tomorrow, would you?"

Daniel shrugged. "Some of them wouldn't care. Mary Ryan said she hoped she never saw her mark."

She took another deep breath. "I'm sorry, Daniel."

Judd finally spoke. "You heard Miss Collins, Daniel. She's had enough for today."

Yes, Miss Collins had had enough.

Holly nodded in response to Daniel's chatter as they walked back to her cabin, the knot of pain inside her twisting tighter. The direction the boy's thoughts had been taking was obvious. He had developed a deep liking for her, and seeing his Uncle Judd and her together had stirred his hopes.

Her pain became excruciating. For a while she had entertained the same childish fantasy as Daniel.

She gathered her strength as they approached her cabin door. Turning toward Judd on the doorstep, she looked up directly into his eyes. She was not ashamed of what she had done. She'd lain in his arms because she loved him. Accepting that reality gave her courage to smile.

"I don't think I'll need to take up any more of your time, Judd. I'm proficient enough now on skates to make a respectable showing at the skating party. I thank you for that."

"B-but we don't mind!" Daniel responded again in his uncle's stead. "We can come back tomorrow to skate with you again, can't we, Uncle Judd?"

Judd's gaze flickered briefly. "I think Miss Collins has other things to do."

"Do you, Miss Collins?" Daniel's voice retained a spark of hope.

Unable to face Judd any longer, Holly looked down at Daniel with true regret. "Yes, I do, dear. I'll see you in school tomorrow."

"You'll skate with us at the skating party, won't you?"

She did not dare look back up at Judd. "I'll be very busy, but I'll try."

"Good-bye, Holly."

"Good-bye, Miss Collins."

"Good-bye."

She entered the cabin and closed the door behind her.

5

On the crisp, clear night of the party, a great, silver winter moon shone down on the community skating pond. An occasional gust of wind raised the titters of the girls and sent them scurrying toward the closest bonfire, while the boys ignored the chill to linger near tables where heaping platters of food had long since disappeared, and a few desserts remained. Aware that the cookies she had contributed were among the first to be consumed, Holly turned to assess the progress of the evening.

Horace Waters, the gregarious community blacksmith, was about to take up his accordion again, to the delight of the skaters. An indefatigable favorite of the locals, he had once again proved that his musical ability was as notable as his brawn. William Tucker was about to plunge a hot poker into another barrel of apple cider as a line of thirsty partygoers, cups in hand, rapidly formed beside him. Skaters young and old continued to circle the pond, laughing, singing, and spilling good cheer. Holly herself had just returned from a turn around the pond with Jeremy Little, one of the community's most eligible bachelors.

She continued her mental checklist. She had not disgraced herself with her skating, her students had performed their individual chores well and with good spirits, and everything was running smoothly. The skating party was a great success. She should be very happy.

Her searching gaze stopped short. Judd was standing a short distance away, speaking to Emily.

Oh, bother Emily! She was such a flirt!

Determinedly blinking away the tears that flooded her eyes, Holly raised her chin. What was wrong with her? Judd had made the situation between them quite clear. She had run into him several times on the street since that day a week ago when he and Daniel had left her at her cabin door. He had been polite and distant, and her pain had been almost unbearable.

Dear Daniel continued to bring up his Uncle Judd's name at every opportunity. The boy was obviously confused about the relationship between his uncle and her. She could almost believe that Daniel suffered as much as she at the distance Judd kept between them.

Holly's gaze lingered as Judd smiled down into Emily's animated face. It was strange. Shortly after being informed about the community skating party and her part in it, Holly had looked forward to this night with great apprehension. All her energy and thought had been directed toward it. She had somehow convinced herself that with its successful conclusion, all her problems would be over.

Oh, Judd.

"How about another skate, Miss Collins?"

Holly turned toward a smiling Jeremy Little. He was a good-looking young man who was perhaps a few years older than she, but he seemed immature. She had the feeling that he had yet to develop in both mind and body, a truly ungenerous thought, considering how helpful and attentive he had been tonight.

She forced a smile. "I have some things to attend to, Jeremy. Perhaps later."

"I'll be back. You can depend on it."

She shook her head, more surprised than pleased at his response. Jeremy actually seemed to like her. She was not accustomed to having pleasant relations with men. Could it be that her participation in this evening's event had effected an acceptance of her by the community in general?

"A glass of cider, Miss Collins?"

Holly turned toward William Tucker, who somehow looked exactly the same in his outdoor skating wear as he did behind the counter of the general store.

"No, thank you. I think I've had my fill."

"Don't say that!" Mr. Tucker's gold tooth glinted in the light of the bonfire. "A pretty young thing like you shouldn't give up so easily!"

A pretty young thing?

Holly suppressed a shudder. The poor fellow meant well.

Emily stood on tiptoe and whispered into Judd's ear. Judd responded by laughing aloud, and Holly turned away, her throat tight.

"Good evening, Miss Collins," Mr. Cartwright said, standing behind her. "We haven't had much chance to talk tonight."

Holly winced as she turned to face him. She was not up to a conversation with the school board chairman at the moment, especially a school board chairman who didn't like her.

Mr. Cartwright saved her from responding.

"I've been trying to catch up with you, but you've been so busy all evening. I was gratified to see that you had at least taken the time for a turn on the ice. Jeremy is a nice fellow, isn't he?"

Really. Did he care?

She managed a noncommittal response. "Jeremy skates very well."

"You seem to be quite proficient on skates yourself."

She couldn't take much more of this.

"Miss Collins." Mr. Cartwright's round, wind-reddened face grew suddenly serious. "Perhaps this isn't the time or place, but there is something I'd like to say to you." He hesitated, then continued with obvious determination. "When you first came here, I felt you didn't quite fit in. I felt you were too young, too hostile, and too progressive, and that given enough time, you would demonstrate those points quite clearly to the rest of the school board members. I expected that what I considered your 'frosty' manner would do the trick at this party and that I would have no problem convincing the others to see things my way. However, the reverse seems to have proved true. Miss Collins"—his pudgy face flushed as he reached into his pocket and withdrew a folded sheet—"I've been withholding this contract, pending the outcome of this evening. I would like to extend my apologies to you for that, and tell you that I'm truly gratified that you've proved me wrong. You've done as excellent a job tonight as you appear to be doing with your students. I hope you will accept my apology as well as the contract we're offering you."

Speechless, Holly accepted the folded sheet

Mr. Cartwright held out to her. She clutched it tightly. A firm contract represented everything she had worked so hard to accomplish, everything she wanted.

Almost everything.

With sudden clarity and true sorrow, Holly knew what she had to do.

She struggled to control her trembling hand as she returned the folded sheet to Mr. Cartwright. "I'm sorry. I can't accept this." Her attempted smile wobbled. "Something has come up and I'm afraid I must return to Boston after the first of the year. I—I would prefer that no one be told tonight about my leaving. The children have worked very hard on this party and I don't want to chance casting a pall on the festivities."

"Miss Collins—"

"I'm sorry, Mr. Cartwright."

Leaving the astounded gentleman behind her, almost as astounded as he by the momentous step she had taken, Holly slipped off into the shadows.

Hoping he had seen the last of Emily Danton for the evening, Judd searched the surrounding area for a familiar slender form. Where was she?

His stomach tight, he scrutinized those circling the ice. When he did not see Holly among the skaters, he frowned.

It had been a long week filled with endless days and fitful nights since he had left her at her cabin door.

Damn! What was wrong with him?

He searched the shadowed forms on the pond's edge. His emotions were out of control, that was what was wrong! They had been out of control since the afternoon when he had made his way back through the snow to Holly's cabin and taken her into his arms.

Memories stirred anew: the wonder of holding
Holly intimately close in his arms; the shattering
response of her lips under his; her scent; tasting her;
the sounds of her sensual awakening when their flesh
had touched for the first time. He had bathed her
breasts with kisses and he had felt the active fluttering
of her heart under his lips, much like a captive bird
struggling to be free. He had set Holly free with his
loving, set her free to soar in the joyous ecstasy of the
moment, and he had soared gloriously with her. And
when she had lain in his arms afterwards, her naked-
ness against his, her eyes a misty velvet that had
touched his heart with the wonder he saw reflected
there, he had shared her wonder. He had drawn her
closer then, willing the moments never to end, knowing a supreme contentment.

His agitation increased. No, he couldn't be feeling
what he was feeling! He couldn't care so deeply for
another woman after Betty, most especially a woman
he had known so short a time. He had known Betty all
his life. The love between them had grown gradually
with the years. It had matured as they had matured,
and when it had finally reached full fruition, he had
known Betty as well as he had known himself.

Yet the days were now filled with Holly's image.

The nights were now filled with longing. As his
sense of betrayal grew.

Those thoughts resounding in his mind, Judd continued to scour the flickering shadows for Holly. He
had seen her skating with Jeremy Little earlier and he
had been overwhelmed with jealousy. Jeremy was a
randy piece for all his youthful smiles. If he had
slipped off with Holly somewhere and was—

No, that wasn't his concern. Holly didn't belong
to him. She never would. He had already known the

only love in his life. He would never love anyone the way he had loved Betty. Betty, his chum, his friend, his lover, his wife.

"Mr. McBain?"

Stirred from his tormented thoughts, he turned toward the anxious boy at his side. Billy Dunn's chapped face was tight with concern.

"Mr. McBain, there's somethin' wrong with Daniel."

Judd was immediately alert. He silently cursed, realizing he hadn't seen the boy since he had joined his classmates at the dessert table over an hour ago.

"Where is he? What's wrong?"

"He's hidin'."

"Hiding? Where? Why?"

"He's on the other side of the pond where it's dark. I think he's sick or somethin' because he's cryin'."

Crying.

Again cursing the intense preoccupation that had made him lose track of time, Judd started immediately toward the area Billy had indicated.

The red-gold light of the bonfires became undulating shadows as Judd reached the far side of the pond. He paused. "Daniel? Where are you?"

Silence his only response, Judd called again. "Answer me, Daniel. Billy told me you're here somewhere. Are you all right?"

His anxiety soared. Where was the boy? "Daniel?"

"I'm over here."

Kneeling beside Daniel moments later, Judd peered down into his nephew's shadowed face. It was wet with tears.

"What's the matter, Daniel? Do you have a stomach ache?"

"No." Daniel avoided his gaze. He shrank from his touch.

"Tell me what's wrong."

Daniel shook his head, refusing to speak.

"If you won't tell me what's wrong, I'm going to ask Doc Peel to come and look at you."

"No! I don't want Doc Peel! He won't do any good. She's going away."

Judd went slowly still. "What are you talking about?"

"She's leaving. I heard her tell Mr. Cartwright that she's going back to Boston after the first of the year!"

"Who's leaving?"

"Miss Collins."

No.

"Why is she leaving? I thought she liked us. She said she did."

Judd drew his nephew into the curve of his arm. He could feel Daniel trembling.

"I know she liked me, Uncle Judd. Her voice was soft when she talked to me, and her smile was real nice."

Judd was numb. "I'm sure she does like you."

"She liked you, too. She smiles when I say your name." Daniel paused. "At least, she used to smile."

"She doesn't smile anymore," Judd said thoughtfully.

"Do you think she's mad at me? Do you think that's why she's leaving?"

"No, no." Judd drew Daniel closer, the numbness turned to pain. "I'm sure Miss Collins isn't angry at you. I'm sure you have nothing to do with her decision to leave."

"If she's not mad at me, do you think she'll stay if I ask her to?"

"Daniel."

"I don't want her to leave. I want her to stay."

"Daniel."

"It was better with her here, wasn't it, Uncle Judd? I thought maybe if we could make her like us a lot, she would—"

"We don't need anybody else but the two of us, Daniel. We're fine the way we are."

"But it was better with her here." His nephew's eyes pleaded his understanding. "It wasn't so lonesome. It's supposed to be that way, isn't it? Like it is at the Sloans', with a father and a mother?"

His pain suddenly too acute to abide, Judd whispered, "Dry your eyes, Daniel. Miss Collins wants to leave. There's nothing you can do."

Judd drew Daniel to his feet and wiped away his tears with a sense of sad finality. Holly had made her decision and it was over and done.

"I don't want her to go, Uncle Judd."

His throat suddenly thick, Judd swallowed. "It's better this way," he said, his voice suddenly hoarse. "Come on, let's go back."

Yes, it was better this way.

It was also the only way it could be.

It was snowing again.

Holly paused at her window. The heavy white flakes were again renewing the landscape, turning barren trees into graceful spires that glittered in the last remaining rays of silver moonlight. She knew she would never forget either the beauty of the forest surrounding her cabin or the intimate beauty she had shared one late afternoon within these walls.

Turning away from the window, she walked back toward the fireplace and stared thoughtfully into the flames. The skating party had dwindled to an end an hour ago and the happy partygoers had gradually wandered home. Unsuccessful in dissuading Jeremy Little from accompanying her home, she had bid the determined young man a firm good-night at the door and slipped inside, grateful to be alone at last so she might review the evening in her mind. Now, with the fire kindled to a glowing warmth and snow falling again, she had reached the same conclusions she had reached hours earlier. The party had been a success, everyone was pleased, she had not embarrassed herself with her skating. And she had never been more unhappy.

Nor had her choices changed. She could not stay in this small community, not now. Once having experienced the wonder of Judd's arms, having known what it was to truly love, to remain so near and yet so far from him was a torment beyond bearing. She had realized in that moment of sudden clarity at the party that she could not spend her life being reminded of what could have been and would never be, without eventually losing all joy in what was. She had to put the hours of love Judd and she had shared behind her, as Judd obviously had.

Judd, who had taught her to love.

Judd, who had taught her to lose.

The silence was shattered by a sudden knock on the door, and Holly jumped. Her heart beating rapidly, she turned toward the sound. "Who's there?" she called, her voice sounding unfamiliar to her ears.

"It's Judd."

No, she didn't want to see him. Her pain was too great.

"I'd like to talk to you, Holly, just for a few minutes."

"No. It's late."

"Holly, please."

Please.

She opened the door. It was Judd, all right, heartbreakingly handsome, the snow that covered his coat emphasizing his overwhelming height and breadth as he stood outlined by the light of the full winter moon. She did not smile.

"What do you want, Judd?"

"I'd like to come in."

"I think not."

"Just for a few minutes."

"Judd."

"It's important."

She hesitated. Then she saw the torment in Judd's eyes and stepped back to let him enter, the ache inside her growing.

Judd removed his hat and shook off his coat. The actions, painfully familiar, returned memories of another time when Judd had come back to her cabin to set things straight between them.

She thrust the bittersweet memories firmly from her mind. "Please say what you came to say and go, Judd. It's late."

His dark eyes searched her face. She saw his regret at her coldness. He hesitated as he started to speak.

"The first thing, the most important thing I want to say, is that I'm sorry." He took a short step closer. His eyes darkened. "You don't know how sorry I am for the way I've behaved. My only excuse is that I was confused. When Betty died, something inside me went numb. I didn't want that part of me ever to thaw, not only because I thought it would be a betrayal of Betty to *feel* again, but because to experience that kind of love again would be to make myself vulnerable to pain I knew I couldn't survive a second time."

His expression tightened. "Then I met you, Holly. Somehow I knew from the first moment I saw you that it was going to be different with you. I couldn't get you out of my mind. You made me angrier than any woman I'd ever known. You tormented me with your sarcasm. You taunted me with your sharp mind. You touched me with brief glimpses of the woman within that you struggled so desperately to conceal. Before I knew it, I was so sensitized to that hidden woman that I suffered her frustrations and pain, shared her hopes, and wanted as desperately as she for that woman to succeed. Then I came to know the total woman that you are, and the slow, inevitable realization dawned that what I really wanted was you.

"I tried to rationalize it then, Holly. I told myself that true love takes years to grow and that feelings that spring up between a man and a woman on short acquaintance have nothing to do with an emotion as noble as love. I told myself that once a man gave his heart completely to one woman, it was no longer his to give again. I told myself that to love again was to make a travesty of that first love, to negate it as if it had never existed at all."

Judd paused, his torment visibly increasing as he searched her face for understanding. "I told myself that the hours we'd spent in each other's arms meant nothing beyond the moment. I convinced myself that my need for you was nothing more than lust, that the feelings you evoked in me were transient emotions that would soon fade. They didn't fade, Holly."

His gaze lingered with an almost palpable touch on her lips, inflaming her aching need for him.

"Strangely, it was Daniel who finally made me recognize where I had gone wrong in my thinking when I realized that Daniel's love for you in no way impinged upon the image he cherished of his mother. Rather, it enhanced it by bringing to life feelings that had lain dormant within him for so long.

"I also realized that Daniel had merely responded instinctively to the love he needed to make his life complete. I wondered then how I could have been so blind not to see that the same applied to me."

His dark eyes filled unexpectedly. The liquid heat there stirred a similar warmth inside Holly.

"With Daniel's help," he continued hoarsely, "I've finally put the past to rest. I know it may be too late for us, that you may never be able to forgive me for the way I treated you, but I had to say what I've wanted to say since the first moment I took you into my arms.

"I love you, Holly," he said in a rasping whisper. "I love you the way a man should love, with my whole heart, with nothing held back. I know that now.

"The only thing left for me to say is that if you can't forgive me now, I hope you'll be able to forgive me someday, wherever you may be, because the truth is that loving you the way I do and knowing how I've hurt you, I need your forgiveness as much as I need your love."

She stood immobile, too moved to respond.

"Holly," he whispered, "say *something.*"

Still unable to speak past the emotion that filled her, she raised her trembling arms to him. She saw the moment of incredulity in his gaze before he closed the distance between them in an anxious step and crushed her in his embrace.

Gasping as his lips closed over hers, as he swallowed her words of love with his kiss, taking them within him to cherish as she cherished him, Holly surrendered to the beauty between them and welcomed him freely into her heart.

Judd. Yes, she loved him. How very much she loved him.

She gazed past him through the window at the

bright winter moon that glittered on the falling snow. Then she looked at Judd and read the pledge in his eyes, a pledge that echoed on his lips.

ELAINE BARBIERI, the beloved, award-winning author of more than twenty novels, has lived for the past twenty-four years in a beautifully wooded area of northern New Jersey and, coincidentally, wrote "Winter Moon" during a winter of the heaviest snowstorms in decades.

She was born in the city, where the "forest" was the park a few blocks away, and the "skating pond" was a tennis court flooded by the parks department. She has warm memories of the many hours she and her brother spent on that flooded tennis court. Like Holly, she was not a proficient skater, and spent much of the time on her knees. As for Judd McBain, the hero of "Winter Moon," he was definitely not at that frozen tennis court, though she always wished he had been.

II

GENTLE RAIN

Evelyn Rogers

1

Spring, l875
Pikeville, Tennessee

"Orem!"

Daisy's voice drifted over the morning air as she headed toward the brow of the hill in front of her. The grass and a scattering of early-spring wildflowers stirred across the meadow; otherwise all was still.

"Orem!" she called again, doubtful of a response from the youngest of her three brothers. She'd never been much good at summoning them, or at calling pigs, for that matter, both handy skills on the Abernathy farm.

Daisy sighed. Not the most dependable Abernathy, nineteen-year-old Orem was the best with animals, and today he was supposed to be tending Daisy's horse. At the end of the month he'd be riding Marigold in the race arranged by the owner of Pikeville's stable, Earl Selfe, and Orem would win the ten-dollar first prize, money Daisy would take with her when she moved to Aunt Clyde's boardinghouse in Chattanooga.

Moving, she thought, breathing deeply. A necessary evil, was the way she looked at it. What with her
middle brother Lucas's recently taking a new bride,
Daisy had little choice but to leave. Her sister-in-law
Maude Louise, the youngest of nine children, had ideas
of her own about running the house and farm, and
now she was little Cleo's mama. Two strong-minded
women on a pig farm was one too many, anyone with a
lick of sense could see that. Daisy's heart might be
heavy these days, but her mind was made up.

As she strode through the pasture, seedpods from
the spring grasses clung to her trousers, and the damp
earth sank beneath her sturdy brogans. Marigold came
over the hill and toward her at a run. She was a beautiful animal, cocoa brown with a mane and tail the same
golden color of Daisy's own hair. The boys had traded
for her when she was a spindly filly, a gift to Daisy on
her seventeenth birthday. That was the same year Cleo
was born and her mama Orodean stepped on a rattler
and died, leaving Lucas a widower and Daisy to raise
her infant niece.

It seemed to her the years in the hills were marked
by births and deaths. And by good-byes.

She shushed herself. What was wrong with her
this morning? Everything around her made her think
of leaving, which was a month away. No one knew of
her plans, but she'd decided she'd tell her family
tonight.

Running, her long, thick braid bouncing against
her back, she met the mare in the middle of the field,
near a lone hickory where the horse's water bucket
rested. She nuzzled Marigold and was nuzzled in
return before glancing at the bucket. Empty. Surely
Orem wasn't somewhere still arguing with their oldest

brother Junior as they had outside her window this morning, awakening her from a deep sleep.

The talk had been about who made the best sour mash whiskey in Tennessee. It wasn't much of a topic, to Daisy's way of thinking, even when it turned to her brothers making a taste comparison. But she knew continued discussion was a possibility.

Since returning from the War Between the States, twenty-five-year-old Junior had shown a dislike for serious labor. He'd caught the malaise, she told herself, using one of the words from the dictionary Aunt Clyde had given her. So it was more than likely he and Orem were off arguing and not helping Lucas in the cornfield or with the hogs.

She found Lucas behind a plow, tilling one of the farm's few stretches of flat land that allowed for crops. Lanky and fair-haired like the rest of the Abernathys, Lucas at twenty-three was the worker in the family, alongside Daisy, of course.

"You seen Orem or Junior?" Daisy asked, shading her eyes with her hand.

Lucas reined in the gray workhorse and leaned against the plow handle, taking off his straw hat and wiping his forehead with his sleeve. His yellow hair clung in a band of sweat around his head.

"Only Junior. He said something about him and Orem setting up a test. Wanted me to be a part of it, but I told him there was work to do. He's with the hogs. You could ask him where Orem's bound."

Her mind working furiously, Daisy tapped a brogan against the fresh-turned dirt. "They were having an argument this morning over who's the best moonshiner around, Jack Daniel over in Lynchburg or Nathan Keene, the Whiskey Man."

"My vote'd go to the Whiskey Man."

"That's not the point, Lucas. They were saying how they needed a sample of Keene's mash to compare with what they already had of Jack Daniel's. It'd be just like Orem to go after it."

Lucas's brown eyes brightened. "That's what they meant by the test." The light in his eyes faded. "Of course, what with Maude Louise being a Baptist and all, I couldn't rightly take part."

Daisy fought her impatience. "Where's this Whiskey Man live?"

Lucas's rawboned face crinkled into a frown. "Why're you asking?"

" 'Cause more than likely that's where the rapscallion's gone."

His frown deepened. Lucas was the slowest-thinking of the boys, but that made him the most cautious.

"You thinking of fetching him?" he asked. "Best not. Keene don't like folks snooping around. He's a genuine recluse, that's for sure."

"I don't want Orem getting into trouble. If I'm figuring rightly, he's after Keene's whiskey, and he hasn't got a penny to his name."

"Whiskey Man sells his moonshine through the Clutter boys down the hill, but Orem knows the way to his place. We came across it last year up in the hills on a squirrel hunt. Keene didn't greet us kindly." Lucas slapped the straw hat back on his head. "I'll go get him."

"You've got planting to do. I'll be careful. Orem's on foot. Chances are I can get there before him, warn Keene what's going on, and then ride on home. He can't take offense at that."

She had to wheedle a little more, but as she'd expected, Lucas gave her the directions she wanted.

* * *

A short time later she was riding Marigold along the twisting paths that led higher into the hills, through woods thick as homespun. The sun was almost directly overhead, the morning mists having long burned away, and the hillsides were fast turning green after the wet, mild winter. Despite the April chill that had her rubbing her sleeves, everything looked so pretty she could almost thank Orem for running out on his chores.

Daisy loved the springtime with its glorious bursts of new life. Stroking Marigold's mane, she devoted her attention to the beauty around her. Too soon she'd be saying good-bye to the hills and to Pikeville, riding the river the hundred miles to Chattanooga, and accepting at last Aunt Clyde's invitation to live with her.

It was all for the best that she go. Lordy, she was twenty-one, an old maid, the best years of her life winging by like crows fleeing a shotgun blast. When her mama was only a year older than Daisy, she'd already borne four children, known the love of a good man, and had her own home.

Daisy didn't have one of those things, but there wasn't a prospective husband between Pikeville and the Tennessee River who interested her, certainly not with Earl running off every suitor who gave her a glance. He claimed he wanted to marry her, but all his money couldn't make her forget he wasn't gentle or kind. Or make her give him the kiss he was always pursuing. She'd take particular pleasure in letting him know the prize money would be sending her out of his reach.

But there was more to it than spiting Earl. That ten dollars was more money than she'd ever had, and after she'd parceled a portion out to her kin, she'd still have enough to make her feel rich, even in the city. She'd also prove to Aunt Clyde and her new husband

that she wasn't just a poor relation taking advantage of
their good will.

As she guided Marigold on the trail that wandered
along the edge of a deep gorge lined with vines and
shrubs, she could hear a creek babbling somewhere
below in the wild growth of the hollow. A dogwood
clung stubbornly to the side of the hill, its white petals
as pretty as pearls against the green slope. Close by, a
redbud was still in bloom. Birds sang from a hundred
limbs of oak and poplar trees. On a day like today she
could think only happy thoughts.

Even leaving the farm, her beloved gardens, and
her four-year-old niece didn't seem so bad. She'd be
taking with her the knowledge that the hills would
keep on turning out all this beauty the way they had
since the Creation. If the city got her down, she could
pull out memories of this morning and know in her
heart that everything was right with the world.

Lordy, Aunt Clyde was right about her. She was
beyond a doubt a deep-dyed optimist. Even in the
darkest of times, hope found its way into her heart.

Wishing she could trill like the birds, she started
to hum, then to sing her favorite hymn from the
Pikeville Methodist Church. She was barely to the chorus of "Bringing in the Sheaves" when she saw a sleek
metal shotgun pointed just over Marigold's forelock
and aimed straight at her.

She reined Marigold to a halt. Her gaze went to
the stock of the gun, to the powerful-looking hands
gripping it, to the blue shirtsleeves, the wide shoulders, strong neck, and lean, suntanned face of the man
blocking her path. Hatless, he wore his whiskey brown
hair even with his collar. With the sun at her back, the
light fell directly on him. He squinted into the bright-
ness, his eyes unreadable.

He had a strong nose and chin and a mouth set a little crooked, so that he seemed about to smile. The gun indicated otherwise.

"Good day," she said with forced cheerfulness. "Out hunting squirrels? I've seen more'n a dozen this morning off the trail chasing one another's tails like they'd been liquored up."

"What are you doing here?" he asked, then glanced past her down the trail. "Are you alone?"

His voice was deep-pitched and mellow, and he took his time speaking. He didn't sound like he came from around these parts. The realization didn't settle her twisting stomach any, or help her draw an easy breath.

"There's lots of folks back down the trail a ways. Menfolk," she said, wishing she were better at lying. "With guns like yours."

"Hunting squirrels?"

She ignored the sarcasm. "I'd be obliged if you would lower the gun, Mister. It makes Marigold all-overish."

His thick brows arched, almost meeting the shock of hair that fell across his forehead. "Marigold would be the mare," he said.

Daisy nodded with more enthusiasm than she felt. "I named her when she was a filly. Because of her coloring."

"And her sex," the stranger said.

Daisy blinked. "Oh," she said, heat rushing to her face. "Yes, *Mari*gold." He wasn't being forward, she decided, just showing he was listening.

"Truth is," she said, "I like anything to do with flowers. I was crazy about her right from the start."

She wished she weren't rambling, but she always talked too much when she got nervous. And she was real nervous now. Then the gun barrel lowered to the ground. Wiping a sweaty palm against her trouser leg, she sighed in relief.

"Were you going to shoot?" she asked.

The stranger's broad shoulders lifted a fraction. "It's not loaded."

Daisy's temper flared. "Then why did you want to scare a body like that?"

"A trespasser, you mean. I've had one too many this morning. You wouldn't know anything about that, would you?"

Daisy started. "Orem. Of course. You're the Whiskey Man."

"Who's Orem?"

"My rascally little brother." She shook her head, her fear evaporating like the morning mist. "You must be awful tired of looking into the sun."

She dismounted, straightening her stiff joints, brushing loose tendrils of hair away from her face. Up this high in the hills the air was brisk, but with the sun's rays and the heavy braid against her back, she felt her shirt clinging damply to her skin.

"Funny how a body can be hot and cold at the same time," she said.

He stared at her strangely, and she felt a peculiar shiver along her spine.

"Yes," he said. "It can be funny that way. You always wear men's trousers?"

Something in his voice unsettled her more than the gun. She thought about jumping back up on Marigold and trotting down the trail toward home, but like all the Abernathys, she had a stubborn streak that Aunt Clyde said would be her ruination.

"I'm Miss Daisy Abernathy, sister to three of the finest men in the world. I'm proud to wear their hand-me-downs when there's no need to slick myself up."

Again a quick flick of his eyes—she saw now that they were amber—seemed to take her in from her braid to her brogans. "No, there's no need to slick yourself up, Miss Abernathy."

"You have the advantage of me, sir," she said. "Are you in truth Nathan Keene?"

"Better that than a revenuer." His comeback was quick.

Seeing as how he was a moonshiner, Daisy took the comment as humorous. "My brothers claim you can't get much worse than a government man." Grinning, she impulsively stuck out her hand. "Pleased to meet you, Mr. Keene."

He ignored her, but she waited. At last his warm hand covered hers. Feeling his calluses against her palm, she silently prayed he wasn't feeling her sweat, and pulled her hand away.

"The trespasser you spoke of could very well be my brother Orem. He and Junior—that's our oldest brother—were having an argument over who makes the best sour mash whiskey, you or Jack Daniel. Only they didn't have a sample from the Whiskey Man. That's what they call you, but you must already know that."

She fell silent, realizing that something unpleasant had crept into his expression. Somewhere a mockingbird sang with wild enthusiasm, but the song didn't sound half as sweet as it had back along the trail.

"My mash can be bought through the Clutters," he said stiffly. "That's halfway down the hill to the west. I'm a private man, Miss Abernathy. I do not welcome intruders."

A yell from the woods at his back stopped her response. "More caterwauling," he muttered as he hurried toward the sound. She followed, Marigold clopping close at her heels.

The trail twisted at a steep angle to the right, then left, and a narrower path took them into a level clearing where the most unusual house she had ever seen came into view. As yellow as fresh-churned butter, it had lots of windows and fancy molding around the top of the porch. Keene hurried around the side of it, and Daisy dropped Marigold's reins and hurried after him.

"Don't shoot!" someone yelled. It was Orem. Before she saw either of the men, she could suddenly smell the whiskey, so strong it almost knocked her off her feet.

2

Daisy halted behind the house. "Lordy," she whispered.

Nathan Keene stood directly in front of her, his shotgun pointed across a square of plowed ground at Orem. Her brother's rangy frame leaned against a barrel that spilled whiskey from its spigot like a waterfall. The liquid filled the furrows, covering the newly sprouted green shoots, and she reeled again from the odor.

Orem raised his hands. "Don't shoot, Mr. Keene. I got the handle turned, then something happened and it wouldn't shut. Only wanted a cup or so." His eyes were wide and desperate as he held up an empty pint jar. "I was gonna pay you for it. Honest." His panicked gaze fell to the ruined garden. "Don't know how I'm gonna take care of this, though."

Keene tossed the gun aside and sloshed across the wet ground to turn off the spout, then backed away, his denim trousers stained with mud and whiskey.

"Orem Abernathy," Daisy said, her hands on her hips, "if I had a willow switch handy, you'd be feeling it on your backside."

Orem gawked, seeing her for the first time. "Aw, Daisy, what're you doing here?" He sounded bothered more by her presence than by his troubles with the whiskey barrel and the gun.

"To stop something like this from happening." She looked in dismay at the ruined garden, then at Keene. He stared back at her with a bemused expression.

As upset as she was, she couldn't help noticing particulars about him: his strong features, the intelligence in his eyes. He seemed to be at least thirty, and he was tall, close to six feet, Daisy guessed.

He wasn't a handsome man, she decided, his features being a little too irregular, but he was a man whose face might linger in a woman's mind. Common sense told her to be afraid of him; he could load that gun fast enough. But it wasn't fear that was twisting her stomach into knots. It was something else she couldn't name.

She tried to speak, but the whiskey fumes choked her.

"Let's go around front," Keene said, his long legs striding past her. She and Orem fell in behind, his whiskey-soaked work boots squishing with each step.

"I'm sorry, Daisy," Orem whispered. "Swear to God I am."

"Now you've taken to swearing."

He sighed, then fell silent.

Keene was waiting for them by the porch, a large brown-and-white cat curled at his feet. "Don't worry about paying me back," he said. "Just get on down the hill and forget you know the way back here."

"We can't do that," Daisy said. "We're obliged to replace your loss."

"I absolve you of any debts."

Orem's face wrinkled in confusion. "You sure talk funny for a moonshiner."

"He's saying we don't owe him anything," Daisy explained, "but he's just being cordial."

"I am not being cordial," Keene snapped.

"Beg to differ, Mr. Keene, no offense intended. I know cordial when I hear it, and I know a debt when I encounter one. Abernathys are honorable folks. How much do we owe you?"

The cat rubbed its back against Keene's legs. He reached down to scratch behind the animal's ears, then stood, his eyes trained on her.

"Fifty dollars."

"Fifty dollars!" Daisy and Orem wailed.

"The garden is ruined for at least this year. I'll be trading good whiskey for vegetables through the winter and into next spring. That's eighty cents a quart I'm losing in whiskey sales, and then there's the inconvenience. A man's got to consider his time worth something."

Daisy suspected he was inflating the value of his time, but maybe that was because she'd never put a price on hers.

"We'll call everything even," he added, "if you two go away and forget you ever saw me."

Now she was certain he had inflated the amount they owed him. He was trying to frighten them off. But she didn't want to leave the hills with a troubled conscience. A debt was a debt and had to be paid.

But fifty dollars! Marigold would have to race from Pikeville to the Kentucky border to make that kind of money.

Her mind working furiously, she looked past him

to the unusual yellow house with its fancy scrollwork along the eaves. It was as pretty as a magic cottage right out of a fairy-tale book. A wicker rocker on the porch seemed to be just waiting for a princess to come along and plop herself down to stay.

"I'll bet you built this," she said.

Keene didn't respond, but she saw right then that he was not only a moonshiner, but an artist with wood as well. Too bad something was lacking, something that made even the humble Abernathy log house look more like a home.

She pictured the farmhouse with its rows of vegetables on one side and flower beds on the other. Only this morning Cleo had pointed out the green hyacinth shoots poking through the yellow-streaked rich black loam. She pictured, too, the lilac bush against the back of the house, its branches already loaded with purple blooms, and the crepe myrtle beginning to fill out.

Where were Nathan's lilac bush and crepe myrtle and flower bed? They were missing, that's what, and whether the solemn-faced Whiskey Man knew it or not, they were necessary to complete the dwelling's charm.

Daisy's consternation vanished like mist in the sun. She saw a way to clear their obligation to Keene, to share the beauty of her flowers and the bounty of her food, to get out of Maude Louise's way, and to keep herself busy enough to stop fretting about leaving the hills.

The idea came so close to perfection she almost laughed out loud.

"Orem," she said, "you start for home. Marigold and I will be along directly. Don't look so worried. Mr. Keene means no harm."

Keene growled something about her being mistaken,

but Orem left anyway. Daisy didn't waste time getting to the point.

"There's no need to lose your vegetables or sacrifice your sour mash in trade. We're leaving now, but we'll be back tomorrow morning early. Don't look so grim. We'll be bringing things, not trying to cart 'em away."

"You will not," he barked.

Paying him no mind, she whistled for Marigold, who was grazing beside the house. "All I ask is that you keep that rifle out of sight. Loaded or not, it gives a girl a fright."

Watching her ride away, Nathan cursed himself for not running her off more efficiently. He also noted how neatly she rode a horse, her trim backside shifting in the saddle, her thick golden braid bouncing against her slender back.

Damnation, he thought, and slammed into the house, Wordsworth slipping through the door behind him. Daisy Abernathy was out of sight and he was still seeing her, both her backside and her front, as she'd stood with her hands on her hips, chastising her brother, her cheeks flushed beneath a dozen freckles, her blue eyes blazing, her lips—

When was the last time he thought about a woman's lips? Or the fit of her shirt over her bosom, or the curve of her hips and legs? She'd been inappropriately clad, that was the problem. He refused to believe he'd been living alone too long.

Solitude was a permanent state for him. He'd seen too much of the world, both during and after the war, to seek out prolonged company ever again. He had his books and his cat and his house, all protected by the hills and woods. He had his work, too. They more than compensated for the lack of a woman in his life.

At thirty, he was done with the urges of the flesh. If today he felt a little heat and tightness in places that hadn't been stirred in a while, it was only because he'd been taken by surprise.

He scooped up Wordsworth and scratched behind his ears. "Old man, Miss Daisy Abernathy is a single-minded woman, the worst kind there is. But she'll soon find out she's no match for a single-minded man."

Wordsworth responded with a skeptical meow. Dropping him, Nathan headed for the back door to work in his woebegone garden. He soon saw all was lost. So for the rest of the day he plowed the fields of corn and rye, walking behind his mule Coleridge, trying to concentrate on turning even rows. But instead of a black tail swishing over the mule's ample rump, he saw a yellow braid bouncing against a straight and slender back. Checking the sky, he saw a pair of smiling blue eyes regarding him with amusement.

At dusk he put Coleridge out to graze with his gelding Browning, then worked at the distillery. He was as proud of it as he was of his house. He'd assembled the rig in a hillside cave. No moonshiner had a more perfect setup—even temperature, seclusion, an underground spring of limestone-filtered water he'd tapped into at the rear.

Venting the cooker had been a problem at first, until he found a break in the cave not far from the spring. Pick in hand, he'd spent a month widening the narrow aperture until it suited his needs.

He grew the corn and rye for the mash. His partners, Claude and Abner Clutter, provided the barley malt. They also hauled the barrels down the hill and sold the mash by the quart. They preferred burned-out pickle barrels, claiming that the residue gave the liquor a special bite.

Splitting the profits with them, Nathan didn't make much money. But with his simple life, he didn't need to. When sales were slow, he dipped into the money he'd accumulated working as a carpenter in his travels after the war.

That night, for the first time in years, he dreamed of the war. He woke weary and heartsick, as grouchy as the bears that once lived in his cave, asking himself if he would ever find permanent peace.

As promised, the Abernathys arrived early the next day while the condensed mist was still dripping from the trees. The girl rode Marigold and her brother walked behind her. They both carried gunnysacks whose contents Nathan could only imagine.

He thought about loading the gun he used to frighten the crows. But they kept returning, like the Abernathys.

Or maybe he could throw stones. It was a good thing for the two young people that his deceased parents had raised him to be a gentleman and that some of their teachings had lingered.

Miss Abernathy didn't seem to notice his mood. After a cheery "Good morning," she tied her mare in a patch of sunlight, then took a few turns around the house, her brother and a reluctant Nathan close behind. She stopped by the whiskey barrel.

"Any reason you picked this place for your garden?"

Nathan bristled. "Is there something wrong with it?"

"Plants need more sunshine this high in the hills.

And drainage. Remember how the whiskey just sat there, the part that didn't soak into the ground? Build up your bed and that won't happen again."

"Good Lord, I hope not."

She grinned, good humor sparkling in her eyes. At one time in Nathan's life the sight would have sent his own spirits soaring, but now it only vexed him more.

"I don't mean just whiskey," she said, hurrying on. "Rainwater, too. It seems to me you've got a way with wood more'n horticulture. That's a word I've been yearning to use. The boys—my brothers—wouldn't appreciate it. I figured you would."

"Appreciation is not uppermost in my mind, Miss Abernathy."

"Daisy. You don't mind if I call you Nathan, do you? If we're going to be working together, Mister and Miss get in the way."

"Stop right now. We are not going to be working together."

She sighed, her face solemn. "Of course we're not. This isn't your work to do. It's mine and Orem's. We'll need to borrow some supplies, though. I brought some cuttings and a few plants today, along with a couple of hand tools, but though Orem deserved it, I couldn't ask him to haul a shovel and hoe up the hills."

She spoke without pause. Nathan took a deep breath, as much for her as for himself. The way she blinked and fidgeted with her hands, he suspected she wasn't as sure of herself as she appeared. If she had been, he would have plunked her on top of her horse and sent her riding home. Instead, she was agitated and eager, and she did owe him a debt.

Nathan had lived long enough and seen sufficient troubles to know when to submit to the inevitable. He would give her one day to make amends for his losses.

One day. Surely he could tolerate that. He got the tools from the shed behind the house, told her to choose where to put her plants, then returned to the fields. Though his head throbbed from lack of sleep, by noon he'd managed to plant half the corn.

He told himself it was weariness that drew him back to the house, but it could have been wariness, too, over the latest Abernathy antics. He found Daisy turning dirt in a half-shaded clearing a dozen yards past his whiskey-ruined plot. Her jacket hung from a nearby limb, and she'd rolled her shirtsleeves above her elbows. Her brogans were covered with mud, a line of dirt streaked one cheek, and wisps of her hair had worked loose to brush against her face.

She would need to get a new shirt before long, he noted, since the one she wore stretched dangerously tight across her bosom each time she wielded the hoe. For such a slender woman, she managed to break up the clods of dirt with amazing efficiency. He watched her longer than he'd intended. When she grinned up at him, he started guiltily, feeling like a Peeping Tom.

"I thought you said the garden needed sunlight," he said.

"This will get it. Morning sun, that is, and most of the afternoon by summer."

"Oh." He looked around at the breeze-ruffled trees. "Where's your brother?"

"I sent him home. He did the hard work with the shovel, but he's not much on details. Besides, his chores are waiting. For a while he'll have to do mine and his."

Nathan didn't care for the sound of *for a while.* "You've done good work. Consider the fifty dollars earned."

She leaned on the hoe handle and regarded him

with open skepticism. "You can't get rid of me so easy, Nathan. Be a recluse all you want, but a debt's a debt. I'll see to your garden, throw in some extras, and we'll call it even."

"Anyone ever call you stubborn?"

"Aunt Clyde."

"*Aunt* Clyde?"

"Jennifer Clyde Abernathy Slaughter. Aunt Clyde for short. She's Papa's sister. Moved in with us after Mama died giving birth to Orem, but she went down to Chattanooga when my brother Lucas got married. The first time, that is. Got herself a boardinghouse and then a husband. Except for the boys, she's the only blood kin I've got left. There's Cleo, of course, that's Lucas's little girl. I mustn't forget her."

An edge to her voice gave him pause. Stubborn, strong-willed Daisy, indomitably cheerful Daisy, had problems of her own.

Problems that did not concern him.

"Miss Abernathy."

"Daisy," she corrected. "Anyone ever call you stubborn?"

"Daisy," he said, a concession that cost him more than she'd ever know. "All recluses are stubborn. It's part of our nature."

She studied him with her disconcertingly probing blue eyes.

"You were at Chickamauga, weren't you? That's what Maude Louise said, and she's up on all the talk. Papa got the wounds that finally killed him fighting there under General Bragg, but I don't suppose you'd remember him. James Abernathy, Senior, kind of lean and fair. We get our looks from him."

Nathan stiffened. "I don't talk about the war."

She nodded in apology. "There's lots around here

who don't. My older brother Junior, for one. Right after Papa came home, he ran away to fight. He was only fourteen, but there was no holding him back. He was fired with energy in those days, but when the fighting was done and he returned, he'd lost all his spark. Papa was dead by then. I was only twelve, but I saw it would be wrong to ask Junior particulars about what he'd seen and done."

For a moment Nathan pictured a young girl fresh from losing her father and wanting to welcome her oldest brother home, but her brother had held himself apart. Like many of her Southern sisters, she'd had to grow to womanhood too fast.

Sympathy stirred within him, so rare an emotion for him that it made him uncomfortable. The feeling lasted until she spoke, which, as usual, didn't take long.

"Maude Louise said you're from Virginia. Someone in Pikeville told her."

Nathan felt the pinch of her words. For a long while he hadn't thought about his long-ago home, and not by accident. Memories were painful things, like burrs prickling the skin.

"Maude Louise talks a lot," he said, wondering who the woman could be.

"Papa said lots of Virginians fought at Chickamauga. Brave men, he said." She stopped a moment, her expression thoughtful. "Sorry to keep bringing up the war."

If he didn't know it was impossible, he would have sworn her eyes teared for him.

"Best keep to what I know and stop the speculation," she said, her voice once again bright. She gestured to the open gunnysack beside the garden. "I brought a few plants today. Green beans, wax beans, some lettuce and onions. Not much, since I didn't know how your tastes ran."

"They run to solitude."

"Which you'll be getting back soon enough. And don't worry that I'll make it a habit of coming up here. I'm leaving the hills before long, moving to Chattanooga. I've never been there, but I hear it's a fine place."

The news didn't bring the relief he would have expected.

"You're getting married, I suppose."

"That I am."

"Congratulations. I'm certain you and your fiancé will lead an active life."

"Maybe. I haven't met him yet."

"An arranged marriage?"

"Nothing like that. I still have to pick him out. Aunt Clyde says I shouldn't have any trouble. I was engaged once, but when Orodean stepped on the rattler, I saw that Baby Cleo needed me more'n my intended, who saw fit to find himself another bride. You're the first person to know I'm leaving. I planned to tell the family yesterday, but with the excitement of coming up here, it sort of slipped my mind."

She turned to rest the hoe at the side of the garden plot, and Nathan tried to interpret her words. She had a way of putting him on a verbal merry-go-round, making him dizzy every time they got into a conversation. He didn't like feeling vexed or pained or dizzy, and especially not sympathetic. Peaceful was his only goal.

A chill breeze stirred the air. He looked up to see a dark cloud high over the tops of the chestnut-oaks.

"Rain's coming," she said. "I know this is my responsibility, but would you mind helping me with these plants? They need to be set out right away. I'll bring stakes for the beans later, before I'm done."

The simplest course was for him to do as she requested. Rolling up his sleeves, he took the small trowel from her and dug the holes according to her directions, watching as she placed a fragile plant in each one, able to identify most, knowing she would provide more than enough information on the rest.

Occasionally their hands touched. If she felt any particular sensation, she didn't show it. But he wasn't so fortunate. What was wrong with him? He'd known painted women and not-so-innocent ladies from Richmond to San Francisco down to San Antonio and all the way back to Nashville. A few had touched him with more than a brush of their hands, but those touches hadn't had the kick of Daisy's muddy fingers.

Springtime, that was the trouble. Promising new life, new hope, or at least most people felt that way. Nathan hated the spring.

Daisy worked as quickly as she could beside Nathan, wanting to finish before the rain and nightfall made the ride home difficult. She tried to concentrate on her task, but strange feelings had set her to tingling.

She'd been courted, and she'd even been kissed— rather thoroughly, she believed, by her former intended— but nothing set butterflies to fluttering in her stomach like one touch of Keene's hand. When she dared steal a glance at him, she understood a little about why Lucas had hurried up his wedding to Maude Louise.

If Earl had once stirred up half the agitation in her that Nathan did, she'd be wed to him now.

She would die right on the spot if Nathan even guessed at her feelings, and so she started talking about onions and beans and that if it didn't rain, he'd have to tote water to the tender plants to give them a chance to take root.

She started to tell him about the cuttings she'd put next to the house, but she figured that was best revealed another day.

On the ride home, she contemplated her situation. Irony was a dictionary word she hadn't fully appreciated until now, and she understood all too well the irony of finally finding a tempting hill-country man just as she was planning to leave.

Not that he was tempted by her, but she wondered if maybe, once she put her mind to it, she could change that. As she rode down the steep, narrow trail, a spattering of rain fell across her path, reminding her that it made little difference whether she could, since she would be leaving in another month.

3

By the end of the week Nathan had dubbed her Whirlwind Daisy. Every day she swept across his land, digging and planting an ever-widening garden, adding flowers along the border, declaring, "You've got to feed the soul as well as the body."

She had even sprinkled rye grass seed over the plot Orem had destroyed, "to cover the mud," she had explained.

"That's a poor use of rye," he'd complained, but she had kept right on planting without comment.

Occasionally, when he wasn't working his fields or tending the still, Nathan had ventured to protest, but there was something so vulnerably innocent about her enthusiasm that he had never spoken up very strongly.

However, when she arrived this afternoon with a bouquet of wildflowers she'd gathered on her ride, he felt he had to put a damper on her high spirits.

"To brighten your cabin," she said as she jumped down from the mare and strode onto his porch. It was the closest she'd ever been to his house.

"Sorry I'm late, but the circuit preacher was in Pikeville and we all went to the Sunday service."

Irritated by her late arrival, an irritation he tried not to admit, he stared at the bright blooms, then looked into her equally bright blue eyes. "They'll just die," he said. "Everything does."

"That's why we have to enjoy them while we can." She smiled as she thrust them into his hand. "I'll get to work. I divided some irises just before I left home. They need to be put in the ground right away." She removed the gunnysack from behind Marigold's saddle, then the saddle itself, sending the mare to crop in the wild grasses that grew by the house.

"I thought I'd put them here across the front. Irises sure will look pretty here in early summer. You'll need to divide them every two or three years and spread 'em out."

I need to dig them out as soon as you leave, he thought as he sought refuge inside his house. A simple, single life was what he wanted, without complications like flower beds.

He had made his house fancy in memory of his mother, who had always appreciated his woodworking skills, but that was as far as he would go. Except for a coat of paint every few years, a house didn't need attention, or worry and care, the way flowers did.

He ought to be honest and tell her so to her face, but he wasn't a cruel man, just a solitary one who was set in his ways.

And so he put the bouquet of wildflowers in a tin of water and set it on the table by his parlor chair. Grudgingly he admitted she was right. The addition did brighten the house, providing living proof of the beauty of nature described in his poetry books. But the flowers would die. The poems would endure forever.

Wordsworth, stretched out in the chair, stared at the bouquet with a mischievous eye. Within a minute he was outside munching table scraps.

Nathan returned to the parlor desk where he'd been working on his accounts when his personal whirlwind arrived. He pictured the horticulturist at work. Horticulturist, he thought again, this time with a shake of his head. It was her word, one she used regularly. A horticultural whirlwind, that was Daisy, a new creation on earth. He smiled, startling himself in the process. To compensate for it, he grunted.

A simple, single life, he reminded himself, emphasizing each word as he opened the letter from the Richmond bookdealer from whom he ordered his reading matter. The dealer informed him of new publications that might interest him, sending them to Pikeville where he picked them up on his monthly visit for supplies.

Otherwise, he remained in the hills, Virginia a world away. He'd grown up not far from Richmond, the only child of a loving mother and gentleman farmer who saw to the education of their son. He'd planned to become a farmer himself, devoting his spare time to reading, having a family of his own if that's the way things worked out. But the war had intruded. At sixteen, filled with dreams of protecting his land, he'd signed up with General Lee.

The bloodshed and mindless savagery of the next four years killed all that was gentle in him. He returned from the Yankee prison where he'd spent the last part of the war to find his land gone and his parents dead from heartbreak.

"They just wasted away," the doctor had said.

"They'd already lost all they owned. Believing you were lost to them, too, they had no reason to live."

For the next few years he wandered, seeing the devastation, the loss, the greed. Maybe there was good in the land, but he didn't find it. Nor did he find peace, until he forced himself to return to Chickamauga, just outside Chattanooga, the site of his most ferocious battle. Calling no place home, he settled high in the hills a hundred miles to the north. Needing a trade, he experimented with sour mash whiskey until he found a formula he liked.

He wasn't a drinking man, but he was still Reb enough to appreciate outsmarting the revenuers with their two-dollars-a-gallon excise. The hated tax had been used by the Yankees to help pay for the war, and at the end of the hostilities they had inflicted it on the former Confederate states. The result was a new kind of combat: the moonshiners against the revenuers.

It was the lone war Nathan still fought. Or it had been until the invasion of Whirlwind Daisy. Looking through one of the front windows, he could see the top of her blond head. She began to sing. Watching just that much of her, listening to her strong, off-key voice, he forgot his books and Richmond, forgot his irritation over her intrusion, forgot he wasn't supposed to enjoy the company of another living soul.

He'd never met anyone like her. Dressed in men's clothing, she looked more delicate, more feminine than the fanciest ladies he could recall, but her true distinction went beyond appearance. He was rude to her; she refused to acknowledge it. He ignored her; she gave him a friendly wave and ignored him right back. He freed her of obligation; she insisted on paying her debt. She was tougher to avoid than any revenuer he'd ever heard of, and impossible to forget.

The singing stopped, and he saw that a soft rain had begun to fall. He walked onto the porch. She was standing, her hands on her hips, surveying her handiwork, oblivious to the rain. Her damp shirt clung to the curves of her body, and droplets of moisture glistened in the golden hair framing her face.

"Come up here," he said.

"I'm dirty," she said, wrinkling her nose.

"It'll wash off." Something possessed him to go inside for a towel. He handed it to her and looked away while she wiped the soil from her hands. She even removed the dirt on her trousers, but she missed a spot on her cheek. He didn't tell her.

They stood awkwardly for a moment under the protection of the porch roof.

"How about a drink?" he asked, surprised to hear himself.

"I don't care for whiskey, thank you."

"Neither do I. I meant lemonade."

"Oh," she said. "That would be fine."

He held the door open, gesturing for her to enter. She hesitated before slipping out of her muddied brogans and walking in stocking feet into the parlor.

"Lordy," she whispered, her eyes on the shelves of books.

He left to get the lemonade. When he returned, she was standing a foot away from the shelves, reading the titles.

"They're mostly poetry," he said, "and a few history books."

She started and backed away. "I didn't mean to pry."

"You're not prying," he said, and meant it. He'd never shown his books to anyone; he found doing so not unpleasant.

"I can read," she said with obvious pride. "Aunt Clyde taught me. Papa never had much use for it, and the boys copied him, but she insisted I learn. All I've got are a medical advisor and a dictionary she gave me for Christmas a few years ago."

"Both handy volumes."

She looked back at the poetry. "But nothing like this."

Setting the lemonade on the desk, he walked to her side. "You can touch them."

She shook her head.

He put a slender book in her hand. "Open to page ninety-three," he said.

For once, she obeyed.

He watched the wonder in her eyes as she read, and a long-forgotten warmth spread through him. "It's by Wordsworth. The same name as the cat," he said, hoping she didn't hear the thickness of his voice. "Read it aloud."

"You'd laugh."

"I promise I won't."

She paused a moment, cleared her throat, and began, stumbling at first, her voice strengthening as she progressed.

> *"I wandered lonely as a cloud*
> *That floats on high o'er vales and hills,*
> *When all at once I saw a crowd,*
> *A host, of golden daffodils;*
> *Beside the lake, beneath the trees,*
> *Fluttering and dancing in the breeze."*

She smiled at him, a child-woman delighting in a new discovery. "That's just the way they look. I've got some in the garden, and when the wind blows, they do seem to be dancing."

Returning to the poem, she rushed through to the final stanza, the words tumbling one over the other, the wonder in her eyes deepening to a satisfied glow.

> *"For oft, when on my couch I lie*
> *In vacant or in pensive mood,*
> *They flash upon that inward eye*
> *Which is the bliss of solitude;*
> *And then my heart with pleasure fills,*
> *And dances with the daffodils."*

She held the book to her breast. "How perfectly beautiful. And true. After I decided to leave, I told myself that whenever I got lonely for home, I could remember the beauty of the hills and feel better. That's just like Mr. Wordsworth."

"I thought you might like it."

Their eyes met. Her childlike innocence faded as she gazed at him with womanly frankness. Nathan felt as if she'd struck him with the hoe, yet all she'd done was lift her lashes and thank him with her eyes. All the defenses he'd built around himself, his conviction that he wanted to live alone, seemed to be crumbling under her gentle assault.

His hands ached to touch her, and other aches were growing in him, too. All he had to do was reach out—

He stopped himself. What in the hell was happening to him? He didn't need her thanks, or anything else she might offer. He needed her gone.

She made no protest when he returned the book to the shelf. "Your lemonade is on the desk."

"Have I done something wrong?" she asked.

He looked past her out the window. "The rain. It's depressing."

"Rain is part of nature. We need it for new life."

"You do. I don't. If I never grew another stalk of grain for the whiskey, it would be all right with me."

He should have left his protest at that, but her wide eyes, parted lips, and gracefully tilted chin drove him on.

"What are you doing here alone with a man? You're too innocent for your own good, Daisy Abernathy. The cruelty of the world will get to you eventually."

With purposeful thoroughness he regarded her face, her mouth, the curve of her throat, the outline of her breasts beneath the rain-dampened shirt. He stopped at her feet curling against the bare wood floor, then his gaze moved slowly upward, lingering at her hips, at last staring into her round, wounded eyes.

"You're going to Chattanooga to find a husband, are you? Parade yourself until the men flock around? They'll run to you for certain, especially if you're wearing tight trousers, but some of them won't have marriage in mind. You'd better build up your defenses before you go. If not, pray Aunt Clyde has some sense."

She looked as if he'd struck her, her hand at her throat. "I'd better leave," she whispered.

"It's raining, remember?" he said, wanting to be cruel, to rip at her the way she was ripping at him. He damned her for the dampness in her eyes.

"It's a gentle rain. I won't melt."

She brushed a tear from her cheek, then hurried from his house, leaving his superior pronouncements collapsing into self-disgust. He hadn't said anything wrong or anything he didn't know was true. So why did he feel hollow inside? Against all common sense, he wanted to rush after her and apologize, to hold her and kiss her tears away, to bring back the wonder in her eyes.

Instead, he watched as she prepared to leave. When she and Marigold disappeared into the gloom, he cursed the manly weakness she had aroused.

4

Until she stepped inside Nathan Keene's house, Daisy had never been hurt by a man, not heartsick-hurt the way she was right now. She spent the first half of the ride home tending to her wounded heart, telling herself he hadn't meant the harsh things he said, that his own hurts from the war made him behave the way he did.

The second half of the ride, when the rain had stopped, she spent pondering what to do about him.

"Should I stop going up there?" she asked Marigold. The animal straightened her ears but kept on putting one hoof after another on the muddy homeward trek.

"I still have the hyacinths to set out. And the daisies, too. A bed of them would look nice by the back door."

They might also remind him of the friendly horti-culturist who had made his house a home.

A host of golden daffodils.

The poem came back to haunt her. "Daffodils can't be put out until the fall. He'll have to take care of those himself."

The suspicion that he wouldn't, that he would neglect what she'd already planted, pinched at her burgeoning optimism. But, she thought gloomily, what he did after she was gone was no concern of hers.

And yet it was. She suffered for him, just as she had suffered for Papa and for Junior so long ago. He wasn't her kin to worry about, yet worry she did. He'd chosen a hermit's life, but she'd seen signs he wasn't without some appreciation of her presence. Sometimes he looked at her in ways that turned her inside out. He wasn't a bad man, just an unhappy one. She'd carried on too much about the poem, a foolish, ignorant young woman who'd come too late to something as fine as poetry.

She was smart with people, though. Nathan Keene was suffering. She would take care of a wounded rabbit, wouldn't she? Why not a wounded man?

She smiled to think what he would say at the comparison. He wasn't rabbity in the least. He was the manliest man she'd ever seen, because, she admitted, he made her feel more like a woman than she'd ever felt in her life.

By the time she sent the unsaddled Marigold to graze in the field, she had made up her mind. Cleo was beginning to take to Maude, the pig farm was coming along just fine without her daily interference, yet she still had more than three weeks until the race. She had to keep busy, or else she would start feeling sorry for herself again.

It seemed to her Nathan Keene was doing just that—feeling sorry for himself. Somehow she would have to ease his pain. And what better time than spring, when the world was bursting with the beauty of creation?

Her intrusions into his life had been to repay a debt. Now she would go as a friend, someone he needed whether he realized it or not.

She wouldn't ask him his opinion of her campaign; she already knew it. Neither would she give him a choice. This time she would be subtle, not invading his house and carrying on over his books. This time she wouldn't be ready to cry like a baby if he spoke harshly. This time she would show him her quiet and steady strength.

Water smoothed the firmest, most jagged rock, didn't it? Like the gentle rain, she'd simply wear him down.

Early Monday she started right in, swallowing her doubts as she rode onto his land. When he didn't come out to run her off, she thought he must be working the fields. So she got right to work and spent the day pulling out the few vegetable plants that hadn't taken, replacing them with others. Just maybe, she told herself, her gifts—her horticultural gifts, she amended— would restore in him the sense of wonder she always felt at the miracle of rebirth.

She added squash, cucumbers, and sweet potatoes to the already planted crops. Later in the summer he would have to plant the rest: turnips, mustard greens, cabbage, carrots, and beets. If he was of a mind. She hoped he would be by then. Before she left, she would give him detailed instructions for the planting, showing him that she could not only read but also write.

He showed up late in the afternoon, just as she was saddling Marigold to return home. The sweat and dirt showed he'd been working hard. He looked strong and handsome, and she turned butter-soft inside as she looked at him across the backyard.

But softness wouldn't do, and neither would silence. He'd done all the talking yesterday. Today it was her turn.

"They don't need me back home so much anymore, and this place does. That's why I'm here, not because I've got designs on you, or want to cause you embarrassment. Don't think you have to entertain me, either. I'm laying out the garden just the way I'm laying out my life."

"Daisy—"

"Beg your pardon, Nathan, but I'm not done yet. I know there's men who aren't as honorable as you and the boys. I didn't tell you the details, but when Aunt Clyde moved south, it was to marry a traveling seed salesman. When she got to Chattanooga, she found he already had a wife and baby. She started to take a shotgun to him, but decided he wasn't worth the effort.

"That's when she moved in with an ailing woman who needed help in her boardinghouse, what with Chattanooga being a thriving town. They struck up a friendship. When the woman died, my aunt inherited the place. She's married to a widower now. The two of them will give me all the watching over I need."

Out of words, she fell silent. He just looked at her with that studied way he had, his eyes peering through whatever she said to the truth of what she meant. He ought to know she didn't lie to him. She never had and she never would.

She pulled herself into the saddle. "It'll take me

another week or so to be sure the plants have rooted. Then I'll be saying good-bye."

She left before he could protest.

True to her word, she returned every day. Sometimes they spoke, sometimes they didn't, although by the end of the second week they were meeting in the morning and sharing a meal at noon. She did most of the talking, telling him about Cleo and how hard it would be to leave her.

"She helps me with the flower garden," she said one day. They sat in the shade by the creek that ran in the hollow nearest the house. Sunlight speckled the leaves, dappling the ground and the water. "She's the only one who likes flowers as much as me." Her eyes misted. "This morning she showed me a ladybug on a hyacinth leaf. She wanted to know where the gemmenbugs were, and I had to tell her my dictionary didn't say."

She talked, too, about the boys and Maude Louise, even about the pigs and how the killing went in the fall.

"Things are going all right with the farm these days. It's fitting the way Maude Louise has taken over. I'm truly glad." She stared into a wall of trees on the far side of the stream. "All I need is for Marigold to win the Pikeville race, and I'll be heading south with the prize money in my pocket. After I buy a few gifts, of course. It'll be the first time I've ever had money for such as that."

"What will happen to the mare when you leave?" Nathan asked.

"When I'm established, Orem has promised to bring her down."

"You've got everything worked out, haven't you?"

"That I have."

They looked at each other they way they had over the book, both of them solemn and still. Daisy's heart caught in her throat. They were as different as two people could be, but something was growing between them, just the way the garden seedlings were sprouting through the loam.

She found herself leaning toward him, studying the bristles on his lean cheeks and the way his mouth slanted into an almost-smile. He had a prominent Adam's apple, and a deep hollow in his throat. If she touched it, would she feel the beat of his heart? Would it be throbbing as hard as hers?

She looked away. Nathan Keene wasn't the man for her. He wasn't looking for a woman, and he certainly wasn't looking to provide her with a home and family and with the love for which she yearned.

But Lordy, he sure did set her heart to thrumming and her blood singing in her veins.

She scrambled to her feet. "I'd best leave. Tomorrow I'll be in Pikeville signing up for the race. Just thought I'd tell you in case you missed me."

He stood beside her. "I'll miss you, Daisy."

A crow cawed in the trees, and a mockingbird trilled its response. She stared at the creek bouncing over the rocks. Maybe if she stood here long enough, he would touch her. Maybe she would touch him, too. Touching seemed right and good, but all he did was clench his hands at his sides. Like she might tempt him too much and he would make a terrible mistake.

Without another word, she hurried away. What on earth was she crying for? He hadn't hurt her. At least not in any way that showed.

* * *

That evening she kept herself busy helping Maude Louise with the homespun dress her sister-in-law was sewing for Daisy to take with her to Chattanooga. She'd finally told the family about her plans, and although they had protested, she could tell they weren't surprised.

Early the next morning she and Orem and Junior rode the wagon into Pikeville. At the country store they picked out the supplies they needed, then Daisy left to sign up Marigold for the race. Registration was at the stable. Daisy would have preferred avoiding Earl, but since she was the one who would benefit from Marigold's victory, she couldn't shirk her responsibilities.

Earl was waiting just inside the stable door. She hadn't seen him in more than a month, but he was still as she remembered him, short and stocky, with a paunch that rested on his belt and a swagger to his walk. His reddish hair was slicked back from his ruddy face and he'd begun a beard, but thus far it was mostly just peach fuzz.

"Well, well, Miss Daisy. Didn't think you could stay away much longer."

She straightened, rubbing a palm against her trousers. "I've come about the race."

"Don't bother. Thunder's going to win."

"That old gelding of yours?" she said with derision.

"The same one. Marigold is nothing but a female. She hasn't a chance."

"We'll see," she said, her voice tight with irritation. No one upset her quite as much as Earl, and he knew it, too. He seemed to take it as a sign she had feelings for him. And she did. Disgust.

"You're sure you want your horse to run?" he asked.

"I'm sure."

"Then maybe you oughta win. That ten-dollar prize will buy you a fine little trousseau. Good as you look in those trousers, as my wife you'll have to get used to a dress."

"I've told you no, Earl."

"I like a woman who teases."

She started to protest further, but Earl was so sure of himself, he wouldn't hear what she said. How different he was from Nathan, who studied her every word.

How different in so many ways.

She stopped herself. Nathan was a long way away, and he'd be even farther once April was over.

"Tell you what, Daisy. You're so sure of winning, how about putting up a little side bet?"

"I haven't any money, and you know it."

"Money's not what I'm after, and you know it. I'll pay you five dollars if Marigold beats my Thunder, and if not . . . " He grinned. It wasn't a pretty sight.

"If not, what?"

"If she loses, then you owe me a kiss."

She shuddered at the thought. "I've told you before, Earl, I don't want to kiss you."

"You won't have to if Marigold is as good as you think she is. Of course, if you're only wishing . . . "

"You've got a bet," Daisy snapped.

Earl licked his lips, the tip of his tongue touching the fuzz around his mouth. "Hot diggity damn, I got me a kiss. Don't worry none, honey. I'll make you real glad you lost."

"Don't you worry. That extra money's going to help me get to Chattanooga."

Earl's grin died. "What're you talking about?"

"I'm moving there. Right after the race."

"The hell you say."

"Aunt Clyde has asked me to live with her." She

didn't add the part about finding a husband, much as she was tempted to rile him more. The way he was puffed up already, he just might explode.

Besides, lately she'd quit thinking about looking for a city man. Her heart just wasn't in the search, especially since she'd started having impure thoughts about someone close to home.

Earl's little pig eyes glared angrily at her. "Moving to the city, are you? Who put such an idea into your head? I'll bet it was the Whiskey Man. Folks been talking about you two, but I've tried not to listen."

Daisy's cheeks burned. "Don't be a fool, Earl. I've been helping Na— Mister Keene with his garden, that's all."

"That what they call it now? Helping with a garden? I've tried to ignore the talk, being as how we're practically betrothed, but—"

"We are not betrothed."

"We will be once we kiss."

Daisy pulled herself up tall, until she was looking down at him. "Just sign me up for the race, Earl. As soon as Orem rides Marigold to victory, your five dollars will be on the way to Chattanooga."

She strode from the stable and down the middle of the street toward the store, taking little notice of the folks watching, her heart thundering faster than her brogans could move. The trouble with towns like Pikeville was that everyone knew everyone else's business. In a city like Chattanooga with more than ten thousand residents, a body could have some privacy.

She found her brothers pitching horseshoes with the regulars in a field behind the general store.

"I'm ready to go," she announced.

"Just a while longer," Junior said, his eye on the game.

Orem looked at her more carefully. "Anything wrong?"

She pulled him aside. "How did Earl know I was helping the Whiskey Man with his garden?"

Orem swallowed.

"Just as I thought. You've been talking."

"I was proud of your work, that's all. I maybe did a little bragging. Word must've spread."

She rolled her eyes, but there was nothing she could say. The damage had been done. Whatever reputation she had was ruined for sure. It seemed more and more providential that she would soon be gone.

She looked at her brothers, then at the half-dozen men who stood in their bib overalls observing the game. A few cast sideways glances at her, and one old codger stared outright at her shirt and trousers.

There wasn't a gentleman in sight, she decided. Then a small voice reminded her that with all her wanton thoughts concerning Nathan, she was no lady, either.

"I'm heading out on foot," she said to Orem. "You and Junior leave as soon as this game is over. I'm mad enough to walk all the way home, but I'm not sure my feet share the feeling."

Without waiting for an argument, she departed.

She was a couple of miles along the trail into the hills when she heard the wagon creaking and bouncing behind her.

"Daisy," called both her brothers, "wait up!"

Wait up? Did they think she could outrun them?

She stopped while the workhorse and the ramshackle wagon caught up with her. Orem jumped to the ground.

"Mr. Keene's in trouble," he said.

Daisy's anger and irritation disappeared. "What are you talking about?"

"Earl was real mad after you left him. Said he'd get that moonshiner if it was the last thing he did."

"Nathan can handle himself," Daisy said, trying to ignore the sinking feeling in her stomach.

"Not against revenuers, he can't. There was some in town, down at the sheriff's office. Attracted a big crowd, they did, when Earl called them out. Must have been a couple dozen witnesses to the goings-on."

"Revenuers?" Daisy asked, not knowing if she wanted to hear the rest.

"Yep. Earl told them about how folks buy whiskey from the Clutters, but if they wanted to get the real culprit, they'd have to make old Claude and Abner tell them where to find the Whiskey Man's still."

He caught his breath. "Those Clutters will do it, too. They ain't got the courage or the sense God gave a 'coon. If we don't do something about it, Mr. Keene's liable to lose everything."

Daisy stared at her brother in dismay. He was right. The government men would trample Nathan's land, including the garden. They'd find and smash the rig. What's more, they'd keep coming back to check on him, destroying whatever privacy he had left.

And like the ruined garden, the losses would be the Abernathys' fault.

She would help him, all right. Determination surged through her. There wasn't much she wouldn't do for the man she loved.

And Daisy loved Nathan.

All the way home the truth of the words rang silently in her ears. She knew a late-night journey up the winding trail was impossible, but she was still tempted to ride up the hill and tell him. Her love for him might not be fitting or convenient, but it was constant and strong. Her heart swelled almost to bursting with emotion.

She didn't need to pull the petals from her namesake flower to know the feeling wasn't returned. On the good days when they were together, Nathan tolerated her, and at times, though he never actually smiled, he seemed amused by her prattle.

On the bad days . . . She wouldn't let herself think about those.

5

She left at dawn the next morning, and found him in the cornfield behind his plow. She could have stood there a month watching his steady stride, the power of his arms as he wielded the reins of the mule, even the patch of sweat that made his work shirt cling to his back. But the revenuers might arrive soon and she had no time to stand there ogling him.

She whistled to get his attention and then waved. Something about her gesture must have told him trouble was afoot, for he dropped the reins and came running.

They met halfway across the field. "Revenuers," she gasped. "They'll be at the Clutters' and then more'n likely here before long. It's all my fault, riling Earl the way I did, and I'm sorry, truly sorry."

"Settle down, Daisy. Slower. I'm catching every other word."

She drew a deep breath and repeated herself, trying to speak more calmly, clearly. Being close to him seemed harder than ever this morning with her feelings so freshly realized. She was tempted to burst out her admission of love, but they had more important matters to discuss than a woman's singing heart.

Not that he saw the difference in her. Mostly he just stood there looking off into the distance, as if he might see the federal agents riding across the field.

"First off," he said, "could this Earl be the owner of the Pikeville stable?"

"The very one."

"Earl's the kind to make trouble."

"He's been thinking to marry me—"

His scowl stopped her. She felt her face grow warm. Nathan wasn't interested in the stableman's intentions. "Oh, that's not important. He knows I've been coming to your place, and I guess it made him jealous." She laughed nervously. "Earl hasn't got a lot of sense, but he's mean to make up for it. He told the agents about you and the Clutters, and Orem says they'll probably be here soon, since Claude and Abner won't last long under their questioning."

She shifted, wishing he wouldn't keep looking at her like that, his eyes dark and threatening. She slapped a palm against her trousers. "Aren't you going to do anything?"

He pulled himself from wherever his thoughts had taken him. "The rig will be hard to find, but there are still signs to hide." He thought a minute. "Most important, we'll need to brush away the Clutters' tracks leading to the cave."

"I'll help."

"Good. You can get started while I unhitch Coleridge."

"Coleridge? The mule? You have the most peculiar names for animals."

"There's a gelding called Browning you haven't seen yet. I keep him in a pasture beyond the corn."

Within the hour, Marigold was grazing in the pasture with Browning and Coleridge. Nathan was frying a trout he'd pulled from the creek, a basket of fresh-picked blackberries beside him. Daisy was stretched out under a chestnut-oak drinking lemonade and reading a book of poetry as if she did it every day.

It must have made a pretty scene, Daisy thought, the two of them relaxing in a patch of shady grass overlooking a hollow, the hills around them blanketed in forest. But what she and Nathan hoped the revenuers would not discover was that the fire had been built directly over the vent in Nathan's distillery cave, hiding the smoke from the cooker.

She peered over the book.

"It's difficult to read a book that's upside down," Nathan said. "The trout will be ready before long."

"They're going to find the cave," she said, aware that it was only a few feet below where she sat. "I just know they will."

"The road up from the hollow is hard enough for the Clutters to find, and they travel it once a month. Besides, we did a good job of covering their tracks."

"I know, but . . . " A thought struck her. "The whiskey barrel! We forgot the barrel."

"You mean the one Orem emptied for me? I never got around to refilling it. Not much purpose, anyway, since I rarely take a drink. And I sure don't have people dropping by for social calls."

She managed a smile. "Orem and Junior never did have that tasting test they wanted." Gazing into the distance, she sighed.

"Quit blaming yourself for everything, Daisy. The revenuers would have been here sooner or later. It was only a matter of time before they got word of the still."

"But your privacy . . . "

He turned the fish. "I'll have it back soon enough."

The edge to his voice twisted her heart. She stole a glance at him. It seemed today she was sensitive to every little thing about him—his take-charge calm, his reassurances, his strength that went beyond the physical.

Not that she didn't notice the way his shirt fit him when he stretched or lifted, and the shape of his trousers across his—

She broke off her thoughts when she saw a pair of suit-clad men ride onto the far side of the field.

"They're here," she whispered.

"Wave to them," he said, "but make it casual. We don't want to appear too friendly."

Reluctantly she obeyed, pulling herself to her feet as if she were greeting ordinary callers.

The men rode directly across the furrowed ground, breaking up the dirt, not caring that they were disturbing the grains of corn Nathan had so carefully planted. They were the ones who ought to be paying a tax, Daisy decided, for disturbing a man's property like that.

Someone ought to tell them, but it sure wouldn't be her. She was so fidgety she was about to jump out of her skin.

She glanced at Nathan, who was setting the frying pan on a rock by the fire. As he turned to the revenuers, he looked at her and winked.

Winked! She didn't know he knew how. Lordy, but he was a man to stay in a girl's mind, and so calm you'd think the law came after him every day. Drawing courage from his example, she shaded her eyes from the sun and watched the enemy approach.

Scowling from under their felt hats, they reined to a halt so close she feared the slobber from the horses might fall onto the fish. Her knees shook, but Nathan didn't so much as blink.

"Good day," Nathan said, cool as you please.

"You're Nathan Keene," said the agent nearest the fish. "I'm Agent Belman, and this here's Agent Floyd. I reckon you know why we've come."

"Can't say as I do," Nathan answered.

He's being ornery, Daisy thought. Good for him.

Neither agent blinked an eye.

"We understand you're operating an illegal distillery on your property."

"Oh?" Nathan sounded as if he were hearing the news for the first time.

"That's right. We have it on good authority."

Daisy snorted in disgust. Only a warning glance from Nathan kept her from asking when Earl Selfe had ever been a good authority.

"We're going to have to look around," Belman continued. He seemed to be the spokesman for the two. "As representatives of the Treasury Department of the United States of America, it won't do you any good to object."

"I'm not objecting," Nathan said. "Go right ahead."

The agents exchanged a look—no, closer to a smirk, Daisy decided—as if they were thinking the Whiskey Man's days as a moonshiner were over.

They took two hours, during which Daisy managed to poke down a portion of the fish, only because Nathan suggested it in that don't-say-no way of his and because, she had to admit, it tasted delicious. While Nathan read poetry to her, she even ate some of the blackberries she'd gathered from the thicket beneath the willow trees by the creek.

It was a shame she couldn't concentrate on a word he said, even though he was reading the words of men named Coleridge and Browning. "So you'll understand where I get my animals' names," he explained, but at the moment she couldn't bring herself to care.

As Nathan had assured her, the revenuers turned up nothing but some newly planted corn and rye. They left more than a little angry, muttering something about the Clutters not having any more sense than a toad.

"What do you say we go down to the creek for a toast of sweet, cool water?" Nathan suggested.

"Sounds good to me."

He carried the pan and the utensils, and she took the berries and the book. They walked through the thick woods, their steps cautious on the steep, slippery ground. They stopped at the creek bank where they'd once had lunch. The air was cooler down here in the hollow, the sun only dotting the foliage, and the scent of honeysuckle made the coolness all the sweeter. As they washed up, Daisy felt the coiled tension in her stomach begin to unwind.

Green, lacy ferns poked out from the rocks on the bank, and fine, thick lichen covered the ground like a carpet, protecting them from the dampness. Phlox grew not far from the water, and there were wild roses, too, and clusters of Queen Anne's lace. She knew beyond a doubt that if she looked hard enough she would find pink lady's slippers.

The woods were like a wall around them, making her skittishly aware that they were very much alone. Seclusion had never bothered her before, but today it did.

Restless, she walked along the creek bank, looking at the pebbles under the fast-moving water, at the ferns, at everything but Nathan, who leaned against an outcropping.

"You own all this?" she asked.

"About a thousand acres in all."

She glanced at him in surprise. "You must be rich."

He shrugged, his muscles working nicely under his shirt, and her heart turned a somersault.

"I would be if it were good for farming. The terrain's bad. That's why I was able to buy it so cheap. I cleared the best land to plant the grain and used the wood to build the house, but otherwise I've left everything pretty much alone."

Which was how he preferred to be, she reminded herself, but on this beautiful day the thought didn't linger.

"That's the longest speech you ever made about anything other than books," she said.

He looked at her so solemnly and for so long, her heart caught in her throat. "You seemed interested. After what you did today, I owe you more than my usual curtness. Thanks for coming to warn me, Daisy. You didn't have to."

Smiling with pleasure, she considered telling him about the lumber business Aunt Clyde described in one of her letters. With all his land and trees, he ought to consider it as a trade, but she'd already interfered in his life enough. Besides, she wouldn't be telling him anything he hadn't considered himself. Nathan Keene was an educated man.

Suddenly she felt silly parading in front of him, and she sat a few feet away from the water. She jumped when he stretched out beside her, but she didn't move away.

Without looking directly at him, she saw everything in detail: his legs that seemed to go on forever, his whiskey brown hair that brushed against his shoulders, his lean cheeks that were shadowed with bristles. His sleeves were rolled halfway to his elbows, and fine dark hair dusted his arms, matching the hairs curling at the opening of his shirt. He had thick lashes for a man, practically as thick as hers. She wished he would tickle her cheek with them, the way she tickled Cleo.

His hands were wide and brown, his fingers long. She could picture them carving the scrolled eaves along his porch. She could picture them touching her cheek, too, and maybe her mouth. What would his hands taste like? And his lips?

"You're not still worried, are you?" he asked.

"Not about the revenuers." She looked him straight in the eye. "I'm worried I'll get away from here without you ever kissing me."

She dug her nails into her palms, amazed she could be so brazen. But she kept on looking at him, and he kept on looking at her.

"Funny you should say that," he said. "I'm worried you won't."

His words astonished her as much as her own.

"You're afraid I'll jump you or something?" she said, letting him see her anger.

"No, Daisy, I'm not afraid of that."

He stood and pulled her to her feet, his hands resting on her shoulders as he held her close. She couldn't move or speak or breathe. His lips brushed against hers, then pressed more firmly, moving back and forth just a little. She tingled from head to toe.

He broke away and she looked at the water, afraid he might read in her eyes what was in her heart. He'd kissed her—at last—and she found the best and worst thing about it was that she wanted him never to stop.

But it was over. She'd practically begged him to

do it, and he had. Collapsing onto the ground, she pulled her knees to her chin and studied the creek.

She heard him walk away, and for a terrible moment she believed he was gone, run off by her forward manner. Then he returned, and relief flooded through her. He knelt behind her, and she felt his fingers working at her braid, unwinding it, spreading her hair against her back. She remained as still as the rocks around her, her eyes closed, picturing his fingers at work. Why he was doing it, she had no idea, but except for the kiss it was the most intimate thing she'd ever experienced.

Unbound, her hair came to her waist. It would be all crinkly from the braid, but if he didn't mind, neither did she. He placed something atop her head. She reached up and touched a wreath of flowers. She turned to him, the two of them kneeling and facing each other and neither saying a word.

"No one's ever brought me flowers before," she said at last.

"You deserve the biggest bouquet in Tennessee."

"Why?" she asked in a small voice.

"Because you're you. You're the princess of the woodland, you know. Gentle as a new bloom, soft as the rain."

Flushing, she looked down at her clasped hands. She was so tight and warm and happy inside, she didn't know whether to laugh or to cry.

"You get that out of a book?"

"I made it up. A poet would have said it better."

Daisy didn't believe him. No one, not even Mr. Wordsworth himself, could have written words more beautiful than Nathan's. She had to thank him, but her declaration would sound awkward and crude after his.

She did the only thing she knew to do. Rising on

her knees, she returned his kiss. Unsure of herself, she made it light, her hands trembling against his chest, but there was nothing light about the heat building inside her, or about the love that had set her heart and head reeling.

The hardest thing she ever did was lift her lips from his. His low moan startled her, but no more than the way he took her in his arms, easing her around until she was flat on her back on the ground, her hair fanned out, his body pressed against hers.

Excitement skittered through her, and even through the thickness of her clothes her skin burned wherever he touched.

He stroked her hair and kissed her eyes. When his lips moved to hers once again, Daisy felt a new world opening up to her, a world where thinking didn't matter, only feeling. Beside this woodland stream, she and her true love were as much a part of nature as the moss on which they lay, as the wildflowers that scented the air.

She stroked his shoulders, then his chest, exploring for the first time the outline of a muscled man, his hardness, his heat. She felt small and helpless beneath him, and as powerful as the sun. Her breasts swelled, a strange and unexpected reaction, and she pressed them against his firm chest because it seemed the thing to do.

He embraced her, his mouth covering hers, and this time there was nothing gentle in the kiss. His tongue forced her lips apart and danced inside her mouth. He tasted of fire and berries and the outdoors, sweeter than honey, and she stroked his hair and his shoulders to let him know she liked what he did.

When his hand moved to the side of her breast, she held herself still, wanting things she couldn't name, trusting him to understand how she felt. Until that moment she hadn't known her body could sing. His hand moved to her waist, to her belly, then upward until he cupped her breast. The heat was building so fast inside her, pumping and throbbing, she couldn't keep still, and it seemed as natural as rain to part her legs and let his thigh rest between them.

Her hips lifted. She was burning for him, and he had to put out her fire.

He broke the kiss and held her, his breath hot and ragged against her cheek. She whispered his name, her hands gripping his shirt, her heart pounding so hard she thought it would burst. When he shifted away, she kept holding onto him, confused because she didn't want so much as a whisper of air between them.

His hands covered hers to break the hold, and then he was sitting beside her. She lay, cold and deserted, and more confused than ever, not knowing what to do with her hands or her heart or her body that still craved him.

He ran his fingers back through his hair and looked toward the water.

"I'm sorry," he said.

Sorry? Feeling ignorant and foolish, wishing she could vanish, she sat up beside him, her hand covering her mouth to swallow the cry rising in her throat. She tried to smooth her hair, but it was hopelessly untamed, like her love for him and her yearning and her spirit that had led her down a path she should not have taken.

He stood, his tall, lean body unwinding with graceful ease. At the creek he splashed water on his face. Instead of looking back at her, he stared into the woods.

"I would have dishonored you, Daisy, and you deserve better."

"Dishonored?" she said, hardly believing she'd

heard right. It was clear he hadn't been as involved as she in their kissing and touching, or else he'd never have been able to pull away or think about right and wrong.

Sitting on the ground, small and insignificant, she felt like a child beside a persnickety grown-up, but there was nothing childlike in the emotions and the bewilderment tearing through her. And there was nothing persnickety about Nathan. He was just being honest; he was being himself.

Which meant that he might be crushing all the spirit in her, but she couldn't hate him or want to hurt him. She carried enough hurt for them both.

She stood. Her gaze fell to the ground where the wreath of wildflowers lay. Pink lady's slippers, she noticed, and she started to pick it up, but what would she do with it? Put it back on her head, as if she were a real princess?

Princess of the woodland, he'd said. Princess of fools, she thought.

"I knew what I was doing," she said, though she saw now that she hadn't, at least not in ways she could explain. It was the first time she had ever lied to him, but pride wouldn't let her do otherwise.

"I doubt you really understood what you were playing with."

"Playing!" Her cheeks burned with humiliation.

"That's right. Kissing is new to you. It's easy to get carried away."

"Hold up right there, Nathan Keene. I was engaged once. I've been kissed."

"Yes, but that's all." He stared at her, his face solemn. "Kissing was only the beginning. If I had continued, I might have gotten you pregnant. Don't you understand? Doesn't that medical book of yours tell you where babies come from?"

He sounded angry, as if she had done something wrong.

"I know," she snapped, her hurt fast turning to anger as well. "I'm not an ignorant country girl, no matter what you might think."

"Forgive me, Daisy. I'm not angry at you. I'm angry at myself for losing control. I wouldn't hurt you for the world."

Too late, she almost said.

Her anger faded. His apology wasn't much, since she knew his opinion of the world, but at least he'd tried. He wouldn't hurt her, but he couldn't love her, either. She wished he'd been blunt enough to say the complete truth.

In that moment she saw the way things were. She loved him, and he honored her. He'd wanted her the way she wanted him, except that his hunger did not come from love. Honor had made him stop. It must have been hard for him, the way it was hard for her to stand beside him and think things through.

She'd known not to start dreaming about impossible things, but her heart hadn't been listening to her mind. No matter how much she wanted Nathan Keene to be the man of her life, her husband and father to her children, he didn't want her for his wife. It mattered little that he didn't want anyone else, either.

"I don't know what got into me," she said with a thin little laugh. "The excitement of the revenuers, I guess." Looking around, she saw the poetry book and the basket of blackberries spilled across the moss.

Handing him the book, she managed to smile. "Take care of this. I know how much it means to you."

Turning from him, she began to climb the hill, thinking that since they might not see one another again, she ought to tell him good-bye. But she didn't have that much hold on herself. When she cried—and she knew she would—she would make certain she was alone.

Nathan didn't move for a long time after she was gone. He hated himself for what he'd almost done. Daisy was all that was sweet and good, and he was a bitter, burned-out wreck. She was a vibrant woman, and he was only half a man.

He'd felt all man, though, when she kissed him. He had begun to think with his body instead of his mind, and he'd almost taken her here in the woods where he'd just called her a princess. A princess needed a prince, not a loner who had abandoned the world.

She thought she had feelings for him. It was in her eyes and in her eagerness. She was ready for love, and that's what she should have. Real love from a real man, not someone who had turned his back on the world. And certainly not some mean-thinking weasel like Earl. The thought of that coarse varmint laying a hand on her turned him cold and empty inside.

With her sweet goodness and honesty, Daisy was spinning him around. The sooner she got to Chattanooga, the better. From everything she'd told him, Aunt Clyde would be more skillful at handling her than a recluse who had trouble sticking to his avowed celibacy. The fact that no woman had ever stirred him the way Daisy did was not a matter for consideration, especially since she would soon be leaving him.

Moving slowly up the hill, he headed for the cave and for the barrels of sour mash whiskey stored inside.

For the first time in his life, Nathan Keene needed a drink.

6

The following week Daisy threw herself into a frenzy of work with Orem and Marigold, practicing runs, making sure the mare and her brother were comfortable with each other but not so worn out they peaked too soon before the big day.

No one was sure of Marigold's ancestry, since she had been bought from a family passing through to Texas, but the way she took to racing, she must have had the sport in her blood. Orem was a little too long-limbed to make a perfect jockey, but his way with animals compensated for it.

Most days, Cleo accompanied Daisy to the pasture and perched in a low hickory branch to watch. Junior and even Lucas and Maude Louise came out from time to time, yelling their encouragement.

As the days passed, Daisy knew that her family must have noticed that she was barely eating or sleeping, or that she couldn't sit still for even a minute, but they never commented. Daisy appreciated their support. Concentrated as she was, grumpy and hollow-eyed, they knew she had worries on her mind. She hinted it was thoughts of losing the race that got her down.

In truth, she was confident of victory, which was a good thing, she told herself, since everything else in her life had turned to disaster. Somehow Nathan and Cleo got mixed up in her mind. She couldn't look at the child without thinking of him and fighting the tears. Maybe, she decided, it was because she was leaving them both.

Everything would turn out for the best, she kept telling herself, but she didn't think her heart was listening.

On the day before the race, the entire family crowded in the wagon for the ride into Pikeville, with Marigold tied to the rear. For a change Daisy wore a dress, one of the few Maude Louise had sewn for her trip. A dress hadn't been her preference, but she knew Maude Louise would be pleased.

Cleo showed the most excitement, shaking the rig with her jumping and sending them all in a tizzy with a million questions about everything they passed.

"Hesh up," Maude Louise ordered more than once, but she didn't put much force behind it, and Cleo kept right on chattering.

They settled in a field near where the race was to begin, almost a mile out of town. For two nights they'd be camping out, the females in the wagon bed if the weather held, and underneath if it didn't. In either case, the boys would be sleeping out in the open. They'd brought their victuals, some early pickings from the garden and a ham from the smokehouse, but when they built a fire to heat them, Daisy thought of

trout frying in a pan and had to leave a spell to pull
herself together.

Other families had come to town as they had, and
there was visiting and the gossip that went with it.
Some of the talk turned to the Whiskey Man's troubles
with the revenuers. More than one woman shifted her
eyes to Daisy, who smiled sweetly as if she couldn't
add a thing to what they already knew.

After supper a fiddle player tuned up and without
any planning, a dance was under way, with romping
and stomping and shouting until it seemed the stars
would shake from the sky.

Daisy especially liked the schottisches. Many folks
around Pikeville, including her family, could trace an
ancestor or two back to Scotland, and the lively dance
came to them naturally. This year, though, she didn't
have much interest in having a good time, even to celebrate her upcoming victory. Looking over the competi-
tion as it arrived, she hadn't seen Marigold's match.

Cleo and some of the other children played "Ring
Around the Roses" and "London Bridge" until long
past dark. At last the lanterns were lowered and everyone settled down to listen to the fiddler playing and a
voice or two lifted in song.

Everyone but Orem, that is. Daisy worried the most
about him, but Junior said he was out testing his mettle.

"What's that supposed to mean?" she asked.

"He's a young man what doesn't get into town any
too often, Daisy. That's enough for you to know."

Daisy disagreed, but since no one else seemed particularly worried, she didn't push for more details. She
woke up a time or two during the night, but all was
quiet and she figured her youngest brother had
sneaked into the camp to rest the mettle that he'd been
testing. She hoped he'd saved enough for the race.

The next morning she learned the bad news. Orem hadn't returned. Junior and Lucas went looking for him, while she stilled her panic by grooming her mare. They returned together to tell her what they had found.

"He's in jail," Junior said right out.

"Jail!" Daisy said, dropping the currycomb.

"That's right," Lucas said. "The sheriff claimed he got liquored up and smashed one of the windows in the general store. Got into a couple of fights, too."

"But town's not so far and we didn't hear anything."

"It was during the dancing," Junior explained.

Leaning against Marigold, Daisy tried to take hold of this latest disaster. "Orem does more talking about drinking than he does drinking," she said.

"Last night he did both," Lucas said. "The drinking got him drunk and the talking got him into the fights."

They stood in silence, the way they would at a burial, Maude Louise keeping Cleo at a distance, and all around them folks getting ready for the race.

"Tell her the rest," Junior said. "She's bound to hear, anyway."

"We don't know it's true," Lucas protested.

"I do." Junior shook his head in disgust. "Talk around town says he didn't come by the liquor on his own, and the fighting was a little too handy to be unplanned."

"I don't understand," Daisy said.

"He was set up by someone who wanted to make sure he didn't ride Marigold today."

"We don't know that," Lucas argued.

"I do," Junior answered.

Daisy looked from one brother to the other. Who on earth would care who rode Marigold? It would take someone worried a powerful lot about the race.

The answer hit her like a thunderbolt. "Earl."

"That's the talk," Junior said.

Lucas refused to confirm or deny the rumor, but planning and carrying through on something so low-down mean was just the kind of thing the stable owner might do.

It was almost too much for Daisy. What with Nathan's being so honorable, and now Earl going as far in the other direction as possible, her everything-will-work-out-right nature was being sorely tested. Nathan and Earl, different as they were, knew what was best for her, and neither seemed inclined to think her opinion mattered much.

The more she thought on it, the angrier she got, and the angrier she got, the more she fidgeted. Finally it all got to be too much. In an explosion of fury, she shoved past the offered comfort of her brothers and headed for town, holding the unfamiliar skirt above her brogans. With each hurried step, her braid bounced hard against her back.

She stopped only once, to tell her brothers to stop following her.

"This is between Earl and me. If I need help, I'll holler." She didn't often speak so sharply, but when she did, her brothers listened. Unaccompanied, she continued on her way.

She found Earl alone in one of the back stalls grooming his black gelding Thunder. She burst in on him with such rage that his eyes showed a flash of fear. Even the horse whinnied and tried to back away.

"Get Orem out of jail," she ordered. "Now."

Earl's fear became satisfaction, enraging her all the more.

He patted Thunder, then walked toward her with a smile and a shrug. "I can't interfere in the sheriff's business, Daisy. Neither can you."

He sounded so all-fired sure of himself. She wished she knew some cuss words to throw at him, but the dictionary was woefully inadequate in that regard and "dad-gum" was about as far as the boys ever went.

She sniffed in disgust. The stable smelled of hay, manure, and sweaty horseflesh, odors she always associated with Earl.

"You wanted to make sure I would lose. Without the prize money, I just might cancel my move to Chattanooga."

"I can't help what vim and vigor'll lead a young man t'do."

"But you can help him along. And you knew it was too late for me to get another rider. I'd be on Marigold myself if I'd worn pants."

"Against the rules," Earl said with a sniff, looking her over. He hooked his thumbs in the belt riding under his paunch. "Honey, you sure look pretty when you're riled. Glad to see you listened to what I said and wore a dress."

Daisy stamped her brogan against the hay-strewn ground. "Earl, you're the stinkweed of mankind. Maybe you fit into the scheme of things in this world, but it would take a head smarter'n mine to figure out how."

If she was hoping to disgust him, she failed. "Looks like I got me a kiss coming," he said with a grin.

Daisy swallowed. She'd forgotten the bet.

"Is that what this is about?" she asked. "A puny kiss?"

He puffed up. "Earl Selfe's kisses ain't puny."

Daisy thought of Nathan, and suddenly all the fight went out of her. Here was Earl scheming and cheating to get what she would willingly offer to another man, only that other man didn't want what she had to give. Irony, that's what it was. Irony, pure and simple.

Life wasn't fair. Never before had she thought so, but now she had the proof. Not only unfair, but also unkind.

She stiffened her spine. If Nathan held her kisses to be worthless, so would she.

"I'll bargain with you, Earl. You get Orem out of jail, and I'll kiss you no matter who wins."

Earl's little pig eyes gleamed with anticipation. "I want the kiss first."

Daisy planted her hands on her hips. "You were just waiting for me to make the offer. It was the kiss you were after, not just the victory."

"I told you, honey, once you kiss me, you'll change your mind about Chattanooga. And about the Whiskey Man."

"The Whiskey Man!"

"Yep. The revenuers left here madder'n hornets about not finding his still. I got my ideas about how he knew they was coming."

"Keep 'em to yourself," Daisy snapped. "You mention Mr. Keene again and I'll cause such a ruckus in here the sheriff'll be throwing me in jail alongside Orem."

Earl looked at her in surprise. "Dad-blame it, Daisy, you look like you'd do it, too." His surprise turned to a smirk. "Ought to save all that energy for my kisses."

Daisy squeezed her eyes closed a minute, fighting down her ire. She *had* made the bet. Nathan wasn't the only one in the hills who was honorable.

"One," she said, sighing, "and then Orem's out."

"I'll do my best on both accounts."

Daisy would rather kiss Thunder than Earl, but

there was nothing she could do but wipe her mouth with the back of her hand and stand with her arms at her side. And not think of Nathan. Why it seemed she was betraying him, she couldn't imagine, but it did, even though he wouldn't care if she kissed every man in Pikeville.

When Earl moved in on her, his lips puckering like a little pink worm caught in his peach-fuzz beard, she tried her best to imagine Mr. Wordsworth's daffodils, but all she could think of was the odor of manure.

Nathan stood in the shadows of the stable watching Earl put his hands on Daisy's shoulders and kiss her. Jealousy like nothing he'd ever felt shot through him. He wished he had his gun. Loaded, and not with buckshot.

The worst part was that Daisy wasn't fighting him the way she should.

She didn't fight you, either, an ugly voice said inside him, making him angrier.

Nathan had got there too late to see what had led to the kiss. At the creek, he'd known she was inexperienced, no matter how she pretended otherwise, but she'd taken to lovemaking right away. Maybe she just wanted more.

He couldn't remember the last time he'd felt such agitation, but he kept it under tight control. "When you two are finished sparking, I've got some business to take care of."

They jumped apart as if they'd been set on fire.

"Nathan!" Daisy said, her eyes wide. Even in the dim light he could see the blush on her cheeks, as if she were guilty of something. "What are you doing here?"

I've been thinking of you night and day, wondering how you were getting along, needing to see you one last time, knowing I had to wish you well.

If he'd found her under different circumstances, he might have put the thought into words, and maybe told her a whole lot more. It was a mighty big *if.*

"I didn't mean to interrupt," he said. "Your brothers were out front, and they seemed worried about you. I told them I'd make sure you were all right."

Earl smiled. "Man's got a right to kiss his intended."

Daisy's mouth dropped open.

Nathan felt as if he'd been punched with a pitchfork. "Fast work," he said, his mouth twitching, his fists clinched at his sides. He hadn't hit a man in years, but that didn't mean he'd forgotten how. "Congratulations."

"You believe him?" Daisy asked, coming at him, stopping a foot away to glare up at him with blazing eyes. "Don't try to deny it, Nathan Keene. It seems to me the men in this town have a powerful lot to say about what I do and why I do it. You claim to have business here? Well, so do I."

She glanced back at Earl. "We made a deal, and don't think you're going to wriggle out of it."

"I'll do my best, honey, but the sheriff don't take kindly to me all the time."

"Don't give me any talk like that. A promise is a promise. I kept my word, and so will you."

"What's the sheriff got to do with this?" Nathan asked.

Daisy sniffed. "I see you decided to start asking questions instead of believing everything you see and hear. Well, put them to Earl. I've had about all of the odor in here I can stand."

Daisy strode past him, her skirt swishing. Her *skirt,* Nathan realized with a start. He'd never seen her in a dress before. She'd never worn one for him. The thought did nothing to put him in a better mood.

He turned to Earl. "I'm asking again, and this time I want an answer. What's the sheriff got to do with this?"

Earl started to strut away, but Nathan caught him by the collar. Earl's neck and face turned fiery red, but his lips clamped mulishly closed. Nathan shook him a time or two, threatening more, and finally Earl sputtered that Orem had got himself in trouble with the law and wouldn't be riding Marigold in the race.

"You wouldn't have anything to do with that trouble, would you?"

"What makes you say that?"

"I know you, Earl. I've seen your kind from here to California and back."

"I'm a simple businessman, that's all."

Earl was simple, all right. Nathan thought a minute. Daisy had pinned a world of hopes on that race, and whether or not he agreed with her plans, she had a right to be entered.

"Sign me up, Earl. I'll be riding Browning in the race."

"You can't do that," Earl whined. "This late it's against the rules."

"Whose, yours?" Nathan backed Earl into the stall, where he bumped against his jittery horse. "Try and stop me. And don't think you can call on the law to enforce your rules. You said yourself the sheriff doesn't always take kindly to you."

He left Earl muttering under his breath and went directly to the jail.

"Boy's gotta curb his rambunctious ways," the sheriff said after refusing to free Orem.

"He's not the one being punished," Nathan said, explaining about the race.

"I already heard about Daisy a hunnert times. Besides, you ain't seen Orem. He's lower'n a creek in a six-month drought."

Nathan gave up trying to reason with the sheriff, the way he'd given up trying to reason with Rebel officers during the war. He would win the race and explain the whys and wherefores to Daisy afterwards. Maybe she would be in a mood to listen then.

He ached to tell her right away more than just about the race. The past week had been about as miserable a time as he could remember, and that was saying something. He'd done a lot of thinking and a lot of arguing with himself, but it seemed clear even to a thick-headed recluse like himself that fate had come along to make changes in them both.

So what had he done but make a fool of himself in the stable? She had a right to kiss anyone she wanted, especially since he'd let her know he wasn't interested. Except that he was so interested he couldn't eat or sleep or even think straight, and he hadn't read a word since she'd left.

And if she thought she could go around kissing just any man, she had better change her mind fast.

That he wasn't being at all rational didn't bother him. He'd been rational long enough. It was time to let his heart take control.

Word about his entry into the race spread fast. By the time the horses were lined up in the field that would serve as a track, the crowd was buzzing about the Whiskey Man. For a recluse, Nathan decided, he surely was drawing attention to himself.

A former recluse, he amended. At least he was trying to be.

A dozen men and a few women came up to wish him well, but the one he wanted to hear from stayed with her family, her eyes wide and wounded, as if he were taking advantage of her situation. She'd said he was too quick to believe what he saw, but she didn't seem to realize she was the same way.

He started to approach her to put her mind at ease, but her brothers stood in front of her like defending knights and he changed his mind. All he needed to make her totally disgusted with him was to start a fight.

Instead, he positioned Browning in a line with the dozen other horses competing in the race. Awaiting the starting gun, he felt her eyes on him, still hurt, still accusing. Unable to find her among the spectators, he concentrated on the task at hand.

He won the race handily. Earl tried to cut him off a time or two, poking Browning with his riding crop, but Nathan was wise to his tricks and simply urged his horse to pour on the speed.

Accepting the cheers from the crowd, shaking a few dozen hands, Nathan walked Browning back to the pasture, where he handed him over to a young admirer to care for. He sought out Daisy right away. She was alone with Marigold not far from the wagon, her protective knights nowhere in sight.

"Congratulations," she said, stiff-backed and proud as she stroked Marigold's mane. He remembered how he'd said the same thing to her not too long ago.

"We've got to talk," he said.

"There's nothing to say. You won. Browning's the fastest horse I've ever seen. He could have beaten Marigold without breaking a sweat."

"That's not true. Anyway, I wouldn't have entered if your horse had been able to race."

"Humph," she said, and it was clear from the set of her mouth she didn't believe him.

Before he could say more, a host of well-wishers caught up with him, surrounding him with words of cheer, cutting him off from the only person in the world he wanted to talk to.

"Great race," one of the men said. "Don't suppose you'd have anything on you we might use to celebrate."

"A sip o' sour mash sure would go down smooth right now," another added.

Others joined in the request, and he had a hard time getting rid of them, until he saw a familiar wagon arrive in the field. "Sorry I don't have any whiskey," he said, "but you might check with the Clutters over there."

Like a school of fish, the crowd shifted their direction toward Claude and Abner, and Nathan started looking for Daisy once again. But she was gone.

"The boys've gone into town after Orem, but Daisy done hiked her skirts up and rode Marigold toward home," Maude Louise told him at the Abernathy wagon. "A day early, too. Said she needed to check on the stock, but a neighbor's doing that." Maude Louise shook her head. "Never seen her looking so down."

Cleo stared up at him with a worried frown. "She said she was a ladybug without a gemmenbug and that was okay."

"She did, did she?" Nathan said, thinking it sounded like something Daisy would say.

He looked toward the hills, rising dark and distant under a cloudy sky. He pictured a slender young woman riding away, a single thick braid bouncing against her back, her heart as heavy as his own.

At least he hoped it was, even though he'd die rather than wish her a moment's pain. He saw right then and there the course he had to follow. He'd been considering that *maybe* he would tell her this and *maybe* he would tell her that. And *maybe* he ought to let her go without a fight.

Like hell.

"Don't worry about her," he said to Maude Louise. "I've got some business to take care of, and then I'll see she's all right."

He spoke confidently, but he remembered too well the way she'd looked at him in the stable. Big words— *I'll see she's all right.* He prayed to a God he hadn't talked to in years that he hadn't been too much of a fool for too long to follow through on his most heart-felt vow.

7

Daisy rode home under low-hanging clouds, feeling for all the world as if she'd been dipped in lye and hung out to dry.

Why, she was a poet, she decided. Like Mr. Wordsworth, only her poem wasn't nearly so cheerful. Wordsworth had one thing going against him right then. Like Nathan and Earl, he was of the male gender, which meant he looked at things his own way.

Men! If she never saw another one, it would be too soon. Aunt Clyde wouldn't believe she meant it, but she did.

Nathan was the worst. Watching all the folks congratulating him, she'd seen him fight for patience. He wasn't a people person, and he never would be. He sure wasn't a one-person person, unless that person was himself.

Lordy, she was getting wordy. It came from thinking

too much, but what else did she have to do besides think and hurt?

She had realized that Nathan had calmed down about Earl and what he'd seen in the stable. But he'd probably decided he didn't care enough to stay aggravated.

By the time she arrived home and put Marigold out to graze in the pasture, daylight was fading fast. Alone for a rare evening in her life, Daisy scrubbed down at the pump by the back door, then went into her room to don her nightgown and brush out her hair. Sitting on the bed, she stared out the window and analyzed her feelings, the way she would analyze a plant that was ailing.

Mostly she thought of Nathan and the way he had betrayed her, making her feel like a loose woman for wanting his kisses. Then he'd reinforced that feeling when he saw her with Earl, never thinking she might have had good reason for kissing him.

And then he'd had the nerve to take her place in the race!

Oh dear, another rhyme, and another reason to hurt.

How many times could a woman's heart break? She brushed away a tear. As many times as she was crushed by the man she loved. To her regret, she loved Nathan as much as ever, even though he'd rejected her. She was a fool for sure, but she seemed to have no choice.

Dejected, betrayed, forlorn. The dictionary didn't have many cuss words, but it had a thousand words to describe her condition.

Thank goodness for Aunt Clyde. She'd regularly offered to send Daisy money for the boat ride to Chattanooga. Well, first thing early tomorrow morning she would write and ask for a couple of dollars. She would pay it back by growing vegetables for the boardinghouse—Aunt Clyde had said there was room for a plot—and by working extra hard at cooking and cleaning. She could even grow some flowers and put fresh bouquets in all the rooms.

Then she remembered she'd once brought flowers to Nathan and that he'd told her they would die. Debt or no debt, she should have ridden away then and there. But if she had, she would never have gotten the flowers he had given her—the wreath he'd crowned her with.

Daisy looked at the plank walls, at her mama's quilt on the bed, at the ruffled gingham curtains she'd made to hang at the window. She loved everything she saw. This was the only bedroom she'd ever known, and she'd been comfortable here, but she knew those days of comfort were at an end.

Sometimes a flower tried to grow in the wrong place. A change of location was usually the answer. Daisy was simply transplanting herself to a more favorable climate.

The sound of horses' hooves drew her to the front door. She watched in surprise as Nathan rode toward her under gathering clouds. He'd said they needed to talk, but she figured he would change his mind once he got back his precious seclusion.

He dismounted and walked toward the porch, one hand behind his back. She stepped outside, and they both just stood looking at each other. She should have been ashamed to stand before him in her nightclothes, but he already thought her a loose woman, so she couldn't see the good of modesty now.

"I brought you something," he said.

"I'm not in need."

*I*f you
have a passion
for great
historical
romance,
here's an offer
you'll love...

4 FREE NOVELS

SEE INSIDE.

Introducing
The Timeless Romance

Passion rising from the ashes of the Civil War...

Love blossoming against the harsh landscape of the primitive Australian outback...

Romance melting the cold walls of an 18th-century English castle —— and the heart of the handsome Earl who lives there...

Since the beginning of time, great love has held the power to change the course of history. And in Harper Monogram historical novels, you can experience that power again and again.

Free introductory offer. To introduce you to this exclusive new service, we'd like to send you the four newest Harper Monogram titles absolutely free. They're yours to keep without obligation, no matter what you decide.

Free 10-day previews. Enjoy automatic free delivery of four new titles each month —— up to four weeks before they appear in bookstores. You're never obligated to keep a book you don't want, and you can return any book, for a full credit.

Save up to 32% off the publisher's price on any shipment you choose to keep.

Don't pass up this opportunity to enjoy great romance as you have never experienced before.

Reader Service.

Yes! I want to join the Timeless Romance Reader Service. Please send me my 4 FREE HarperMonogram historical romances. Then each month send me 4 new historical romances to preview without obligation for 10 days. I'll pay the low subscription price of $4.00 for every book I choose to keep--a total savings of at least $2.00 each month--and home delivery is free! I understand that I may return any title within 10 days and receive a full credit. I may cancel this subscription at any time without obligation by simply writing "Canceled" on any invoice and mailing it to Timeless Romance. There is no minimum number of books to purchase.

NAME

ADDRESS

CITY   STATE   ZIP

TELEPHONE

SIGNATURE

(If under 18, parent or guardian must sign. Program, price, terms, and conditions subject to cancellation and change. Orders subject to acceptance by HarperMonogram.)

Indulge in passion, adventure and romance with your

4 FREE

Historical Romances.

TIMELESS ROMANCE
READER SERVICE

120 Brighton Road
P.O. Box 5069
Clifton, NJ 07015-5069

"It could be I am."

Always thinking about himself, she thought.

He dug into his pocket, then held out a small leather pouch. "Here," he said, "take it. It's yours."

Reluctantly she walked to the edge of the porch and took the pouch, careful not to touch his hand.

"It's coins," she said, surprised.

"The ten dollars from the race."

She dropped it as if it scorched her fingers. "It's not mine."

"I rode for you, not for myself."

He sounded so sure, so strong. She shook inside, but she couldn't let him know it. "So I'd be certain to have the money for Chattanooga? That's kind of you, Nathan, but it's still not mine."

"I didn't do it to be kind. And I don't want you to go to Chattanooga."

Daisy hugged herself. "You're confusing me. Can't you make up your mind?"

"I want you to make up yours, and that's the truth. You've got to have choices, Daisy, so I'll know for sure how you feel about me. It wouldn't do to ask you to marry me if that was your only option."

She stared at him open-mouthed, but no words would come.

Stepping onto the porch, he pulled a wildflower bouquet from behind his back. She saw phlox and ageratum and Lord only knew what else.

"They're not as pretty as they were when I picked them. I'll do better next time." He thrust them in her hand. "You said no one had ever given you flowers. I wanted to be the first when I gave you the wreath. And I want to be the only man ever to give you flowers for the rest of your life."

Speechless, her mind whirling, she stared down at

the blossoms in disbelief. Wilted or not, they were the most beautiful flowers she had ever seen.

He held her by the shoulders and kissed her, gently at first, and then hard, but he didn't crush her against him the way she wanted him to do.

"I love you, Daisy Abernathy, and I want you for my wife. I want you to bear my children and I pray they'll have your beauty and your goodness and spirit and that they inherit damned little from me."

Daisy dropped her head. She couldn't even look up from the flowers. Her heart was pounding so hard it was like a roar in her ears. She couldn't be hearing Nathan right. He couldn't be saying all the things she had longed to hear from him.

A cool breeze stirred the air. He stepped off the porch. "I've got my answer. I love you, Daisy, more than life itself. I'll always wish you well."

Rain began to fall as he backed away, then headed down the path that took him by the flower garden at the side of the house.

Suddenly she came to her senses. "Nathan," she cried, dropping the flowers, running barefoot through the grass and dirt, catching up with him by a bed of hyacinths and irises in full bloom.

"Get on back to the porch, Daisy. You'll catch cold."

"It's only a gentle rain," she said, gesturing toward the light moisture layering the multitude of color at their feet. Her hair was curling from the dampness and her gown clung to her body, but she didn't care. "I once told you rain was needed to make things grow."

"You're the gentle rain, my love. Without you, everything in my life would shrivel and die."

They stood looking at each other. Then Nathan smiled. For the first time since she'd met him, he truly smiled. She saw it on his face and in his eyes.

"I love you, Nathan Keene. I want nothing more in this life than to be your wife." She pressed her fingers to her lips. "Oh, dear, I'm afraid I've been making terrible rhymes lately. But you know—"

He didn't let her finish. Sweeping her into his arms, he kissed her, so many times she lost count, and neither of them gave any sign that the rain mattered in the least.

At last he held her close. "I used to hate the springtime, can you believe it? But you have a way with all living things. You bring flowers to life, and you did the same with me."

He cupped her face, his thumbs brushing the raindrops from her cheeks. "There's ugliness in the world, I still know that. But there is also beauty. The beauty of love. I needed you to show me the wisdom I hadn't found in my books."

Daisy knew he was giving her too much credit, but she wasn't about to correct him. Let him think she'd brought him back to life. He was right about so many things, maybe he was right about that, too.

Lifting her into his arms, he carried her to the porch, though it seemed silly to her since they were both soaked to the skin. She cuddled against him. If there was ever a time for silliness, it was today.

"We need to get out of these clothes," she said as he set her down. With a grin, she added, "Don't think I'm suggesting anything improper. After all, I'm an honorable woman and you're an honorable man."

"Are you poking fun at me?" he said with a mock growl.

"Would you mind if I were?"

"Not in the least."

She saw the abandoned flowers at her feet. She picked them up and tried to plump them back to life, then stopped. "There's one thing I've been thinking about. The revenuers are liable to return, aren't they?"

He shrugged. "I imagine they will."

"And with our children and all, seeing their father hunted down by the law . . . I was wondering if you'd ever given any thought to the lumber business? You must have thousands of chestnut oaks on your land. Aunt Clyde says they provide the best tan-bark in the country."

Nathan's eyes glinted. "Something else Aunt Clyde knows all about?"

"Her husband does. We wouldn't have to cut them all down, just a few and replant as we cut."

He opened the door for her. "Anybody ever call you a managing woman?"

"Just me," she said over her shoulder, returning the wink he'd given her a week ago.

He shook his head. "As you said, we have to get out of these wet clothes, but you may need to remind me about being honorable." His eyes trailed over her clinging nightgown. "On the other hand, we're both getting on in years, you up in your twenties already and I'll be thirty-one next month. Wanting babies the way we do, maybe we ought to get started right away."

Daisy eased into his arms. "Whatever you say, Nathan Keene. Whatever you say."

The author of fifteen historical romances and four novellas, *EVELYN ROGERS* lives in San Antonio, Texas, with her husband of thirty-eight years. Parents of two married children, they spend as much time as possible traveling, recently to Germany and Austria in celebration of her husband's retirement.

Before her first book appeared in 1987, she experienced a variety of careers: crime reporter, Air Force service club director, teacher, and librarian. The twenty-five years she spent as teacher and librarian in Texas middle schools were challenging and exciting, she says, but writing is the best career of all.

III

SUMMER STORM

Karen Lockwood

1

Summer, 1891
Mesquite Junction, Texas

Rose had borne up under the merciless heat for weeks now, but today she could not stand it any longer. She reached for one of the cast-iron pump handles and cranked, welcoming its squeak. The water tumbling over her hands and into the bucket was a blessed respite, cooling her burning skin.

The screen door slammed, setting ripples in a kettle of water on the stove. Rose turned, wiping her hands on her apron, and at the sight of the figure in the doorway, she tensed and her heart beat faster. Baxter Yates, her employer's son and heir, leaned against the door.

"Lunch isn't ready," she said.

"I didn't come to eat."

He took off his Stetson and with the other hand held out a yellow rosebud plucked from his late mother's garden. Another peace offering. Well, he could bring a hundred and it wouldn't change anything.

"I told you I don't want any more roses."

"But I like giving them to you."

Ignoring that, she went on, "Well, if you're here to lecture me about your cowhands again, save your breath."

He tossed his hat onto the table and closed some of the distance between them. "Jess says you might like a practical gift better than roses."

"I won't be bribed with presents."

"Not even blue-enameled crockery?"

She looked up. "The set at the Mercantile?" She could save it for her restaurant.

"Yes. It's nearly as fine as what I could get in Boston."

Just because he'd left home for four years of college at Harvard, Baxter acted so uppity at times. Though for a brief moment she entertained accepting his offer, she knew she could take nothing from him.

"No. I won't be bribed with roses or crockery or— or anything. I don't need protecting. If you and your father want to fire me for passing the time of day with the hands in broad daylight, then go ahead. I'll survive."

Of that, she had no doubt, for she had come a long way to get from the mission kitchen to Oliver Yates's ranch.

She stood at the stove, pretending to stare at the bubbles in the kettle. As it started to boil, she reached for a wooden spoon and a cupful of dried beans.

"Rose," Baxter said quietly.

She turned, reminding herself to remain polite. That was easy. Remaining unaffected was difficult as her eyes traveled over his tousled sandy hair, his eyes the color of the wide Texas sky, and his ripcord muscular arms exposed by his rolled-up denim sleeves. And those fancy boots. The ones his father had passed on to him. As the heir to the Lazy Y, Baxter was walking in old Oliver's footsteps, all right, grooming himself to inherit half the county. But even if he owned nothing more than a shack and a swayback mule, Rose still would have thought he was the handsomest man in all of Texas.

But he only saw her as a child, a girl in need of protection. "What? What do you want?" These talks with Baxter, which had been going on for the past few weeks, were becoming more and more difficult for her to handle, not to mention making her working here more and more intolerable.

Her pulse beat in her throat so hard that she yearned to loosen the neck of her dress.

"To talk to you without fighting," Baxter answered.

She bit her lip, afraid she'd blurt out things she shouldn't.

"I only want to help," he went on. "I'm looking out for you."

She turned away and continued stirring. "You had no call to chase off my suitors." Her voice was so soft she could barely hear herself. Especially now that Oliver was feeling poorly, Baxter was the boss—her boss—and she had to try not to lose her temper.

"The Lazy Y pays them to be ranch hands, not suitors," Baxter said in a level voice. "You were distracting them from their work."

She lifted the spoon and laid it across the pot, then faced him. "The men were only resting in the shade. If you had any sense, you'd care about them getting out of the sun, Baxter. They're not a bunch of cattle."

He stared at her. "There's shade in plenty of other places on this ranch besides the veranda."

"Well, what does it matter if one of them had courting on his mind? Are you the only one around here who's allowed to go courting?" She regretted the words as soon as she spoke them. She didn't want him to know she'd even noticed he was an eligible bachelor, the most eligible bachelor in all of Mesquite Junction. She grew warm under his gaze. His meddling in her life was as embarrassing as having him catch her in her nightgown. And what business was it of his anyway? She was only the kitchen help. "By rights, you've got no claim over my time."

"When you spend my butter-churning time courting, I do." He picked up his Stetson and rotated it in his hands. "The men can court you at the dance this weekend properly, like it's done in Boston." His voice was husky and soft and added to the warmth she always felt when she was near him.

She reached for the pepper shaker. "I don't care how it's done in Boston." There he was, being uppity again.

Pivoting back to the stove, she liberally seasoned the beans. It wasn't fair that he got to court whomever he pleased while chasing away her suitors. She hated the hypocrisy of it. Baxter could do anything he wanted, while she couldn't. Stirring the beans more vigorously, she tried to banish the image of him standing behind her, looking like a penitent little boy. If she wasn't careful, she'd end up like her mother, wanting and loving a man she could never have, wasting years of her life on Oliver Yates when she could have moved on to a respectable relationship.

Then another suspicion arose—her usual one. She had known her share of prejudice because of having Milligan for a last name and black hair and brown eyes. So had her Mexican mother, Maria, and her Irish father, Rory. But instead of defeating her, the prejudice had bred a fierce pride in her. So far, Baxter had shown no prejudice toward her, and she hoped it stayed that way.

She began to pump water into the coffee pot. "Is it because I'm half Mexican? Is that why you don't want the ranch hands around me?" She looked over her shoulder at him.

She wouldn't have expected a man who'd been to school back East to blush as Baxter did now. "It's not that," he said. "You just shouldn't be alone with the men. It's not right."

"They like to talk, that's all."

"And next thing you know one of them will make improper advances."

"You mean, try to kiss me?" She wondered what it would feel like to kiss Baxter, to go soft in his arms, the way she'd seen her mother do with Oliver. "Is that wrong? Why can't I kiss a gentleman just because he's a cowhand?"

Baxter raked his fingers through his hair, then touched the rose she'd rescued from the mud. Snapped from its stem, it floated in water in an empty peach tin.

"I'm saving it for Elmer," she said.

"Don't change the subject, Rose."

"What was the subject?"

"You know," he said uneasily.

She looked up into his eyes, blue as lupine. "You're toying with me, Baxter. You have been ever since you came home." He was, and she feared if she let down her guard he would use her the way all gringos did with women of half-Mexican blood. Use her when the whim suited him, the way Oliver had come and gone from her mother's life. Oh, she had no doubt Oliver had loved Maria, but that love had caused pain to his wife, whom Rose had come to care for. Never would she cause pain to any man's woman.

"You're quiet, Rose," Baxter said softly.

"I was thinking."

"About what I said?"

"Yes. And I still don't see what's wrong with having my own suitors on the veranda, Baxter." She took a step toward him. Her heart pounded in her ears. She didn't want to kiss any of the cowhands; she just wanted to pass the time with them. But Baxter was different. Though she could never be courted by him, that didn't matter now, standing in this large kitchen, so close to him. She felt lightheaded and closed her eyes. "Tell me."

Without warning, he bent his head and his mouth brushed hers. She felt his warmth, as his kiss deepened. The kettle began to boil, like an alarm. She placed her hands on his shoulders and pulled away, shaken with desire. "You had no call—"

"You asked me what might happen," he cut in. "One of the cowhands might forget himself and do that."

She stood still while the taste of his kiss evaporated off her lips and his words burned in her mind. She struggled to regain her composure, her dignity. She took two deep breaths, counted to six, and felt in control again.

"Baxter, you're like a devil sent to guard the church, you know that?"

He looked abashed and moved away. She turned back to the stove. Since Baxter had arrived home four months ago when his mother died, it had become more difficult for her to remember that she was a servant and had no right to these yearnings. No right to tell him off, either.

He was close behind her now, so close she could scarcely breathe.

Lazily, he ran his hand up her arm. "Now, Rose, you might be right about that, but I couldn't help myself. I've been wondering how it'd be to kiss you for months now."

She'd been wondering too and wishing. But now that he had finally kissed her, she was angry and rueful that he had waited so long. But she'd never tell him that. He was already too cocksure for his own good.

"Unlike you, your ranch hands manage to behave like gentlemen," she pointed out.

"You're too good for the ranch hands."

Words locked in her throat. She felt rooted to the spot. Then he was kissing her neck. His arms spanned her waist and he turned her to him. She melted against him, her emotions reeling. He made her hot and cold, like air colliding before a storm.

Again his lips dipped to hers and her mouth parted.

Just in time, she came to her senses. She placed her hands on his forearms and shoved him back. "Oh, I see. And you're better than them. You are the most conceited man in Mesquite Junction."

"You asked me why you shouldn't let the ranch hands come hanging around the porch so much, and all I'm trying to do is show you."

"Then am I supposed to die an old maid?"

He pondered that. "I'd marry you if I could." His mouth lifted in a half-smile.

"You're teasing me now!" Oliver had said the same thing to her mother. *Maria, I'd marry you if I could.* And then he'd left for his ranch and his wife. Someday, too, Baxter would marry one of the fine rosewater-scented ladies who batted their lashes at him. Like father, like son.

"Your mother and I got real close before she died, and she said I had a right to have beaus and to never mind the town ladies with all their stuffy airs. Maybe you better go sweet-talk one and rustle up a lunch invitation."

He peered into the kettle. "What are you cooking?"

"Beans in molasses and hot mustard. If it was just you eating, I'd serve it up."

He gulped. "Now, Rose, don't take this the wrong way, but can't you make some plain gringo food? Does it always have to be hot and spicy?"

"You'll eat what I cook. That was the condition for my taking this job." Tears blurring her eyes, she grabbed at the apron strings behind her back and ripped off the apron.

"You know, you look pretty when your eyes are on fire."

"Quit your sweet-talking, Baxter, and leave me alone."

She slammed out of the house, marched straight for the vegetable garden, and began hoeing the weeds. No man told Rose Milligan who to spend time with. No one. And Rose had no intention of letting any man use *her* as a plaything. Especially not a rogue like Baxter Yates.

Oh, the sooner he got married the better. For then he'd be branded, roped, and fenced in, and he'd have better things to do than "protect" her.

Yet longing filled her, an awful ache for what could never be. But she'd learned, watching her mother pine for Oliver in his younger days, not to set her sights on the wrong man. How many times had Oliver kissed her mother, filled her heart with fiery words of love, only to return to his wife, sweet, perpetually homesick Ellen Yates. Rose would have thought it impossible to love her mother's rival, but Ellen's long bout with tuberculosis had brought them close, so close that they had been on a first-name basis.

Ellen had known about Rose's mother and had forgiven Oliver and Maria, and Rose had loved her for that, too. But Rose had made a vow never to be in Ellen's position—forgiving a man, taking morsels from him, and then finally being discarded.

She hoed harder, for she was not going to repeat her mother's or Ellen's heartache.

She peeked up, saw Baxter striding toward the barn, and caught her breath. Then she outright stared—at his broad shoulders, his straight back, his light brown hair curling beneath his dark Stetson. Disgusted with herself, she looked away.

She had made up her mind. As soon as she had enough money, she'd leave this ranch and strike out on her own. She was in a better financial position to do that now than when Ellen had died. If the previous cook hadn't retired the day of Ellen's funeral, and Oliver hadn't offered Rose the job, Rose didn't know what she would have done. Besides, she had learned to cook at the mission and she enjoyed it.

At least she *had,* until Baxter had come home. Tension had simmered between the two of them ever since, the undercurrents growing hotter with each passing day. But no one, especially not Baxter, would ever see her shed a tear over him. For like a Texas rose, the hardy kind, the wild kind, she would not wilt easily in the heat.

2

In the barn, a bewildered Baxter touched his face to make certain it matched the one the Boston ladies had swooned over. No woman had ever rebuffed him like the Lazy Y's cook, he thought as he worked in the tack room. He hung up a fallen halter, rearranged a few horseshoes, and hammered one over the door. Mindless chores of no consequence. That was his mistake. They weren't important enough to take his mind off Rose.

He left the barn and headed for the veranda. He stood on the top step, looking at the rocking chair where Rose usually sat and held court with his ranch hands. He wanted to fire every single one of them. But for what? Courting the ranch house cook? He pushed back his Stetson, wondering if the heat was getting to him.

The screen door slammed and his father's uneven footsteps moved across the porch. Oliver Yates limped toward the rocker, sat down, then turned his stern gaze on Baxter.

"What was going on in the kitchen awhile ago, Baxter? Rose hit you in the forehead with a frying pan, or what?"

"She didn't like me picking the roses from Mother's garden. I guess I ought to try bringing her a wild prickly one. A whole batch of them grow up the side of the bunkhouse, but I guess if she doesn't like specially bred ones, she won't like those either."

Oliver snorted. "You expect me to believe that? Your ma loved picking those roses. The house was filled with them when she was alive, and Rose was quieter then, never lost her temper."

Only one man dared talk to Baxter in that imperious tone of voice—the white-haired patriarch of the Lazy Y.

"I guess the heat's getting to Rose," Baxter said. "Heck, it's getting to all of us." There couldn't be any other explanation for their short tempers with one another. Everyone had been on edge, especially him and his father.

"You and I need to talk."

"Here?" Oh, no, Baxter thought, not again.

"In my den. It wouldn't be right if anyone else heard what I have to say."

Oliver motioned him into the house, then into his green-wallpapered haven dominated by an enormous rolltop desk.

"Let me see," his father began, easing himself with painful slowness into the leather chair at the desk. "It seems the only thing the ladies can talk about is catching your eye, only so far they haven't been very successful. Word is you spend more time in the kitchen with Rose than in town with the ladies of refinement."

Baxter pulled a green shade a bit lower to keep out the relentless heat. Someday this room, and all of his father's vast spread, would be his—one reason the young women of Mesquite Junction were as relentless as the summer sun in their pursuit of him.

"Any truth to what they're saying?" Oliver asked. "Is Rose a distraction?"

"To the ranch hands, yes. That's what I keep trying to tell her. Only she keeps getting angry, and I keep trying to make peace. Only she hates my peace offerings." He released the shade's braided tassel, watched it twirl and finally grow still.

Oliver stared at him a long time. "There's something you're holding back. What are you saying to rile her? Not asking any questions about her family, are you?"

"Of course not." This was harder for Baxter than confessing he'd branded the neighbor's calves when he was sixteen. Harder even than learning his way around Boston. "I tried to, uh, explain . . . Heck, she needs a woman to look out for her."

His father snorted. "Well, there is no woman on the ranch. None of those hands have kissed her, have they?"

Baxter knew any mention of the kiss he and Rose had shared would be a grave mistake. He shook his head as he sat down. "Not yet."

"That's a mercy. Town folks are still clucking about us keeping Rose on after your ma died. At least when she was alive, she kept an eye on Rose, but now . . . "

"They wouldn't cluck if Rose had a companion. What about Nettie?"

"Our housekeeper? She's got a family and only comes twice a week. And I don't need her any more than that."

Oliver leaned back against the rocker and stared out the window. His rheumatic hands gripped the arm rests.

Baxter decided the silence was worse than the heat. "What are we going to do?"

"Do? That's fairly obvious, Baxter. You're going to be her chaperone."

"Her what?"

"It's only right. You're the only man on the ranch I can trust not to take advantage of her. You can be like a big brother to her."

The notion struck Baxter as wrong, but he wasn't sure why.

"Chaperoning Rose won't be easy," he argued. "Heck, it would be ten times easier learning how to breed and fatten cattle. She's got a tongue sharper than barbed wire. I'd rather chaperone a Boston lady any day." Though secretly he had to admit it wouldn't be as interesting.

"Well, she ain't got no one but you and me. Now, her mama was, well, a friend, and Rose, she came and cared for your ma, so we owe it to her to make sure no one does wrong by her. She hasn't got anyone in the world to look out for her like those ladies in town do, and you know a ranch hand can get mighty lonely. Hard to know what they'll try with her at the town hall dance. And then there's the annual picnic. So it'll be your job to keep the cowhands at bay."

"You could do it," Baxter argued.

"I'm too old and too arthritic—which reminds me. Elmer's got a new potion he's invented, some powder to mix with water." His father closed his eyes as if weary. "Keep Rose pure, and don't worry. I wager she'll marry Elmer one of these days and then she'll be his woman and his responsibility."

Sometimes Baxter wondered if his father had gopher holes in his head where good sense should be. "Elmer Hughes? What does he know about women? He's always got his nose in a book of potion recipes, or else he's gossiping."

Oliver opened his eyes and smiled at him. "He'll do for Rose. Might as well put the word out, too. There doesn't need to be any fighting over a woman on this spread. A good rancher can run his outfit and scare off coyotes without creating a commotion."

"That's not going to be easy either."

"Nothing out here is easy. But you set the example and start courting a real lady, mind?"

"Rose is a lady."

Oliver's face darkened. "Of course she is. But there are ladies and then there are ladies . . . with rich papas."

Baxter got to his feet, ready to leave. His father could lecture him all day about how to run the ranch, but when it came to women, Baxter was his own man.

"Where are you going?" Oliver asked.

"To town."

"To court?"

After a pause, Baxter said, "To the bank. You want me to pick up Elmer's new potion?"

Oliver nodded. "And be sure to do all your errands where there are eligible ladies."

Something in Baxter snapped. He'd been arguing about his getting married for four months now. A grown man could take only so many orders from his father. He turned in the doorway. "Maybe I don't want to marry for money. I want to do it different from you and Mother."

Oliver's eyebrows rose. "Son," he said at last, "you've got no idea what went on between your ma and me."

"I know her father put up the money for this ranch and made a good profit. I know she was homesick for Boston."

Oliver looked out the window into the distance. Then he linked his hands behind his head, turned and gazed at the old wedding photo on the bookcase. "It was a fine arrangement. I never regretted it."

"Did Mother?"

"Never," Oliver thundered, half rising. "Love is a bunch of fluff. Cattle don't love. They mate. Produce offspring. You don't ever have to love, but you have to produce heirs for this ranch. It's your duty."

"A man could spend a lot of lonely nights in the name of duty," Baxter observed.

"You telling me you'd throw away this ranch for some fool romantic notion?" Oliver's face had grown red.

"I didn't say that." And he guessed he never would. He'd had it ingrained in him from his youth that his first duty was to the Lazy Y. "I didn't ask to inherit this ranch."

"Well, you're going to, and the only way you'll get rid of it is to sire an heir. Now the ladies in Mesquite are few and far between, so you'd better get busy and choose one before some other rancher beats you to the draw."

"Courting's changed from your day. People marry for other reasons than needing heirs."

His father blinked his faded blue eyes and looked at him. "What other reasons are there? What nonsense did they teach you up there at Harvard?"

"I learned courting. The new way."

"Don't you humor me, you hear. Duty comes first."

Baxter had come to see his duty as a yoke around his neck. But his father wasn't physically or mentally strong enough for too many more of these arguments. The old man had not been himself since Baxter's mother died. Baxter tolerated his lectures, but knew better than anyone that his father's health was waning. By now, Baxter had decided the only way to handle him was to go into town, and go through with the pretense of courting.

He picked up his hat and headed for the door.

"I like Carrie Snyder," his father called after him. "You ought to take her for a buggy ride."

"Her father thinks she's too young to wed."

Oliver waved an arthritic hand. "Oh, lots of papas say that. But if the heir to the Lazy Y came courting, they'd change their minds. Preacher Snyder ain't dumb. He knows who fills the church collection plates. Yep, her pa's got a lot of influence in town, and when times get tough on a ranch, the most important thing a rancher needs is that influence. God knows you can't count on the weather. A woman, you can count on."

Baxter wanted to lash out, but he restrained himself.

"Where are you going?" Oliver asked again.

"Like I said, to town, to get your medicine and do some courting."

Oliver leaned back, his white hair pressed against the rocker. "I knew you'd finally see the light."

Let the old man think what he wanted. There was a limit to playing the dutiful son, and Baxter did not intend to marry anyone of his father's choosing. Oh, he was going to town all right. But not to please his father. He was going to make Rose jealous. She'd be sorry then that she had acted so high and mighty.

Women! They were more trouble than twisters.

*   *   *

Rose gripped the hoe tighter and chopped away a clump of weeds. The loamy smell of newly turned earth that filled the still, hot air had calmed her some. She was glad to be outside, even though it wasn't much cooler than the kitchen, her beloved domain that boasted the biggest, fanciest cookstove in the county, and a sink that was a curiosity for ten counties. It was the only one with two cast-iron water pumps, each drawing from a separate well.

The grand-sized pantry was something, too. It was always stocked with more food than Rose had ever seen. Besides the staples like cornmeal, sugar, and lard, fancy things like tinned peaches and home-canned tomato sauce were kept on hand. And her prized red chili peppers from the vegetable garden hung to dry beside the blue gingham curtains framing one of the kitchen windows. Yes, she was proud to work at the Lazy Y, but someday she'd be even prouder to have a place to call her own. She'd be free of the Lazy Y—and Baxter.

The sound of a horse's hooves disturbed her reverie, and she looked up. In the distance, far across the ranch, a dust devil played with the mesquite. She shaded her eyes and peered closer. A horse and rider emerged from the dusty cloud, and as he drew closer, her face relaxed into a smile.

Elmer Hughes. The only one in town who'd befriended her from the start, and behaved like a true gentleman, she might add. An apothecary, he'd hand-delivered potions and tonics to Ellen dozens of times, and Rose greeted him now as she had so often in the past.

Elmer whipped off his hat, the brim of which was too narrow to protect his oversized nose from sunburn. His corn silk hair hung lank, and sweat stained his shirtsleeves.

"Hello, Rose," he said. "Put on your bonnet or else I'll have to sell you some of my salve."

She smiled and then rested the hoe in the crook of her arm while she picked up her bonnet from where it had fallen amidst the green peas. As she tied it under her chin, she looked at Elmer skeptically. "I haven't seen you in a while. I guessed you were too busy inventing new potions to care about the Lazy Y's rose petals anymore."

"You haven't stop saving them for me, have you?"

She shook her head. "Of course not." Not at the rate Baxter brought roses to try to pacify her. She had a bucket full of drying yellow, pink, and red petals, all heavy with fragrance.

Elmer's face relaxed. "I'll buy all you've got. Baxter's been in town every day this week, and the ladies have bought me out of rosewater and rose lotion. I do like your boss, you know. Ever since he came home, my rosewater's been selling like hotcakes."

Her heart clutched as a stab of envy pierced her. A lady, Elmer had explained on occasion, could never wear too much scent, especially since, in this dreadful heat, scent evaporated quickly. And when Baxter rode into town, Elmer had also reminded her—well, it seemed entire bottles of it evaporated.

Elmer frowned. "You're looking peaked, Rose. Maybe you need a potion yourself."

"No, I'm fine."

She made a pretense of hoeing again. Applying rosewater was, in her opinion, like decorating a tumbleweed with ribbons and lace. A pure waste. "You know what I think, Elmer? Mesquite Junction smells like a lot of things, from molasses to manure, and all the rosewater in the world won't change that."

Elmer grinned. "Maybe not. But with the money

I've made from it, I'll soon be able to reroof the shop. And by the time Baxter picks a bride, maybe I'll be able to afford a coat of paint, too." He paused. "Mighty hot to be hoeing so hard."

She stopped and looked up. "Mind your apothecary business, and I'll mind my kitchen garden."

"You're mad, aren't you?"

She shouldn't tell Elmer about Baxter, but she needed to confide in someone, and Elmer always treated her decently. He didn't act as if he thought he was too good for a homespun cook. "Baxter kissed me."

"What'd he do that for?"

Rose spun around. "Is there something wrong with kissing me?"

"You're just . . . I mean, heck, Rose, Baxter's supposed to court a lady with a rich papa. That's what his pa wants. You're just the cook."

"I know that. And he wasn't courting me. He was showing me what the cowhands might try if they got me alone."

"The rattlesnake."

"I know. He thinks he's better than the hands, toying with me when he says it's wrong."

"Right hypocritical of him."

"Mmm-hmm."

"If Baxter takes liberties again, you should slap him good. The man needs breaking."

"I guess I'll do that," she said calmly.

"I imagine old Oliver would have a conniption if he knew his son was kissing the cook."

He'd have heart palpitations. Oliver had struggled to put down solid Texan roots. It meant a lot to him to keep his bloodline pure, like breeding new cattle and not wanting them to get mixed up with the old Spanish Longhorns. It wouldn't matter whether Rose Milligan were a cook or the wealthiest woman in town, she'd never be good enough for the likes of Oliver Yates.

"It's too bad Oliver doesn't judge the ladies by their canned goods or their beef stew instead of their fathers' bank accounts," Elmer said, interrupting her thoughts.

She nodded. "Well, come in and get the petals. As for me, I like the wild roses better."

"They've got no scent, Rose. Don't mix them in."

"Don't worry. I haven't."

She slung the hoe over her shoulder and strolled beside Elmer, who was leading his horse toward the house and veranda. Rose had learned the difference between wild and cultivated roses when she'd cared for Ellen. She'd made a promise to look after the dear woman's precious Eastern roses. So she watered and tended them and when the petals fell, she gathered them. When the blooms faded, she clipped them and put them with the petals in an old bucket, saving them as Ellen had for Elmer, who paid her for them. That money augmented her cook's wages, but even if Elmer hadn't paid for the roses, she'd have collected them for him anyway. After all, he was her friend and confidante.

"By the way, Rose," Elmer said, "I won't tell anyone Baxter kissed you. It'd go hard on him if that got out."

"I wouldn't want to do anything to harm his chances with the ladies." She could barely conceal the sarcastic edge in her voice.

"I didn't mean to make you mad, Rose. I think you're nicer than all of them."

"Thanks, Elmer, and for that, I might buy some of your hand salve. And I'm not mad. I really don't care what Baxter does. I don't plan on staying in this town forever."

"Where would you go? Somewhere cooler?"

Well, she didn't know—yet. "I'm going someplace where I can have my very own restaurant someday, one with a paper menu and cornbread with gravy on the side. And a dish of sweet pickles sitting on every table beside a rose in a vase. And there'll be table-cloths, white ones."

Elmer whistled and stared at her from where he'd perched on the step outside the kitchen. "I always wondered what you think about in between rolling out pie dough. I wondered if you were like the other ladies, dreaming about Baxter."

"Of course not," she lied. "My only dream is of a place of my own."

A big dream perhaps. But a dream gave a woman something to live for. After all, when you were stranded in a town like Mesquite Junction with only an apothecary for a friend and a man bent on destroying your chances of finding a suitable mate, dreams were important.

Elmer stood up and opened the screen door for her.

Inside the kitchen, she reached amidst the canned tomatoes where she kept the bucket of rose petals.

At once, Elmer got busy weighing bunches of petals on her kitchen scale. He'd brought a gunnysack of supplies and his own bucket. He layered the petals in it, alternating them with a sprinkling of salt and a layer of absorbent cotton, which he dipped into a bottle of olive oil. From this unlikely mix, he had explained to Rose, he would in ten days or so, extract the oil from the roses, which he then turned into rose-water.

Fascinated as she always was with Elmer's work, Rose watched him as he finished layering the petals. "Who's your best customer—for the rosewater, I mean?"

He opened his gunnysack and loaded it with his supplies. "Well, they all buy it, but mainly three. Carrie, Effie, and Annabelle. I thought you didn't care."

"I don't. But having no one to visit with, I get lonely for company. And you always bring me such good gossip, Elmer." Her stomach fluttered. Which one had Baxter kissed? Carrie was fluff-brained, and Effie and Annabelle were snobs.

"Does the rosewater work? I mean, has Baxter paid any attention to them?"

"Not so far. You don't see Baxter leading any of 'em to the altar, do you?" Elmer reached for his coin purse. "Now, if Baxter took a shine to you, that'd sure rile up a storm. And it'd be mighty fine for business."

Rose, her face hot, scraped out a chair, sat down, and began snapping early peas while Elmer laid a few coins on the kitchen table.

Tendrils of hair clung to her neck. It was too hot to think straight. What was that Elmer said about a storm? "I don't know how you can be so sure there's a storm coming."

He plopped his hat on his head, and then, his gunnysack in one hand, his bucket in the other, he stood to leave. "I wasn't talking about the weather, Rose," he said, and went out the screen door. It slammed behind him.

3

Later that afternoon, as Baxter rode toward town, Mesquite Junction rose up like a mirage, with dust devils skittering on the outskirts. Main Street stretched out like a snake sunning itself as he headed down it, viewing the buildings that were all the same peculiar shade of pitch yellow, fronted by unpainted boardwalks.

Dependent on the ranches for its financial survival, the west Texas town was designed to offer services rather than to please the eye, and the only important social activity was finding eligible ranch hands for the unmarried young women. The more designing mothers had set their caps on Baxter, a thought that made him shudder.

He stopped at the bank and then at the barber. As he walked to Elmer's Apothecary Shop, he knew what to expect, since it was the one shop where single ladies could go unchaperoned. Everyone in town knew that

Elmer's most regular customers were a bosom trio of girls whose fathers were wealthy pillars of the community and had settled here a few years ago. Carrie Snyder, the preacher's daughter, had been here the longest, but Effie White, the banker's daughter, and Annabelle Simmons, the lawyer's daughter, were the prettiest and the most stylish, too, as far as calico and muslin would allow.

Baxter entered the shop and had been inside a scant five minutes when the girls walked in, looking like three rosebuds, one peach, one pink, one yellow. But unlike the real Rose, they did not arouse any passion in him, only a longing to get back to the ranch and see Rose's snapping brown eyes, her wild black hair, and her calico dress clinging to her body.

He tipped his Stetson. Though he wasn't Preacher Snyder's most regular customer, he sent up a quick prayer that he could extricate himself from this situation without having to promise to dance with the girls at the weekend event.

"Afternoon, ladies," he said stiffly. "It's awfully hot to be out for a stroll. I hope all of you are feeling well." Elmer, after all, did dispense more than rosewater.

Annabelle and Effie exchanged a giggle. Carrie simply smiled smugly. "We're quite well, thank you. Did you know that in this heat a lady can cool off by dabbing her handkerchief in rosewater and patting it to her temples?"

The shop was filled with the sweet, cloying scent of herbs that, combined with the heat, threatened to choke him. "What a novel remedy," he finally managed to say.

"Taken in the shade, of course," Carrie said. "Under the oak tree outside the church. You know the one?"

Baxter didn't blink. "That's the best piece of shade in town." The only piece. And small at that. The oak tree had, after all, been planted only last year.

"Of course, the cottonwoods at the river are taller." Carrie dimpled flirtatiously. "That'll be the picnic site again this summer. Where do you go to cool off, Baxter?"

He felt a bead of sweat trickle down his temple and swiped at it. The veranda. But that made him think of Rose. "Well, anywhere really. Even in the storm shelter."

"Oh, Baxter, that's not at all a proper place for a lady to take the shade."

"But it's cool, and on a hot day like this, I'm usually reminded to restock it with supplies."

"You're so smart, Baxter," Carrie said, twirling her parasol. "We don't have a storm shelter at the church or parsonage, so I'll have to sit alone in the shade of the oak tree, and dab on my rosewater."

She turned to Elmer, who stood behind the counter, grinding his mortar and pestle. "I'll have this ready for you ladies as soon as I can," he said, his eyes moving from one girl to the next. "Rose petals do take a while to turn into liquid scent," he added apologetically. "One more ingredient to stir in . . . "

"I told Mama I'd be right back," Effie whined.

"That's all right, Elmer," Carrie said as she gave her companion a poke in the ribs with her elbow. "We're in no rush. No rush at all. So you just grind away at that potion and tell us the news." She smiled up at Baxter. "Unless, of course, Baxter is in a hurry to be waited on."

That was an understatement. Luckily, Elmer had the rheumatism remedy all ready except to record it in his account book and package it.

Baxter ran his finger around his collar. "I am. It's growing hotter by the minute, and I'd like to get this medicine back to my father as fast as I can. He doesn't do well in the heat."

Carrie anchored her parasol tip into the floorboards and twirled it again. "Aren't you going to tell us who's coming from the ranch to the dance this weekend? The ranch hands? Rose?"

"Aw, everyone's coming to the dance, Carrie," Elmer said, looking up from the account book. "Ain't that right, Baxter?"

Elmer could stir up gossip faster than he could any potions, so Baxter had to tread carefully.

"Well, if Rose comes, are you going to dance with her, Elmer?" Carrie said this with a sideways glance at Baxter.

"Maybe," Elmer answered, continuing to write.

"Well," Carrie said with a sniff. "You can dance with her, I suppose. You and Rose would make a good match, but in my opinion it's not right for servants to go dancing. It's improper, but then I don't suppose Rose learned much about proper behavior with a family background like hers. What do you think, Baxter?"

Baxter rolled his Stetson in his hands. "It's not as if this were Boston, Carrie," he said. "That's why I wanted to come back to Texas. At the Lazy Y, everyone counts for something."

The girls' faces flushed, but it was Carrie who spoke up. "Oh, Baxter, we know that. But admit it, even in the smallest of towns, there are some social distinctions." She lowered her voice to Annabelle. "Everyone knows that Rose has Mexican blood in her. Why, that makes her an enemy of Texas and—"

"Rose is a native of Texas," Baxter said, his tone brooking no argument. He stared straight at Elmer as if willing him to hurry up and wrap that bottle of potion. For a preacher's daughter, Carrie had an uncommon mean streak. "Rose isn't an immigrant." That much Baxter knew. Oliver had brought her with him on his return home from one of his business trips, from somewhere near Galveston.

"Well," Carrie said, "Texas born or not, she's still half Mexican. Too bad. Such a pretty girl to be left behind at the ranch while the rest of us are enjoying the dance."

Baxter had been thinking of forbidding Rose to attend the dance to protect her from the ranch hands. Now he wanted to make her go so that the likes of Carrie Snyder would see her as an equal.

"Rose gets a night off." Baxter had heard enough from this petty-minded piece of fluff. "She can do what she wants with it."

With that, he doffed his hat, took his father's medicine, and left. He hurried down the boardwalk, and when he had placed enough distance between himself and Elmer's shop, he turned around and looked back. He saw the three females file out, first peach, then pink, then yellow. Somehow, Baxter preferred the unpainted boardwalk and the wide blue sky to their showy array.

It was a relief to watch them stroll off, clutching packages of rosewater wrapped in brown paper. None of them inspired him to drape himself on a veranda railing the way Rose did.

Rose. The veranda. The heat.

Suddenly worried about how long he'd been gone, he snapped out of his musings. He mounted his horse and ran it at a faster pace than usual all the way to the Lazy Y.

As he rounded the corner of the big house and the veranda came into sight, Baxter stopped dead in his tracks. There was Rose, sitting in the shade, churning butter, her calico skirt bunched up at her knees. The once-green fabric, now faded from the sun, was molded to her voluptuous figure, and clung to her curves. No wonder the ranch hands couldn't work. *This* Rose might have a prickly temper, but she begged to be plucked from that chair and held.

At least six other men apparently thought so, too. He counted again. There were so many men that there was scarcely any shade left on the veranda. Draped all over the railing, they had eyes only for Rose.

Jess, the rangy foreman, spotted Baxter first and quickly stood. One by one, the other men noticed and straightened too.

"Uh-oh," one of the cowhands muttered, dusting off his shirt. "I think I've about had enough shade. Afternoon, Baxter. I was passing by on my way to the barn to check on the branding irons."

At the mention of his name, Rose stopped churning and shaded her eyes. "Baxter," she said, "now there's no call to get riled up. It's hot enough to fry eggs on the barn floor, and I invited these men to sit a spell, just long enough to wet their whistles with some lemonade."

"How kind of you. But if they wet their whistles any longer, they'll have to miss the dance to catch up on their work."

Just like that the men scattered, heading back to the barn and their chores.

Rose lowered her eyes. "How was your trip to town?"

"Hot."

He walked up the steps to face her, uncertain of what he was going to do. She had flagrantly disobeyed him.

"I could, by rights, fire you."

She looked up at him with her big brown eyes, her face framed by tiny black ringlets. They clung to her face limply, but she was as pretty as a picture.

He caught himself, annoyed at his attraction to her. She was the cook, a servant.

"If you do fire me, Baxter, could you please wait until after the dance? I've promised a lot of dances, and I don't want to break my word. Besides, I've been looking forward to an evening out."

Doing what? he wondered. With purposeful strides, he walked toward her and towered over her in the rocker.

"They weren't doing anything," she whispered.

"Exactly. They should have been working." Even to his own ears, his voice sounded unusually husky.

"I meant, to me. They were only watching me churn the butter."

Baxter looked down at her. She was staring up at him, her expression filled with the same longing he felt. Her breasts, outlined through the thin material of her homespun dress, revealed that she wasn't wearing a corset.

"I'm not at all sure it was the butter they were watching."

Her face set in sudden stormy lines.

"Now don't take this wrong, Rose, but you have to wear a corset to the dance."

"Will the men think I'm loose if I don't?"

Maybe. Maybe not. "It's the women I'm more worried about. Now, have you got a pretty dress to wear?"

"Your mother gave me some clothes."

His mother had had impeccable taste. "Then wear one of them. And her corset."

Rose blushed. "You're carrying this role of protector

too far. As if I don't know how to dress." She rose and picked up the bowl full of butter.

As she passed him, he could smell her fragrant hair, more tantalizing than Elmer's rosewater.

He moved up close behind her, touched her shoulders just slightly. She half turned. At that moment, he still could have left. But his feet were weighted, as if someone had put lead in his boots.

Beneath his hands, her shoulders rose and fell, and his heartbeat quickened. His hands moved down her arms. He took the bowl from her hands, and then she was in his embrace.

They kissed, just a touch of the lips, and she pulled away.

"Baxter, you said you wouldn't—"

"I never said that."

"You're such a hypocrite."

"Maybe, but I can't help it."

"You have to. Your father—"

"Doesn't own me."

She pushed him away. "Well, I don't like it." Tears pooled in her eyes. "I don't want to kiss you."

"You're lying, Rose. I may be hypocritical, but you like it."

"I don't," she cried. "It's wrong for us to kiss and touch."

"Because you're the cook and I'm heir to this spread? I'm getting tired of hearing that."

She was shaking her head. "No, it's not that."

"Well?"

"It's like you said. Hypocritical. To tell the men one thing and do another yourself."

"You kissed me back. Does that make us both hypocrites?"

"I—I can't help it. I've never kissed anyone before."

"Well, I have kissed a few ladies, but that doesn't mean . . . I mean, heck, Rose, I just wanted to kiss you."

"Rose!" Oliver called from inside the house.

Rose backed away, smoothing her dress. "I—I'd better see to supper."

He held open the screen door for her. "Rose," he said, and their gazes locked. There was longing in hers, he'd swear there was, but she'd never admit it. Proud girl. "Tell me again you didn't like kissing me."

"Baxter, you've no right to ask that."

He shrugged. "Well, just don't let anyone else kiss you like that, hear?"

She nodded. "No one."

Baxter strode off. He hated the thought of those cowhands pawing over her at the dance. But he dreaded trying to keep away from her himself. For the sake of appearances, for her sake, he'd have to try.

The evening of the dance, the sun set in a clear sky and early stars were beginning to appear as Rose wrapped an angel cake, her offering for the midnight supper, in a linen dish towel to keep the dust off.

She was so excited about her first summer social event that she had served a cold supper and gotten dressed early. She had put on one of the dresses Ellen had given her, a rose-colored muslin with short-capped sleeves and a lace-edged V neckline. The color set off her dark eyes and upswept hair. At the neckline she'd pinned her mother's cameo. She'd also plucked a red rose and placed it in her hair.

Holding the cake with one hand, she was tucking the dish towel under the plate when the screen door squeaked open. Whirling, she nearly dropped the cake. Icing clung to her fingertips.

"Baxter!" There he stood, looking too handsome for his own good and far too appealing for hers as well. "You shouldn't sneak up on me that way," she said, turning and placing the cake on the table.

He moved to the table and picked up another dish towel. His gaze traveled up and down her dress, then he tossed the towel to her. "Here, wipe off the icing."

She ignored it and moved to the sink. "I'll wash." She cranked the pump and glanced at Baxter over her shoulder. "You're ready for the dance?" Turning to face him, she picked up the hand towel near the sink and wiped her hands.

He was staring at her. "Yes, and I'm giving you a ride into town."

"I can go with the others—with the ranch hands."

"No, you can't. I have strict orders from Oliver. I'm to be your escort."

She knew that it would do no good to argue. But he never moved, nor took his eyes off her. "Is—is something wrong? Should I change my dress?"

"It's pretty. The color suits you."

"It was your mother's. You said to wear it. Do you mind after all?"

He shook his head, his gaze transfixed. "She gave it to you and she'd be proud to see you in it. I was just thinking how different you must look from when you first came here, hauled in by my father."

"You weren't even here then, Baxter."

"Mother had a knack for describing people in her letters, especially the people who cared for her. She wrote about what a little thing you were, but how well you'd learned to cook at some mission school."

She hated being reminded. "There aren't many other places for a girl whose gambling father threw away all of the family's money and died in a barroom brawl, and whose mother was Mexican. At least not in Texas there aren't."

"You found the mission."

"And it's a good thing I liked cooking, or I'd have ended up a nun."

"That would have been a loss to the Lazy Y."

Suddenly flustered, Rose finished securing the dish towel covering the cake around the plate. "Well, maybe so. And I got to like the place while nursing your mother, so it was a relief to me that your father needed a cook. I still miss your mother, though. She didn't fit in here, she told me that, but I know she tried, Baxter."

"What's done is done," he said, never taking his eyes off Rose as she bustled about the kitchen. She was a pretty sight, a lot happier, too, than he remembered his mother being.

Nothing he had done or said alleviated his mother's homesickness for Boston. But she'd as much as bought his father with the dowry Baxter's railroad baron grandfather had settled on her. She had often told Baxter that her sole happiness was him and that without him she would never have been able to stand the bleak Texas landscape. Several times during his boyhood she had taken him by train to see her relatives, and it was during those visits that Baxter's longing to go to college in Boston had formed. And the irony was that he'd been there when his mother had become ill.

Now there's no need for you to come rushing home, she'd written him. *This is a passing malaise. Your father has brought in a lovely girl to help me. Her name is Rose Milligan. She's half Irish and half Mexican and not very welcomed here, but I feel all the more for her because of it, and her Irishness reminds me of Boston. This small town is as class-conscious as*

Boston, and though that's a pity, I'm the one who gains because Rose is all mine. Elmer stops by, too, with his potions, and he is so enchanted with Rose that I took the liberty of sharing with him my secret recipe for aromatic rosewater. The poor roses are so wasted here.

"You miss her still, don't you?" Rose asked softly, running a hand over her dress, smoothing the skirt. "Your mother treated me like a lady, Baxter, and I liked her for it."

He nodded and said, "That dress is pretty." His gaze swept down her figure and back up again. "My mother knew what was suitable."

"And what ladies were suitable, too." Of all the women in the world, she was the last one his mother would have wanted him to marry. Ellen had befriended Rose, forgiven her her family even. But never, ever, had she said, as mothers were wont to do, that Rose and her son would be the perfect match.

"Rose, I'd like to dance with you tonight."

Disturbed, she turned away. "Oh, you'll forget about me once the ladies see you. They'll be preening and vying to see who you're going to ask to the picnic. Besides, your ranch hands are waiting to dance with me."

"Then I'll never get to dance with you."

She ducked her head to wipe a speck from her skirt. "No, I guess not."

Strangely, Baxter felt disappointed. "Maybe I should steal a dance now."

She faced him. Her chin came up, and her beautiful brown eyes looked straight into his, a sparkle in them that had not been there before. "Maybe."

He moved to take her in his arms. He never really asked her if he could have a dance here in the kitchen, nor did she refuse him. There didn't seem to be a need for words. It was like white lightning the way they came together. Their music was a lone cricket chirping in harmony with the dripping of the pump. A dog whined somewhere in the distance.

Rose put her arms around his neck, and his arms circled her waist. They swayed to music only they could hear. For a second. Or five minutes.

Then footsteps intruded, and hastily they broke away. Rose quickly busied herself with the coffee pot.

"What the heck's going on? Dancing? In the kitchen?"

4

Rose looked over her shoulder. Oliver limped in, his expression stormy.

"I thought I'd leave the coffee pot filled and ready to boil," Rose said. "In case anyone wants coffee after the dance."

"And I'm escorting Rose to the dance," Baxter added. He stood straight and looked his father in the eye, as if daring him to argue.

As Oliver's bushy white eyebrows shot up a fraction, Baxter hastily added, "And I was about to ask Rose to make me a picnic basket—you know, for the annual barbecue."

"Since when do the men have to bring food?" Oliver asked.

"They don't, but I don't like eating food from Mesquite Junction when everyone knows Rose is the best cook around—except for her hot sauce."

Oliver, apparently pacified, nodded. "Well, that's all fine, but you get along now and go courting. Those ladies may not cook like Rose, but they've got other assets a lot more important than kitchen skills."

Baxter clapped his Stetson on his head and squared his stance. He wasn't going to march to Oliver's tune any longer. "I'm going dancing, that's all."

"Well, call it what you want, but nature always takes its course at these affairs."

Baxter walked out, Rose on his heels. Quickly she got into the wagon and turned to wave good-bye to Oliver.

"He doesn't mean to push you," she said softly.

"Yes, he does."

"Why are you boiling over like a pot left on a too-hot stove?"

He flicked the reins and slanted a glance at her. "It's just the heat, I guess."

"I guess so," she said. But heat or no heat, tempers or no tempers, tonight she intended to enjoy herself. She sat ramrod straight, and the couple of times Baxter spoke, she answered pleasantly.

She turned once to look at his profile. His Stetson hid his handsome face and fair hair, but the moonlight gleamed off his white shirt. He half looked at her and she turned away, pretending to be interested in the scenery, the bleak stretch of mesquite between the Lazy Y and town. Only the squeak of the wagon wheels broke the silence.

Finally Rose heard the fiddle music from about a quarter mile away. An annual event on the first day of every summer, the dance was held in the town hall, where the mayor ran the town meetings and the circuit judge presided over weddings and trials. Rose always looked forward to it. She liked dancing. And dance she would. For Mesquite Junction was no different from any other Western town: men outnumbered women three to one.

But when she walked beside Baxter into the hall, she felt ambivalent. She looked around. One or two daring couples were dancing on the veranda, and their shadows danced off the walls from the kerosene lanterns. The scent of hay rose from the floor, and the prevalent perfume on this sultry June night was rose-water. As it wafted around her, it seemed every woman was doused in it.

"You want me to drive you home after the dance?"

Baxter's voice, unexpected, startled her. Just for a moment, watching everyone dance, she'd forgotten about him. Now shivers went down her spine. Yes, she wanted him to drive her home. She wanted him to take her in his arms. She wanted to melt against him the way she had in the kitchen. But she couldn't have any of those things.

Elmer made a beeline through the crowd to them. "Howdy, Rose. Can I have the first dance?"

She hesitated. Baxter was still standing beside her, and at least three young girls were eyeing him over their shoulders. One by one their gazes moved to her, and there was scorn in their eyes.

She tossed her head proudly. "Baxter, you know I don't need you looking out for me. One of the ranch hands will bring me home."

"Maybe."

"And maybe you'll want your wagon to escort some *fine* lady home. Excuse me now. I'm going to dance with Elmer."

*   *   *

Elmer had no sooner given Rose a turn around the sawdust-strewn floor than she was surrounded by the hands from the Lazy Y, each eager for a dance.

"You promised me first, Rose. Now come on," Jess the foreman cajoled her, after elbowing Elmer out of the way. "Baxter got to drive you here, but we get the dances you promised, remember?"

She did remember. Her heart melted at the anticipation in their faces, scrubbed and shaved, at their shirts still wrinkled from laundering them in the bunkhouse. Of course she said yes, and with an understanding shrug Elmer walked away.

Across the crowd, she caught a glimpse of Baxter. He, too, was surrounded, by a bevy of lovely girls, many chaperoned by a financially secure father. Baxter was laughing, attentive to Annabelle and Effie in their stylish ruffled gowns. Carrie walked up to them and said something that made Baxter smile. Rose's heart sank.

"Rose," Jess said again, "will you dance with me?"

She turned back to him. "Of course, Jess," she answered with a quick smile, and went into his arms, vowing to give each of her dance partners her undivided attention. It was a beautiful summer night, she was young, and she wanted to dance. Baxter could do what he wanted.

Baxter did what was expected. He started by leading Carrie in a two-step and strained to catch a glimpse of Rose. True, there was a shortage of women dance partners, but the men from the Lazy Y didn't have to look so eager to touch Rose. It didn't help that the fiddler played one soft tune after another, the kind that made a man long to hold one woman in his arms. Not just any woman, but a special woman. And Carrie definitely did not fit the bill.

He tried to enjoy himself, but Carrie giggled too much. Then she started talking. "Papa says a man has a powerful streak of right and wrong in him and that his churchgoing habits tell a lot about him."

"Does he?" Baxter felt optimistic. Since he had rarely darkened the church doors this spring, Reverend Snyder would probably discourage Carrie's pursuing Baxter to the altar.

"I think Papa's wrong. I think a man's dancing tells more about him."

He had the good sense not to reply.

"Don't you want to know what I think of your dancing?" she asked.

He was peering across the room trying to decide if Jess was a good dancer. He held Rose entirely too close for propriety.

"Baxter, do you?"

"It's too hot to dance my best." He tried to loosen her hold on his hand, but she clung like glue.

Resigned, he watched Rose change partners. The next ranch hand enveloped her in a bear hug. Baxter stepped on Carrie's toes.

"Baxter, you're shockingly forward," she whispered, "but don't worry, I won't tell Papa. You can hold onto me if you're tipsy or dizzy."

He straightened. "I'm fine. It's just crowded. And hot." Crowded with too many men from the Lazy Y, all of them ogling Rose.

From across the room, he could almost feel her in his arms. It was him pulling her close, not one of his hands.

Someone tapped him on the shoulder. He turned to face Preacher Snyder.

He relinquished Carrie with relief. But when Preacher Snyder stepped aside, the crowd parted, and there stood an entire wall of young girls, blushing and hopeful. From behind him, in the crowd of dancers, he heard Rose laugh gaily, and clenched his fists in frustration.

One by one he danced with them, and each time he took one onto the dance floor, he looked to see where Rose was. Each time he hoped she'd be in the line of wallflowers.

But she wasn't. She was dancing. His ranch hands were making up for all the times Baxter had chased them off the veranda. Dance after dance, Rose was in some yokel's arms, held too close, twirled too fast, breathed on too near, and talked to with too much enthusiasm.

Rose was in bloom tonight, Baxter thought, as he saw her black hair shimmering in the lanterns' light, her rose-colored dress glittering, her laughter filling the air. She never had time to look at him. And every time he looked for her, she was with yet another man, laughing, flirting, dancing too close. Naïve girl. She didn't know what she was asking for. It hurt so much to watch, he finally turned his back and tried to pretend he was enjoying having Annabelle step on the toes of his fancy boots.

Every time Rose looked, Baxter was with a different girl. She finally quit looking because it hurt too much, and she pretended that every ranch hand who asked her to dance was the only man in the world.

Finally she ended up again in Jess's arms. He smiled down at her. "How about I get us some lemonade and we can go outside where it's cooler?"

That sounded good to her. It was so hot, and she was so heartsick trying not to notice Baxter's latest dance partner.

"Yes, thank you, Jess. I really would like some. Nettie made the lemonade, so it should be delicious." And Rose knew Nettie would be guarding it and doling it out.

Jess escorted her out to the young elm tree back by the parked wagons and then reentered the hall. She took the opportunity to catch her breath, rearrange her hair, and pat her skin with a hanky. A scented hanky, but *her* scent was violet. Anything to be different from those other women.

Too soon, Jess returned. "Nettie's rationing the lemonade now. I could only get one cup between us. Do you mind sharing?"

Rose smiled. "I guess we've got no choice."

Jess handed her the cup and watched as she sipped. Then he took it, drained the rest, and set the cup on the floor of the nearest wagon.

"That was good," Rose said. "Can we go back now?"

"Not yet. Doesn't it feel good out here?"

It did. But suddenly she felt uneasy alone with a man she didn't know very well.

"I think we ought to stay out here a while longer and cool off."

"Cool off?" Even though it was slightly cooler than inside the hall, the heat was still stifling.

"Yeah," he drawled, as he skimmed his fingers over the sleeve of her dress. "Best way is to go swimming."

Rose gulped. "Swimming? Here?"

"Naw, over by the cottonwoods, by the creek."

"It's nighttime."

"Water's just as cool at night, maybe cooler."

His suggestion was so audacious Rose didn't

know what to say. For once her fiery responses had been quenched.

"You ever been skinny dipping, Rose?" Jess asked, his hand roving up to touch the flower in her hair.

She had, but she'd been a child. Her heart began to pound and fear raced through her.

His chuckle cut through her like a knife. "I thought so. You little hot tamales like taking off these gringo dresses, don't you?" Now his fingers tugged at her cameo brooch.

Immediately she covered his hand, then pushed it. His laughter deepened.

"Come on, Rose, don't play innocent now that you're out of the kitchen. You're not like those cool little gringo prissies. You're one hot little gal, I know that. Take after your ma, I bet, and I know about her and Oliver Yates. I've seen you kissing the other fellows, like Baxter."

"Liar." She'd kissed no one—except Baxter. And there was no way Jess could know that. How dare he insinuate that she let Baxter toy with her! It was an insult!

He was touching her cameo again, so Rose lifted her foot and stomped on the toes of his boots, hard.

She jumped out of the way and backed into someone. Whirling, she gaped, half in surprise, half in relief.

Baxter.

Even though it was dark, she could see the anger on his face, feel the tension leap between the two men like a bolt of lightning.

"Jess, you're fired." Baxter's voice was thunderous.

Jess hooked his thumbs through his pant loops. "What for? I ain't workin' now and it's my time off. Last time I heard, they didn't string men up in Mesquite Junction for dancing."

"They string them up, though, for messing with a lady's virtue. Go back and pack your things. Be out of the bunkhouse by dawn. I'll send your wages down from the big house."

Jess shrugged. "Whatever you want. I was just having some fun with Rose, but if you're so goldarned possessive, I'll move on. But you'll wish you had me to teach you the ranch workings."

"I'll figure them out just fine."

With a careless flip of his hand, Jess faded into the night.

Rose took a step forward. "Baxter—"

"I told you what would happen if you let the likes of Jess hang around you."

"We were dancing, and then drinking lemonade, and then . . . "

Then she'd gotten in over her head. Skinny dipping. Why, anything could have happened. "He thought because—because of my mother, because . . . " She couldn't tell Baxter, she just couldn't.

But actions could say what words couldn't, and it seemed like the most natural thing in the world to move into his arms. She clung tightly, half ashamed of her shaking. It wasn't like her at all. But she enjoyed the way she fit against Baxter. He was solid and strong and gentle. She wished he could be hers forever.

He held her and at last as her trembling subsided, she realized the compromising picture they made. She pushed him away and lowered her voice. "I'm sorry. I didn't mean to do that."

"Yes, you did. You know you want me to hold you, Rose. Did you want Jess to hold you, too?" he asked, his voice husky.

"No. He took advantage of me."

"Maybe so, but all the men you've danced with have held you too close."

"So what?"

"It isn't proper."

"And who are you to decide that?"

"I'm the one who's in charge of these men, that's who. And you're the Lazy Y's cook."

Her anger flared. "You mean I'm not good enough for any of them."

"No, I didn't mean it that way."

"Oh, just leave me alone, Baxter. Please, stay away from me. And I don't want you touching me anymore."

She turned away from him, but he grabbed her arm and spun her around.

"I know what you think, but this has nothing to do with your background or your mother. As far as I'm concerned, you're better than all the other females. It's me who's different." His voice was cool and almost believable. "I'm the one who doesn't fit in. I live with my father's expectations, and if I argue back, or fight for what I want, I figure it might kill him. Heck, if this was Boston, if this was anywhere but—"

She placed her finger on his lips. "Hush up, Baxter. This is Texas, and I'm a Texan forever, so don't go making me wish I could be something else. Some things can't be changed, no matter how much we wish."

But despite her words, she wanted so much to believe she was the only woman for him. She wanted to mold her body against the work-hardened contours of his and sway in the age-old rhythm.

He drew her closer, and a current went between them, as swift as lightning. Oh, Rose wanted to melt into his arms all right, but he was too arrogant for his own good, worse in a way than the likes of Jess.

Then, before she could protest, he pulled her

behind the big oak tree shading the well and kissed her again. Finally they broke apart.

"I said not to touch me." She meant to sound stiff with indignation, but the words came out soft like runny pudding. That's how he made her feel.

"I heard you. That doesn't mean I won't touch you if I want to."

"Oh." She stamped her foot. "The trouble with you, Baxter Yates, is that no woman has ever turned you down, so you don't believe one when she does. You should worry less about your skinny cows needing grass and water and more about your manners needing improvement."

"Maybe I'll do that."

Picking up her skirts, she ran off into the darkness to hide the tears pricking her eyes. She'd do anything to change the way things were. But she was bereft. Orphaned. Alone in the world. And less worthy than anyone in this town.

She stopped in front of Elmer's apothecary and leaned her head against the cool glass of the door. What was she going to do? How was she going to stop this flirtation that could never be more than that? She'd refused his roses, yelled so loud that anyone within five miles could have heard her, and pushed him away. But she'd also kissed him.

She looked up at the star-filled sky and realized that she had been wrong all along. She was as good as any of the young women in town. She might not have their pedigrees or their wealth, but she had something more. She knew how to survive.

"A survivor," she whispered. More than anybody knew.

It didn't matter where she had come from or what she had gone through. It was where she was going that counted.

She smiled. Well, she was going to the picnic. Then she chuckled. That wasn't very far. But it was a start. Maybe one of the ranch hands could make her forget all about Baxter, and the ache in her heart.

5

For a week after the dance, Baxter decided to stay out of Rose's way. Out of sight, out of mind, his father was fond of saying about women. Then he remembered another of the old man's favorite adages. "Pretend your mind has two corrals, Baxter. The marrying kind of woman belongs in one corral, and the one for sport in another. Remember, the only one you're going to brand is the marrying one. But keep the corrals separate. Build a high and sturdy fence between them." It was the gospel according to Oliver.

And in which corral would his father say Rose belonged? Oh, of course he knew what Oliver would say, but he didn't agree. His mind stopped short of putting Rose anywhere, and anyway, Baxter didn't like thinking of women that way.

Besides, Rose was special, too spirited. She couldn't be corralled. Nor could his thinking about her.

No matter where he went on the ranch, thoughts of her trailed him, like a stray foal looking for its mother. Rose was an orphan after all, and she had no home, except for the Lazy Y. He couldn't see her corralled in that kitchen forever. But what could he do about it? It was too hot to think. When it cooled off, maybe then he could ponder the problem.

Meanwhile, he wanted nothing more than to invade the kitchen and take her in his arms. But he wanted to keep the peace, too.

So, with reluctance, he decided to go into town. It was easy to come up with excuses for going. Another haircut. Another trip to the bank. Another visit to Elmer's to stock up on his father's rheumatism potion. It pleased his father to think he was going to see the eligible young girls. But Baxter had only one reason. He had to put some distance between himself and the pretty black-haired cook in the kitchen.

He had no doubts, of course, of his welcome in town. The ladies hadn't seen him since the night of the dance, and they would be all atwitter about the picnic. Not a happy prospect.

As he strolled up Main Street, Baxter was greeted by the shopkeepers and merchants. The fathers of marriageable daughters were respectful to the heir to the Lazy Y and rushed to give him a warm welcome.

Baxter's response, a tip of his Stetson, was the same to all.

"Hotter than usual today, Baxter," Mr. White said, choosing to open the door of his house and sweep off the welcome mat at precisely the moment Baxter came by.

"Hot indeed," Baxter noted politely for at least the tenth time.

"Effie has fresh lemonade if you'd liked to cool off a spell."

"Thank you, but I have to pick up my father's medicine from Elmer."

He'd no sooner tipped his hat and continued on than the banker hurried inside. Voices floated through the open windows. "Papa," Effie wailed. "You let him get away. Now he's going to Elmer's, and you know Carrie's already there waiting for him."

"Then you have to outsmart Carrie."

"I can't. Oh, it's just not fair."

Baxter lengthened his strides. Forewarned was forearmed. He braced himself to keep Carrie at arm's length. Why the preacher didn't put her to work planning Sunday school lessons or visiting the needy, Baxter didn't know.

Tipping his hat, he smiled at the barber and then strode up the boardwalk, his fancy boots clicking on the wooden boards.

He doffed his hat to Mr. Simmons, and Annabelle peeked over her father's shoulder as he stood in the doorway of his office.

"Afternoon, Baxter," Mr. Simmons said, "must be something special to bring you out in this heat."

"An errand for my father."

"Oh." Like the banker before him, the lawyer's face fell, as did his daughter's.

"June's turning out to be uncommonly hot. My wife says it's a good thing there aren't any weddings planned yet," Mr. Simmons said. "Later in the year when it's cooler maybe—"

"Pa, hush up or I'll never be able to show my face again!" Annabelle chided him.

Smiling at the beleaguered man, Baxter continued on.

He should have been flattered by the interest in him as husband material. He'd always puffed up about it before, just as his father did. But something had changed at that dance. It had irked him the way the cowhands manhandled Rose, and he hated their ogling her as if she were a steer on the hoof.

What's more, now the townsfolk were giving Baxter a taste of the same treatment. For the first time he realized that the anxious mothers and fathers made him feel like a piece of beef on the hoof, too. Looking him up and down like buyers up in Kansas, assessing his value before they railroaded him off to the slaughter-house. That's what marriage to one of their daughters would be, too. The end of the line.

He wanted, he realized, to be wanted for himself, not for his wealth or his ranch. His father could go on pretending he would make some rich alliance, but it would never happen. Even if he didn't consider his own happiness, he would never wed a woman for money as his father had, never want some woman to be as anguished and feel as unwanted as his mother.

He wanted happiness on his terms.

The way . . . the way he felt with Rose.

Of course, he couldn't marry Rose.

But that kind of feeling.

Somewhere he'd find it. There was no rush.

He reached his destination and glanced in the window, newly polished and smelling of vinegar. As he entered the shop, he heard Elmer dispensing gossip along with his rosewater and castor oil.

Unnoticed, Baxter listened.

"Oh, Elmer," Carrie said, placing both hands on her parasol handle. "Do tell me more."

"Now, Rose is my friend, so I told her that she has to watch out for Baxter. He takes after his pa, you know, and his pa was never a man to settle down, Carrie."

The girl gasped. "Why, Elmer, you're trying to shock my sensibilities, and of course it's not ladylike to gossip . . ." She lowered her voice and whispered, but her voice carried. "Everyone knows how those Mexican women are, but I had no idea about the Yates men."

Baxter cleared his throat and tapped Elmer on his shoulder. Elmer turned to him and jumped, his face reddening.

"I came for my father's rheumatism medicine," Baxter said, "but I've changed my mind."

"Why? Has he quit ailing?" Elmer asked.

"No, but you just dishonored my father's name, Elmer. Maybe I'll just have to order his potion from a mail-order catalog or wait for a traveling peddler."

Elmer pushed back his stringy blond hair. "It's just harmless gossip, Baxter. The ladies expect a little gossip. It's good for business."

"Well, you repeat it, as fact or gossip, and you'll never get any more rose petals from the Lazy Y. Your rosewater business will go down the drain. See if the ladies come calling then."

"I can get roses petals anywhere. The Lazy Y doesn't have a monopoly on anything, cattle or roses."

"Where are you going to find roses in Mesquite Junction? From the blacksmith? All he has is used horseshoes, and they don't smell all that pretty."

"I—I'm sorry, Baxter. I didn't mean any insult."

"Well, my father built this county, and no fly-by-night is going to use our roses to peddle potions and then badmouth the Yateses. It's not the way things are done here—or anyplace, not among men who claim to be our friends."

"I—I said I was sorry. But since that doesn't seem

good enough for you, I won't be needing your rose petals anymore. I can order all the ingredients I need for my rosewater from back East. I also have my sources for other scents. I can make lily of the valley and violet scents just as well."

Baxter pulled his hat lower over his forehead. "I'm glad to hear that, Elmer. I'm sure that's put Carrie's mind at ease about her rosewater. That is, if she's willing to wait a long time to get it."

"Baxter," she said, "I don't need it. It just helps pass the time to come do business with Elmer. You need to cool off with a nice lemonade. Why don't you come home with me and have some?"

He backed toward the door. "I'm not that thirsty, Carrie."

Her face fell. "I'm sorry, Baxter. I'll never gossip again. You'll still help me haul the picnic baskets to the picnic won't you? I told Pa you would. You said so at the dance. They're for all the needy families."

He was the one who felt corralled now. Corralled by a promise he didn't even remember making.

"Now, Baxter," Elmer said. "I think you ought to accept our apologies."

"What about Rose?"

"You think we ought to apologize to Rose? What for?"

"She's part of the Lazy Y, too."

Carrie drew an impatient breath. "Very well. I'll be nice to her at the picnic. Promise you'll be nice too."

"And don't worry," Elmer said. "I'll stay away from the ranch and your roses."

Oh, but Baxter hated those roses. All they did was remind him of his mother's unhappiness. Some women weren't suited for this parched place, and it had killed his mother. Maybe that's why he had no interest in courting. He didn't know. He only knew he'd rather not court at all than put a woman through what his mother had endured. Women had no business out in this godforsaken land. Period.

Back on Yates property, Baxter rode across the sage-covered land, heading not for the cattle but for the ranch house and the rosebushes growing outside the parlor window.

He reined in his horse and grabbed an ax from the barn. He took it to the pink rosebush. His mother's favorite.

Whack! With one stroke, it was felled.

Rose pushed open the door. "Baxter!" she said in a half whisper. "What are you doing to your mother's roses?"

The sight of Rose, gingham clinging to her curves, her black hair piled up in a soft cluster of curls, the sun spilling off her creamy skin, made Baxter temporarily forget his mission. He stood staring at the way the light shone right through her dress, highlighting the shape of her legs. Miss Milligan needed a slip. The ax fell to the ground.

"What are you doing? Going loco from the heat?" she asked.

"Maybe. I don't know."

"You were at Elmer's, weren't you?"

He nodded.

"Did he gossip?"

"That's all Elmer does."

"About you and me?"

Baxter was silent. Only a muscle twitched by his mouth. It took all his control to keep quiet.

"Did Elmer gossip about your father?"

"How'd you know?"

"I didn't. I just guessed. Since Elmer knows about my past, I figured he'd might have said something. I'm sorry if—"

"You told Elmer something about my father?"

"Did he say anything about Oliver . . . and my mother?" she asked, not answering his question.

Baxter stared at Rose a long time, then walked toward the lone oak tree. He leaned against it, wishing he had not heard Rose. Wishing he had never gone to town. Wishing Oliver had never asked him to pick up his rheumatism potion. Wishing Rose had never come to the Lazy Y.

The heat must be getting to him. That was it, and he'd heard wrong.

Rose touched his arm, and he shut his eyes.

"Baxter, I never meant for you to know."

"My father and your mother." All those times Oliver had been gone from the ranch . . .

He looked at Rose questioningly.

She smiled. "I'm not your sister, Baxter. Oliver didn't see my mother again until after my own father died. They'd known each other when they were real young. School age. Their fathers fought against each other in the Mexican War. So Oliver could never marry my mother. It was forbidden."

He hadn't realized he'd been holding his breath until he exhaled. He swallowed hard and gulped in the still afternoon air. It burned. Rose. The daughter of his father's mistress. Oliver's forbidden love. And now his father had decreed that Rose and he were forbidden to each other as well.

Baxter had never been in the eye of a tornado, but he knew what it must feel like. Calm, with disaster swirling all about. He was amazed how calm he felt, and how clearly he could still think. No wonder old Oliver had told Baxter to stay away from Rose. For if Baxter gave in to his feelings for Rose, he'd be no better than his father. Selling out in marriage to a woman with a rich papa, and then being unfaithful with Rose—for he had no doubt that if he ever gave in to his desire, if he had one taste of Rose, he'd never be able to give her up.

"What about my mother?"

"She knew but she forgave them. I nursed her the best I could to make up for it, but she said not to do it for that reason. Love was nothing you had to make up for. She'd made her choice, and had to live without love. She said she envied my mother, but never wanted to know more about her. She was good to me."

"You know," he said, "my mother told me a long time ago not to sell myself for money. I never knew why she felt so strongly about that till now. Because that's what she did, and money wasn't enough to hold my father's heart."

Rose bowed her head. "I guess not. I never knew much. Except I was eight when your father came to see my mother who was newly widowed, and I knew by the look in her eyes that this was someone special, maybe even more special than my own father. I never even saw them kiss. I never saw them do anything but walk and talk and laugh and gaze into each other's eyes. My mother did tell me that she made Oliver promise to take care of me if anything ever happened to her. And when my mother—"

"Maria?"

"Yes. So when she died, your father kept his promise and asked me to take care of your mother. Though she knew everything, she didn't think it was right to burden you with your father's secret.

"I didn't want to come here, but I had no choice, and I had no choice about meeting you."

"Are you sorry we met?"

"No, but I won't live the kind of life my mother did, and I won't make some other woman live the way your mother did. And I think I know you well enough to know you don't want that either. Your father's got good reason to keep you away from me. The best reason of all."

When Baxter looked up, she was gone, and it seemed as if the sun had dimmed in the sky. But if it had, its absence did nothing to lessen the impact of the heat.

He understood things a lot better now. That didn't mean he liked it. He understood now why his father had tried to forge a big-brother relationship between him and Rose. But it would never work. He'd kissed her once too often for that. Touched her silky skin. Breathed in the rich fragrance of her hair. Oh, it was far too late for him to think of her that way.

But above all, he understood why he'd have to keep his distance from Rose. Even if it killed him.

Rose avoided Baxter until the day of the picnic, but now she had to ride into town with him. Well, she thought, she might have to sit beside him in the wagon, but that didn't mean she had to talk to him any more than necessary.

It was too hot to make conversation anyway. The heat was making everyone cranky, especially the young ladies of Mesquite Junction, because it was practically the end of June, and Baxter had shown no signs of proposing. Rose knew this piece of gossip from Nettie, now that Elmer had stopped coming for the rose petals and the ladies were experimenting with new scents. Nettie had also told her about the argument between Baxter and Elmer, and that Baxter had warned him to stay away from Lazy Y.

"Go easy on that hot sauce now, Rose," Baxter told her, finally breaking their mutual silence and interrupting her thoughts.

She bristled. In charge of basting the side of beef for the barbecue, she'd make it as spicy as she wanted. "You can scrape it off if you don't like it."

"It's too hot for spicy barbecue. There's not enough water in this county to cool down everybody's throat."

She shrugged, determined not to let him have his way. "Then you don't have to eat any barbecue." She looked at him, daring him to argue back. One look, and her heart melted. He looked so handsome. His hair was tousled, his shirtsleeves were rolled up, and he was wearing his fancy cowboy boots.

"You've packed me a picnic hamper, haven't you?" he asked.

Rose knew he wanted a hamper so he could go off riding with one of the eligible girls. It was to be expected. The only mystery was which one he'd choose.

"I made you a special hamper all your own," she said.

"Without spicy food?"

He was still carrying on about her hot sauce. Well, she'd show him. Smiling to herself, she decided he was going to have food in that hamper he'd never forget, something to ruin whatever romantic picnic he had in mind. Suddenly she couldn't wait to get to town.

*   *   *

Baxter drove halfway down Main Street and slowed to a stop in front of the Mercantile, where they had to pick up kegs of root beer, one of the Lazy Y's contributions to the picnic. The others were the side of beef and the dishes and tablecloths, which Rose was in charge of. While Baxter went inside for the kegs, she climbed in the wagon bed and rearranged her boxes of supplies and Baxter's hamper.

After Baxter loaded the root beer, he helped Rose put the food baskets for the needy from the Mercantile into the wagon.

Finally, he noticed Carrie on the store's porch. "You aren't waiting for the shade to move, are you, Carrie?"

"Oh, Baxter, you're such a tease. I was just waiting for you to finish putting the baskets for the needy families in the wagon. You know you promised we'd ride together to the picnic." She stood twirling her parasol and squinted at Rose.

At that moment Elmer drove up in his wagon and offered to drive Rose to the picnic, saying that Baxter's wagon was too crowded for three. Oh, the apothecary was very polite and on his best behavior, all right, and Baxter figured he was trying to get back into Baxter's good graces. He'd probably checked on the price of shipping rose petals from back East and realized what a bargain he'd been getting buying from the Lazy Y.

Oh, yes, Elmer was being nice. Too nice. Baxter seethed. He had thought that if Rose was with him, he could hold Carrie off.

Now Elmer had ruined everything. He had Rose, and Baxter had all the root beer, supplies, beef, food baskets—and Carrie Snyder.

Rose showed Baxter where his hamper was in the wagon bed and then climbed up into Elmer's wagon.

"Much obliged, Rose," Baxter said, wishing that she had refused Elmer's offer.

"*I've* brought a hamper for us," Carrie reminded him, with a nasty look at Rose. "And mine has nice cool food, like boiled eggs and blueberry muffins."

"Well, we'll eat from both," he said.

"I'm sure you'll like what I've made. I put in one of my specialties just for you," Rose said, giving him the sweetest smile he'd ever seen.

"Thanks again, Rose," he said looking up at her beautiful face. He remembered what it felt like to hold her in his arms and yearned to hold her again. He turned away. It could never be.

"My goodness," Carrie noted, turning around to look at the back of the wagon. "The Lazy Y donates so much. Your father must be as rich as my pa says."

"Rich enough."

"It'll be a grand picnic," Carrie said.

"Barbecue," Rose said automatically.

"It's a picnic." Carrie glared at Rose. "And I don't appreciate having a ranch cook contradict me. Tell her, Baxter, tell her that in Mesquite Junction, we call it a picnic."

Wearily, Baxter ran his fingers through his hair. A great debate had raged in past years over whether to call the event a picnic or a barbecue, with Republicans and Democrats lining up on either side of the issue. "This summer," he said, "what with the heat and all, I doubt no one much cares what it's called. We'll bow our heads with Preacher Snyder and pray for a cool spell."

Carrie's mouth opened in an O, and her eyes sparkled with delight. "You mean that, Baxter? Will you stand by Papa during the blessing?"

He scuffed the toe of his boot in the dirt. "Yeah,

sure," he said, realizing he had no way out. Oh, but Carrie was dying for him to get close enough to her father so that he might remember to ask for her hand.

He watched as Rose rode off with Elmer and jealousy sliced through him so thick you could have spread sauce on him. Bitter sauce.

But there wasn't much he could do about it. It was one thing for him to scare off cowhands who stared at Rose while she worked on the veranda, or who danced too close with her. But he had no reason to scare off a decent man like Elmer, whose only fault was that he had gossiping in his blood.

6

SUMMER STORM

"Why'd you ask Rose for a hamper?" Carrie demanded, drawing his attention back to her.

"I'm not in the mood for spicy barbecue. I wanted something plain, like fried chicken and cornbread."

"Well, my hamper's got plenty of food and even some apple pie, so you see, if we get delayed, we won't go hungry." She stared up at him and batted her eyes.

"What makes you think we'll get delayed?" he asked, looking down Main Street, feeling uncomfortable. He never could relax when a woman batted her eyes at him. It made him want to swat flies.

"Well, you never know when something could happen."

Not liking the sound of that, Baxter set her hamper in the back of the wagon next to where Rose had moved his. Then he helped Carrie up.

As they rode along in silence, Baxter stared glumly at the passing mesquite and every so often up at the clear sky. Anything to avoid looking at Carrie, who sat primping and fussing with her hair. Heck, nothing would make Carrie's mousy hair as pretty as the midnight black that framed Rose's face.

Carrie laid a hand on his arm. "I know a shortcut to the picnic, Baxter. If we take it, we'll get there much faster."

Now that was the most sensible thing he'd ever heard Carrie say. Getting there fast was exactly what he wanted. But first there was a little detail to clear up.

"What shortcut?" he asked. This was his first summer back home in four years, and he didn't think he'd forgotten the landscape that fast. "There aren't any shortcuts to the cottonwood grove on the creek."

"Either you were gone too long at your fancy Harvard, Baxter, or you spend too much time on the Lazy Y. Of course there's a shortcut. Coming right up, we turn off and cut through the back of the school road. There's a fine road there the children use to ride to school. You'll see."

Baxter was skeptical, but he was in a hurry. If Carrie could be useful for once, he wasn't about to object.

At the schoolhouse, he turned off and headed the wagon into the sage. The dust swirled around them, and the mesquite grew a bit too thick for his liking. But the road stirred an old memory. Long ago, he used to ride this way. And if he remembered correctly, someone lived nearby. An old couple. It was indeed a shortcut. He couldn't wait to see Rose's face when she and Elmer arrived at the picnic and saw Carrie and him already there.

He pushed the horse and wagon through thicker and taller mesquite. Slower and slower the horse walked. Finally they came to the old shack. Baxter recognized the place now. He hadn't been here in a long time, since he'd come with his father. But now he remembered that even years ago, south of the cottonwoods by the creek the road had been barely passable.

Now the dirt farm was abandoned and wild roses had spread out on the sunny side of the old shack.

"Oh, Baxter, aren't the roses beautiful? We could stop and pick some and then—"

"There's no time."

"Oh, Baxter, we're not out herding cattle. We're going to a picnic. We can take our time. Isn't this the most charming place?"

"It's abandoned."

"The Hendersons died while you were gone. Right after you left. Didn't anyone write you?"

If his mother had mentioned it, he'd forgotten. "We have to keep moving. The root beer'll get warm and we've got the beef for the barbecue."

But he did admire the wild roses as he passed by. They were like Rose. She'd taken root at the Lazy Y, just like these flowers. He couldn't forget the taste of her lips, the feel of her soft body in his arms, and he grew wild with longing. That's how a man should feel about a woman if he was about to propose. But there he was thinking of Rose again, when it was Carrie he was escorting.

Carrie, who wore boned corsets. He'd felt it when he danced with her. Carrie, who batted her eyes and giggled, like a silly schoolgirl. She couldn't hold a candle to Rose.

"Where's the road?" he asked tersely as he reached the spot where he thought it had been.

"I'm not sure. I guess we're lost, Baxter." And with that announcement, she snuggled next to him and put her arms around his neck.

He draped his hands on his knees, defeated. Damn, but Carrie Snyder, the minister's mischievous daughter, had pulled the wool over his eyes and taken him the long way around. He knew he was right, for he was familiar with the old female ploy to trap a husband. But he wasn't about to let Carrie's mischief succeed.

Carrie seemed to sense that his thoughts had wandered, for she touched his arm. "If we're lost, maybe we should turn back. We could have our own picnic in town."

He gathered the reins while the horse pawed the dirt nervously. "We're not lost. The mesquite has grown so thick and higher here that it's hidden the road, that's all. I'll find the way."

He squinted, saw only dust and mesquite, but he would not turn back.

"But we can hardly see anything. What if we get lost even more driving through it, Baxter? Why don't we just stay here? We've got plenty of food, so we could still have our picnic."

Baxter thought fast. "Carrie, I don't want to look down the barrel of your preacher father's shotgun. If you're hungry, get out the hamper and eat, but we are not going back the way we came."

He unraveled her arms, arms scented liberally with rosewater, from around his neck.

Carrie's lower lip protruded in a pout. "Is that all you can think about? Food?"

It might be his salvation in this situation. "Come to think of it, I'm hungry," he announced suddenly. "I need some strength for the bumpy ride ahead." He reined in. The mesquite was tall enough to tickle the horse's nose. Its tail flicked back and forth in an attempt to sweep the branches off its rump. Baxter reached for Rose's picnic basket.

"Well," Carrie said, crossing her arms, "suit yourself, but I don't like Rose's cooking."

"I told you, I asked her to make just plain food." He reached into the back of the wagon. "Let's open up my basket, and yours, too. Come on, show me that apple pie."

Carrie bit her lip and stared guiltily at her knees. "I guess I left it with Pa and my sisters."

Well, he was certain that Carrie's pie crust couldn't match Rose's anyhow.

"That's all right. I'll treat you to the good food in my hamper."

Actually, he was eager to see what Rose had packed as he lifted the lid, his mouth watering for fried chicken and cornbread.

Reaching in, he pulled away a red-and-white checked napkin and stared at jars. Jars? He pulled one out. It was a jar of red-hot chili peppers. Well, that was a side dish she'd packed by mistake. He put the jar back with the others and looked for the main course. And stared down at red-and-white checked napkins.

"Chili peppers!" Carrie, her eyes widening, leaned over and peered in. "Nothing but jars of chili peppers from your favorite cook."

"It must be a mistake."

"Might be, or else Rose deliberately packed them for you. Obviously, she's mad at you. What did you do to her?"

A hot fury stole over him. He knew what he'd do to Rose Milligan if he had his hands on her now. He'd defended her to the town gossip, protected her, and this was his reward? To make matters worse, Carrie giggled.

He looked again to be sure the heat wasn't making his eyes play tricks on him. No delicately spiced chicken, no jars of fruit preserves, no cornbread, no angel food cake. A suspicion grew. He climbed in back and pulled the cork on a keg of root beer. When it trickled out, he leaned over and tasted it. It was warm, too warm. Hot. Pepper hot.

She'd spiced the root beer. With an angry flick of his hand, he jammed the cork back in the keg. The vixen had gone too far.

"Well, we might as well go back to town. There's no sense delivering peppered root beer to the picnic," Carrie said smugly.

Baxter was too busy settling back on the wagon and gathering up the reins to reply. Oh, yes there was a reason to continue on. To confront Rose.

The wagon lurched over a gopher hole, and mesquite brushed across Carrie's skirt. She squealed and pulled the sides of her bonnet close to protect her face.

He ignored her.

"You'll never find the cottonwoods," Carrie predicted. "If we get stranded out here all night, my pa will be angry." Tears made twin tracks in the dust on her face. "Angry enough to condemn your worldly ways, Baxter Yates. You're putting me in harm's way all because of that—that half-breed cook."

"Rose is a Texan, not some lily-white import like you and your town friends." Baxter cared more about straightening out Rose than he did about Preacher Snyder declaring he was as useless and as wasted as a piece of dried-up hardscrabble land.

As he guided the wagon, Baxter didn't say a word to Carrie. He ignored her every squeal and screech.

The smoke from the barbecue pit gave away the picnic site. And, oblivious to the mesquite clinging to everything from his shirt to the spokes of the wagon, and to Carrie's taunts, he reined in in a cloud of dust. Carrie started crying.

"Here now," Mrs. Snyder said, rushing up to Carrie, who jumped down from the wagon. "It can't be that bad, girl."

"Baxter got us lost," she cried, running straight for her father.

"That so?" Preacher Snyder looked up at Baxter.

"It ain't so," Elmer spoke up. "Baxter knows his

way around this entire county, from the skinny-dipping holes to the quail nests."

"Where've you been, then?" the preacher asked.

"We took the shortcut," Baxter admitted as he got down from the wagon, "but it was so overgrown we had a hard time getting through it. No harm done."

"That ain't so either," Elmer piped up. "I heard Carrie telling her friends she was going to take Baxter on the cutoff by the old shack. She knows there's no road there anymore, not since the Hendersons died three years back. But Baxter's been gone and didn't know the place is grown over with mesquite."

Carrie glared. "See if I ever buy any of your rose-water again, Elmer. You traitor."

"You'll buy. Who else have you got to make it for you?"

"Oh!"

As he rummaged through his hamper in the wagon bed, Baxter saw Carrie sobbing on her mother's shoulder while Elmer spoke with the preacher, offering apologies for tattling on Carrie. Well, at least Elmer's gossiping had paid off for once. He'd gotten Baxter off the hook. Maybe he just might let Elmer buy his rose petals from the Lazy Y again.

But right now he wanted satisfaction, and he'd get it from the Lazy Y's cook.

It didn't take long to spot her, sitting surrounded by ranch hands. They looked at Rose with so much hunger in their eyes that Baxter would have thrown them all in the creek, if it weren't half dried up.

He circled the group, tapping one man after another on the shoulder till one by one they slunk off. Then it was just Rose sitting there looking pretty as a picture in her yellow calico dress. Her black hair fell down her back in luxurious curls. "Is something the matter, Baxter?" she asked, oh so innocently.

He held up a jar of red chili peppers. "You call this the perfect fixings for a picnic hamper?" Before she could answer, he raised the jar high. "You put these peppers in the root beer, didn't you, Rose? What were you trying to prove?"

She raised her chin a notch. "I'm the cook, and I'll cook the way I like. Besides, those are my prize peppers. They won first place at the fair last summer. If they were good enough for the judges, they ought to be good enough for you."

"I've told you time and again I don't like hot spicy food, and I didn't expect to find it in my hamper, much less the root beer."

"Well, then you shouldn't have insulted my hot barbecue sauce. Go ahead, fire me like you did Jess."

Fire her? That wouldn't solve the slow simmer he felt for her. He looked around briefly. Everyone at the picnic was hanging on their every word. Gently he took Rose by the arm and steered her off a ways. "We've got to talk—in private. We've got to put a stop to our always fighting."

She looked him right in the eye. "I'm not fighting. You are. You hate me because of my mother. From the minute I laid eyes on you, I knew there would never be anything but trouble between us." Picking up her skirts, she ran through the wagons and down toward the dried-out creek, where the oaks shaded the bank and wild grass grew scraggly amidst the mesquite.

Baxter watched her, too dumbstruck to act. The heat was making all the women act loco, but this wasn't like Rose at all.

He quickly followed her and found her leaning against a tree wiping her eyes. He turned her in his arms and reached up and brushed away the last of her tears. One little swipe, and then he held her hands. "I want to talk to you, Rose." He stretched out his hand. "Walk with me along the creek."

Rose stared at his hand, as if debating the wisdom of going anywhere with him. She tossed her head, shook out her long black hair, and sighed. "All right, let's get it over with." She stalked ahead of him.

"Rose, that wasn't funny what you did, especially to the root beer," he said, catching up to her.

"Don't you have a sense of humor, Baxter? You mean you're supposed to dish it out to me whenever you feel like it, but you can't take a taste of your own medicine?"

"Is that your idea of humor, giving me peppers when I asked you nicely to pack me a picnic basket?"

She shrugged. Innocent brown eyes looked up at him. "Maybe I thought it was my turn to play some mischief. Look, if this is going to be another lecture about my behavior, you're wasting your time. If you ask me, you're the one whose behavior hasn't exactly been decent. You were off spooning with Carrie, weren't you? I've heard from Elmer that the girls giggle about that road and that shack covered with wild roses. It's the place to go spooning."

"That has nothing to do with you and what you did with those peppers. I thought the Lazy Y had cattle that are hard to handle, but compared to you, they're chicken feed. You take the prize for being contrary and ornery."

She placed her hands on her hips, her face red with anger. "How dare you! You're an arrogant know-it-all thinking you can lay rules on me, tell me how to act without having to live by any rules yourself."

"That's not true, Rose. I'm only watching out for you."

"Really? And what do you see?"

A woman who disturbed him, a woman who made his blood roil, made him hot under the collar.

"Well?" She tapped her foot. "Don't I remind you of the woman your own father was unfaithful with?"

"Stop it, Rose."

"Well, you know what, Baxter? Your father loved my mother. They couldn't have each other, but at least Oliver was man enough to tell her how he felt. They had that at least, and your mother forgave them. You've got to forgive too, Baxter."

"Why?"

"Because I'm hungry and I want to get back."

They stared at each other, and then he smiled.

Goldarned her pretty black hair and big brown eyes. He closed the distance between them and lifted his hand to cup her face. He gulped and felt his body go rigid with longing. He felt as if he were locked in a storm cellar, and only Rose had the power to unhinge the door. But if she did that, she'd bring the storm in with her.

His hands moved down her bodice to her waist and he pulled her close and kissed her. He couldn't stop himself. Just fleetingly, he knew he was doing exactly what he'd warned her against with other men.

They knelt by the creek bed, sweet mesquite filling the air, the fragrance wafting over them in the hot dry sun, and it ceased to matter to him what other men might do. Only what he did made any difference.

Rose touched his cheek, gently stroked it. "Why are you always so angry with me?"

His throat worked, and for a minute he couldn't form words. He laid his hand over hers, pressed her palm closer to his skin, and shut his eyes, drinking in her scent, her touch. "I think I'm angry that I can't have you."

For a minute she was silent, but he felt her take a deep breath and sigh. "You'd be tempting fate to want me, Baxter. Repeating history," she said so softly he could barely hear her.

The heck with the past. This was now. He kissed her, hard, and together they slid to the ground. Their mouths met with urgency. They kissed, barely breathing. They were by turns still and breathless and longing for the storm within them to break. She moved away, and he pulled her back. Her arms came up around his neck, and she molded her body against his.

Then, moving away from her, he stood and bent down to pick her up in his arms. He carried her off through the mesquite, his long strides taking them to toward the creek, far away from the picnickers. He clasped her tighter and marched right into the water.

"Baxter," she cried. "Where are we going?"

"Somewhere where no busybodies will find us."

The creek was at its lowest this time of summer, the heat having taken its toll. He waded through the waist-high water till he emerged on the other side where a secluded grove of trees shaded them.

He set her down and held her at arm's length, fighting his longing, trying to hold the storm at bay. She reached out to smooth his rumpled shirt front, and as her hand grazed the fabric, his desire built and built and built. He pulled her close and his fingers unfastened her dress, then slid the calico off her shoulders and down to her waist. He marveled at the sight of her, corsetless. Beautiful. Bedeviling. As God made her.

Below the waist they were both drenched, and he motioned toward his wet pants. "That was to put out the fire in me," he said, unable to take his eyes off her.

"Did it work?"

"Afraid not."

He molded his hand to her breast. She stood still, barely breathing, and shut her eyes. She tilted back her head and he bent and kissed her throat. "Rose," he murmured, burying his face against her cool skin.

The embers they'd been trying to douse, the fire they'd tried to ignore, ignited. She ran her hands inside his shirt and eased it off his shoulders and down his arms. The two of them clung, as closely as skin would allow, molding themselves to each other, desperate for the shelter of each other's arms, yet desperate to give way to passion. She began to kiss him, sweet and slightly wet little kisses that teased his lips, his neck, his shoulder. He couldn't keep up with her or stop her.

His hand caught her chin. "Rose—"

"Baxter, I don't feel like this with anyone else. No one," she said, pinning that liquid brown gaze on him.

Then he kissed her, deeply, slaking the drought he'd felt within himself. Kissing and touching her breasts, her waist, he pushed her dress over her hips and it pooled at her feet. He pulled her against him. He was on fire, and only having her close could cool him. He kicked off his boots and quickly removed his pants. Then she moved into his arms. He lowered her to the ground and his passion broke like a summer storm and he and Rose were lost in their own private world.

A world with no small-town rules, no prejudice. No petty jealousies. No corrals, one for him, the Lazy Y's heir, and another for her, the orphaned cook. Their passion washed all that away, and when they came together, they created a new world. A place where ecstasy was all that mattered.

His hands lingered over her every curve, his heart pounding at the gift of her, and when she gave herself he took her gently, and more shyly than she received him. He wrapped himself in her—her sweet scent, her velvet touch, delicately unfolding to him like a rosebud—deeper and deeper until she moaned softly, the way she did when she buried her face in roses. Then, silence as they lingered together.

As they lay side by side in the heat of the sun, Baxter was stunned at how much he needed Rose. Forever. As endlessly as the horizon.

He turned to stare at her face and at the storm cloud of black hair that had fallen out of its pins and floated around her shoulders. He raised himself on his elbow and, twining a curl around his finger, planted a kiss on the bridge of her nose. Then a kiss on her chin. And then her lips. A tiny kiss. Another, and then they were kissing again, his hands tangled in her hair.

Stunned at the suddenness of their desire, Baxter broke off their lovemaking. "Rose, you should get back to the picnic. Leave," he said sharply, getting up and putting on his clothes and boots.

She got to her feet, her eyes filled with sadness. "You mean, you had your way with the kitchen help. How like you. No one else can come near me, but you can. Use me and dispose of me." She donned her dress and started walking along the creek bank, her bodice unfastened in back. "You are a miserable failure as a chaperone. You realize that, don't you, Baxter?"

He scrambled after her and caught her by the arm, stopping her. She never turned, nor did he move, except to fasten her dress.

She bowed her head, her back to him, her hair hiding her face. "Did you use me?"

"No," he whispered. "I never meant to touch you at all. It just happened."

"Do you care for me?"

"Of course I do."

"How much?"

"Rose," he said, letting his hands drop to his side. "Don't ask too much of me."

"Of course not. Asking for Baxter Yates, heir to the biggest ranch in Texas, to say what he feels to a lowly cook would be asking too much, wouldn't it?"

She smoothed the skirt that had dried and he watched the emotions playing across her face.

He knew she was upset. She'd given herself to him, with no price on it but the passion of the moment. He was glad it was him. How could he tell her, though, what she meant to him?

A blinding light zigzagged across his heart, just like lightning in a slow-building storm, and the darkness was lifted from his soul. In that moment, he realized he loved and wanted Rose. Not the ranch. But Rose.

She lifted her arms to pin up her hair and the yellow calico stretched across her breasts.

"Rose, it's not—I'm going to give up the ranch. I don't want my inheritance."

She gave him a sad smile. "You can't do that, Baxter. You can't, any more than I can walk away from who I am."

"Rose, you know what I think? You belong with me more than any other woman in Mesquite Junction."

Tears shimmered in her eyes, and her hands fluttered, pinning up the remaining strands of hair. "Maybe, Baxter, you're forgetting who I am."

"I don't care."

"You *have* to care," she said. "You belong to the Lazy Y. No woman comes first when it comes to that ranch. And nothing can change that."

Then she was gone, vanishing through the mesquite. It seemed he was destined to repeat his father's ignoble frustration with women, whether he wanted to or not.

7

The next day Rose avoided the veranda, and though it was hotter than ever, she stayed in her kitchen. She'd heard from Nettie this morning that everyone was gossiping about her and Baxter leaving the picnic, and she didn't want to face any of the hands.

She didn't care so much about what people said, but she did feel guilty. She'd given in to temptation and allowed Baxter to make love to her. She was repeating her mother's fate. Oliver had never been free to marry her mother, any more than Baxter would be free to marry Rose. She should never have allowed him to touch her. His father had made it all too clear that Baxter was to marry for money, not love, and nothing could change his stubborn mind.

So what if she loved Baxter? He could never be hers, and she was doomed to live a life of regrets, just like her mother.

She finally realized that she couldn't put off her

chores any longer and that she had to go outside. She
walked to the hen house to check the hens. No eggs. If
this heat didn't let up, the town would have a lot more
than that to complain about.

As she walked back to the ranch house, she saw
Oliver sitting on the porch, looking pale. She suggested
that he move into the den.

"No, I'm waiting for Baxter."

Rose knew that Baxter had gone far out on the
range today to brand and round up some strays and
wouldn't be home any time soon. It wasn't healthy for
Oliver to sit in this heat, waiting for him, and he was
acting as jumpy as a steer next in line for the butcher.

"I'm feeling all hot and prickly like," Oliver complained good-naturedly. "What'd you do, give us another dose of chili peppers?"

"Is there something wrong with your stomach?"
she asked.

"Stomach's fine, but I feel funny."

"It's the heat, so don't you go blaming my food."

"Never known heat to feel like this. Not in many a
year. Even the cattle are acting skittish."

"Which is why Baxter's out with some of the
ranch hands today, checking on them."

She glanced up at the blue sky and blinked. Was
the sun playing tricks on her eyes? Why, off in the
horizon she could swear she saw huge masses of
clouds moving in.

She finally felt her crestfallen spirits lift. "See that,
Oliver? Clouds. Maybe we'll get some rain."

She waved him into the house and settled him in
his den. Then she went out again and poured muddy
water on the rosebushes just in case it didn't rain. It
was the best she could do, but the roses looked as
droopy as she felt.

She knew without a doubt that Baxter would never respect her again. Every woman knew what happened when she gave in to a man. He lost interest, especially a conceited man like Baxter. Instead of curing his conceit, she'd merely made it worse. Oh, yes, the only way she'd ever get Baxter's attention again was through his stomach. No more kisses. No more roses. No more tempestuous arguing over him toying with her. No more touching. No more anything.

Oh, it must be the heat getting to her, she told herself as she wiped her brow with her hand and stared out at the parched land. A couple of chickens darted across the yard by the pump and scared up dust. Other than that, the air was still. The clouds had scooted a little closer and lower.

As the morning gave way to a muggy afternoon, there was still no sign of Baxter, and despite her intention not to think about him, Rose missed him. He was like all her favorite foods—cinnamon taffy, peppered eggs, and spice cake—all in one, and she couldn't resist him. She yearned to have him walk in with one of his mother's rosebuds and try to soften her mood. She wanted to smile back at his interfering advice and tell him off. But most of all, she ached to feel him against her.

She was so confused. She feared her attraction to Baxter was wrong, the way her mother's love for Oliver had been wrong. Oh, how she wished she had another woman to talk to, but the only woman in whom she could have confided was gone, and she would never have been able to tell Ellen her feelings anyway. It would have hurt the older woman, reminding her of her own betrayal and heartache.

She should never have come here. She should have left the day she first laid eyes on Baxter.

But she would leave soon. She had almost enough in the bank to be able to leave in another month. Then she would make her dream of opening a restaurant come true. She'd call it Pepper Stew and the menu would offer a mixture of Mexican and Irish dishes. In a city like Houston or San Antonio, she'd be a success. As her mother had told her over and over, a woman could survive without a man, as long as she didn't fall in love with a man she could never have.

She sighed. It was so hot her own breath was swallowed up in the air, and though she dreaded heating up the kitchen even more, she lit the oven.

She decided to make Oliver's favorite meal—fried chicken, cornbread, and an enormous sweet potato pie.

By now her dress was sticky, her hair plastered to the back of her neck and to her forehead. But she kept working.

A few minutes later she walked onto the porch to shake out the white muslin tablecloth. It billowed in a wind that had come up. She glanced up at the sky. More clouds were moving in. Big clouds, fluffy and as white as a hundred damask tablecloths floating low in the sky. She looked closer. They were thunderheads.

And then a drop of rain fell on her face.

Plop. Another drop landed on her arm.

At last, it was going to rain, and at once she thought of Baxter. Wished he were here beside her on the porch. She'd like to stand with him, feeling his warmth while they watched the rain together. She shook her head. She had to stop wishing for what she couldn't have.

*   *   *

An hour later, she opened the window to set the sweet potato pie on the ledge to cool. It hadn't baked as she'd hoped. The oven had not cooked properly today. A few raindrops hit the pie. When, oh, when would the storm break and get it over with? She removed the pie and started to close the window, but first peered out.

The hair on the back of her neck stirred. Lightning flashed in the distance. The clouds had grown dark and were roiling lower. A frightening thought crossed her mind—instinctive, sudden—and then from the base of those clouds a pair of tails snaked down, then just as quickly disappeared. The wind slammed a door shut somewhere out in the yard as more rain fell.

Another little white tail slid down from the clouds, clouds that looked like the underbelly of a thousand milking cows. Teats formed, ready to burst. Rose had been a little girl the last time she'd seen such clouds.

It was a Sunday, and she had been in church with her mother. The windows had all been opened because it was so hot, so oppressive. Then it hit and there was no feeling like it in the world. You had to have lived through it to know what it meant.

Tornado.

Rose's heart thudded in her ears, and instinctively she propped open the back door and pushed up the window over the sink as high as it would go. She remembered that the only building that had blown apart had been the schoolhouse, the one place that had been all closed up. Rose knew from cooking that if too much hot air was trapped in a pan with a lid on it, then the pan blew up. If you cracked the lid, the pan might bubble over and splatter the stove, but at least it wouldn't explode all over the ceiling like the first time she'd ever made pressure cooker pudding.

So she figured the same applied to the house. Open the lid on the place. As she pushed up one window sash after another, the wind blew rain inside, soaking the blue gingham curtains, beating against Rose's face. And all the while, the wind grew louder, the black clouds more menacing.

A potted geranium blew off a ledge and shattered all over the floor. The rain wet the braid rug and the walls. And then a gust of wind tore through and flattened Rose against the kitchen wall. She managed to hold up her hand to shield her face as dishes clattered off the counter and table. It looked as if Mother Nature were having a fine old tantrum right here in the kitchen, in this house. This house! Oliver!

Clinging to the walls for dear life, one arm still shielding her face, Rose ran into the den where Oliver usually took his afternoon nap. Sure enough, he was asleep, completely oblivious to the crashing wind outside.

She raised the shade and tried to budge the open window higher.

Oliver jerked awake. "Now, Rose," he said as he stretched in his leather arm chair, "what are you up to?"

She gave up on the window, which wouldn't move, and turned to the old man. Rain slashed at the panes. "Oliver, we have to get to the storm cellar."

"The storm cellar?" He glanced at the rain-swept window. "By damn, but we're finally getting some cooler weather. I don't blame you for opening the windows and letting it in. Feels good, girl."

"Oliver, you have to leave the house with me now!" Was he deaf? "Can't you hear it coming?"

He stared at her as if she'd pulled a gun on him. "What? What's coming?"

She rushed to kneel at his side. "A tornado. We have to—"

"Tornado?" he shouted, cutting her off. "We haven't had a tornado in Mesquite Junction since Baxter was a boy. You must be overreacting. You ain't seen a good rainstorm in a while, that's all."

The old man levered himself out of the chair, hobbled over to the window, and placed his gnarled hands on the ledge to lean out. When he drew in his head, his white mane was wind-tossed. "Where's Baxter?"

"On the range somewhere." For the first time her voice wavered. "I'm sure he's all right, but we have to get into the shelter now, or the storm will be on top of us."

She grabbed his hand.

"Storm shelter? We ain't used it in years. Likely to have mice in it."

The wind howled through the den and knocked over a vase that Ellen had brought from Boston, and outside Rose could have sworn a freight train was coming at the house. Only there weren't any trains near the Lazy Y. Only wind. Twister wind. A giant bolt of lightning lit up the sky, an eerie yellow glow.

Suddenly Oliver's face drained of color as lightening and thunder crashed about them. The old man gripped her hand tightly. "Let's go. Duck your head. Watch out and run."

He dragged her out of the den to the front door. He opened it and tugged her outside into a wind so wild, a sky so black, that Rose was swallowed up in the storm. The wind whipped her hair and skirt into a tangle and tried to push her backwards, but she and Oliver managed to barrel forward step by step. An empty crate crashed against the veranda, followed by the butter churn, and the rocking chair went rolling end over end into the dark.

Oliver never let go of her hand until they reached the storm doors set in the ground behind the house.

It seemed like an hour to Rose as she and Oliver tried to lift the wooden doors out of the wet earth, but at last they were inside and clambering down the ladder. Above them, Oliver pulled the doors shut. Rose knelt in the dirt and covered her hands with her ears. Nothing shut out the sound of the wind or of the thunder crashing.

They were underground in a pitch dark, mouse-dung-smelling hole lined with wooden walls. Rose tried to calm down for Oliver's sake. She felt around and found a musty blanket and then a kerosene lantern. Oliver's hand touched hers and she plucked a match from his fingers. She groped until she felt his boot sole and when she struck the match, it flared to life. Moments later they huddled on either side of the lantern, the blanket slung over the old man's bent shoulders.

Overhead, a hellish wind battered at the shelter's doors, rattling them, tossing debris from the yard at them.

"Where's Baxter?" Oliver asked over and over. "Where's my boy?"

Rose gulped. As the wind howled, she had visions of Baxter lying on the ground somewhere. The twister could pass him by or pick him up and toss him a mile away, as if he were a rag doll.

"Are you scared?" she asked between chattering teeth.

"Oh, a tornado's not something to take lightly," came the stern reply. "But we're safe. And though I always was afraid of the dark, that bitty lantern helps some. I just can't help feeling uneasy about Baxter."

Rose's survival instinct kicked in. This wasn't her first tornado, and it wouldn't be her last. She'd do whatever she had to to live through it and make sure Oliver did, too. But the old man, despite his gruff assurances, was trembling. He was holding her hand again, and his was shaking worse than hers.

"Now, don't you worry about Baxter. He's resourceful. I wager he's weathering this out in some town lady's storm shelter, or at least in a ditch out on the ranch."

"The Lazy Y has got a lot of ditches."

"Dry ones, too," she pointed out. "The heat's left them dry. They'll make good hiding places. The tornado won't get him there."

"One good thing. Maybe this storm will shake the man up so he'll see the light and settle down and run the ranch for me. That's if there's a ranch left after this storm blows through."

One more crash vibrated off the doors above. Rose gulped, then steadied herself. "Maybe Baxter doesn't want to settle down especially with any of the ladies you keep pushing at him."

He was silent, and around them the wind howled louder than ever. Rose hugged her body to keep warm.

Finally he answered, "Well, that may be. But we can't always have what we want in life, Rose, like me and your mama. I couldn't have her. Loved her, but I already had a wife—a decent woman."

"But don't you want Baxter to have the things you couldn't have?" she asked, every word punctuated by the crash of debris above, every pause filled with the ugly wind.

"I do," Oliver insisted. "I want him to have the money to keep the ranch growing and prospering."

"Maybe he wants something else." Rose said the words slowly.

He pulled the blanket closer. "Can't imagine what."

"I admired your wife and I loved my mother. I don't mean any disrespect to Ellen, but you missed out on having my mother for your own. Was the ranch worth more than that? What if your fear is correct? What if there's no ranch left when this twister's gone?"

He didn't answer and she changed the subject to something easier. Talk of her restaurant, and while the wind and rain raged above them, she tried to keep Oliver's mind occupied on anything. Except Baxter's whereabouts.

For an eternity it seemed she knelt in the dark with the old man. Talking about recipes. Listening to Oliver talk about cattle. But Rose knew that Oliver was as worried as she about Baxter. Was he safe?

Finally, as the wind abated somewhat, Oliver said, "You know, Rose, you got me to thinking about what Baxter wants. That son of mine always was a mite too confident for his own good, too many pretty women turning his head. So I wasn't sure he knew who the right woman would be for the ranch. That's why I came up with different ones for him." He half snorted, as if laughing at himself. "Sounds silly now."

Rose sighed. She loved Baxter so. She knew that no matter what happened to her, or who Baxter married, that would never change. Her heart ached, and it was her turn to shiver. "Oh, you shouldn't have worried about that. Women have a way of rising to the need. Whoever he picks will make a fine mistress for the Lazy Y."

"I hope you're right, Rose."

"I am. Just be warned. I won't be staying on to cook for her, whoever she is. In fact, I might be gone before Baxter weds."

Oliver cleared his throat and passed the blanket to her. "Somehow you wouldn't be Maria's daughter if you didn't say something like that. You really think Baxter's all right?"

"He knows how to take care of himself," she said, as much to reassure herself as his father.

Finally, mercifully, the wind died down, the rain stopped. And she dared to crawl up the wooden steps and lift one of the doors just a few inches.

Quiet. The tornado had blown through, leaving in its wake a yard full of debris. She let the door fall shut, and hunched on the top step, wondering if she should let Oliver see the mess.

"How's it look out there?" he asked.

Rose paused, thinking of a way to break it to him easy. "Well, I think maybe Nettie's going to need some help with the cleanup."

At that moment, the doors were ripped open. She gasped, startled, and then relief washed through her. Baxter stood there, his hair and shirt plastered to his skin.

"Baxter, you're all right! Where *were* you?"

"Flat on my stomach behind the church in town, praying hard I'd see you again."

He hauled her out into the yard, littered with fallen limbs and shutters and hay. She saw some of the ranch hands venture out of the barn and bunkhouse, their shirts plastered wetly to their skin, picking through the debris. Half the roof of the ranch house was torn off.

But she had no time to look around further because Baxter pulled her into his arms right in front of everyone.

"Rose, Rose, I couldn't find you. I looked everywhere—the house, the barn."

Warmth seeped through her even though a thoroughly wet Baxter held her close.

"Why, I took your father down to the shelter. Don't you think I know how to take care of him and myself? I tried to tell you for weeks I didn't need chaperoning. No Texas-born-and-bred lady does."

Oliver climbed out of the shelter and walked toward them. He didn't seem surprised to see her in his son's arms. "She took care of me, Baxter. Guess she don't need any chaperone as bad as I do. She took care of me right nice. Got me out of that house and into that shelter as quick as you please. Why, she saved my life."

He glanced around. "Worst tornado in twenty years."

But Baxter had his own storms to weather still. "I want to take care of you. Marry me, Rose."

"What?"

Before he could repeat his proposal, his father's voice chimed in. "I was wrong trying to foist a woman on you, son, because of her papa's bank account."

"You're darn right you were. I had to go to town to get more rope when the twister hit, and you should see those rich fathers' businesses now. They're totally flattened. The bank. The mercantile. The law office. Even Elmer's apothecary. Flatter 'n a pancake, and some of those eligible young ladies are packing up to move on. Leaving Texas. Crying over what the tornado did to their hairpins and ruffle petticoats."

"Even Carrie Snyder?" Rose asked.

"Naw, the preacher's going to rebuild his church, but she's crying in Elmer's arms, and he's promising if she marries him he'll build her a house with the biggest storm shelter in ten counties."

"Well, that's that," Oliver said. "The twister might have messed up the town a little, but it shouldn't scare off a ranch wife. Not a Texas ranch wife."

Baxter looked at Rose. Her hair was wet and bedraggled, her dress plastered to her skin. She looked like a drowned rat, but she was here and she wasn't crying over the mess.

"You aren't going to set up a Texas-size to-do," Baxter said, "because if she'll have me, I'm marrying Rose. So if you object, don't say a word. You'll just be wasting your breath." He looked at his father, daring the old man to argue with him.

Oliver shook his head. "I guess I've given you everything, son, but the one thing I can't give you is the right woman. I want you to have the one you want, and that's Rose. I learned down in that storm shelter that she's more woman than any of those hothouse ladies in town. I see that now, and I envy you—not meaning any disrespect to your mother."

"She would have understood better than anybody."

"Yeah, I expect you're right." With a nod, Oliver hobbled over to examine the damage to the ranch house, the house he'd built for Baxter's mother. "Some of us live a lifetime and work for everything. Others just get lucky and find it. Don't lose it, Baxter." He stared at the battered roof of the house, then squinted. "Well, look at that."

Baxter and Rose didn't move.

"Come see this, Rose. Baxter."

Rose allowed herself to be tugged along by Baxter, and she didn't mind a bit, not the way she'd minded when he'd followed her outside at the dance because the ranch hands were dancing too close. And not the way she'd minded when he'd come storming at her for playing a practical joke with his picnic basket and the root beer. No, it felt good to have his hand in hers. To be walking side by side with him. Like she was his equal.

Suddenly he stopped. "Look, Rose, tell me what you see."

"The well's been sucked dry, ripped away. And the veranda, it's gone." Sick at heart, she could scarcely talk.

"Yeah, but look." Oliver pointed. "Over there."

"They're gone. Every one of Ellen's rosebushes is gone. Oh, she'd be heartbroken."

"I think she'd accept it," Baxter said. "She accepted a lot." He moved behind Rose and wrapped his arms around her, then loosened his hug and pointed again. "Look what the tornado set down in place of those fancy roses."

Rose stared, afraid to believe what her eyes told her was true. "A wild rose bush." Covered with pale pink blooms. She knew that the nearest wild rosebushes had climbed up the bunkhouse, which was now in shambles. But its wild rosebushes still stood. That meant that this new rosebush had to have been blown here from somewhere else. It now lay in front of the big house, as if it had been pulled up gently, whirled off in the center of the tornado, and set down without so much as disturbing one wild petal, just waiting to be replanted.

Baxter walked over, plucked a tiny bloom, and offered it to Rose. "The wild roses survived that twister. And so will you, Rose. With me."

After only a brief hesitation, Rose took his offering and bent her head. She brushed its velvet petals against her cheek.

Then Baxter raised her chin, his touch as soft as the petals. His kiss tripped off her heart more wildly than the storm had.

"I love you, Rose," he said. "You never said if you'll marry me. Will you?"

"The gossip, the town—"

"Hang the town. Together we'll show 'em we can weather any storm. You belong here, Rose. You and no other woman."

She stared into his eyes, intense with longing. For

once, she was tongue-tied, but words finally tumbled out, soft words. "Oh, Baxter, yes. I love you so."

They stood there, clinging, until Rose became aware of all the gawking and the grumblings from the disappointed cowhands who, now that the veranda was gone, had no place to find shade and spend time with her. Well, she could at least talk to Baxter about a new veranda so they'd have shade. As for her . . .

Well, Baxter was kissing her, and though the air was cooler, she knew that things were going to heat up around here again. Real soon. And if another storm broke, this time they'd weather it in the shelter of each other's arms.

KAREN LOCKWOOD's stories are known for their tender portrayals of courtship and first love. The author of three historical novels and two previous novellas, she is a graduate of Western Washington University with a degree in English and Education. She and her husband have raised three sons.

IV

GOLDEN HARVEST

Lori Copeland

1

Fall, 1873
Branson, Missouri

"*By the way, what are you* wearing to the dance?"

Aster glanced up from the pan of apples she was peeling. Her sister stood over the wood stove, stirring a large pot of apple butter. The aroma of tart apples and cinnamon filled the air—the smells of fall. Oh, how Aster loved the crisp air and the trees of red, yellow, and orange carpeting the Ozarks, painting a picture she could carry in her mind throughout the cold, snowy months.

Her gardens were sporting their last offerings of squash and pumpkins, and the corn shucks were already tied and standing in tall rows.

Though the last of the vines was pulled and she had hired two farmhands, Arthur and Mason, work was never done on the farm. But it wouldn't be long before they could all rest.

There was only one fly in the ointment: fall meant the annual Harvest Barn Dance.

"Mmm, I suppose the blue calico."

Sally blew a strand of hair out of her eyes. "But you wore that last year. You need something new. Something . . . prettier."

Aster smiled, knowing that Sally's restlessness had been wearing on her these past few weeks. Sally had been in school in Philadelphia when John passed away. The moment she'd received Aster's letter, she'd returned to the farm to be with Aster. That had been two years ago, and in spite of Aster's protests that Sally needed to finish school, Sally had stayed, and Aster loved having her there. She didn't know what she'd have done after John died without Sally's help, even though she wasn't at all suited for hard physical work, which she hated. For that reason, they'd divided the farm duties, Aster tending the animals and garden, Sally doing the housework.

For the briefest of moments Aster's mind wandered back to her husband. It was easier to think about him now, but his death had come as such a shock. So like her kind, caring John, he had died while helping fight a fire on a neighboring farm. Everyone Aster knew had been wonderful at the time, but she'd needed her sister.

"What I wear won't have any effect on whether I have a good time," Aster finally said.

"Yes, it will. Wearing something new and bright always makes me feel better, have more fun. You should do something with your hair, buy a new dress."

"The blue calico will do just fine."

"But you ought to wear something more than will 'do.'"

It was an old argument, but Aster knew that Sally was determined to make her socialize more and stop

acting like an old maid. In Sally's opinion, it was time
for Aster to move on.

"You're only twenty-four, Aster. Not eighty-four."

Aster stuck her tongue out at Sally in an impish
gesture she hadn't used since she was fifteen and Sally
twelve.

"What would you suggest? I haven't the time to
make anything, and the dance is only three days
away."

Sally stirred the apple butter, staring up at the
ceiling in contemplation. "Yellow."

"Yellow?"

"Yellow check. With lots of lace around a scooped
neck."

"Sally, I look horrible in yellow, and besides, I told
you, I don't have time to make a dress."

"You don't have to! I saw one at Brown's Mercantile just this week." Sally gestured with the wooden
spoon, scattering droplets of sticky apple butter
around the kitchen. "Long close-fitting sleeves, a narrow waist with a V in front and back, and a gathered
skirt that will swirl perfectly when you whirl in a
dance." She squealed. "You'll love it."

Whirl in a dance? Aster flicked a drop of apple
butter off her nose. "You didn't happen to notice the
price, did you?"

"I did, and you can afford it. And it's just your
size. I had Meredith hold it for you."

Aster shook her head, knowing the dress
wouldn't be what she wanted but also knowing she'd
have to try it on because Sally wouldn't rest until she
did. Once her sister got something in her head she
was like a dog with a bone, hanging on until the bitter
end.

"We'll go try the dress on this afternoon," Sally

said. "It will be perfect for you and you'll love it. Then we'll do something about that hair."

Aster was alarmed. "My hair?"

"Yes. You wear it like Grandma did."

"I wear it pulled back because it gets in the way when I work."

"That doesn't mean you have to wear it skinned back like a monk. My word, if I had all that glorious red hair I'd make sure everyone saw it!"

Aster grimaced. "If you had it there'd be no way anyone could miss it. Red sticks out like a geranium in a field of daisies."

"Back to the dance," Sally said. "You'll wear the yellow dress and I'll do your hair and you'll dance with every man who asks you. No more hiding behind the food tables."

"I'm on the food committee," Aster reminded her.

"That doesn't mean you have to be there every minute. No one else does."

"Everyone else has a husband or suitor."

"You would, too, if you'd put forth a little effort."

Sally was certainly on her soapbox today, Aster thought. And once Sally got on the subject of Aster's eligibility, there was no stopping her.

"I'll try on the dress. And you can 'do something' with my hair, but if I don't like it I won't wear it."

"Agreed," Sally said.

The sun gilded the maple trees as Aster and Sally made the five-mile trip into Branson. Aster didn't mind taking the afternoon off, since sixteen quarts of apple butter were cooling on the cabinet, evidence of their morning's work. Tomorrow they'd can the pumpkins.

The twenty-five-year-old Brown's Mercantile, in

the center of town, offered everything from threads and laces to saddles and harnesses. The bell over the door rang as Aster and Sally entered.

"Oh, I know what you're here for," the elderly Meredith Brown said with a laugh. "I've got that dress right over here."

As Aster put on the dress, she had to admit that it was everything Sally had promised. The heavy golden yellow cotton cloth had an almost indiscernible pattern, set off by ivory tatted lace around the scooped neck and sleeves. The deep V bodice cut into the gored skirt front and back, and the skirt swirled perfectly around her ankles.

"Turn around," Sally directed, her face pensive. "It's perfect. Simply perfect."

"I look awful in yellow." With her hair, Aster thought she resembled one of the colorful maples out front.

"You look stunning."

"That's what I'm afraid of."

Fifteen minutes later they were back out on the sidewalk, the dress wrapped in brown butcher paper to protect it on the way home.

"See, didn't I tell you!"

There was nothing worse than Sally in a righteous mood.

"You did. I admit it." The dress was gorgeous.

"And I'm right about your hair, too. You just wait."

The day of the dance, Aster bathed in the kitchen late in the afternoon, allowing herself the privilege of a long soak and the liberal use of lilac-perfumed soap that she kept for special occasions. She washed her hair twice, and rinsed it carefully with rainwater so that it shone like silk when she brushed it out. The only problem was, as soon as her hair was dry, its curliness became even more evident.

"You're lucky, you know," Sally said as she carefully combed the waist-length mass. "If your hair was as straight as mine you'd have something to complain about."

"At least you can braid it and expect it to stay where you pin it," Aster returned. She eyed the scissors on the table anxiously. "Be careful what you do with those. I don't trust you."

She was perched on a stool in the middle of the kitchen, a towel draped around her shoulders. Sally stood in front of her, holding the scissors, contemplating Aster's face.

"I'm just going to trim a little . . . here." She snipped a strand of hair over Aster's forehead. "And here."

"Sally—"

"Sit still. I know what I'm doing."

Aster wasn't at all sure of that, but when Sally was finished and let her have the mirror, Aster had to admit she definitely looked different. To tell the truth, she could hardly recognize herself.

Her carrot-red hair was pulled up in a soft pouf to frame her oval face. Soft bangs graced her forehead, making her grass-green eyes seem larger and wide withsurprise. Excitement pinked her cheeks and even her lips seem a tad softer. Leaning closer to the mirror, she frowned. Wasn't the neckline a bit low?

"Well, what do you think?"

"I think— I don't know. Is that really me?"

"It is, dear sister. The way you should look all the time."

"Oh." Aster laughed. "I'm sure the cows and chickens would appreciate that!"

"I don't know about the cows and chickens, but I bet the bachelors around here surely would."

Aster laid the mirror aside. "You know I'm not looking for a husband."

"You should be," Sally returned.

"I loved John—"

"I'm not disputing that. I'm just saying that he'd want you to be happy, and you're not. You're a woman who wants a family. That means a husband."

"A husband means children, too, and I can't have children. We were married four years and there were no babies. What man wants a woman who can't have babies?"

"Plenty, I'd say."

"Farmers want sons to help with the work, inherit the farms. Carry on tradition."

"If that's all they want a wife for—to be a brood mare—then who needs them? What you need is a man who loves you. That's all. And you've got to give them a chance. You hide yourself in corners. Get out in the light. Give them and yourself a chance. Tonight you get out from behind the food table and dance!"

Aster laughed at her sister's persistence. "We have to get there first."

"I'll be ready in thirty minutes."

Sally disappeared up the stairs and Aster could hear her moving around in the room she'd occupied since birth. The room was next to Aster's. Sally was right about one thing. Aster had always wanted a home and family. Facing the fact that she was barren had been the hardest thing she'd ever done, besides burying John.

*   *   *

The dance was in full swing when Aster and Sally arrived. After helping Aster with their food contributions to the pot-luck supper, Sally disappeared with Philip Greenly, the handsome young schoolteacher she'd been seeing for the past six months. She danced away with him in a blur of pale green-and-white petticoat lace to the tune of "Fire On The Mountain" played by two fiddlers and a guitar picker. Aster watched the young couple whirling around the floor and smiled when she realized that their relationship was becoming serious.

Good, she thought. Philip would be a stabilizing influence in her impetuous young sister's life.

Aster inhaled the aroma of freshly cut hay. The opened doors at both ends of the large barn kept a welcome breeze stirring inside.

The floor had been swept clean and tables had been set up to one side. Punch had been assembled in a galvanized tub, but Aster knew that several of the men would have brought their own "kick" to add to their cups later on.

After rearranging the food on the table as other dishes were given to her and speaking to the other women, Aster didn't know what to do with herself except wait and help serve when it was time to eat. Sally, meanwhile, had already danced with two other men besides Philip, and was laughing up into the face of a third. Aster almost wished she had some of her sister's spirit, but like Mama always said, Aster was the quiet one in the family.

Aster was talking pumpkins with Ada Broom when she felt a light touch on her elbow.

"Excuse me, ma'am. May I have the pleasure of this dance?"

She turned in surprise and found herself looking up into the face of the handsomest man she'd ever seen.

"Why—"

"You go on," Ada urged. "We've got more than enough help here."

Before she could protest, Aster found herself caught up in a fast reel, whirling round and round in her partner's arms. Almost before she could catch her breath, the musicians began a waltz and she was being held a little closer than she felt necessary.

"I really must go."

"They don't need your help." Spinning her around, he held her shamelessly close. "Miss Ada Broom said so."

His hand was warm on her back and his other hand held hers against the broad expanse of his chest in a far too intimate gesture. He was a stranger, after all.

As if he read her mind, he said, "Dane Gordon, ma'am. I know I haven't seen you around before, either." He flashed her a devastating smile. "I most surely would have noticed."

His smile was engaging and his hazel eyes, crinkling at the corners, seemed to see right through her. His hair was the color of new straw and gleamed in the light of lamps hanging from the rafters. His firm jaw was clean-shaven and his cologne had a woodsy aroma that made her think of the spice rack at Brown's Mercantile. He was also the best-dressed man at the dance.

"Are you going to tell me your name?" he asked.

"I—it's Aster Harris." Her voice sounded light, breathy. She hardly recognized it.

"Aster. Like the flower. Tall and willowy, with a face that turns up to the sun."

She felt her face grow warm beneath his gaze. "You speak very pretty words, Mr. Gordon."

"And you hardly talk at all," he teased. "Where do you live? Why haven't I met you before? And is there a husband or suitor I should be avoiding?"

He was much too charming. When he looked at her as if she were the only person in the room, it made her heart race in a way it hadn't in a very long time.

"N-no, there's no one."

Leaning closer, he whispered, "Then all the men who live around here are fools." His tone seemed to sing along her senses.

The music changed three times and Dane never let her go. As he guided her around the dance floor, it seemed everyone else melted away.

The tune changed from a fast reel to a slow waltz and still he held her, his gaze holding hers as if he couldn't look away. If the truth be known, she was mesmerized by him.

"Who are you?" she whispered at last, too uncertain and unnerved to speak in her normal tone of voice.

"I told you my name."

"Dane."

His eyes softened. "I like the sound of it coming from your lips."

"But *who* are you?"

"I'm a traveling salesman. I sell everything you need, from buttons to bow saws, lace to lavender, medicines to the moon."

She laughed at his absurdity. "The moon?"

He leaned closer. "If you want it. Yes, ma'am, I can make your kids nicer, your husband more considerate, and you, my lovely . . . " He pretended to study her. "No," he mused, "there is nothing in my wagon that can improve you. You're perfection."

"Oh, for heaven sakes," she murmured.

"No, wait. Perhaps I could make your hair redder.

Yes," he said, "perhaps a little redder, and add perhaps a little more curl here and there."

Suddenly she found it hard to breathe. Dane Gordon was a natural born charmer and much too much for her to deal with.

"I—I think I'd like some punch," she managed, hoping to distract him until she could think more clearly.

"Your wish is my command." He laughed, leading her off the floor.

She watched him make his way through the crowd toward the punch. Desperately looking for Sally, she stood on tiptoe and searched the crowd, finally spying her in Tom Carter's arms.

Threading her way through the crush, Aster caught Sally just before she returned to the dance floor.

"I'm leaving," Aster whispered. "Right now."

"But the dance isn't over. I haven't—"

"I have to leave. Can you get a ride home?"

"Why, I'm sure Philip will see me home," Sally said, studying Aster's face. "What's wrong? Are you ill?"

"No, I'm fine. I just need—I just have to leave. You have a good time."

Though it was plain that Sally wasn't happy about her leaving, Aster quickly slid through the nearest exit and ran to their wagon.

The sounds of the fiddles and laughter floated on the air, growing faint as she hurried the team back toward the farm. As she drove, she thought about Dane Gordon. He was a handsome devil all right, a man naturally born to turn a woman's head. And while he made her feel beautiful, and made her heart beat like a trapped sparrow, she just wasn't ready to cope with a man like him.

Not ready at all.

2

"*What on* earth *got into you?* Why did you leave the dance like that?" Sally asked the next morning when Aster returned from milking and gathering eggs.

"I—I just felt like it."

"Well, who was that man I saw you dancing with? I've never seen him around before, but he certainly seemed taken with you. Wouldn't hardly let you out of his sight." Sally frowned. "Did he say or do something he shouldn't? If he did—"

"His name is Dane Gordon and, no, it wasn't that at all."

Aster poured milk through the gauze cloth they used as a strainer, then poured out a little for the black-and-white cat who earned his living as a mouser.

"Then what was it?"

She'd lain awake most of the night thinking about why she'd been so disturbed by Dane's flirting, and she'd come to only one conclusion.

"I just—I just can't seem to talk to men. Not like you can."

"It's so simple. They're just like us." Sally was obviously exasperated. Then she grinned. "Only slightly different."

Aster felt warmth flood her face. "It's that 'slight' difference that's causing the problem."

"What are you talking about?"

Sally took the bucket of strained milk and set it next to the back door, ready to carry it down to the spring house where it would cool throughout the day.

"Men. Men other than John." Aster wiped her hands on the dish towel and tried to come up with a rational explanation. "I've never been with anyone but John. We started courting when I was fifteen and he was seventeen. I've never kissed another man, never even held hands with anyone else but him. We got married when I was seventeen, and I've never been . . . drawn to another man until . . . "

Sally's face cleared with understanding. "You liked this man last night, but—?"

"He's just too sure of himself. He said all the right things, as if he'd practiced them a hundred times with other women. He knew just the right way to hold me, how to smile, how to look into my eyes."

"So? What's wrong with that? I'd take that over a man who stumbles over his own feet. Lord knows there's enough of those around."

Aster stared out the window without seeing the gloriously beautiful Missouri hills blanketed in autumn colors. "John was gentle," she said, almost to herself. "So loving, so caring."

"But John is gone," Sally said softly. "It's time you laid him to rest."

"I can't."

"You can," Sally said firmly. "But you've got to try. Do you want to spend the rest of your life alone?"

"No." The thought of that made Aster ache with loneliness.

"Then you've got to change. Look what happened when you spruced up and got around people. You attracted the most handsome man in the whole room!"

"But—"

"Don't 'but' me, sister mine. All you've got to do is bait the hook and the fish will come snapping at your heels."

Aster almost laughed at the vision those words conjured. "I can't think of a single man within fifty miles I'd want to 'hook.'" Of that she was certain, since she'd known most of them from when she was a girl.

"How about Mr. Gordon?"

"He's a traveling salesman."

"Don't say that like it's a nasty word. He's making a living. A good one too, I'll warrant." Sally leaned against the cabinet so she could look at Aster. "You're not getting any younger. Unless you want all these young girls of seventeen and eighteen catching the few eligible bachelors around here, you've got to dress up, use your feminine wiles, flirt a little."

"That's easy for you. You've never had any trouble flirting with men. Why, the moment you came back they were flocking to the front door like flies to watermelon."

"And why was that? Because I pride myself on looking good. You've got to do your hair, dress pretty, smile more often, talk. Men are people, Aster. They want the same things you want. A home, family . . . "

"Babies. Have you forgotten? I can't have babies."

"Don't you think some man will understand that?

Do you think that's all they want? Babies? Haven't had a one speak to me of it yet!"

Aster had to smile.

"There now. That's better."

Sally grasped her shoulders and turned her around to face her. "You're a beautiful woman, Aster Elizabeth Harris. Don't let yourself shrivel up before your time. Listen to me for once."

That evening after her chores, Aster wandered outside to escape the hot kitchen. Sally had been baking all afternoon, and the room was like an oven.

It was that intangible time between daylight and dark when the farm was settling down for the day. The smell of woodsmoke hung in the air; cows dotted the pasture as they grazed after milking. In the west, a glorious full harvest moon was just rising.

She wandered at the edge of the woods that flanked the east side of the farmhouse behind the garden. As she walked she picked the last of the summer flowers, thinking that they would look pretty on the supper table—snapdragons, marigolds, wild sage. For years there had been a strip of sunflowers on this side of the garden, their blooms full and inviting, their seeds feeding the birds through the long winter.

Every evening after supper, hand and hand, John and she had walked until dark, talking about their future. They'd had big plans: to clear more fields, build a second barn, put shutters on the old two-story house that her parents had built not long after they'd married.

Tears stung her eyes and she blinked them away. John had been her only love. She'd expected to grow old with him. They'd been deeply in love and shared every-

thing. She'd been just a girl when they'd married at the
old church down the road, and in his arms she'd
become a woman. Their marriage had been strong and
secure. Even when they'd had to accept that there
would be no babies, John had been gentle. Each month
she'd cried tears of bitter disappointment, but he'd reas-
sured her that though he was as disappointed as she, it
didn't change his love for her.

She'd loved him more than life itself, and he'd
been taken from her far too soon. She'd been alone for
two years, and the rest of her life stretched long and
empty ahead of her.

Sally was right. John was gone. And he wouldn't
want her to be alone. A home, with a loving husband,
was her dream, a dream she longed to fulfill again. But
with the right man. A man who would love and cherish
her as John had. A man she could love and trust, build
a future with. A man who would accept her inability to
give him a child.

As Aster dusted the cellar shelves, she took stock of all
that she and Sally had accomplished. The pumpkins
were harvested, peeled, cooked to a pulp, and canned
along with the squash. Their lively color stood out
among the green beans, peas, tomatoes, apple butter,
and peaches.

Baskets of apples and dried corn were ready to
sustain Aster and Sally through the winter. Cured
hams and bacon hung from the rafters of the smokehouse, and Aster sighed with contentment. It had been
a good year. A prosperous year.

Aster left the cellar and returned to the house. She
stood at the front window, taking a break from her fall
cleaning, when she noticed a covered wagon coming

down the road. It had been a long time since a tinker had come their way, and she was curious about his wares.

"Sally. A tinker's coming!"

"Wonderful!" Sally's voice floated from upstairs. "I need some lace and ribbons for my new dress."

A man in a fine brown suit jumped nimbly from the wagon seat. When the sun shone on his straw-colored hair, Aster recognized him at once. Dane Gordon!

"It's been a long time since we've had a tinker come by," Sally said, entering the room. "I wonder if he'll make this a regular route."

Dane was coming toward the house. Aster didn't want to see him, not now, and especially not looking like this. Her hair was a mess and her dress was a faded green that was far too tight in the bust.

"You go see if there's anything we need," she urged.

Sally peered out the window. "Why, it's that fellow you were dancing with. Dane Gordon, right?"

"Yes," she hissed, "and I don't want him to see me."

"Well, I don't blame you." Sally cast a critical eye her way. "I wouldn't let the undertaker see me looking like that, much less a man like Dane Gordon. I'll stall him while you run upstairs, comb your hair, and change into a decent dress. Then you come outside like you've just noticed he's here."

"I will not!"

"And why not?" Sally said crossly. "He's clearly interested in you. It was as plain as the nose on your face the night of the dance. And now he's here, by plan or God's providence—it doesn't matter which. You've got to take advantage of it either way. Now get going!"

"I'm not changing my dress. And—I just—I just can't think of anything we need."

"Nonsense, buy anything! Go on." Sally shooed Aster with her apron flap. "Hurry up! I can't keep him here for hours!"

Realizing that Sally wasn't going to relent, and that she'd just as quickly embarrass her in front of Dane as not, Aster hurried upstairs. She heard Sally open the front door and speak to Dane, but then the words were lost as the door closed behind them. Oh, she wouldn't put it past Sally to tell Dane she was changing. She'd have to do it quickly and get down there before Sally made a complete fool of her.

Grabbing a powder blue dress off a hook in her closet, she pulled it over her head, then seized her brush and quickly ran it through her hair. Reflected in the mirror, her face was flushed with an excitement she tried to deny, and her eyes were bright with an anticipation she didn't want to feel.

Still, she practically ran down the stairs, pausing at the door to gather her wits before casually stepping out on the front porch.

"Oh, here she is now," Sally said. "Wasn't that blue ribbon you wanted, Aster?"

Bless you, she said silently, glad that Sally had had at least a moment of sanity.

"Yes, blue." Aster smiled timidly at Dane.

"While you look," Sally said, "I'll get Mr. Gordon a cool glass of water." She bestowed a triumphant look upon Aster as she returned to the house, ignoring Aster's warning glare.

"Well, well, if it isn't our disappearing princess," Dane said softly. "Where did you go the other night?"

"I wasn't feeling well," Aster lied, knowing he'd recognize it as one.

"I missed you. When you left, the life went out of

the party." His eyes skimmed over her in frank appraisal. "I like your hair loose. It becomes you."

"I'm a farm woman, Mr. Gordon, not the belle of the ball. I'd like to see some ribbons, if you don't mind."

She was being short with him, but it seemed some demon had invaded her tongue. Because she didn't know *how* to flirt with men, everything she said came out caustic—the very thing Sally had warned her against.

Dane reached into the back of the wagon and brought out a flat wooden box. When he opened it, carefully folded ribbons in bright and inviting hues of every color caught the sunlight.

"You were the 'belle' the other night."

"I like that blue there."

"And I liked dancing with you. It's been a long time since I enjoyed an evening so much."

His charming blarney brought a rush of heat to her face. "I'll take a yard of that, and I'd like to see some skillets, please."

He unhooked three cast-iron skillets of various sizes from a rack attached to the side of the wagon and arranged them on the open tailgate.

"I was looking forward to having a cup of punch, and learning more about you, but when I came back you were gone."

"I'll take that eight-inch size, please."

Unhooking the skillet, he grinned. "I'll have to say, Miss Aster with the bright red hair, thinking about you kept me awake most of the night."

"And three of those wooden spoons there."

"I thought about how all that glorious red hair glowed in the lamplight, and how your eyes were full of question—"

"Mr. Gordon, you're much too forward."

"That I am. You're a beautiful woman. I enjoyed dancing with you. I'm hoping to convince you to let me come by to see you."

She cast a skeptical look at him and he smiled.

"Why do you look at me as if I've lost my mind?" he asked.

"Because you have. I'm a farm woman. I milk cows and gather eggs and work the fields. I don't have time for dances and such."

"Ah, what a waste. Even a 'farm woman' should make time for fun," he teased.

As he spoke he reached inside the wagon and drew out a long, narrow box. "I have something to show you. Something that reminded me of you the moment I saw it."

He opened the box and Aster's breath caught. Lying against a black background was a gold necklace with green stones that captured the late-afternoon sun. The exquisite piece of jewelry glowed with warmth.

"The stones are the exact color as your eyes. I'd like for you to have it."

As if a thief had stolen her mind, she couldn't think of anything to say. Sally would have had some cute, clever retort, and they would have had a good laugh, but Aster's mind was a complete blank.

"I—I can't buy that. I haven't the money—"

His features sobered. "I didn't intend for you to buy it. It's a gift—for a beautiful woman. Something to remember the dances we had together."

"Please—" she stammered. "I can't—I can't accept that. It's too much."

He acknowledged her refusal by closing the box and returning it to its place in the wagon.

"Then if you won't accept my gift, will you ride

with me awhile and direct me to some of the outlying farms? I'm not familiar with this area, but I plan to be this way every two weeks."

She made herself meet his searching gaze and wished she could be as glib and natural as Sally.

"No, I can't go with you. I have chores to do." Noting the disappointment on his face, she relented slightly. "I could—I could draw you a map, if that would help."

He smiled. "It surely would, Aster with the glorious red hair."

He handed her a small pad and pencil, and she quickly sketched directions to three farms that were off the main road between her farm and Branson.

She handed the map to him, imperceptibly flinching as his hand brushed hers. "You shouldn't have any trouble."

"Thank you, though I would rather have had you beside me for the afternoon."

She met his gaze again. "You are far too silver-tongued, Mr. Gordon."

"I'm a man taken with a charming and lovely woman. The sight brings poetry to my lips."

He bent, lightly brushing her lips with his, taking her totally by surprise. But when he kissed her again and his lips lingered for a moment, her mouth clung to his for just the briefest of moments. She was rewarded with his surprised look and warm smile as he brushed her cheek with the backs of his fingers.

"Yes, beautiful lady, you put poetry in my mouth," he whispered.

She stepped back to create some distance between them. This was much too sudden, much too overwhelming, and he was, after all, a mere stranger.

"I'll be back in two weeks. May I bring you something? A bolt of cloth? A piano?"

She had to smile at his absurdity. A piano, indeed.

"A bolt of wool for a winter dress."

"In a rich green, pine-tree green. You will be beautiful in it."

"How you do go on, Mr. Gordon."

He leaned closer. "And how you do tempt me, Aster Harris."

With that, he leaped to the wagon seat and slapped the reins against his horses' rumps.

Aster stood, holding the yard of blue ribbon, her wooden spoon, and her skillet, as he drove off down the road.

Just before she turned to go to the house, he leaned out and waved back at her.

"I'll be back in two weeks and we'll have that ride!"

It was only after he'd disappeared from sight around the bend that she realized she hadn't paid him.

3

Sally was nowhere in sight when Aster came back into the house.

"Sally?"

"Up here," Sally's voice came from upstairs. When Aster went into her bedroom, she found Sally standing at the window.

"What are you doing up here?"

"Getting a better look at what's going on."

"You were *spying* on me?"

"I didn't see him kiss you," she denied.

"You *were* being nosy!"

Smiling, Sally straightened the curtain that she'd held back to look down on the road in front of the house.

"Was he good?"

Aster's face flamed. "I refuse to dignify that with an answer."

"Oh, he was, wasn't he! I can see it in your face! Is he an open-mouthed or close-mouthed kisser?"

Aster was practically sputtering now. "I— Well, of all the gall. I—"

"Oh, forget it. Open-mouthed, I think." Sally sighed.

"So, what did he have to say?"

"A lot of nonsense," Aster said with disgust.

"What kind of nonsense? Sweet talk?" Sally almost crowed. "I'll bet he did! Why, he's taken with you, Aster. How wonderful!"

"I don't know how 'wonderful' it is. There probably isn't an ounce of substance to him."

"You're not buying a milk cow, Aster."

"I'm certainly not buying anything *he* said."

"And what did he say that was so bad?"

"He tried to give me a necklace."

"A necklace! What kind of necklace?"

Sally was obviously intrigued, and Aster wished she hadn't said anything.

"A gold one, with green stones. He blathered something about the stones matching my eyes."

"Oh," Sally said with a grin. "He's a sweet talker. Give me a sweet-talkin' man over a shy one any day. A man who knows how to say the right things." She winked. "And knows what to do after the talking's all done."

Aster flushed with embarrassment.

"Well?" Sally asked.

"Well what?"

"When's he coming back?"

Aster shrugged, trying to act nonchalant, though her heart raced when she remembered Dane leaning near and talking to her in that soft, intimate way.

"Oh, two weeks, I think he said. He's bringing me a bolt of wool to make a dress." Aster hesitated, not sure she should tell Sally about Dane's invitation. "He wants me to show him the farms off the main road."

"Now we're getting somewhere! Let's see, what would be suitable attire for an afternoon, show-that-good-looking-man-a-farm, ride?"

Suddenly Sally was throwing open the doors of the armoire and tossing dresses, skirts, and blouses across the big double bed in which Aster and John had slept during their short married life.

"Sally! Have you lost your mind? Stop that!" Aster grabbed for a skirt as it went whizzing by. "Put my clothes back."

"Aster, I don't know how you ever expect to catch a man. Why, these sad excuses for dresses have been outdated for years! And they're all brown!"

"They are not." Aster snatched a skirt from Sally's hands. "My clothes are lovely. Why, half of them belonged to Grandmother. There is no reason to throw them away just because—"

"Because a man finally looked at you?" Sally was plainly exasperated. "Mourning time is over," she announced. "You're a young woman, a woman with a man interested in her. Now, for an afternoon—"

"I can't go with Dane Gordon!" Aster exclaimed. "It's one thing to dance with a man in public, but to go gallivanting with him all over creation? That's not proper. What will the women think when they see me with a complete stranger when we visit their farms?"

"Gossip is the curse of the idle brain. You can't worry about what someone might say—or think, for that matter! Besides, riding beside him in a wagon doesn't mean you have to marry him!" Sally picked up another dress and examined it critically before tossing it aside onto a growing pile of rejected garments. "Anyway, it's only a mild flirtation. Lord knows you could use the practice."

Aster's cheeks burned. Sally could be so blunt!

Still, Aster supposed it wouldn't hurt to have a new dress.

But only one, and certainly not because a silly afternoon ride with Dane Gordon warranted it.

Dane sat on the wagon seat, idly daydreaming. The reins were slack in his hands as he allowed the horses to plod down the road at their own speed.

"Aster," he murmured aloud, testing her name on the wind. Like her name, she was tall and slim and as lovely as any woman he'd ever met. Her hair shone like copper, and her green eyes had been full of indignation and wonder when he teased her.

Though she called herself a farm woman, he sensed that she was more than that. She was a homey kind of woman. The kind who made even the most humble dwelling warm and inviting.

Sitting up straighter, he tightened the reins. What did he know about warmth? Or about homes, for that matter? Orphaned at two years old, he'd lived most of his life at St. Mary Catherine's Home for Foundling Children.

Over the years there had been a few couples who had thought about adopting him. They'd come and looked, but in the end somebody else had always been chosen. Consequently, he'd stayed at St. Mary's until he was seventeen.

He'd had a variety of jobs to keep his head above water—a dock worker on the East Coast, a stock boy in California, a stableboy in Arizona. But since he'd wandered into Missouri five years ago, he'd been selling goods from his wagon.

It was a life that fit him, he supposed. Glancing at the finely cultivated fields around him, he knew farming didn't appeal to him. No, he had a roving spirit, liked seeing different things, different people. His insatiable curiosity about what was just over the next hill had taken him across the country and back.

He enjoyed sleeping in a different bed every night, and if there was a woman willing to share it, so much the better.

He wasn't a settling-down kind of man, though he'd met plenty of women who'd tried to change his mind.

Now, Aster Harris might make him think twice. There was something about that woman that drew him. Her shyness, the uncertainty he'd seen in her eyes when he'd bent close to her. He'd wanted to know more about her, but she'd bolted from the dance like a scalded cat.

The morning following the dance, the talk over breakfast at Sterling's Boarding House in Branson, where he'd taken a room, had been about the previous night. He'd taken a chance and asked about Aster. When he'd learned she was a widow, he couldn't deny he had been pleased to know she was available. Furthermore, he'd been told that with her looks and fine womanly figure, more than one of the local bachelors had beaten a path to her door, only to be politely rebuffed. Yet rumor had it she was ripe for a new man.

A spurt of jealousy went through him. Well, what was that? he thought. Him jealous over a woman? Ha. It was the other way around. Women, drawn to his out-going nature, had always vied for his attention. The sisters at St. Mary's always said he was a charmer, sure to break a woman's heart. Well, he could safely say he'd never broken any woman's heart because he never stayed around long enough. His gift of gab and winning smile had won him many a sale, and made him a fine living, but he wasn't hooking up with any woman. Not him.

A picture of Aster Harris flashed through his mind.

Are you crazy? he chastised himself. She's a stayin' kind of woman, and you're a ramblin' kind of man. The two just don't go together.

"Are you seriously going to wear that old rag?"

Aster stopped halfway down the stairs and stared at her indignant sister. First, it was unusual for Sally to be awake and downstairs before she was. Secondly, Sally had a determined look on her face, especially for so early in the morning.

"What?" Aster asked.

"That dress. You're not seriously going to *wear* it, are you?"

"No, Sally, I'm going to eat it for breakfast."

"It's not even fit for that. You just march back up those stairs and put on that russet cotton with the tatted lace at the neck that we bought last week. It'll be perfect."

Aster frowned. "For what? The cows and chickens don't care what I'm wearing."

"But Mr. Gordon will."

"Dane Gordon?"

"Today's the day he's due to come by, isn't it?"

Aster continued down the stairs, sweeping past Sally on her way to the kitchen.

"He may be, but that doesn't mean I'm going to see him."

Sally followed her. "And why not?"

With a butcher knife, Aster sliced bacon with sure, swift strokes. "Do I need a reason?"

"For me you do."

"Then it's because . . . there's no point in it."

"No point? No point!" Sally threw her hands up in her typical dramatic fashion. "Does there always have to be a point to everything you do? Couldn't you just spend some time with him because you want to?"

Aster laid the bacon in the heated iron skillet. Sally was tenacious, all right. "Why would I want to?"

"Because—he's—a—good-looking—man," Sally enunciated carefully as if she were speaking to a simpleton. "Because—he—likes—you. Because—you—need—things—in—your—life—besides—this—farm!"

"Things meaning men?"

"Meaning something more than this!"

"I have you," Aster said dismissively.

"You won't forever. I, unlike you, *want* a man in my life."

"I've had my man," Aster said quietly. "You don't love the farm like I do, Sally. This land, this house—they're my life."

"Fine, but share it with someone, a man to work the ground with you, to fill this house with—"

Aster turned to her. "With babies?"

"I didn't mean—"

"That's exactly what you meant. This house was made for children. You don't know how I dreamed of having those bedrooms filled with sleeping babies, to hear their footsteps on the stairs, to hear their laughter. But it's not going to happen. Men want families, and I can't give a man that."

"Perhaps if you and John had consulted a doctor—"

"No. John didn't want that. It's me, it wasn't John."

"I've told you again and again men don't marry for the sole purpose of having children. They marry the woman they love and want to spend the rest of their lives—"

"Even though they lose that life in some senseless fire. Sorry, but I've had enough disappointment and pain to last me a lifetime, thank you. I'm not anxious to go through it again. You go with Dane Gordon. You know where everyone lives."

Aster was tired of arguing. She was sick of hearing about "living again" or "finding love again," Sally's most popular themes of late.

"That was just an excuse Dane used, Aster, and you know it. He wants to see you again, spend time with *you*. What's wrong with that?"

"It's wrong if he expects anything else!"

She turned the bacon, and buttered the bread to put in the oven to toast.

"How do you know what he expects?"

How did she know? Because of the way her heart raced when he touched her, because when she looked up into his laughing hazel eyes, feelings came alive in her that she had thought were dead.

"Do you want eggs with your bacon this morning?"

"Ohhh," Sally grumbled. "You drive me crazy!"

"Well, then I'll just go out and take care of the stock while you eat. And when I come back I don't want to hear any more about Dane Gordon."

Yet that afternoon she donned the russet dress and brushed her hair, having convinced herself that she just wanted to look nice for a change.

She was sitting on the front porch, rocking and appreciating the glorious Indian summer weather, when she heard his wagon coming down the road.

Her pulse tripped double time and her palms grew damp. Stop it! she chastised herself. He was just a traveling salesman, for heaven's sake.

But when Dane drew the team to a halt in front of the house, she crossed the brown grass toward him.

"Aster, my love! Have you missed me?" He leapt agilely off the wagon seat, walking to meet her.

"I haven't said I'm going with you," she warned, realizing she hadn't yet said she wouldn't.

He grinned. "I ordered that material for you. I couldn't get it right away, but I'll bring it next time."

She cocked her brow. "And when might that be?"

"Exactly two weeks from today, ma'am. Not a moment longer. I couldn't bear the wait."

"What do I owe you from the last time?"

His eyes danced with merriment. "A kiss?"

The man was impossible. He was a charming scourge with an infectious smile that could turn any woman's head. "In dollars."

"One dollar and sixty-five cents."

She pulled a small leather purse from her pocket and counted out the money.

"Thank you. Is your sister here?"

She was a bit taken aback. "Sally? Why, yes. Why?"

"Tell her we won't be back until sundown."

"Oh." Relief flooded her. For a moment she thought he had come to see Sally.

Dane just stared at her. "We'll ride a bit, you'll show me some of the farms I don't know, tell me about the people, and we'll enjoy one of the last warm days of autumn," he coaxed. "I'll have you home in plenty of time to do the milkin'."

She wasn't at all sure she was doing the right thing. Not sure at all. "All right, I'll tell her."

He watched her walk quickly toward the house, noticing her russet skirt swaying around her ankles, her hips flowing from a waist so narrow he could span it with both hands.

"Fool," he muttered aloud.

She was a winsome woman he'd spend time with, then he'd drive away until spring. Maybe he'd be back this way, maybe not. More than likely not.

"I'm ready," Aster said.

Dane dragged his thoughts back to the present. "So am I."

Helping her aboard the wagon, he made her comfortable. Aster realized she was so nervous she could hardly breathe. What was wrong with her? She'd never been this way around John.

A nagging voice reminded her that this wasn't John. This was a man about whom she knew almost nothing.

"Tell me, where are you from?" she managed.

He slapped the reins lightly, and the wagon rattled onto the lane.

"All over. I spent some time in Boston, in Maryland, Virginia, Kentucky, Tennessee, California, and finally came to Missouri."

"So many places. What were they like?" She'd never been more than ten miles from Branson.

"Cold winters in Boston, rolling fields in Maryland and Virginia, brown tobacco in Kentucky."

"I've never lived anywhere but here."

He glanced at her. "Well, I've never lived anywhere more than a year."

"Really?" She couldn't imagine such a life. "Do you like moving around so much?"

She couldn't conceive of not being at home, sitting at her own table each night, sleeping in her own bed and waking to the raspy sound of Old Ned the rooster who ruled the barnyard.

"Liking it has nothing to do with anything. It's what I do, how I earn my living." He shrugged. "I guess I like it. It's served me well."

"What about family?"

"Don't have one. Never really thought about having one."

He looked at her out of the corner of his eye. "Someone mentioned you're a widow."

"Yes. John, my husband, died while helping a neighbor put out a barn fire."

"No children?"

"No." Her hands twisted nervously in her lap. She might as well tell him the truth and get it over with. If he wanted to marry and have a family, he should know right away that he was wasting his time on her. "I—I couldn't give him children."

"Lots of people don't have children and they seem perfectly content."

"I wasn't. I wanted babies," she said in a rush, then was embarrassed at what she was telling a man who was almost a stranger.

"But that didn't interfere with your marriage, did it? I imagine that would make a man and a woman closer, if anything."

"No, it didn't make any difference in the way John and I felt about each other, but I surely did want them."

She studied his profile. A broad forehead, crisp straw-colored hair that covered the tips of his ears and lay against his neck, that straight nose and those curved lips made him a very handsome man. The kind of man any woman would be proud to claim.

"Do you want to marry and have children?"

"No, ma'am." He slapped the reins lightly. "Children are for people who have time and money for them. I've got neither."

That put her mind to rest—temporarily. Perhaps it was only a simple, afternoon outing. One that wouldn't upset her comfortable life.

"That's real pretty."

She looked at him. "What?"

"Your smile. I want to see it more often."

She looked away, but his words sang in her heart. He liked her smile.

A warmth that had been missing for a long time settled around her heart.

4

They spent the afternoon visiting neighboring farms. Aster chatted with the women, held the babies, and charmed the little children while Dane showed his wares. The women told him they were delighted to have a mercantile wagon come to them, since they were too busy to make trips into Branson. Even if they could, they'd have to take their children, which would shorten the trip out of necessity.

If they had any questions about Aster's accompanying him, they didn't voice them, though Dane did catch a glint of curiosity from the men.

The new orders, combined with those from the stores in town, and a nice order from the woman running the boardinghouse, had made this a profitable trip. By tomorrow he'd be on his way back to Kansas City to arrange shipment of the larger orders.

As happy as he was with that prospect, the time

spent with Aster also had proved fruitful. Today he'd seen a far different Aster. She wasn't shy with the women. She'd laughed, sharing canning stories, boasting of how many jars of this or that she'd put up this fall. For the first time, he'd shared in her laughter, seen her eyes dance with merriment.

Seeing her like that made him wonder what unruly passions she kept deeply hidden. An ache began in his groin and burgeoned. He'd be heading back to Kansas City tomorrow, but right now he had a powerful urge to make love to Aster Harris.

He wanted to hold her until the sadness was gone from her eyes, until his was the only name that escaped her lips.

Riding beside him, Aster studied Dane from the corner of her eye. She was aware he was watching her. What was it Sally had said? Flirt with him. Make him aware you're a woman. Sally just hadn't said exactly how to do it.

Well, at least Aster had "poufed" her hair as Sally had advised, and worn the dress she had laid out for her. She had to admit that the russet dress was more flattering than her usual uninspiring drab brown.

She glanced at Dane sideways. She could look "deep into his eyes," as Sally had stressed in her how-to-catch-a-man plan.

From there she supposed she could ever so lightly touch his arm, laughing up at him and babbling inanely about the dance, the weather—anything to get his attention.

Well, she thought, drawing a deep breath, she guessed she could give it a try.

During the following few awkward, strained minutes, she laughed, looked deep into his eyes, and touched his arm more than necessary, all the while commenting about the weather and the dance, and in general acting as if she didn't have good sense.

Dane, aside from a few curious sidelong glances, kept up his end of the conversation.

Goodness, Aster agonized when she realized she was exhausted from her incessant chatter. She didn't know why she listened to Sally anyway. Her advice was foolish. Acting like a simpering ninny wasn't like Aster at all. Wasn't mutual attraction, love, supposed to be a spontaneous thing?

Aster reached up to repin her hair, and Dane's eyes were drawn by the pull of her bodice against her full breasts. She was ripe, like the fruit hanging heavy on the trees lining the road, and the ache in his groin grew more insistent.

The orange ball of a sun was slipping below the horizon when he turned the horses into the Harris lane.

"Thanks for giving me a hand." He looked at her and smiled. "It helped ease the women's fears that I had something more in mind than selling ribbons and skillets. Farm women are a great deal more wary of strangers than city women."

"Women alone find it necessary to be wary."

He pulled the wagon to a halt in the shade of a brilliant scarlet maple. When he turned to her, she looked away nervously.

His fingers brushed her cheek, then followed her stubborn jaw line.

"Do they?" he asked.

Her skin was soft, her lips inviting. The mix of anticipation and wariness in her eyes was so appealing that he was compelled to lean forward and touch his lips to hers.

"You are so lovely, Aster Harris," he whispered. "How you do sorely tempt a man."

He had wanted to hold her again since the night of the dance. She'd felt so right in his arms, so perfect.

His lips were warm and well-tutored when they closed hungrily over hers. For one glorious moment she was tempted to surrender. As his hand slipped to her breast, sanity returned and she jerked away.

"Mr. Gordon!" she gasped, her back to him.

Gently turning her to face him, he touched the tips of his fingers against her mouth, where his lips had been only a moment before. "Aster?"

"Don't touch me."

"Aster, don't be afraid." He grasped her upper arms and tried to draw her to him, but she pulled away.

"Stop it!"

"Why? You want me to hold you as much as I need to hold you. Don't be afraid," he urged softly.

"Stop . . . it's too soon . . ."

"Aster . . ."

Before she was aware of what she was doing, she slapped the side of his face. She put her hands to her mouth, appalled. She had never struck anyone in her life.

He blinked in surprise, and then anger slowly crept across his face. "You act like an outraged virgin," he said, grabbing up the reins and slapping them briskly.

"I told you to stop!" she sputtered. "I don't appreciate being . . . pawed!"

"Pawed?"

"Yes, pawed! Now take me home, Dane Gordon, and don't come back!" She'd become a gnarled old woman before she ever listened to Sally again!

"You don't need to be worryin' about that, Widow Harris. I'd just as soon visit a polecat!"

"Widow Harris!" she bristled. Tossing her head, she refused to look at him. "Take me home. Right now!"

"Yes, ma'am! I'd be happy to!"

He slapped the reins again, hurrying the two bays along. Aster saw the firm set to his jaw, his tight grip on the reins. He was angry with her, but she didn't care. Who did he think he was? Why, she was barely out of mourning!

Why had she listened to Sally? Why hadn't she trusted her own instincts?

Dane drew the horses to a dust-boiling halt in front of the farmhouse. Before he could get down to help her, Aster had scrambled down from the wagon seat and was headed toward the house in a fast stride.

"Afternoon, Widow Harris," he called, tipping his hat.

Damned woman. Flirting with him like a tart, then practically accusing him of attacking her in plain daylight. Why, he had been on his best behavior! Damned woman.

He slapped the reins and urged the horses forward, never looking back.

Aster slammed the door behind her, leaning against it to catch her breath.

"Goodness, what's all the noise?" Sally's face

brightened when she saw that it was Aster. "Ohhh, good! Tell me everything that happened."

"There's nothing to tell," Aster said, pushing away from the door, "unless you mean almost being seduced on a wagon seat in plain sight of God and everyone."

"Seduced? Oooh, my, he is a cad, isn't he?" Sally grinned.

"*You* go riding with him next time. Frankly, I wish I'd never heard of Dane Gordon. And"—she pointed a finger at Sally—"from now on you just keep your words of wisdom about catching a man to yourself."

Sally's eyes widened. "Did he really try to seduce you?"

"Yes," Aster snapped.

"A kiss?"

"And more!"

"Did you kiss him back?"

"Yes," she snapped again, "but only until my sanity returned."

"Then what's all the fuss?"

"He—he tried to—Oh, it's just too embarrassing." The way he'd touched her breast? The impertinent—tinker!

Sally laughed. "Oh, he tried to—Well, it sounds to me like he really likes you!"

"Well, I don't like him," Aster said, striding into the kitchen for a drink of water. She was burning up. "And when he comes around again, you tell him I've changed my mind about that green wool!"

"You don't want it?" Sally asked, trailing her into the kitchen.

"Sally, he tried to—to have his way with me! Right there in the wagon! It's my own fault. If I hadn't been trying out those silly suggestions of yours, it wouldn't have happened!"

"That's true. It wouldn't have happened. And you wouldn't be so blamed overheated!"

Taking a long drink, Aster set the glass on the table. "I'm embarrassed, Sally. Can't you tell the difference between passion and embarrassment!"

"Hmmm, embarrassed, huh? Are you sure you just haven't smothered your emotions for so long you don't know how to act around a man?"

"I should say not! I know how to act around a man, I just don't happen to want to act that way with Dane Gordon."

"And why not? He's handsome, charming, obviously doing well in his business. He'd be a fine catch for any woman."

"Not for me." Aster stared out the window, across the fields that were plowed and ready for planting winter wheat. "Not for me."

"Nonsense. You hardly know him."

"I know enough about him to know he's wrong for me."

"Well, let's look at this logically. What *do* you like about him?"

As soon as Aster calmed down, she considered the question. "Well, he's funny, and he can charm birds out of the trees."

"And you like how he looks," Sally helped.

The corners of Aster's mouth turned up in spite of herself. "Yes, I like how he looks." He was a handsome devil.

"Then what's not to like about him?"

"He hates farming. Thinks children are a nuisance. He likes moving around, living in hotels and boarding-houses," Aster ticked off automatically. "All the things I love, he dislikes intensely. He has no intention of ever settling down. Never were there two more opposite people."

"A woman can change a man's mind," Sally retorted. "Give him a chance, Aster. You owe it to yourself."

Sally's blithe statement pricked her temper. "If you think Mr. Gordon is so wonderful, you go after him!"

"He's perfect for you, not me! Besides, Philip and I have . . . well, a kind of understanding."

Aster had figured as much the night of the dance. Of course, she approved, for Philip was one of Branson's most upstanding citizens. In fact, now that she thought about it, Philip was a lot like Dane, except that he was settled in a profession and had already purchased a small house.

"You haven't given Dane a chance. It isn't fair to rule him out just because of one silly little misunderstanding."

Aster moved her glass to the sink. "Don't worry, he won't be back."

"He has to bring the cloth you ordered."

"He won't. Not after the way I acted." Aster's cheeks warmed at the thought of her overreaction.

"Yes, he will, in two weeks. When he brings it, we'll invite him to dinner."

Aster spun around. "To dinner!"

"I've never met a man who could turn down a home-cooked meal, especially a man who lives in hotels and boardinghouses."

"I wouldn't dream of inviting him to dinner."

"Well, that's what we're going to do. I saw a new recipe in one of those fancy ladies' magazines in Brown's Mercantile. We'll try it out on him."

"That's ludicrous!"

"No," Sally mused. "I believe it was Mexican. Anyway, we'll invite him. You'll see, he'll jump at the chance."

"Absolutely not!"

"Then I'll invite him myself."

"Sally, if you persist in this, you have to promise me you'll be there the entire evening. No running out to see Philip, no going to bed because you're tired."

"Of course."

"Do you swear?"

"Not often, but I feel like it a lot lately. With you." Sally smiled.

The next two weeks flew. Besides the usual chores on the farm, Sally insisted that they make two new dresses for the night Dane came to dinner—assuming that he would.

"I still think you should wear the dress you were married in. It's so beautiful."

"Wear my wedding dress!"

"It's the prettiest dress you own."

"Never. I wore that for John. My wedding dress? You must be out of your mind."

"Well, then, this plain old blue one should do." Sally flicked the material Aster was sewing.

"It's not plain, and it certainly will do. I don't want him thinking I've set my cap for him."

"Well, you should," Sally murmured.

Aster's eyes narrowed. "What?"

"What do you plan to cook for dinner?"

"I don't know," Aster muttered around the pins in her mouth. She adjusted the turn of the hem. "Baked ham, I suppose."

"Ham!" Sally protested. "That's just ducky." She tossed aside the dress she was sewing, and picked up a ladies' magazine she'd bought at Brown's Mercantile that morning. "Here's that recipe for a Mexican dish I've been wanting to try. Cornbread should go well with it. Then . . . lemon meringue pie. You make the best lemon meringue pie I've ever had. I bet Mr. Gordon will be in the marrying mood once he gets a taste of it."

"Mexican," Aster groaned. She hated to try a new recipe on company.

"Oh, he'll love it. He's been everywhere, hasn't he? He won't be satisfied with ham and gravy. We do want to impress him, don't we?"

"You do, not me."

"All right, I'll make the pie if you want."

Sally's lemon meringue left an awful lot to be desired.

"No, no, your crust tastes like sawdust. I'll make the pie."

"I think we ought to use Granny's china."

"Sally, you're making too much of this."

"He's our guest," Sally insisted. "And I think the cream-colored linen tablecloth. Flowers! Candles!" She ran over to search the cupboards. "Candles on the table. Perfect," she exclaimed, holding up two new ones.

"Candles? It will still be daylight."

"Who cares? Candles will make the table look elegant. We're trying to get him to think about settling down, aren't we?"

"No, *we're* wasting our time. A mere dinner won't change him." He'd made it perfectly clear that he liked his roving ways.

"I don't know," Sally said, concentrating on her sewing now. "Many a man has offered a ring after a fine Mexican dinner."

Aster turned to shoot her a dirty look. *Mexican* dinner?

Good heavens.

5

During the next few days, Aster awaited Dane's return, vacillating between thinking Sally had lost her mind, and telling herself that Sally had so much more experience with men that she must know what she was doing.

Certainly none of the women in the community would know anything about preparing a fancy meal. A fancy *Mexican* meal. They fed their families and harvest hands common fare, giving no thought to fine crystal and Granny's china. They would laugh at the notion of putting candles on the table unless they'd run out of lamp oil.

She and Sally made more trips to town than they normally did in two months. There was always something more they needed for the dinner, or another bit of lace or ribbon for a dress.

On the day of Dane's expected arrival, Aster felt as if she'd harvested a whole field by herself. She had to admit, though, that she felt more alive than she had in a long time. She had a purpose again. Thinking about clothes, whether to wear her hair up or down, planning a meal for a man. It was all, well, exciting. Her only real concern was Dane's reaction to all this effort, considering she'd slapped his face.

"It's time to take a bath and get dressed," Sally reminded her at three o'clock.

"What I need is a long nap," Aster complained. She was exhausted by all the goings-on.

Sally ignored her grumblings. "Wash your hair and let it dry naturally. We'll need the extra curl for the style I've planned."

Sighing, Aster set her sewing aside. "I wish I'd never let you talk me into this."

"If you're going to catch a mouse, you've got to bait the trap."

Thinking of Dane as a mouse was almost funny. He was more like the prowling cat and she the mouse.

By the time Aster heard Dane's wagon coming down the road, she was a bundle of nerves.

"I can't do it," she said frantically, running her palms down the skirt of her new blue dress.

"Yes, you can," Sally soothed. "We've put in too much time on this project to back out now."

Aster looked out the window and saw Dane jump down from the wagon seat. His hair gleamed in the late-afternoon sunlight, and when he reached into the wagon, his white linen shirt stretched over his broad, manly shoulders. Tobacco brown gabardine trousers encased his slim hips and strong thighs.

Aster was absolutely certain this evening would be a disaster.

Pulling a brown-wrapped package out of the back

of the wagon, Dane strode toward the house. A knock sounded at the door a moment later.

"You get it," Aster snapped.

"No, you get it," Sally snapped back.

"You get it, or he'll stand there till kingdom come!"

"You are never going to catch a man." Sally left the room and went downstairs.

"Mr. Gordon! How nice to see you," Sally said, opening the door.

"Afternoon, Miss Sally!" Dane craned his neck to see around her shoulder. "Is the Widow Harris in?"

"Yes, she's here." Sally opened the door wider. "Won't you come in?"

"Thank you. I've brought the material your sister ordered. It's a moss green, and will make her a fine garment." He handed her the package.

"I'm sure it's lovely." Sally tilted her head to one side and smiled up at him. "How was your trip?"

"Very nice, thank you."

"You travel so much," she cooed.

"That's my job, ma'am."

"You know, I'll bet a traveler like you would enjoy a home-cooked meal."

Dane looked mildly surprised. "Well, now, I can't recall ever turning one down, Miss Sally."

"Then you *must* stay to supper. Aster has tried a new recipe and I know she would love your opinion!"

As he entered the house, Dane searched the room for Aster, wondering where she was. Hiding, he guessed. Grinning, he thought about her reaction when she found out her sister had just invited him to supper.

"Why don't you take your horses around back to the watering trough?" Sally suggested. "Supper'll be ready soon."

Yet it was Sally again who met him at the door when he'd taken care of his team. "Come in and make yourself comfortable."

"You say your sister's around?" Dane asked. Aster was still nowhere in sight.

"She's in the kitchen, but she knows we're having company. She's thrilled."

Sally ushered him into a cheerful sitting room where a rock fireplace dominated the east wall. Dane could picture the two sisters sitting before a fire on a cold winter night, sewing or reading.

He was surprised at the hominess. Other farm houses he'd visited were functionally practical, plain but serviceable. Aster's home had carpets, bright and cheery wallpaper, doilies on the tables.

Sniffing, he tried to identify the spicy aroma mingling with the scent of wax and furniture oil in the air.

Sally chatted incessantly, talking about this and that, people with whom they had a mutual acquaintance. She was a born vixen, and he enjoyed the repartee. Still, it was Aster who interested him.

"Well, this has been nice," Sally said, "but I should check on supper. Excuse me a moment?"

Dane came to his feet. "Tell Aster I'd be happy to help."

"Certainly not! Why, you just sit right there and relax, Mr. Gordon. Aster wouldn't dream of letting a man turn a hand around this house."

"Yes, ma'am. I'll just wait here." Dane sat back down.

*   *   *

Aster was nervously pacing the kitchen when Sally
sailed through the doorway.

"This is never going to work," Aster agonized.

"Silly, everything is fine." Sally opened the oven
door and peeked in. "Is supper ready?"

"I don't know about that . . . that thing." Aster
gestured to the oven, where the Mexican dish bubbled
away. "It doesn't look right."

"How's it supposed to look?"

"I don't know, Sally! I've never made a Mexican
dish!" Oh, if she only had a ham in the skillet, she
wouldn't be so nervous!

"Relax. You followed the recipe, didn't you?"

"Yes, but—"

"Then don't worry. What could possibly go
wrong?" Closing the oven door, Sally smiled. "He
brought you the green material, and he's asking for
you."

"Nonsense. He's just wants his money and his
supper."

"No, he's—" Sally stopped, casting an appraising
eye over Aster. "Isn't that your wedding dress?"

Aster flushed. So, she'd caved in at the last
minute. The cream satin with lace trimming at the
neck and dropped waist *was* more eye-catching than
the nondescript blue dress.

Sally's eyes softened. "You look really nice."

"Sally," Aster began, her courage failing her
now.

"Hush!" Sally reached out and turned Aster
around to the stove. "It's too late to back out now."

And it was; much too late. Dane was in the sitting
room, patiently waiting to be fed.

*   *   *

"Well," Sally said, breathlessly coming out of the kitchen, Aster on her heels. "I do believe everything is ready. Hope you're good and hungry."

"That I am," Dane said, coming to his feet again. He smiled at Aster, then frowned. Was that a wedding dress she had on? "Evenin', Widow Harris."

Aster nodded coolly, avoiding his eyes. "Tinker Gordon."

The two sisters carried the large serving dish toward the dining room. Trailing behind the women, Dane suddenly stopped, his eyes curiously searching the table. Candles in glass holders, good silver, china, a predominantly large bouquet of marigolds, snapdragons, and fiery-colored sage eclipsing the table.

What was going on here? Realization suddenly dawned on him. He started backing up. "I'm sorry—I didn't know you were having a wedding . . . "

Sally glanced back at him. "Wedding?"

His eyes went to Aster. "I had no idea you were promised."

Aster's face turned the color of a ripe persimmon.

"Oh." Sally laughed. "We're not having a wedding! We eat like this quite often." Hooking her arm through his, she pulled him further into the room. "It's ever so easy to fall into the habit of eating at the kitchen table. One forgets the joy of dining elegantly, wouldn't you agree?"

"You do this often?" His eyes skimmed over Aster.

"Oh, every now and again. Now, you sit here, Mr. Gordon." She indicated a chair at the head of the table. "And, Aster, you sit right here, next to our guest. I'll sit in Papa's chair."

Papa's chair happened to be at the opposite end of the table.

Dane hurried to pull Aster's chair out for her.

"Thank you," she murmured.

Leaning close to her ear, he whispered, "You look mighty fetchin' in that dress. Your husband must have been a proud man."

Straightening, he took his seat, casually unfolding his napkin on his lap.

Sally picked up a dish and peered into the bowl skeptically. "My, my, this does look tasty," she exclaimed.

Dane peered down the long table. "What is it?"

"A *Mexican* dish." Aster's tone dared him to make something of it.

He and Sally slid to the edges of their chairs, trying to get a better look at the smoldering ingredients.

Snatching up the bowl, Aster rammed a spoon into the casserole, grimly dishing it up.

Sally cleared her throat. "Tell me, Mr. Gordon, how long have you been a traveling salesman?" Her eyes nailed Aster, who kept her head down.

"Oh, around five years," he said, watching the play between the two sisters.

As he accepted the basket of bread from Aster, his hand brushed hers briefly. For a moment their eyes met. He smiled, but she looked away.

"I imagine you've seen quite a bit of the country, then."

"My fair share." He picked up a bowl, offering it to Aster. "Corn?" It had been a while since he'd eaten a home-cooked meal, and he found himself anticipating the unexpected pleasure.

"My," Sally exclaimed. "I don't think I'd care to be so unsettled. I prefer having roots. Why, people around here have lived on the same land for generations."

"I like to know what's over the next hill," he said

nicely. He'd made the statement many times, but tonight it had a hollow ring to it. "New people, new places, new things to see. That's the life, ladies."

"I suppose that would be exciting. But haven't you ever thought of settling down, putting down roots?"

"Señora Rosa's Mexican dish, Mr. Gordon?" Aster interrupted, thrusting a plate in front of him.

"Well, doesn't this look . . . interesting." Dane studied the smoking mound on his plate. Señora Rosa must have had a snoot full of tequila when she thought this one up.

Sally hesitated briefly as Aster handed her a plate. "My . . ."

"I followed the recipe!"

"And doesn't it look wonderful! Mmm." Sally picked up her fork, smiling.

Dane convinced himself it couldn't be as bad as it looked. Forking up a large bite, he slipped it into his mouth, nodding and smiling amicably. "Interesting."

The moment the food hit his tongue he knew he was in trouble. Yet he chewed, swallowed, then smiled, and chewed some more. It was like biting into hell. His eyes started watering as the heat in his mouth built.

"Is it all right?" Aster asked expectantly.

Nodding, he loaded his fork again, and took another bite.

Smoke belched from his ears, and his nose was running like White River during a spring gullywasher.

Aster turned to her sister. "Sally?"

Nodding, Sally chewed, tears rolling down her cheeks.

"Well, I must admit I'm not surprised. I thought the recipe called for entirely too much red pepper," Aster mused.

Grabbing his napkin, Dane gagged. Glancing up,

he struggled to breathe. "A tad . . . spicy," he whispered raggedly. "But delicious . . . "

Sally was on her feet immediately, thumping his back, offering him a glass of water. "Are you all right?"

"Yes, ma'am. Just got choked up there for a minute."

He eyed Aster as she quickly tasted the food. Coughing, she jumped up, hitting the table and knocking over a crystal goblet of water. Her eyes streaming, her nose running, she ran from the room, and then he heard the back door slam.

"I'll go after her." Pitching his napkin on the table, he left Sally sopping up spilt water.

He found Aster a moment later, sitting beside the barn.

"You must think me the perfect fool," she uttered.

"Perfect? No. You're a terrible cook."

A slight smile curved her lips. "You didn't have to gag."

"I'm sorry. Did you taste it?"

She nodded. "And I had to gag."

They both laughed then.

"That Sally. I could strangle her," Aster complained.

"I gather she's playing matchmaker?"

Nodding, Aster apologized, then added, "If you can wait, I'll fix you a decent meal."

Straddling a bale of hay, he noted the full, harvest moon. "Let's sit for a while and enjoy the moonlight."

They sat for a long while, talking, sharing their thoughts, discovering their likes and dislikes.

"My stomach thinks my throat's been cut," Dane teased as the air took on a seasonal chill.

"Of course. I'll get supper started right away."

She was about to walk away when he caught her by the arm. "Just your home cookin' this time."

She grinned. "My plain home cookin'."

He kissed her, and she didn't pull away.

Aster stoked the fire, set a kettle of water on to boil for the potatoes, put the cast-iron skillet on the stove, then ran upstairs to change out of her satin dress. Pulling on a faded gingham, she hurried back downstairs, threw a spoonful of lard into the heated skillet, and ran to the spring house to fetch the baked ham she'd cooked yesterday for Sunday dinner. She had settled Dane comfortably in the parlor reading *The Farmer's Almanac.*

Sally came into the kitchen a while later. "Need any help?"

Flour flew in the air as Aster prepared the gravy, then cut slices of ham, dropping each piece carefully into the hot grease. "None at all, thank you." She knew she could handle it from here on.

Forty minutes later, ham, mashed potatoes, gravy, and hot biscuits were set before Dane. Smiling, Aster watched him dig in, her confidence soaring. Now *that* was a man-catching meal.

Later, as Dane said good night at the door and she paid him for the green wool, he hesitated, then leaned down and kissed her lightly. Surprised, she kissed him back, her lips clinging to his longer than necessary.

"I'll be back soon," he promised, the tips of his fingers brushing her cheek.

As his wagon disappeared, she was still clinging to the word *soon* he'd left hanging in the air.

6

To Aster's relief, Sally never spoke of the disastrous dinner again.

Dane, on the other hand, was becoming a regular visitor, stopping by every day or two while in the area. Though she wouldn't admit it to herself, Aster kept a watchful eye on the road, hoping to see his matched bays appear on the horizon.

As she bustled around the kitchen preparing supper, she thought about his gradually developing the habit of staying for dinner. Afterward, they'd sit on the front porch until it was too cool, then go inside to sit by the fire in the parlor until it was time for Dane to leave. Each evening he brushed an impersonal kiss across her lips, always leaving her wanting more.

Later she'd lie in her lonely bed, her pillow crunched beneath her cheek, watching the moon rise, wishing for . . . she wasn't sure what.

Dane was exciting, charming, even dependable. He

knew how to make a woman feel desirable. When she was with him she felt not only wanted but unique, one of a kind. He made her feel as if he'd never looked at another woman the way he looked at her. The emptiness inside her had been replaced by a glow that made her giddy over nothing. When he touched her, it was like striking a match to kindling. And when he left, she wanted to call him back, to keep him with her forever.

"Will Dane be here for supper?" Sally asked, peeling potatoes, and jarring Aster from her wool-gathering.

"I hope he will." Aster bent over, checking a roast in the oven.

"And what other plans are you making?"

The oven door banged shut.

"Concerning what?"

Sally grinned. "He's courting you, you ninny. Where's it going to lead?"

"I wouldn't say that he's actually 'courting' me," Aster said slowly, wishing she had a better explanation. Actually, she'd asked herself the same question for the past two weeks. What were her plans?

"If it's not courting, then what is it?"

"We're . . . friends."

Sally snorted. "Friends. A man who looks at a woman the way Dane looks at you doesn't have friendship on his mind."

Aster was almost afraid to hope Sally was right. She had seen the look in Dane's eyes, almost as if he did want more stability in his life.

"But like any man, he needs a push in the right direction."

Alarm rose in Aster. "Don't you dare push this, Sally. Whatever is happening between Dane and me, I want us to explore on our own, with no interference from you."

"I'm only trying to help."

"I think I've had enough of your tutoring."

"But how are you going to get him to the altar, string pieces of meat down the aisle?" Sally asked, wide-eyed.

Aster laughed. "I don't think I have to resort to such drastic measures."

"Well, it's going to take more than supper every night and sitting on the front porch to hook him. It's going to take a little teasing, giving him a taste of what married life would be."

Aster nearly dropped the bowl of cherries she was sweetening. "Surely you're not suggesting—"

"No!" Sally exclaimed. "Though what could be so wrong about two people who love each other—"

"Sally!"

"Aren't you the least bit curious how he'd be . . . "

Aster's face burned. "I'm content just spending time with him right now."

"Don't set the hook at the precise time, and he'll get away," Sally warned.

"But if Dane doesn't love me, then . . . "

"Then?" Sally asked. "A man isn't quick to admit how he feels. Sometimes you've got to give him a little shove in the right direction. You've got to romance him, Aster, and that takes more than a good meal. What you're trying to arouse is slightly lower than his belt."

"You're outrageous."

"Maybe, but I know men."

Sally set aside the pan of potatoes and tossed her paring knife onto the cabinet as she stripped off her apron.

"That's not enough for supper," Aster said, glad for a change of subject.

"Oh, I forgot to tell you. I'm spending the night with Jane. We're planning her wedding and it seemed silly to ride all the way over there only to start back in an hour. I'll be back by noon tomorrow." Sally wiped her hands on a towel and filled the pan with water. "By the way, you're ignoring my question."

"I don't like the idea of setting a hook for a man, Sally. That sounds as if he has no choice in the matter. I want a staying kind of love, not one won by hook or by crook."

Aster could see that Sally didn't agree, but she let the subject drop. But the questions were still in Aster's mind as she finished making supper. She liked having Dane sitting at the head of their table, liked having him around, liked the way she felt when he looked at her, the way he sat with his arm around her shoulders when they were together on the porch swing. And she especially liked the way he held her when they finally got around to saying good night.

Admit it, Aster, she chastised herself. *You've fallen in love with him.*

Dane was lost in thought, letting his team set their own pace as they approached Branson. In the next couple of days he'd have to start back to Kansas City, his fall tour completed. For the first time he found himself reluctant to leave.

What was there about Aster that made him want to stay? Quiet, shy, home-loving, she was all the things that had never appealed to him before. But when he sat with her in front of the fire, something besides his sexual urges responded.

What did he know about home and hearth? Nothing. Absolutely nothing. And he didn't want to know. A wife meant responsibilities. Children. Settling down. Things he'd never thought about until now.

He liked his life. New places, new people, no one to answer to but himself.

"It won't work," he muttered. "She's a woman who needs a farmer. I'm a tinker. Farming and tinkering don't mix."

Realizing he'd wasted half the afternoon talking to himself, he slapped the reins and stepped up the horses' pace. He'd never been tempted to stay with a woman for more than a day or two, and he didn't intend to change now. He was a man who liked women. Lots of women. He was a rolling stone, he told himself, and tomorrow he had to roll on. Tonight he had to tell Aster he was leaving.

When Sally left for Jane's around four o'clock, Aster ran upstairs to change her dress and comb her hair. By the time she heard the wagon pulling into the lane, she'd checked the table four times, rechecked the potatoes and vegetables three, and glanced in the mirror at least ten.

Running to the door to meet him, she admitted she was excited. She was wearing the golden yellow sprigged dress she'd worn the night they first met.

The lamplight turned her hair to fire and her lips were parted in anticipation as he approached her front door. Smiling, she tilted her face to accept his usual kiss, and he called himself a fool just before he drew her hungrily into his arms.

"Hi," she whispered.

"Hi," he murmured.

Their mouths met again, savoring another long kiss.

His arm encircled her waist as they entered the house.

"How was your day?" she asked.

"Tiring," he conceded. A cold rain had begun falling that morning and he was chilled to the bone. All he'd thought about was tonight, a warm fire, and Aster to share it with.

"Where did you say Sally was?" Dane asked later, setting his napkin aside, having finished eating.

"She's helping a friend plan her wedding. Jane. You've heard us speak of her."

"Yes . . . Jane. She's marrying Edward Langston next month."

"Uh-huh. Going to be a large wedding. Sally's her maid of honor."

Aster began clearing plates from the table. "Let's have our coffee before the fire," she suggested. "You seem tired."

"I'm fine," he declared. He didn't want her mothering him. He neither wanted nor was accustomed to maternal clucking. A man could get too comfortable, even come to look forward to that sort of thing.

He searched for the proper way to tell her he was leaving, feeling his collar growing tighter by the moment. Every move she made beckoned him, from the sway of her hips to the tilt of her head, to her soft, unassuming laughter. For weeks now he'd wanted to make love to her. The chaste kisses at the door weren't enough anymore. He wanted more. No, he wanted less. That's why he had to tell her. No sense letting her go on thinking anything could come from the past few weeks.

She was like an itch he couldn't scratch, her face haunting him as he drove from farm to farm during the day. Her smile, the light in her eyes when she looked up at him, kept him awake nights. More than once, when her lips had clung to his, her breath warm against his face, her hand against his chest measuring his heartbeat, he'd almost swept her into his arms and carried her upstairs.

He ached to remove the pins from that glorious hair and bury his hands in it. Just once. If he could hold her just once, then he'd be free of her obsessive sweetness.

She sat on the settee pouring coffee. The lamplight surrounded her, bathing her in an ethereal light. The room reeked of domesticity.

"Coffee?"

"Yes, please."

The tension between them was noticeable. Aster wondered why, since they were usually comfortable with each other. As she handed him the cup, their fingers brushed, and warmth rushed through her.

Startled, she glanced up and caught Dane's pensive gaze. Time was suspended as they each held onto the saucer. She hardly dared breathe.

"Aster," he said, his voice breaking tentatively.

"Yes," she whispered.

She suddenly felt on the brink of something unknown, exciting and totally wonderful. For one giddy moment she could almost hear Sally's voice urging her to forget what was proper and run to meet the unexpected.

She barely knew when he set the cup aside and reached for her. They slipped to their knees, and he kissed her, passionately, lustfully, their need for each other openly acknowledged.

Holding her hands, he lifted her to her feet and drew her down onto the settee. Her body melded with his and his eyes drifted closed as he tasted her with a fervor that matched her own. Her lips clung to his, and his touch was like a fiery brand against her body.

Her mind whirled with emotions. Trembling yet exhilarated, eager and full of passion, she pressed closer, famished for a man's touch. His tongue teased and excited her as she tried to experience all of him at once.

"I can't promise I'll be here in the morning," he whispered between frantic, hurried kisses.

"That's all right. I can't promise I'll even remember how to do this." It had been a long time since she had sought to appease a man's sexual demands.

"Mmm, you taste good."

"You, too."

When he rose, she stood, too, unaware of her feet on the stairs as she led him to her bedroom.

Their hands were busy now, trying to see who could undress the other quickest. They couldn't divest themselves of their clothing fast enough. Desire consumed them and clothes scattered like petals in the winds.

Moonlight bathed the bed as they fell across the wedding-ring patterned quilt. They were aware only of each other, all questions, all doubts, all sanity momentarily lost.

"Aster," he whispered as his hands closed around her breasts. "I don't want you to have regrets in the morning." His voice was soft, raspy, needy, as he nipped at her lower lip.

She knew she would feel nothing in the morning but the physical ache between her thighs to remind her that she was alive, a woman once more—a woman deeply in love.

"Shush," she whispered, bereft when his lips left hers for the briefest of moments. "I know what I'm doing, Dane."

"Aster . . . I want this night to be unforgettable . . . for you . . . for me . . . "

"Oh, Dane," she whispered. "You are unforgettable." She realized she had known that practically from the moment they first met.

"My beautiful Aster. The loveliest of all blossoms, the pride of a golden harvest."

She slipped her legs around his waist, and the smile she knew so well lit his face, his tone teasing now as she yielded willingly to him.

"Why do I have this feeling that you can be wicked, Widow Harris—that I'm about to fly into the spider's very own web?"

Her breath mingled softly with his. "Oh, I can be, Mr. Gordon. Infinitely wicked." Her hands stroked him gently, conveying her promise.

Lowering his mouth, he kissed her breasts, skimming a torturous path down her body. She moaned as she arched her back and cradled his head more tightly to her.

Lifting his head, he touched his lips to her upper lip, then to her lower one. Their eyes met, saying everything, nothing, as he entered her.

They settled into a slow, experimental rhythm, occasionally smiling, at other times growing solemn.

Wildly passionate, then slow and tentative, their lovemaking exploded into moments of laughter, tears of happiness, of wonder, joyful elation, and unbridled hunger.

The end came too swiftly. Shattered by the intensity, they collapsed, catching their breaths. They lay on their sides, spooned tightly together as they basked in the afterglow.

Outside, a branch tapped lightly against the rain-spattered windowpane.

"Wind's comin' up," he whispered.

"Uh-huh." She was so relaxed, so utterly at peace in his arms. "Stay the night?" Her heart raced as she awaited his answer.

"I believe I will."

They made love twice more during the night. When the rooster crowed the next morning, they were still wrapped tightly in each other's arms.

7

Aster awoke, full of wondrous feelings and not certain why. She slowly opened her eyes, absorbing the sunlight that flooded the room. What on earth . . . It had to be nearly noon!

Then she remembered. Dane.

Her hand went automatically to the pillow on the other side of the bed. Empty. Her eyes closed. It had to have been a dream. A crazy, wonderful, too-good-to-be-true dream. She sat up, dragging the sheets and the quilt with her, hoping to hear Dane in the dressing closet. But silence mocked her.

Then she saw the sheet of paper lying in the hollow Dane's head had made in the pillow. Her hand trembled as she reached for it, and she almost didn't pick it up. She knew what it said. She didn't need it spelled out in writing.

Perched on the side of the bed, she stared at the piece of paper, wrapped in a cocoon of sheets and quilts, her hair tangled around her face. Closing her eyes, she could still hear his whispered, passionate murmurings as his hands reacquainted her with the rhythms of love. He had made love to her as if he had planned to be around forever.

Opening her eyes, she stared at the pristine white ceiling of her room; the room she'd lived in as a little girl, the room she'd shared with her husband. She should never have brought Dane to this room. It was wrong, just as surrendering to love had been wrong.

A sob caught in her throat. If it was so wrong, why had it felt so good? Never before had she felt so complete, so wanted, so loved. John had been a gentle lover. In their own, inexperienced way, they had learned the ways of love together.

But Dane was an experienced lover. A man who knew how to please a woman. She closed her eyes against the humiliation that flooded her. She'd done and said things last night that she would never have done or said with another man. Not even John.

She groaned, burying her face in her hands. "Oh, Sally, what have I done?"

When she reached for Dane's note, she did so with grim determination. Whatever he'd written, she had no choice but to accept it.

Aster,

Please believe me when I say that I've never known a woman like you. You were an unexpected gift in my life. A gift I don't deserve.

You know who and what I am. A traveling salesman.

Traveling. Going from place to place, selling my wares, meeting people . . . and leaving them.

I'm a man who needs new challenges, new

horizons. Knowing that, I tell you with the deepest regret that I'm not the kind of man you deserve.

I wanted to be. And for that brief time last night when I held you, and loved you, I told myself I could be. But we both know differently.

If I stayed, it wouldn't be long before I'd wonder what was over that next hill, and soon I'd go find out, and then you'd be unhappy.

I wouldn't want that.

I want you to be happy. I want you to have a man who can be there for you every night, take care of the farm, sit across the table from you, hold you until you fall asleep.

I wish I could be that man, but knowing I can't . . . I wish you love.

Dane

Aster's fingertips trembled against her lips as she finished reading. "I wish you love, too, Dane," she whispered.

But wishing wouldn't change anything. He was gone. He'd come into her life like a whirlwind and left just as quickly. If she had followed her first instincts, she wouldn't be sitting in a bed that still smelled of his soap, her body so branded by his that she didn't feel like herself anymore.

"Aster?"

She started at the sound of Sally's voice and the banging of the back door.

"Where are you?"

Scrambling out of bed, Aster quickly grabbed her robe off a hook on the back of the door, then hurriedly ran her fingers through her tangled hair.

"Aster?"

Sally opened the bedroom door, a frown creasing her forehead. "What's wrong? Are you all right?"

Aster knotted the cord at her waist. "No, I'm fine," she said, trying to think of a plausible excuse for lying in bed until nearly noon.

"You look pale. The monthlies?" Sally guessed.

"Yes," Aster said, relieved that her sister had provided her with an excuse. "I'm better now. I'll dress and be down in a few minutes."

"Maybe you should just be lazy today. Arthur can do your chores. What's a hired hand for?" Sally's smile was back. "I'll fix us some hot tea, and then I'll tell you all about Jane's wedding plans. You'll never believe it."

Dear Lord, how could she listen to someone's wedding plans when she'd hoped—She'd been a fool even to let the thought enter her mind.

She'd known Dane wouldn't stay, and she should never have dreamed of finding love a second time. Certainly not with a man like him.

He was right. He *wasn't* the man she needed.

Then why does it hurt so much to know he's gone forever? her heart cried.

" . . . and she's going to have Christmas decorations! Can you imagine?"

Aster dragged her mind back to Sally's ramblings and tried to look interested. "Uh, no, I can't," she murmured, wishing her head would cease its pounding. "I, um, think I'll take a bath, then do the chores."

"I said I'd asked Arthur to—"

"I said I want to do them, Sally." Aster hated the tone in her voice, but she knew that Sally could be relentless.

"All right. I'll heat water for the tub. How was Dane?"

Aster turned away. "How should he be?"

"Were his sales up around Ozark? I'd have thought they'd be very good this time of year."

"I'm sure they are. We didn't discuss his sales."

"What did you talk about?"

Aster busied herself making the bed. "Nothing, really."

That much was true. They'd done little talking. Certainly nothing she could repeat.

"Well, I guess I'd better put the water on to heat," Sally said.

"Thank you. I'll be down in a minute."

For the remainder of the day, Aster avoided Sally. As she started supper, she gazed out the window at the fields of gold. Arthur and Mason ambled up the lane, finished with their evening chores.

The day had been warm, but at sunset a cool breeze had sprung up. This was Aster's favorite time of day, when she usually was satisfied that she'd accomplished something, that the farm was still prosperous, and she could rest contentedly. But not today. Not tonight. She was lonely again. The noticeable ache was nearly as debilitating as it had been during the dark days following John's death. Only now another man's name was on her mind and in her heart.

She stood with her hands in a bowl of water, the carrots she was peeling forgotten. Last night had been a mistake. What had she been thinking?

She *hadn't* been thinking. That was the problem.

When she'd first met Dane she'd known instinctively that he was not right for her. But she'd been so alone, felt so discouraged that she'd never meet anyone she could love, that she hadn't listened to her own common sense.

Lord, how naïve she must have seemed to the experienced, worldly Dane. How young and untutored. And he had taken full advantage of her stupidity and vulnerability.

In the clear light of day, she saw her mistake. Dane made his living manipulating people. He'd known exactly what would appeal to her. His laughter, his wit, his charm, had all been used to convince her to let down her guard. And she'd been taken in completely.

She felt like the biggest fool who ever lived, but at least her disastrous mistake was behind her now. Dane was gone. No one ever need know how foolish she'd been. Dane Gordon was out of her life. She'd never have to see him again. Should he ever be brazen enough to come to her door selling his wares, she would slam it in his face.

The reins rested lightly in Dane's hands as the team plodded down the road. If anyone had asked him where he was, or where he was going, he couldn't have answered.

The sun was setting as he approached Springfield. He'd stay there the night. He wasn't particularly looking forward to another hotel room, or to meeting his merchants the next morning.

A week had passed since he'd left Branson. One week since he'd lain beside Aster. He'd watched her sleeping that morning, knowing that what he was about to do would shatter her life once again. A sadness had come over him, one he'd been powerless to shake.

He'd let a strand of her coppery hair float through his fingers, memorizing its texture, her essence. He'd counted the pale freckles scattered across her nose and cheeks, knowing she didn't find them nearly as attractive as he did. Her lips had been slightly parted and he'd ached to taste them again, but he had known that if he woke her she'd cling to him, and then he wouldn't have had the strength to leave her. He'd even hesitated to write the letter, but he had known he couldn't go if he didn't. She deserved that much from him.

When he pulled up at the livery, he left his horses and headed for the hotel. After he'd put his suitcase in his room, he went back out to find a place to get an evening meal.

The cafe two blocks from the hotel was busy, but he was able to find a small corner table. The hand-lettered menu offered a variety of meals. His eyes scanned it: beef stew, soup, biscuits. Nothing sounded good. He could go back to the hotel, but it was too early. The night stretched endlessly ahead of him.

He would have traveled farther, but there wasn't another decent place to stay for miles. As it was, he'd have to camp out the next two nights, and he didn't look forward to that.

Finally he chose the beef stew and coffee because he had to order something.

Sipping his coffee, he let his gaze drift over the crowd, watching the other diners. They were talking and laughing. Some looked to be young marrieds, others appeared to have been married a long time. Those couples ate in silence.

There was one older couple who sat by themselves, intent on their food. As they got up to leave, the man's hand drifted to his wife's back in a gesture of practiced affection of which neither seemed to be aware.

Couples. Families. Everyone seemed to belong to someone.

The waitress brought his meal and he concentrated on eating. He realized that everyone had a mate but him. It had never bothered him before. So why did it bother him tonight?

It was dark when he walked back to the hotel. Sitting in the lobby, he dawdled over a newspaper until it got so late the hotel clerk began to eye him suspiciously.

Finally he mounted the stairs and strolled down the hall toward his room. A door opened next to him and a woman stepped out, her back to him.

Another time he wouldn't have paid much attention, but when the lamplight fell on a wisp of her red hair he felt his gut twist with emotion.

He paused, and the woman turned and looked at him warily.

"Is there a problem?" she asked.

"Uh, no. I . . . I thought you were someone else."

She stepped around him and disappeared down the stairs, leaving him staring after her.

He unlocked the door to his room and entered, tossing the key onto the dresser. Sitting on the edge of the bed, he looked out the window. Rowdy street sounds drifted up to him.

He knew that the woman he'd seen in the hallway couldn't be her, but this wasn't the first time it had happened. He'd see a woman ahead of him on the street and the way she walked made him think of Aster. A waitress with a certain tilt to her head, a woman with red hair, a yellow dress—time and time again he'd thought he'd seen her.

Damn.

Rolling onto his back, he closed his eyes, trying to block her out of his mind.

For the next month, Dane slowly worked his way back to Kansas City. The farms along the way were large and prosperous, and business was good. Ordinarily he would be pleased; this time he wasn't.

He studied the farmers in the fields, plowing their

ground for winter planting, sometimes gathering the last of the corn harvest.

The women who answered his knock were generally strong women used to hard work, with little children peeking from behind their skirts.

Some, who had never encountered traveling salesmen, were suspicious. Others greeted him warmly and offered him a cup of coffee or a cool drink.

Occasionally, when he stopped at a farm near noon, or late in the afternoon, the farmer himself picked through the wares with his wife. Some even invited him to share a meal. Because some towns had no hotel or restaurant facilities, he learned to accept a hot meal wherever it was offered. He should have been happy, but he wasn't.

For the first time in his life he became aware of the bond between family members. A look, a touch, a feeling. The emptiness inside him grew larger, the ache more acute. Aster's face, her smile, her laughter haunted his sleep. The days grew longer, the nights darker and lonelier.

Six weeks after leaving Branson, he was driving along a road when the cool, dreary afternoon was shattered by the sound of frantic screams. Glancing up, he saw a woman running toward him.

"Help me! Dear Lord, help me!" Tears streamed down her cheeks. "My son—he's been hurt! Bad!"

Dane leaped off the wagon and ran with her to a nearby field where a small boy lay beside a row of furrowed ground. The horse stood beside the cultivated rows, still hitched to the plow.

Kneeling beside the child, Dane felt for a pulse. "What happened?"

"The horse—I didn't realize Matthew was so close. Oh, I told him to stand back! A snake startled the horse and he kicked back." The mother was beside herself with fear.

"Go for the doctor. I'll stay with the boy."

"No! I can't leave him—"

"Go!" Dane ordered. "And hurry!"

The woman seemed to be in a trance now, sobbing hysterically.

"I'll stay with Matthew," he coaxed. He couldn't go for the doctor not knowing the area.

The woman finally calmed herself and ran off down the lane while Dane loosened the child's collar. The boy was pale, unresponsive.

A half hour passed before Dane heard the rattle of a wagon and team racing down the lane.

As the wagon came to a halt, a tall, lanky man jumped out, followed by the child's mother and the doctor carrying a black bag close behind.

"Is he breathing?" the doctor asked.

Dane stepped back to give him room. "Yes, he's breathing."

"Get him into the house," the doctor said grimly.

The farmer gently picked up his son and carried him up to the house, laying him carefully on the kitchen table. The boy's mother stood with trembling hands covering her mouth, tears coursing down her cheeks.

The farmer's hands rested on his wife's shoulders, as they waited, united in fear, to learn their son's fate.

After what seemed an eternity, the boy finally opened his eyes.

"Matthew?" the woman cried, moving to the table.

"Mama?" The child stared up at her vacantly.

"Yes, my darling?"

"I'm hungry."

Relieved laughter filled the room as they all rejoiced over the boy's recovery.

Satisfied that the child would live, Dane tried to leave, but the boy's father stopped him.

"I'm Robert Andrews." The young farmer extended a work-callused hand. "I'm much obliged to you for helpin' to save my boy's life."

"I didn't do a thing," Dane said modestly. "I just happened along at the right time."

"Nevertheless, thank you," Mrs. Andrews whispered, gently cradling her slightly cranky son in her arms. Her eyes were filled with gratitude. "If you hadn't come by when you did—"

A sob caught in her throat and her husband drew her to him, his arm tight around her shoulders.

"I don't know what we'd have done if you hadn't been here to help my Mary," he said. "God bless you."

Later that evening, Dane checked into a hotel. After a bath and supper, he lay across his bed staring into the darkness. Matthew's still body, the pale faces of his parents, the way they turned to one another, comforted one another, kept gnawing at him.

Questions plagued him, ones he'd never asked himself before. If something happened to him, who would care?

The truth hit him like a train.

No one. Absolutely no one would care.

He lay there, remembering. Those evenings he'd spent with Aster and Sally at the farm had been different from anything he'd ever known.

When Aster had talked about her marriage, there

had been such a look of contentment, such love, on her face. No woman had ever looked at him like that. No one except Aster.

Tears burned his eyes, and for the first time that he could remember, he let the pain of never belonging, of never having anyone special to care about him, spill over.

Turning on his side, he sobbed like a baby into his pillow.

8

Aster sagged against the bedpost limply, eye-ing the chamber pot. She had told herself for weeks that all she was suffering from was an upset stomach, or that for some unknown reason certain foods no longer agreed with her. But by Thanksgiving her com-mon sense had finally won out and she had to face the fact that she was pregnant. And the father was Dane Gordon.

That day tears of shock, of joy, and of fear had rolled down her face. From her wedding day, she'd longed for children, but when the months, then years, had passed and there was no baby, she'd accepted that she was barren. But with the undeniable proof that it wasn't she who couldn't have children, but John, she had laughed, then covered her mouth with both hands in shock.

She heard her bedroom door open and Sally entered the room. Aster looked up at her.

"What's wrong? Aren't you feeling well?" Sally asked, a worried expression on her face.

"I'm fine. I'm just pregnant," she answered matter-of-factly.

"Oh, my gosh. What are you going to do!" Sally murmured.

"I don't know," Aster admitted. "It's scandalous, actually. I'm not married, and everyone will know I'm having a baby. There will be talk, Sally—vicious talk—but I don't care. I want this child."

"We've got to find Dane."

"No!"

Aster sprang to her feet, starting to pace. When she had finally accepted that she was indeed pregnant, she'd told Sally the truth about the last night Dane had been at the house, but she had not mentioned her pregnancy. Sally had been surprised and sympathetic, then angry at Dane for leaving Aster.

"That's the last thing I want to do. He *left* me, Sally. And I felt . . . used. I was nothing more than a dalliance, among who knows how many others. I was hurt." Aster stopped in front of the window, her hand resting on her still-flat stomach. "But now . . . he's left me a wonderful gift. A gift that's mine alone."

"Aster, Dane has to know—"

"No!" Aster spun around. "No. He doesn't deserve to know, to share this child. We'll raise him. Right here on this farm where we grew up."

"But you're not married."

"I don't care! I didn't want this to happen, I never expected this to happen, but now it has and I'm going to make the best of it. I don't need Dane. I just need this baby." She drew a ragged breath. "And you're going to help me because you got me into this in the first place."

"Aster . . . I'm sorry. I never dreamed it would turn out this way."

"But you will help me."

"Of course I'll help you."

Aster saw the regret in Sally's eyes and knew she would not desert her.

It was the first of December and the weather had turned cold. Aster tossed three sticks of wood into the stove and quickly slammed the door. Straightening, she automatically rested her hand on her stomach as she did a hundred times a day. Perhaps it was to reassure herself the child was real, that at last she was having a baby. Or perhaps it was to remind herself that in only six months she would hold her dream. A tiny scrap of life.

"Whooo, it's getting worse out there. Looks like snow," Sally said, unwrapping her muffler from around her neck.

"Could be," Aster said, glancing out the window again. "I think I'll go to the cellar and bring up some apples to bake for supper."

"Sounds good. Need me to do anything?"

"No, everything's done."

Aster took Sally's coat and let herself out.

Sally stood at the stove, rubbing her hands together, warming herself. When she heard a knock at the front door, she was surprised, but hurried to see who would venture out on such a cold afternoon.

She swung the door open and stared in shock. "Dane?"

"Is Aster here?"

"Yes, but I don't know that she'll talk to you."

He twisted his hat in his hands. "Where is she?"

"Honestly, Dane, she is going to be upset—"

"She has every right to refuse to see me, but I have to see her."

Sally hesitated, then stood back and held the door open. "Come in the kitchen. You must be frozen. Aster's in the cellar getting apples."

He was holding a cup of coffee and standing beside the stove when Aster opened the back door. Holding the pan of apples, she stared at him. He was as handsome as ever, though there was a weariness around his mouth that hadn't been there before. His hair was a little long. He needed a shave, but he looked awfully good to her.

He nodded. "Widow Harris."

Sending Sally, who was sitting at the table, an accusing look for allowing Dane into the house, Aster shut the door and set the pan on the table.

"I'd like to talk to you," Dane stated quietly.

"I think everything's been said," Aster answered.

"I, uh, I'll go light the fire in the sitting room." Sally rose from her chair.

"Don't bother," Aster said. "Dane won't be staying."

Sally met Dane's glance.

"Find something to do, Sally."

Sally nodded, leaving the room.

"You can't get rid of me that easy." Dane's eyes met hers and held momentarily.

"You left easily enough three months ago," Aster said bitterly.

"Yes," he admitted. "I left. But you're wrong if you think it was easy. I'm back," he pointed out.

"For how long?"

She shrugged off Sally's coat and hung it on a peg beside the door. For a moment she let her hand linger, delaying turning around. Would he guess her secret? Was there anything to alert him to her pregnancy?

"As long as it takes."

"To what?"

"Aster, look at me."

She faced him, but didn't look at him right away. She looked everywhere but at him.

"I'm here to stay, Aster."

Moving to the stove, she lifted a lid and stirred the contents in the pot. "How nice."

"I love you."

The words came out so softly she wasn't sure she'd heard them. She stared blankly into the pot for a long moment.

"You must be confused. I'm Aster Harris. The woman you seduced and left with just a note."

"I know exactly who you are, and for the first time in my life I know exactly who I am."

Refusing to meet his eyes, she started setting the table. "You're talking nonsense."

"No. For the first time in my life I'm making sense. I love you, Aster. I honestly do. I want you to marry me."

She turned, her eyes meeting his. "What?"

"Will you marry me?"

She stared at him as if she didn't understand. "Have you lost your mind?"

"No. Found it." He smiled.

"But you were the one who said you liked moving around, would never settle down. A rolling stone. Marriage, especially to me, would mean staying. Settling down. No more exploring what's over the next rise."

"I know what I said, and believe me they've been tough words to eat."

"What's the matter? Lose your job?"

"No. Quit it."

"Thinking of taking up farming?" She knew better than that. Dane had no interest in farming.

"No. Taking up merchandising."

She frowned. "What nonsense are you talking now?"

"Bought Brown's Mercantile."

She didn't believe him. "No, you didn't."

"The few times I saw Margaret and Ben, they talked about retiring. I bought the store, and they're moving to Springfield to be near their daughter."

With a skeptical glance, Aster strode out of the kitchen. Dane followed her through the hall to the front door. She flung the door open and pointed to his wagon. "That wagon, I take it, is full of your merchandise. You're still selling on the road, Dane Gordon. Don't tell me your tales. I don't buy them anymore."

"I'm stocking the store with that and everything else I've bought."

She let the door slam shut. Marching toward the kitchen, she tried to collect her thoughts. He was lying. He wouldn't buy Brown's Mercantile! That was too permanent, too settled.

She stopped and, turning, looked at him. "You really bought Brown's Mercantile?"

"Sure did. Except it'll be Gordon's Mercantile by Friday. Come into the kitchen where it's warm. We need to talk."

"I don't have anything to say to you," she insisted, walking ahead of him.

Entering the kitchen, she whirled, facing him again.

"What are you really doing here?"

"I told you. I came to marry you."

"And if I say no?"

"Then I'll run Gordon's Mercantile and grow to be an old and bitter man waiting for you to accept my proposal."

"I thought that was the last thing you wanted. What changed your mind?"

"You."

When she was about to turn away again, he caught her by the arm. Pulling her to him, he kissed her, long and hard.

As their lips parted, he ordered softly, "Sit down. I have something to tell you."

Curious, she sat at the table, watching as he calmly poured himself a cup of coffee before sitting opposite her.

"I was driving down the road one day, minding my business, when I heard screams. A woman came running toward me, saying her son had been kicked in the head by the plow horse." He sipped his coffee. "I did what I could for the boy while the mother went for the doctor.

"The child was unconscious, and for a while I wasn't sure he was breathing. When the mother returned she had the boy's daddy and the doctor with her. For the next few hours all we could do was wait."

He ran his fingers through his hair and hesitated. Then he continued, "I watched them, the mother and father, together, waiting, hoping, praying. The husband held his wife close, she kept looking to him for reassurance that their boy would make it. If he didn't, I knew they'd have each other. If he did, then the three of them would be a family again."

Aster waited for him to go on, imagining how she'd feel if the boy were hers, theirs.

"To make a long story short, the boy finally woke up. But—I don't know. I couldn't get that family out of my mind. They were like one person. Depending on one another, taking comfort in one another. And I had to ask myself, if something happened to me, would anyone care? Would there be anyone who would give a damn if I lived or not?"

Aster held her tongue. She was sorely tempted to say that she cared, that she gave a damn. But she couldn't. No matter the reason, he'd made love to her and then left her.

"And the more I thought about that, the more I realized that no one would have a reason to miss me." He stared at his hands. "I wish I had the eloquence to say what I feel, but I don't. All I know is that when I die, there won't be a hole where I've been, no one to mourn me. I have no reason, no purpose, no grand design in this world. In short, I've never given a damn, and no one has given a damn about me." He met her gaze then. "Until I met you."

She swallowed, biting back tears. He couldn't do this to her. Her mind was made up. She would spend the rest of her life with her child, living on the farm, just the two of them.

"I came to Branson with no idea of what was going to happen. All I saw was a pretty woman at a barn dance, and I wanted to hold her for a while. When I learned who you were I thought, well, that I could romance you and—It wasn't right, but I haven't always done the right thing."

"Why are you telling me this?" Her voice was hardly above a whisper.

"Because I want you to know who I am. I want you to know what I'm thinking. I want to be honest with you."

He stood and began to pace. "I . . . I love you, Aster. I never thought I'd say those words, never wanted to say them. But it sneaked up on me. That day I spent with you visiting the farms, the night I came here for supper, seeing you and Sally together. The way she came here to be with you after your husband died. I've never known that kind of love.

"I'm no farmer, Aster. I'm a merchant. But you've had hired help all this time and that could continue. I do know how to sell merchandise. I'll make us a good living, and I'll try to be a good husband to you."

He reached in his pocket and pulled out a narrow box. "I tried to give you this before." His eyes mirrored his deep love. "This time I hope you'll accept it."

He opened the box and placed it on the table. The green stones set in gold winked up at her.

"There's a ring that goes with that. I want to put it on your finger. I want you to be my woman, Aster Harris. For the rest of your life."

She stared at the necklace, wanting so badly to believe him that it hurt.

"Dane . . . there's something you should know," she said softly.

"I love you, Aster. If there's another man, I intend to fight for you—"

"I'm going to have a baby," she blurted.

His face went blank. "What?"

"I'm going to have a baby." She swallowed hard, then met his shocked gaze. "Your baby."

He stared at her a long moment, and then he began to laugh. Pulling her out of the chair and into his arms, he danced her around the kitchen before stopping and looking down into her face.

"A *baby*? You're sure?"

She managed a frail smile. "There's little doubt at this point."

"But I thought—"

"I know. I was sure I couldn't have children. I thought—Well, imagine my surprise. But I wouldn't change it. I want this baby, Dane. I wasn't going to tell you because I thought, well, I thought you wouldn't want it."

His lips met hers hungrily. "You might have been right, once. But not now." He hugged her tightly, lifting her off the floor. "Oh, Aster. You've got to marry me! I've got to make an honest woman out of you!"

Suddenly her doubts crumbled. The love crowding her heart told her he finally belonged to her. "Yes."

"Yes?"

"*Yes.* Yes, yes, yes!"

His whoop of joy echoed through the house, and Aster knew that at last, as the first flakes of snow falling outside signaled the end of autumn, she had found a bountiful harvest of love.

LORI COPELAND is the author of more than forty romance novels. Her warmth and humor have earned her numerous awards, including a Lifetime Achievement Award for Love and Laughter. Having lived all of her life in the Ozarks, she's eager to share a small part of rural Missouri's beauty and appeal with her readers. Since autumn is her favorite season, writing "Golden Harvest" was a breath of fresh air for her—gloriously cool, crisp, apple-scented, woodsmoke-filled autumn air!

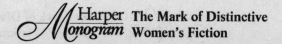

La Flamme by Constance O'Banyon

Lady Sabine pledged herself to the powerful Garreth Blackthorn, Duke of Balmarough, and then managed to escape him after he betrayed her and her family. Years later, in the guise of a provocative Parisian actress known only as "La Flamme," she plots her revenge, but eventually truth and love triumph.

A Purrfect Romance by Jennifer Blake, Robin Lee Hatcher, and Susan Wiggs

Three bestselling, award-winning authors bring together a collection of historical romances filled with fiery passion, glorious love, and fearless felines.

Return to Camelot by Donna Grove

Arthur Pierce's boyhood had been brightened by Arthurian legends, though reality taught him not to count on dreams. But when he came across an ancient document that provided a clue to the whereabouts of King Arthur's fabled sword, Excalibur, he teamed up with the lovely Chelsea Delafield and the two found more than they bargained for.

Lucien's Fall by Barbara Samuel

Lord Lucien Harrow was a tortured rake slowly self-destructing—until he met Madeline, a beautiful woman betrothed to another man. Despite her resistance, Lucien seduced Madeline and drew her into his tragic past. Only sacrifice and true love would be able to save them both and keep them together.

Young Man's Darling by Lee Scofield

Jesse vowed never to be lured into a lifetime of heartache by any sweet-talking, rascal of a young man. *If* she married, she would be an old man's darling, treasured by a mature husband. But when Luke, a young Wyoming rancher, showed her laughter, love, and adventure, Jesse discovered that she might just like being a "young man's darling" after all.

Lord of Forever by Patricia Simpson

When Olivia Travanelle agrees to design the gardens of a historic Charleston estate, she finds herself hopelessly drawn to her enigmatic and highly reclusive employer, Alexandre Chaubere. Then her painful past comes back to haunt her, forcing Alexandre to reveal a deep, dark secret of his own—one that threatens to destroy them both.

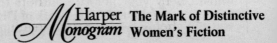

101 Days of Romance
BUY 3 BOOKS, GET 1 FREE!

CHOOSE A FREE BOOK FROM THIS OUTSTANDING
LIST OF AUTHORS AND TITLES:

HarperMonogram

____LORD OF THE NIGHT Susan Wiggs 0-06-108052-7
____ORCHIDS IN MOONLIGHT Patricia Hagan 0-06-108038-1
____TEARS OF JADE Leigh Riker 0-06-108047-0
____DIAMOND IN THE ROUGH Millie Criswell 0-06-108093-4
____HIGHLAND LOVE SONG Constance O'Banyon 0-06-108121-3
____CHEYENNE AMBER Catherine Anderson 0-06-108061-6
____OUTRAGEOUS Christina Dodd 0-06-108151-5
____THE COURT OF THREE SISTERS Marianne Willman 0-06-108053-5
____DIAMOND Sharon Sala 0-06-108196-5
____MOMENTS Georgia Bockoven 0-06-108164-7

HarperPaperbacks

____THE SECRET SISTERS Ann Maxwell 0-06-104236-6
____EVERYWHERE THAT MARY WENT Lisa Scottoline 0-06-104293-5
____NOTHING PERSONAL Eileen Dreyer 0-06-104275-7
____OTHER LOVERS Erin Pizzey 0-06-109032-8
____MAGIC HOUR Susan Isaacs 0-06-109948-1
____A WOMAN BETRAYED Barbara Delinsky 0-06-104034-7
____OUTER BANKS Anne Rivers Siddons 0-06-109973-2
____KEEPER OF THE LIGHT Diane Chamberlain 0-06-109040-9
____ALMONDS AND RAISINS Maisie Mosco 0-06-100142-2
____HERE I STAY Barbara Michaels 0-06-100726-9

To receive your free book, simply send in this coupon **and** your store
receipt with the purchase prices circled. You may take part in this exclusive
offer as many times as you wish, but all qualifying purchases must be made
by September 4, 1995, and all requests must be postmarked by October 4,
1995. Please allow 6-8 weeks for delivery.

MAIL TO: HarperPaperbacks, Dept. FC-101
             10 East 53rd Street, New York, N.Y. 10022-5299

Name_____

Address_____

City_____ State_____ Zip_____

Offer is subject to availability. HarperPaperbacks may make substitutions for
requested titles.   H09511